Good Eggs
and
Hoover Bags

Dawn Cairns

POOLBEG

Published 2002
Poolbeg Press Ltd.
123 Grange Hill, Baldoyle,
Dublin 13, Ireland
Email: poolbeg@poolbeg.com

13 5 7 9 10 8 6 4 2

A catalogue record for this book is available from the British Library.

ISBN 1-84223-056-5

Cover designed by Slatter-Anderson
Typeset by Patricia Hope in Sabon 10/14
Printed by Cox & Wyman
Reading, Berkshire

www.poolbeg.com

About the Author

Born in Belfast, Dawn Cairns now runs the marketing department for an Estate Agent. Recently married, she lives with her husband and cat in Holywood, Co. Down. *Goose Eggs and Hoover Bags* is her second novel. Her first novel *Tulips, Chips & Mayonnaise* was an instant bestseller.

Acknowledgements

I would like to thank the following people who gave me a hand, a push or a shove in the right direction while writing this. To my darling Brian, who stayed with me during the tracksuit months and took endless walks with me to discuss the problems I was having with the plot and just for generally being the love of my life. To Mum and Dad with much love and thanks – again. To Roy Cairns for taking the time and talking me through some of the finer details of criminal investigation. To Cathy K for some invaluable advice and a couple of ego boosts! To Gaye for facing the mammoth editing task through gritted teeth and good humour. To Ingrid for the red pen. To Lottie, Janey and Carlin, what would I have done without you on the email? To George and Claire for being great mates and calling for cups of tea and to keep me updated on the gossip. To Michael Shields for unwittingly suggesting the title. To Pat for loan of props. To Paula and all at Poolbeg for all the hard work that you have done, thank you. Finally, to everyone who bought and read my first book, your support was very much appreciated and I hope you enjoy my latest effort.

To Brian
My little rock in a stormy sea

Chapter 1

It's funny how just when you're feeling totally in control of your life, one small thing happens and nothing can ever be the same again. In Alice's case, it was a telephone call on a chilly October afternoon as she was digging through some seemingly endless case notes while making futile attempts to turn off the radiator in her rabbit hutch of an office before she baked to death. As she sat with her glasses on top of her head, chewing the end of a pencil, her phone rang, jolting her out of the exciting world of head versus pavement. A young man was trying to sue his local council for being drunk, falling over and hitting his head on the pavement.

"Yes, Louise?"

"There's a gentleman on the phone. His name is Ted Dunbar and he says it's personal."

Ted Dunbar . . . Ted Dunbar . . . Nope – didn't mean a thing to her.

1

"Does he sound nice?"

"He sounds old."

"Oh, well, put him through."

"Miss Watson? Alice Watson?"

Alice immediately recognised the Ulster accent – it couldn't be anywhere else.

"Yes, speaking."

"Ted Dunbar, from Dunbar O'Toole, Solicitors, in Belfast. I'm acting on behalf of the estate of Miss Jean Maguire. We've had quite a job tracking you down –"

"I'm sorry," Alice interrupted. "The estate of?" She stared at the telephone receiver.

"You haven't yet heard? In that case, Miss Watson, I'm sorry to inform you that your aunt has passed away."

"But she wasn't ill – was she?" Alice tried to remember the last time she had spoken to her Auntie Jean. It was about a month ago and she had seemed quite chirpy on the phone.

"No, Miss Watson. Quite unfortunate actually – your aunt was picking blackberries at the side of the road. It seems that she slipped off the grass verge and fell into the path of an oncoming bus."

"You're joking, right? Fell in front of a bus? Picking blackberries? I've never known her to go out blackberry-picking. At the side of the road? "

"I can assure you, Miss Watson, that it's true. She was still holding the basket when the ambulance arrived." Mr Dunbar sounded a bit irritated that Alice wasn't taking him seriously.

"Oh my God! I'm sorry, Mr Dunbar – it's just that this is truly unbelievable!" Alice was stunned. She picked up her chewed pencil and stared at it, her mind trying to comprehend what she was hearing. She brushed her leg against the boiling radiator, burning it and making herself jump.

"I can only tell you what the police have told me. It was indeed a most unusual thing for your aunt to be doing. I did know her personally – she was a client with our firm for many years." There was silence on the phone as if Mr Dunbar was thinking of what to say next. "She died instantly, Miss Watson. I'm very sorry to be the bearer of this sad news."

"Well, I suppose I should thank you for letting me know." Alice didn't know what else to say.

"I presume you will be attending the funeral?

"Yes, of course. When is it?" Her reply was automatic – she hadn't even thought that far ahead.

"Monday, noon, at her church in Groomsport. It's the only one on the main street – you cannot miss it." He paused. "Miss Watson, there is one other matter I need to discuss with you."

"Yes?"

"She left a will, which is why I have gone to such lengths to contact you. She left you a large portion of her estate, such as it is."

"Pardon?" Alice's mind was whizzing. What on earth had Jean left her? Surely she didn't have much money?

"She has left you her shop and her house."

"No!" Alice couldn't believe it. She burnt her leg again and dropped the pencil.

"Indeed she did. We will of course have a formal reading of the will, but your aunt had no family other than yourself so I have taken it upon myself to inform you prior to it being officially disclosed."

"Oh, um, yes, of course." Alice could hardly take it all in.

"We can discuss the details when you come over . . . there are some, em, clauses . . . there will be a few papers for you to sign."

"Oh, yes, absolutely." Alice tried to regain her lawyerly composure – failing abysmally.

"I'm sorry I had to let you know so abruptly."

"Well, thank you. I will, um, I'll see you on Monday then."

"Yes, indeed, thank you for your time. Good afternoon, Miss Watson."

"Good afternoon, Mr Dunbar."

The line disconnected immediately.

Alice was left sitting, staring at the quietly buzzing handset.

What the hell? Auntie Jean was dead? Picking blackberries? She'd have no more thought her aunt would be out picking blackberries than she'd be a referee at a boxing-match!

"Shit! This is totally nuts!" she said aloud.

* * *

4

Alice Watson was a twenty-nine-year-old solicitor living in London. She was starting to accumulate the trappings of a successful life. She worked hard and enjoyed the comfortable life she had created for herself.

Years before, her mother had died from cancer – a long and painful death that Alice and her father had to witness. It was a cruel way to die and having to watch his wife suffer in a pain that he would never fully understand was more than Mr Watson could bear. After her death, he virtually forgot Alice existed, leaving her with friends of his late wife, so that he could forget by focusing his attention on finishing all the alcoholic spirits in the house. When he had finished those, he bought a lot more at the off-licence. No-one was able to help; he seemed to have already decided he had had enough. Alice lost her father to a broken heart and whiskey in the same painful way she had lost her mother months earlier to cancer. Her dad was buried beside his beloved wife and Alice was left at eleven years old with a semi-detached in Belfast and a series of relatives who didn't really want to help. She didn't like to be reminded of any of this if she could possibly help it.

Alice's early memories were mainly happy ones – she had all but succeeded in blocking the unhappy ones out. She could remember her mum and dad when she was about eight. There had been holidays abroad, friends staying in the house, home-cooked meals, help with her homework and the bedtime stories which always culminated in the Princess Alice saving the kingdom and the handsome prince falling madly in love with her. Later it had been carers, strangers moving quietly round her home, wheelchairs, her dad sobbing quietly to himself in front of the television. Then there was Jean – thank God for Auntie Jean. Jean was a fairly tenuous relation but, when Alice's mother was diagnosed, Jean insisted that Alice spent part of the summer with her in Donaghadee, County Down.

At first, Alice had not wanted to leave Belfast, but her parents persuaded her otherwise. She ended up spending two carefree months living with the slightly eccentric Jean in her terraced house by the sea. Jean had the kindly look of a granny and Alice automatically warmed to her. Attached to the house was a slightly haphazard, Aladdin's Cave of a hardware shop which Jean ran with the help of her even more eccentric assistant, Emlyn. After that, Alice spent every summer, even after her dad's death, with Jean and her interesting life – a life a million miles away from Alice's own.

Hours of fun were had, looking through all the bits and pieces Jean had collected over the years. Broom-heads hung from the ceiling, while plastic bins and buckets lined the shelved walls. Plugs, nails, rubber plungers, rakes, screwdrivers, Stanley knives, spades, tins of varnish, furniture wax, hangers, plant-pots all had their own place in her shop. Jean and Emlyn had the amazing ability to put their hand on any particular item that was requested, items it would have taken the uninitiated several days to locate.

Alice loved Jean, the shop and the seaside village. It

was another world compared to her claustrophobic and depressing home in Belfast city, only fifteen miles away. Her memories of those holidays were of the dark, waxy smell of the shop; the brilliant sunshine when you went outside after being in there for any length of time; the beach which filled with seagulls padding around looking for food when the tide went out; and men and women out collecting the seaweed they would dry and sell in the shops, calling it dulse. Paddling with her trousers rolled up to the knee, Alice would look for interesting shells and pebbles that Jean would help her varnish when she brought them home. Alice still had a collection of varnished seashells in a box somewhere. Home-made ice cream, water pistols, walking along Donaghadee harbour to the pier where a boy a few years older than herself would dive in and retrieve ten-penny coins. The water was a good twenty metres deep – he must have been mad.

Her aunt would go to great lengths to keep her occupied. She was not a great cook and encouraged Alice to experiment with food in the kitchen saying: "It's not like it could be any worse than something I would make you." So when Alice wasn't helping out in the shop or playing with the other kids on the beach, she and Jean would try out recipes in the galley kitchen. They would pretend all the while they were actually on television demonstrating the ease with which one could make this delicious pudding, pie, casserole or whatever they had decided on.

As she grew older Alice saw less of Jean, but always kept in touch even if she hadn't visited for months. Jean always seemed instinctively to know when to talk and when to stay quiet. She never berated her for not visiting more. As soon as Alice turned eighteen and left her boarding school behind, she packed her bags, took one last look at Belfast and caught a flight to Heathrow. She put herself through university with the last of the money left from her parents' estate and the sale of the semi. She worked her way through four years of a gruelling law degree, supplementing her income by working in bars or typing for post-graduate students. Her reward was an honours degree and a job with a fairly well-established law firm in Covent Garden. By constantly pushing herself, she now had a small one-bedroom flat in Hammersmith, a one-eyed cat called Gary, a mild shopping addiction and a string of less than successful relationships to her name.

The last visit Alice had made to see Jean was about six months ago and she could only manage to stay a weekend. Jean had been delighted to see her. Visiting Ireland was always hard for Alice, as memories filled her head as soon as she got off the plane. They had spent the weekend chatting over coffee in the shop, a glass of wine in the kitchen, and a few pints in the local pub – Alice telling Jean how wonderful life in London was and Jean making her laugh with tales of the folk who came into her shop with odd requests and tall tales. Jean had seen it all.

* * *

Alice thought back. The last time she had spoken to Jean was about a month ago, when Jean had phoned her at work to ask a legal question. It hadn't had anything to do with a will . . . in fact, it was a rather odd question . . . something to do with antiques. Alice had to research it for her – something to do with ownership rights.

Alice leant back in her chair, narrowly avoiding banging her head off the wall behind, and her eyes filled with tears. Slowly they ran down her cheeks. She brushed them away with the back of her hands.

"Alice?" Louise stuck her head round the door.

"Yes?" Alice bowed her head so that Lou couldn't see she had been crying.

"Oh duck, what's the matter? Man trouble?"

Louise, her forty-seven-year-old secretary, was an odd mix of motherly concern and the attitudes of a woman whose husband had recently left her for a younger model and was now convinced that men were largely to blame for everything. Usually she wasn't far off the mark. Louise had quietly reinvented herself from a Surrey housewife into a legal secretary who ran her office as efficiently as she ran her home. With her children now at university, she had sold the family house and bought herself a bright flat in Barnes with a garden and a spare room so her kids could still come and stay during the holidays. The Shit (as her ex, Gerald, was now officially known) tried to maintain his relationship with the children, but they found it very hard to accept his new flashy girlfriend who seemed hell-bent on spending all of his money. Alice admired Louise and enjoyed her sense of humour. She had to share her with another solicitor but she was Alice's only perk in the job. She still didn't quite know how she had ended up with the best secretary in the firm.

"No, I just got a bit of bad news." Alice took the hanky that Louise proffered. She relayed her conversation of ten minutes ago and her surprise inheritance. Twenty minutes later she was finishing the coffee that Louise had made and massaging her burnt calf while Louise was booking her a flight to Belfast.

* * *

Walking home later that evening, Alice tried to prepare herself for what was going to be a very strange week. She still had Jean's old house-key on her key-fob – somehow she had just never got round to taking it off. She was booked on a flight to Belfast City Airport first thing on Saturday morning. She had also booked herself into a local guesthouse as staying in Jean's house would seem too odd, to say nothing of inappropriate since it wouldn't be officially hers until her meeting with Mr Dunbar.

Alice walked the whole way home. It was over five miles so it was something she rarely managed to do – she usually ended up catching a bus for the last mile or two. She wandered past Harrods, taking the long way home. She watched the tourists *oohing* and *aahing* over the window displays of the huge store. Funny, most of the time she didn't even observe it as she passed.

Taking off her shoes in the hall of her flat, she was suddenly aware that her feet ached and that her head throbbed. She poured herself a big glass of red wine, lit a cigarette and collapsed on the sofa in front of the early evening news. She watched it the whole way through – right to the sport, something else she rarely did. Usually she listened to the headlines before channel-hopping for something more light-hearted. Tonight the soothing voice of John Suchet explaining the intricacies of international terrorism took her mind off Jean and stopped her having to think about the future.

Chapter 2

Two days later Alice landed in Belfast. It was a wet morning and of course there was no-one to meet her. She realised there wasn't anyone to phone. No-one knew her. It had been so long since she had spent any real time back home.

She climbed into the back of a taxi, throwing her bag in front of her.

"Donaghadee, please."

"Certainly, love – though it would be much cheaper to catch the bus into the city centre and get a taxi from there."

"I really don't mind."

Alice suddenly had an urge to see Jean's house; just from the outside, just to see if it was still the same.

The taxi driver nodded and started the engine.

Forty minutes later he pulled up outside the little seafront terrace. The shop was attached to the house, which in turn was attached to a row of about ten houses.

"Alright here?"

"Yes, that's great." She pulled thirty pounds out of her wallet and handed it to the driver. She shook her head at the single he tried to hand her back.

"Thanks, love. OK with that bag?"

"Fine."

It had stopped raining and the sun had come out. Alice stood, bag in hand, staring at 20 Shore Street, the house where she had spent so many summers, now devoid of it's heart – the person who had occupied it. She touched the bunch of keys in her pocket; one of them was for the door to the house in front of her.

She pulled the keys out of her pocket. The dull brass one was the one she needed and she pushed it into the lock. She turned it clockwise, the lock clicked back and the door opened. She stepped in and set her bag down on the floor beside her.

She peered up the gloomy hall: nothing had changed since last time. She pushed open the door to the front room. It was full of the ornaments that Jean had been so fond of; she particularly liked putting lacy doily-type things underneath them. Alice was always amazed at the amount of dust they collected.

She was surprised she didn't feel at all weird. She had expected to be a bit creeped-out at being in a dead woman's house, but she got an odd, comforting feeling that Jean was very much still there.

"Jean?" she asked the dusty room, half-expecting to hear a reply.

Complete silence, bar the ticking of the clock on the mantelpiece.

"Silly cow, now you're talking to ghosts!" she told herself off. Anyway, rooms were supposed to be icy cold if there was a ghost and Jean's living-room was as tropical as ever. No-one had thought to turn off the heating.

She pulled back the curtains, letting the light flood into the room, banishing any traces of gloom. Dust particles danced in the air, highlighted by the sun. Even though Jean hadn't been gone a week, the house gave the impression it had been vacant for months. She opened the windows to get rid of the imagined stale air. She went into the small back living-room and the little kitchen that opened off it and opened the curtains and windows there too.

She looked in the fridge – sour milk, a rotten lettuce and an old piece of cheese. She threw them all into the bin.

She went back into the living-room which looked out onto the back garden. The sideboard was cluttered with photos in frames, some of them family, most of them people she didn't recognise. She picked one up. It was of her mum and Jean over twenty years ago. They both looked so happy. Alice wasn't in the photo but she knew she was running round on the sand nearby while they posed for the holiday snap.

Putting the photo back, she sat down on the old

armchair that Jean loved, mainly because the arms were so wide she could put her plate there, enabling her to eat dinner and watch *Eastenders* at the same time. Alice looked at the ring left by years of hot plates set directly onto the faded fabric. Before she could stop herself, tears were streaming down her face. She made no attempt to stop them. The sense of loss that filled her was indescribable. She hugged her knees into her chest and hid her face, not wanting to see any more of the family photographs that Jean had so proudly displayed.

Minutes slipped by. Alice had lost track of the time. She had gone back twenty years to the time of the photograph and was imagining her mother and her aunt teaching her to swim in the freezing Irish Sea.

The doorbell rang, jolting her back to Saturday morning. She suddenly felt awfully self-conscious being in Jean's house without permission. The bell rang again, and she moved to answer it. Through the textured glass of the front door she could make out a small figure waiting in the porch.

"Ah, Alice, I thought it must be you!" Emlyn, Jean's shop assistant and friend of many years, was standing in the doorway looking not in the least bit surprised to see her. He was holding an umbrella – it had started to rain again.

"Oh, Emlyn, I'm so sorry, I just walked in – I didn't even think," Alice blurted out.

"Of course you walked in! Where else would you go?" He gave her a gentle smile. "Now why don't you come next door to the shop and have a cup of tea and tell me how you are and what's happening in London!"

Emlyn – the little man looked the same as he did the very first time Alice had met him all those years ago. On more recent visits she imagined he was gay – he had a slightly androgynous look but it was very hard to tell. In all the years that she had known him, and that was as far back as her memory went, there had never been a girlfriend, or a boyfriend for that matter. He did occasionally mention women he thought attractive, but people like Hilary Clinton and Cherie Blair did make her wonder. Princess Diana would always have a special place in his heart and, even years after her death, the mention of her name and Emlyn's eyes would mist up.

He was also slightly lottery-obsessed. In the few years it had been running Emlyn had never missed a week and always tuned in on Wednesday and Saturday nights. Needless to say, he had never actually won more than £10 – but he was convinced one day his numbers would come up, and wouldn't he be sick to his stomach if that was the week he hadn't bought his ticket? Auntie Jean was forever telling him he was mad wasting his money as he had more chance of sprouting wings than winning millions.

Emlyn had always been Jean's shop assistant and he had grown to become a very good friend. Alice thought Jean enjoyed his eccentric sense of humour and interesting dress sense. One rarely saw Emlyn without his tweed waistcoat and jeans, with a spotty cravat tucked into the open neck of his shirt.

Today, however, he was not bedecked in his usual finery – he was sporting a black polo neck and cords.

"Waistcoat is in the dry-cleaners for Monday," he said, observing her glance. His small mark of respect for Jean was to have his favourite item of clothing spotless when he said his final goodbye.

Alice hugged him. It was good to see a familiar face on this horrible day. She closed the door. Picking up her bag, she linked arms with him under his umbrella and walked round to the shop.

* * *

It was the smell that hit her when she walked in: it was that creosote, rubbery, birdseed smell that had always been there. She nearly laughed out loud when she saw the large galvanised metal bins with smiley faces painted on them.

"Whose idea was that?" she asked, pointing to the bins.

"Oh, a man came a few weeks ago and insisted they were all the rage. He was a bit pushy so Jean bought two to get him to go away." Emlyn shuddered when he spoke.

"Real aggressive type, you know."

"An aggressive smiley-bin salesman? Interesting." Alice grinned.

She sat down on a stool beside the counter and rested her elbows on the chipped Formica.

"Oh, what do you think you'll do with the shop?" Emlyn shouted from the depths of the back store where the kettle and tea-making accessories lived.

Alice was taken aback. She hadn't expected him to know. It was out of order for Mr Dunbar to have told him.

"Alice? Can you hear me?" Emlyn bellowed.

"Yes, yes, I can," she shouted back. "Just a bit surprised that you knew about it."

"Well, you don't stay chums with Jean for years and not know who was getting what in the will, do you?"

"I didn't even know she had one. I guess I thought she was the sort of person that didn't believe in them."

"What? A will?" Emlyn appeared out of the gloom, steaming cups in hand. "She loved all that stuff. She said it made her appreciate what she had."

"Really? That's kind of odd, don't you think?"

"That, my dear, was your aunt all over."

Alice took the cup of tea that was proffered and, pushing a tray of nuts and bolts out of the way, set the cup down on the counter.

"Poor Jean, who would have thought she would get hit by a bus! Emlyn, what the hell was she doing picking blackberries at the side of the road? Isn't it even a bit late for them?"

Emlyn seemed to hesitate. "Oh, she sometimes went out just for a walk – the blackberries probably meant she was worried – she used to say pulling them off the hedgerows helped clear her mind."

18

"Really? I never heard her say that. Did she do it a lot?" Alice felt like he was describing someone else – Jean had abhorred exercise.

"Only in autumn."

"What? Only walked in autumn?"

"Oh, sorry, I thought you meant the blackberry thing. Yes, she walked nearly every day."

"Hmm . . ." Alice rested her chin on the palm of her hand, which was a bit sweaty from holding the tea.

"I don't believe she fell in front of that bus anyhow."

"Pardon?" said Alice.

"I really do not believe Jean fell in front of an oncoming bus. I mean, she just wouldn't."

"Emlyn, I admit I was as amazed as you are when I heard – but if the police say she got hit by a bus, then she must have got hit by a bus."

"Of course she got hit by a bus – the poor woman virtually had tread-marks on her back."

Alice cringed at his tactlessness.

"Doesn't mean it was an accident though, does it?" he continued.

"What are you saying?"

"I think she was pushed." Emlyn took a swig of his tea, and didn't flinch as the scalding liquid went down his throat.

"You're serious, aren't you?" Alice was stunned by his comment.

"Completely. It makes sense, doesn't it?" Emlyn folded his arms across his chest.

"Sense? Not really! Who would want to kill her? You mean she was mugged? For money? It's not like she'd have been carrying masses of money, is it?" Alice pushed strands of hair out of her face as she struggled with what Emlyn was telling her.

"No, I don't think it was money. I think it was something else." Emlyn didn't catch her eye.

"What?" Alice felt a strange mixture of intrigue and disbelief. She wanted to laugh at Emlyn and tell him not to be such a camp stirring little bastard – her aunt was dead and that was that. Something stopped her. He was too good a friend to Jean to ever make something like this up. It was far-fetched, but she hadn't believed the business about the bus either when she heard it for the first time.

Emlyn smoothed the neck of his jumper and continued, "I don't know, but I think she had . . ."

"She had what?" Alice waved an arm and knocked her lukewarm tea into the tray of nuts and bolts, leaving them swimming in a light brown pool of rusty bits and liquid. "Oh, sorry!" She looked about for something to mop it up with, Emlyn's last sentence still hanging in the air.

"Never fuss, never fuss." Emlyn waved his hand at the mess. "Anyway, it's your mess now, your nuts and bolts, your shop."

"Jesus – don't remind me!"

"It's not that bad – this is a pretty good little shop. Our customers are an interesting bunch and no two days are the same."

Alice realised the conversation had shifted, but she

20

didn't feel like discussing Emlyn's fanciful ideas about Jean's strange fate any longer. "Oh, Emlyn. I'm a solicitor not a shopkeeper. What the hell do I know about running a hardware shop? I don't even know what half the bloody things in this place are for!"

"I'll teach you."

"I'm not sure I want to learn."

"You may have to." Emlyn looked stern.

"Why? I have a busy job in London, which I love – slight exaggeration – and I was kind of hoping you could run it until I can get a buyer for it." Alice was giving him her best look of hope.

"Oh Alice, Jean wouldn't want you to sell this place!" He looked genuinely upset at the thought.

"Emlyn, this place doesn't really fit into my life plan! I don't mean to seem ungrateful, but of course I'm going to sell it! I have no intentions of coming back to Northern Ireland – ever!"

"What about the house?"

"What about my career?"

"Are you going to sell that too?"

"My career?"

"No, the house."

"What about it?"

"Are you going to sell it?"

"I don't know – I haven't had time to decide. I don't know why she left it to me in the first place."

"How else did Jean think she was going to get you to run the shop – if you didn't have anywhere to live?"

Alice just stared at him, not sure what to say next. Emlyn seemed to have all the answers, only she didn't feel like asking all the questions.

"Well, you've been handed a business and a home," he said, as if it was the simplest thing in the world and Alice was being totally thick that she hadn't already worked it out.

Alice wanted to scream at him, to try and displace some of his neat hair-sprayed hair.

"Now clear up your tea," he said. "You can spend the rest of the day here with me. Of course, you'll be staying in the house tonight."

"I've booked into a guesthouse." Alice was mulling over their conversation. Her Saturdays usually consisted of visiting a few well-known high-street shops, finished off with a meal based on some kind of fried carbohydrates eaten out, or a trip to the local with her friends. Sitting in a hardware shop with a man of indeterminate age discussing the merits of hardware versus the legal profession was a different kettle of fish altogether.

"Cancel it, you'll want to get yourself all settled."

"Emlyn! I'm not bloody staying! OK?"

He just smiled serenely and smoothed the neck of his jumper.

"I need to use the phone," she muttered.

"It's in the back, beside the kettle."

"Thanks."

She felt bad for yelling, but everything was going slightly pear-shaped and she felt that she needed a bit of moral support. Time to call Bernie – he might know what to do.

Bernie was the guy who owned the flat beneath her and who had become a good friend. He ran his own restaurant/café and was extremely practical – she prayed he was in work. Sitting on an upturned plastic bucket, surrounded by a huge array of household products she hadn't known existed or what use they could possibly have, she dialled Bernie's number. Thank God – he answered on the third ring, a good sign that he wasn't too busy.

"Hi, good afternoon, Logan's."

"Bern, it's me, have you got five minutes?"

"Hi, Lice, long time no chat, sure thing, fire away."

Thank you for giving me Bernie! Alice offered up a silent prayer through the ceiling of the back store. Other than the fact he had nicknamed her 'Head-lice', he was an absolute diamond.

"I'm in Donaghadee."

"I thought you were going to Belfast? Donaghawhat sounds much better – so what's the problem?"

"I've inherited a shop."

"I know, you told me on Thursday night, right? From your aunt who fell in front of a bus."

"Right, only she may not a fallen."

"Sorry?"

"Never mind. Here is the problem. Emlyn – I've told you about him before, haven't I?"

"You have, the camp shop assistant who loves the lottery?"

"That's the one. Well, he apparently knows all about Jean's will – which as you may imagine is most unusual – most people like to keep it totally private –"

"Stick to the point, Al."

"So, I'm in the shop right now and Emlyn has just told me that not only have I inherited the shop and her house, but her intention was for me to run the business and stay over here!"

"Wow!"

"Bern! What am I going to do with a shop and a house in Northern bloody Ireland? I live and work in London!" She could virtually hear him smiling.

"Can't Emlyn run the shop for you – say, as your manager – and you pay him? And then you could just rent out the house – you always said it was in a nice area."

Alice considered his idea – pure brilliance as usual.

"Bernie Logan, you're a wonder. Did I tell you I loved you – in a purely platonic way of course?"

"Not as much as you should. I'm your friend, cat-sitter and trusted advisor. Listen, I've got to run – I think the Gruyère quiche is burning."

"Quiche, Bernie? Are you sure you wouldn't like to meet Emlyn?"

"I'll tell Susie you said that!"

"Only messing, thanks again, send Susie my love. I should be home soon." She had her fingers crossed.

"We'll see you then. Oh, and Gary sends you his love. He misses you quite badly – keeps going and lying on your bed looking most forlorn."

"Scratch his chin from me."

"Will do – bye, Lice."

"Bye, Bernie."

Gary, Alice's cat, of the silver tabby variety, was one of her pride and joys. Formerly a stray she had found lying at the side of the road outside her flat, she had taken him to the vet's where he had to have one of his eyes removed. The vet told her a car had probably hit him. Judging by the state he was in, he hadn't been looked after for quite some time. After a bit of wrangling with the Cat Protection League as to who would be best suited to look after the cat, Gary became Alice's flatmate/ hot-water bottle. It took a little bit of encouragement to make him eat properly. Initially he used to take his food and eat it under the sofa, which was not popular with Alice. Very soon he had made himself at home and was happy to eat out of his bowl, without strewing the contents all over the floor. The loss of one eye didn't seem to bother him and Alice thought it gave him character. With that new added character, she felt he was too battle-scarred to have a traditional name like Tiddles so she named him Gary, which suited him down to the ground.

She hung up the phone and made her way back to the front of the shop. Emlyn was helping a man who was looking for wood preservative.

"You'll only need to use this once every couple of years." Emlyn spoke most knowledgeably with a tin of something unpronounceable in his hand. The man nodded in agreement. "Now, would you like it in a dark stain or a light?"

The man considered this and then settled for the light option. They continued their transaction, Emlyn chatting all the time and the man nodding at intervals. Once money had changed hands, the man continued chatting for several minutes before leaving. He checked out a couple of light-pulls in a box beside the door before walking out.

"Get through all right?" said Emlyn.

"Pardon?"

"On the phone."

"Oh, yes, thanks. I rang Bernie, my friend in London."

"Oh? Is he your boyfriend?"

"No, he certainly is not – he has a girlfriend, Susie, who he's very much in love with."

Emlyn held his hands up, as if surrendering. "Sorry I spoke!"

Alice was starting to get annoyed – not with Emlyn in particular, just annoyed in general. "I think I'll go for a walk, if you don't mind."

Emlyn looked slightly put out. "I was going to show you how we carried out stock control . . ." He tailed off as if realising that would be the last thing on her mind.

"Not today. Show me another time, OK?"

"You're the boss."

Alice glared at him.

Two minutes later she was out of the dark shop and into the contrasting brightness of the rainy Saturday afternoon. She walked along the seafront, heading towards the harbour.

She thought back to what Emlyn had said about

Jean's accident. It all seemed so far-fetched, but it had seemed as if he had been about to tell her something significant. She wondered if she should just put it down to Emlyn finding it hard to let Jean go. She really should be more sympathetic towards him; it was a really big blow for both of them.

The wind whipped her hair round her face. Pushing it back, she looked out over the sea and watched the fishing boats. There were a couple of container ships in the middle of the channel and a group of brave little boats with their red sails were out there too. Alice watched the boats until they were almost out of sight. She put her hands in her pockets to keep them warm and shrugged her shoulders so the collar of her coat came up higher. She walked right up to the lighthouse and round its circumference, watching the seagulls float on the wind.

Smelling the salt in the air brought back more memories. After ten minutes, and having passed only one other person – a man walking a King Charles Spaniel on the seafront – she turned and walked back.

She stopped outside the house again.

"Why am I here?" she asked herself.

"You're here because you're nosy and you want to have a look round the house – your house," her voice of reason answered back.

She had worked hard for anything of great value in her life – what on earth was she going to do with a house and a shop in a little town in County Down?

"Auntie Jean, you old nutter, what were you thinking of?"

But whatever she was thinking, Alice was now going to have to make some pretty big decisions.

She unlocked the front door and walked in. The house was brighter this time, as the curtains were open. The front room had a view straight out over Belfast Lough. An old sofa, formerly of the velveteen variety and now very threadbare and a little sad, sat on its own against the far wall. Heavily patterned wallpaper, badly faded by the strong sunlight, was starting to peel in the corners of the room. A bureau, its lid closed, had a photo-cube sitting on top, again badly faded, with pictures of people Alice didn't recognise. There was a sideboard, its top faded, and pushed up against the window was a small uncomfortable-looking chair where Jean used to sit and admire her view. Alice wondered why she had never got round to getting a decent chair.

The back living-room, which had the kitchen off, was slightly smaller than the front room and every bit as tatty. Jean's favourite old chintz armchair didn't match the old sofa, which in this case was leatherette, with worn patches from years of bums sliding across its surface. There was an enclosed fire; the old-fashioned kind where you had to open a glass door at the front to put coal in. Above it was a mirror, the nicest thing in the room. Gilt-edged and simple, its clean lines appealed to Alice among the rest of the clutter.

The kitchen was galley-style, with orange Formica

doors, and a little gas cooker at one end. Everything looked as if Jean had bought it twenty years ago or more. Outside the little garden was overgrown, but pretty. Jean had loved her garden, though not many plants liked the salty air and constant battering from the wind and rain.

Upstairs there were three bedrooms, the largest being Jean's. The other two had single beds and small wardrobes. Jean's had a double bed, which had seen better days, and a huge dark wood wardrobe, which looked circa 1950s. The bed had a pink wool blanket and a rather horrid floral duvet on it, with mismatching pillowcases. The bedside tables had lace doily-type things under sheets of glass. The sunlight had faded the bedlinen and warped the veneer of the bedside tables. There was a bright pink lipstick and a little bottle of Tweed beside the bed, along with an overdue library book and small ornament of a dog with its paw broken off.

The bathroom was a profusion of bottles and jars. Jean had obviously sampled several of Boots' '3 *for* 2' offers and the place was coming down with shampoo, conditioner, vitamins and vile cheap perfumes.

Even upstairs Alice could hear the ticking of the clock. Funny – she had never noticed it before, but then the house had never been so quiet.

Back downstairs again, she decided she would ring the guesthouse and cancel her booking. She would stay here in the house after all.

Chapter 3

"Ouch! Crap!"

Alice rolled over in bed, and nearly fell out. It had been years since she had slept in a single bed. Her bed at home in London felt like three times the size. Interestingly enough, this bed seemed to come with hidden lumps and bumps. Alice felt like she had spent the night sleeping on a small hill. She got out of bed gingerly, since she had turned off the tropical heating yesterday and the floor was wooden and very chilly. She had decided against sleeping in Jean's bed, as that had felt too creepy.

"Ohhh!" She rubbed her aching back and wished she had slept on the floor. She padded downstairs in a thick pair of woolly socks and her reindeer pyjamas. The water would be cold so she would have to wait for it to heat up.

Catching sight of herself on her way down, in the mirror in the back room, she grinned – hair on end, mascara panda-eyes. Anyone would think she had been out on the razz, rather than spending the evening familiarising herself with the town and unpacking her not-warm-enough clothes from her suitcase.

"Shit!" she muttered to herself as she looked for the immersion heater. Then she remembered: opening the back door, she made the dash across the concrete yard to turn on the switch for the oil boiler. It gave a little roar, satisfactorily announcing that it had started. Waiting for everything to heat up, Alice made a cup of coffee and turned on Jean's telly, which was from the pre-remote-control era. Curling her feet under her, she sipped coffee and watched the *Hollyoaks* omnibus.

"Thank God for continuity," she said to no-one in particular. In London, *Hollyoaks* was compulsory viewing in her flat on a Sunday morning.

The rest of the day was spent buying a few provisions for the house and trying to find a decent Chinese which would deliver. On closer inspection of the cupboards in the kitchen, she was horrified to discover condensed milk that cost seven pence. There was also an assortment of Angel's Delight packets, all at four pence and a variety of other tinned goods which looked like Jean might have picked them up at the end of the Second World War. While binning these undesirable items she decided to clean the cupboard from whence they came and ended up scrubbing the insides of all the cupboards, the kitchen floor and the inside of the cooker. Afterwards the kitchen gleamed orange, smelled of bleach and Alice

31

had ruined a top with bleach spots and melted her fingertips.

After the kitchen, the front and back rooms followed, then the hall and finally the bedrooms and bathroom. Alice inspected all the beds and discovered that Jean's was by far the comfiest and if she were to sleep at all tonight in relative comfort, she would have to sleep there. Stripping all the beds, she put the sheets into the washing machine – top-loading twin tub, of course.

After her bleach-fest she decided to get a bit of fresh air. At a bit of a loose end, she wandered along the seafront to a park and watched big children pushing smaller children too high on the swings. They screamed, half with excitement and half with fright.

Emlyn was obviously not working on a Sunday and Alice couldn't remember where he lived. Strange she hadn't thought to ask him yesterday. She had gone back to the shop later in the afternoon but it was closed up, no sign of Emlyn. She knew she would see him at the funeral tomorrow, strange wee man. She almost felt that if she walked about for long enough he might appear.

She walked until her hips hurt and then she decided it was time for that Chinese and for plonking down in front of the TV. Unfortunately, Jean had never got round to buying a video or a Sky dish, so it would have to be terrestrial television. Lying on the leatherette sofa, shovelling chicken chow mein down her throat forty minutes later, Alice found it hard to believe that tomorrow she would receive the news officially that she was now the owner of one hardware shop and adjoining seafront terraced house in Donaghadee, County Down.

"What the hell am I going to do?" she asked the room. "Well, possibly a paint-job inside for starters. God no! What am I doing? I'm not staying, I'm going to sell this place or rent it out. I have to get back to London as soon as possible."

Then she started thinking about her rabbit-hutch office, and the vicious radiator she shared it with.

"Why hurry back? Remember Louise? You have never been so organised." That voice was back inside her head.

"I think maybe I need some company, before I start talking to myself out loud," she said to herself out loud.

* * *

Monday morning was a bit drizzly. Thankfully Jean's bed had been comfortable and Alice had slept well without dreaming. She had left the heating on, so the house was bearable when she got up. She thought carefully about how she should dress, not sure what tone she should set. Finally she settled on the navy suit she had brought with her for the occasion. It was an office suit, but it would look suitably sombre today.

Brushing her blonde hair back into a ponytail, she noticed her roots had come through rather badly, so quickly decided to leave it down and not draw attention to her neglected bonce. A smattering of make-up and a few squirts of Donna Karan's Cashmere Mist and she was ready.

The funeral was at noon; it was only 10am, so she had a bit of time to kill. She rang the office and spoke to Louise.

"Everything is absolutely fine, ducks. You just relax and try and get through today, OK? Mr Balfour is in meetings all day so he won't be looking for you. I let his secretary know where you were, so you're covered."

"Thanks, Lou, what would I do without you?"

"Don't be silly, dress nice in case there are any nice men there."

Chance would be a fine thing.

"I will, Lou, and thanks again."

Work was fine without her. Her boss Mr Balfour was a bit of a stickler but if Bettye his trusted secretary had the message then she was fine. Bettye was Louise's new best friend – Louise had made sure of it. With Bettye on her side, Mr Balfour was a pussycat as she ran his office with military precision and he trusted her implicitly. Alice was wandering round the house, at a loose end, when she noticed someone had put a letter through her door. As she opened the envelope, a key fell out with a note stuck to it: *"Your key for the shop. See you at noon, Emlyn."*

God, he hadn't even knocked. Alice opened the front door and looked up the street – no sign of him. She wondered how long the envelope had been sitting there.

"Well, at least I have something to do for an hour or so." She pulled on her coat and closed the front door behind her.

The shop blinds were drawn so it was in complete

darkness when she opened the door. She felt about on the wall, searching for a light-switch. Her foot slipped on something and she wobbled for a moment trying to regain her balance.

"*Ohhh, shiiiiit!*"

Flailing her arms, she tried to right herself, but in the dark she could see bugger-all. She keeled over, pulling boxes off the shelf as she struggled to stay upright. Then, lying half-in and half-out of one of Jean's smiley-bins, with tacks and nails in her hair, she attempted to regain her composure. The navy suit was covered in dust and she guessed her smattering of make-up had been joined with a more generous helping of dust and DIY accessories.

"*Oh, arse!*"

Struggling to get her bum out of the bin, she realised that the light had been switched on.

"Yes, it does seem to be your arse, doesn't it?"

Alice stopped struggling with the bin and looked up at the voice. It was American and belonged to a kind-faced youngish man, who looked like he was going to a funeral.

"Oh, God. Sorry." She tried again to free herself from the bin and only succeeded in looking like a drunken tortoise stuck on its back with its legs in the air.

"Here, let me help you." As the kind-faced man leapt forward to assist, his sudden movement dislodged a box of broom-handles which proceeded to fall down on top of them both, creating a massive din.

"Perhaps I'm causing more harm than good," he said as he pulled the smiley-face galvanised bin off Alice.

35

"Thank you," Alice giggled, dusting herself down.

"How did you know I was in here?"

"I could hear you from the street, and since the light wasn't on I presumed you must be Jean's niece, or a very badly organised thief."

"Ah, right, was I that loud?" So he knew about her.

"No, no, I just have a very keen sense of hearing."

"Thanks." Alice blushed.

"I'm Bill, by the way." He extended his hand towards her.

"Alice." She took his hand and shook it. "I was looking for the light-switch, but I seem to have been intercepted by some household items."

"So I see, but if it's any consolation they seem to have come off worse!" He started to pick up the broom-handles. "Emlyn told me you're taking over the shop."

"Did he indeed?" Alice could have cheerfully swung for the little polo-neck-wearing, interfering pain-in-the-arse right about then.

"Well, I think he *hoped* you would, rather than anything else."

"Nothing is official, of course – the will hasn't been read or anything." Alice suddenly realised that she didn't have to explain anything to this total stranger.

"Sorry," as if reading her thoughts, "you must think I'm terribly nosy. I was quite a good friend of your late aunt. She used to stock goose eggs just for me."

"Oh, right, I didn't realise." Goose eggs?

"No reason why you would," he said cheerfully. "Would

you like a hand to clear this mess up?" He had a bunch of broom-handles in his arms and looked like he didn't know where to put them.

"Oh, no, don't be silly, I'll sort it out straight away." She took the broom-handles and put them back in their box.

"It would be quicker if I did." He bent down and started picking up the nails which had scattered all over the linoleum.

"OK, great." Alice picked up the bin and the remaining broom-handles.

"So, you're from London?" Bill asked her conversationally.

"Not originally." Alice wondered what else Emlyn had been telling him. "You're American?"

"That obvious, huh?"

They continued chatting while they tidied up the mess – Alice guardedly, Bill without seeming to notice that.

By the time they had finished it was nearly twelve.

"How are you getting to the funeral?" he asked

"I was going to order a taxi."

"We'll share one. I'd drive but I thought I'd have a few drinks at the wake."

Alice looked at him, thinking how inappropriate that last comment was and how she would rather go alone. But before she could voice that feeling, Bill was already chatting to the taxi firm. So he knew where the phone was and had no problem making himself at home.

Sitting in the back of the taxi, Alice surreptitiously

tried to touch up her make-up. Bill was sitting in the front while the taxi-driver relived most of Saturday's match for him, whether it interested him or not.

When they arrived, Alice saw Emlyn standing alone at the side of the church. Leaving Bill to pay for the taxi, she walked over and joined him. He was smoking and offered one to her. All good intentions of giving up had disappeared about the same time Mr Dunbar had called, and she took one gratefully.

"How was the rest of your weekend?" Emlyn asked, inhaling deeply on his cigarette.

"OK. Thanks for dropping the shop key in. Were you supposed to do that?" Alice cupped her hands round the lighter to stop the wind blowing it out as she tried to light it.

"Don't know, but thought you might want to have a look round the place by yourself. I see you met Bill."

"Jean's goose-egg man."

"The very same."

"What's he like?"

"Bill? He's a pretty nice guy actually. Easy-going and always nice to me. Been coming into the shop for a while. Nice, for an American."

"Funny, Jean never mentioned him."

"Why would she? He was just one of her customers."

"He seemed to know his way round the shop well."

"He normally would stay for a cup of tea – he usually made it too."

They smoked the rest of their cigarettes in silence,

38

watching the other mourners arrive. She recognised quite a few of the people from her previous visits to Donaghadee. She tried to spot the solicitor, but no-one who passed looked appropriately old or wise. In fact, she was very surprised by the amount of people who did pass. In her relative inexperience, this was a big funeral. Jean must have known a lot of people: it seemed every DIY enthusiast in town had come to pay their respects.

Alice felt detached as she sat in the front pew reserved for relatives. Emlyn sat beside her. Other than that the pew was empty. The rows behind her were packed. The coffin with Jean's body was about five feet in front of her. A pale wood coffin with brass handles specified by Jean and no doubt dealt with by Mr Dunbar. Alice hadn't really imagined Jean going into such detail. Her own wreath of flowers lay on top of the coffin with a simple message expressing her love and thanks to the woman who had made her formative years bearable.

The rest of the service was a bit of a blur. Hymns were sung, kind things said about Jean, uplifting things about life going on. Alice stared straight ahead, feeling very alone.

When it was over, four pallbearers came forward to carry the coffin out of the church. Alice followed them down the aisle and a very tall man followed closely behind her. Outside, he touched her on the shoulder.

"Miss Watson?"

"Mr Dunbar?"

"Very pleased to meet you, Miss Watson." He shook her hand warmly.

Together they stood and watched the mourners leaving the church.

"Come with me in my car. We can follow the hearse to the crematorium."

Alice had no idea Jean had wanted to be cremated. They walked together to a shiny green Jaguar. Mr Dunbar was clearly a very successful solicitor.

"Your aunt was very specific in her requests."

"Oh?"

"In particular her funeral."

Alice said nothing, waiting for him to elaborate.

"After the crematorium, the wake will be held in Ned's bar, in the centre of Holywood."

"She wanted her wake in a pub?" Alice raised her eyebrows. Maybe Bill, the goose-egg man, hadn't been so far off the mark after all.

* * *

The following day, when she and Emlyn had gone to hear the reading of the will in his office in Belfast, Mr Dunbar explained that, besides Alice, Emlyn and the Cancer Research Foundation were the only beneficiaries of Jean's will. Alice was amazed that Jean had so much to leave.

Apparently she had amassed a small fortune and she had left the business in pretty good shape. Alice shouldn't have too much difficulty selling the shop.

"Jean did however make one proviso in regard to your inheriting her property," said Mr Dunbar.

"Oh?" Alice looked at Emlyn. He shrugged and returned his attention to the solicitor.

"In order for you to take over numbers 20 and 21 Shore Street, Donaghadee, you must live in number 20 and work in number 21 for a full six months. If you can do this and run the business successfully, then the properties will be yours to do with what you wish."

Alice was stunned. Six months? Was Jean mad? What the bloody hell was she going to do now?

"Miss Watson? Are you OK?" Mr Dunbar peered over his bifocals at her with the kindly look of an elderly uncle. "I realise this information has come as a bit of a shock."

Alice looked again at Emlyn. He didn't seem in the least bit surprised at the news.

"Did you know about this?" she asked him with her voice lowered, trying to retain her temper.

"Me?" Emlyn gestured in a not very convincingly innocent way.

"Yes, you!" she hissed.

"Might have," he grinned.

Alice was again rendered speechless.

Mr Dunbar told Alice to take her time to decide whether if she would accept Jean's terms. Then Emlyn drove her back to Donaghadee. They drove in total silence, Alice angry that he hadn't told her what Jean had planned and Emlyn quiet because he understood, but he had made a promise to his old friend. It was his last obligation to her and he had carried it out.

Chapter 4

Alice flew back to London on Wednesday without saying goodbye to Emlyn. She had to get back to work for one thing. She landed in Heathrow with her head full of questions about her future. It would be the easiest thing in the world to tell Mr Dunbar that she did not accept the terms, and the proceeds of the sale of the shop and house would be given to Cancer Research. But something told her to take more time before she made her decision.

Back in her flat Gary was delighted to see her return.

"Hello, my darling!" she greeted him, stroking his furry tabby head. He purred like a little engine and wrapped himself round her ankles as she lugged her bag into the small hall. She felt as if she had been away forever rather than five days, so much had happened.

That evening she called to Bernie and Susan's flat downstairs and filled them in on her trip. They opened several bottles of wine as they discussed her options.

"Well, it's a major decision, Lice."

"I know, Bern. I'm totally flummoxed as to what I should do."

"Are you happy in London?" Susie asked her.

"I hadn't thought about it until yesterday. I just thought I would let Emlyn run things until I could sell everything or rent it or whatever. I hadn't actually gone into all the possible permutations."

"Do you love your job?" Bernie asked

"Well, I worked bloody hard to get where I am! Admittedly it isn't quite what I expected, but it's good – I'm doing well."

"But are you happy?" asked Susie.

"I've never really asked myself that. I can afford stuff, I've made a life for myself, I have a cat."

"Apart from us, Alice, do you ever see anyone or are you always working or sleeping?"

"I guess when you put it like that . . ."

"I'm not having a go – it just never struck us that this was your life's work."

"And becoming an expert in wood preservative would change all that?" Alice asked, surprised if not a little annoyed that they weren't trying harder to convince her to stay.

"OK, look at it another way." Bernie tried changing tack, realising she was getting cross. "When was the last time you came home and thought to yourself, 'I love my job, this is what I want to do for the rest of my life'?"

Alice helped herself to the packet of Marlboro Lights

43

on the coffee table. Lighting the cigarette she sat back on the sofa and blew a plume of smoke up towards the ceiling.

"Do *you* love *your* job, Bernie?"

"At the moment I do, but I know I won't do it forever. I see myself in five years moving down to Dorset and opening a seafood restaurant and being able to work to my rules rather than anyone else's."

"But you run your own place now!"

"My seafood restaurant will be a friendly little place, with a great wine list and top-notch fresh seafood. I won't have to worry about the fickle and ever-changing market in the city, where one minute traditional restaurants are all the rage, and the next it's ultra-modern. One minute, people can't get enough of you, the next you're yesterday's news. I think smaller towns are more real. I want to be able to grow vegetables myself, work at my own pace and maybe start a family. Susie and I have discussed it and when we both feel ready we're going to sell up and get the hell out of here."

Alice looked at Susie as if for the first time. Susie was fairly high up in a marketing job for Harvey Nicols and Alice thought she had it all. She had never considered that she and Bernie were just biding their time.

"We don't want to bring kids up in London, Alice, and we would both like a slower pace of life."

"But what about your amazing job?"

"Discounted designer clothes do not a happy person make!" Susie laughed as she said it.

44

Though it was easy for her to say as she sat there looking gorgeously glossy and groomed.

"I do like my job, and the clothes are definitely a perk, but let's face it, it's not rocket science and there is definitely more to life than sitting around all day with a bunch of fashionistas discussing the merits of Gucci or Prada. Not everyone wants to be Tara Palmer-Tomkinson."

Alice was stunned into silence for the second time in as many days. Listening to her two friends talk quite seriously about their futures made her consider her own.

"Where do I see myself in five years?" she asked herself, looking into the bathroom mirror later on that same evening as she scrubbed her face with a facial cleansing wipe, which didn't appear to be removing all traces of make-up as the packet had promised.

"I don't want to wake up in my thirties and still be alone," she thought as she brushed her teeth with her electric toothbrush with its oscillating head.

"Could I live in Donaghadee again?" she wondered as she smoothed age-defying moisturiser into her face and neck – well, you're never too young to start.

"Will I be able to run a business I have no experience in?" she considered as she brushed her hair free of any tangles.

"Would moving to Donaghadee be admitting that I couldn't make it on my own?" she worried as she climbed into her bed. Gary was purring at the bottom of the bed, both because of the fact she was home and because she had produced his favourite Whiskas in gravy for his dinner as her way of an apology.

She lay there wondering about Emlyn's comments concerning Jean's death. At the time she hadn't given him much credence, but the more she thought about it, the more she couldn't see Jean out picking blackberries in October at the side of the road.

She sat up, turning her light back on.

Gary looked up from his curled position by her feet.

"Gary, I think there's something that Emlyn is not telling me."

Gary blinked at her.

"I'm going to ring him." She looked at her digital alarm clock. The time glowed 01.15am at her.

"Well, I'll ring him in the morning." She realised that it was very late, that she was slightly pissed after all the red wine round at Bernie and Susie's and that she had work tomorrow. "God, work!"

For the first time Alice was aware she was actively dreading going back. The idea of dragging herself through London for her commute to work almost had her in tears. She lay back on her pillows in her big bed, screwed her eyes shut and tried to sleep.

She tossed and turned and couldn't get comfortable. She looked at her clock: the red digital numbers indicated it was now 02.04am.

"Shit, shit, shit." She pulled the duvet up over her head, dislodging Gary in the process. She heard the quiet thud as he jumped down off the bed and padded out of the bedroom to sleep in the living-room as he often did when his mistress had insomnia.

Flicking on the television as a last resort to try and tire herself out, Alice passively watched crap on Sky One. *Ibiza Uncovered* was on. The narrator was explaining that this week they were following the fortunes of a gay couple in their late thirties as they tried to set up a bar in San Antonio.

"Jeez, that poor sod looks like Barry Gibb," Alice murmured before she started channel-hopping. There was absolutely nothing else on, so she was soon back to Barry Gibb and his partner and witnessed what was presumably a highly edited version of their trials and tribulations. She wasn't sure if it was a good idea to have called the bar 'The Back Door', but she was glued when she recognised their accents as being from Belfast.

* * *

Alice woke up the following morning with Gloria Estefan singing in her head. She rolled over in bed and nearly had a heart attack when she saw the time – she should have been up thirty minutes ago! Jumping out of bed, she sprinted into the shower, narrowly avoiding tripping over her open but not yet unpacked suitcase full of crumpled clothes. She slathered herself in grapefruit shower-gel at breakneck speed, shampooed, conditioned and towelled herself dry, all in less than five minutes. Grabbing the first thing that came to hand from her wardrobe, she flung on an ironed blouse, zipped up a pair of bootleg trousers and shoved her arms into a jacket. She threw down some dried cat food for Gary, and rushed out, pulling the front door shut behind her, hair still dripping wet.

Sitting on the bus, she noticed the less than admiring glance from the man sitting opposite her. Looking down, she saw that her trousers were black, her blouse deep blue and her jacket brown. She hoped like hell that she didn't have any clients coming in to see her today.

By the time she reached her stop, her hair had dried sufficiently for her to realise that in her haste she had forgotten to rinse the conditioner out. Instead of the freshly washed and fragrant hair she had seen in the adverts, she looked like she had been shallow-fried – and she didn't have any make-up on.

Entering her building, she made a beeline straight for the ladies' loos to see what repair job she could possibly do before she reduced Louise to a giggling mess. There was nothing she could do about her hair now – she dragged it back into a ponytail, making a mental note to try and rinse it at lunch-time. She found a bronzer, an ancient mascara wand and a rather nice MAC lipstick lurking at the bottom of her bag. She applied all three liberally and was relatively pleased with the results. Obviously she would look better when she stopped sweating, she told herself.

She sped down the corridor on her floor, rushed into her office and flicked on her computer while throwing her jacket over the back of the chair – it was nine fifteen and Alice thought she had got away with it. Thirty seconds later Louise popped her immaculately coifed head round the door.

"Looks like someone could do with a coffee." She smiled, her smile faltering as she inspected Alice more closely. "Were you mugged on the way to work?"

"Sorry?"

"By the Bad Taste Fairies?"

"Louise!" Alice tried to pretend she had no idea what Louise was talking about.

"I'm sorry Alice, but you look a complete mess. Mr Balfour wanted to see you at some stage this morning, but I think I should put him off, at least until you've had time to brush the lard out of your hair and get dressed with the lights on. Have you been on a sunbed?"

"I slept in."

"They have a big sink with good mixer taps in the disabled toilet. I could help you rinse your hair. You can borrow my make-up if you like."

"Is it that bad?"

Louise nodded. "It's that bad."

Half an hour later Alice felt as if she had had a make-over at Christian Dior. Louise seemed to own every product they made and she had to admit that she was really very pleased with the results. Alice's hair had been rinsed and re-shampooed and the results were as good as the make-up job.

"You could meet the Queen today – well, from the neck up," Louise commented, making a face at Alice's outfit.

There was nothing Alice could do other than take the jacket off and quietly freeze.

"Thank you! Thank you so much!" she repeated all the way back to their office.

"Now go and see Balfour and give him what for."

"Actually, now that you mention it, what does he want to see me for?"

"Bettye didn't say."

Alice shrugged. She was tired from her awful night's sleep and, with everything else that was going on, she felt her boss was the last person she could deal with.

Chapter 5

"I don't understand. Why don't you want children? All women are supposed to want children, it's like you're programmed that way."

"For Christ's sake, Derek, do you really have to carry on like you're straight out of the Dark Ages. We can vote now, you know!"

"That's not what I mean."

"What do you mean then?" Maggie's green eyes flashed at her husband who was driving her nuts.

"I just thought women of a certain age start to feel maternal – you know, the biological clock," he countered.

"Of a certain age! Jesus, Derek, ask the charm school for a full refund as they don't seem to have been able to help you!"

"Isabel has kids," Derek said, as if by way of explanation.

"I know, Derek, but I'm clearly not Isabel, nor do I have any wish to be."

Isabel was Maggie's best friend, who had twins. But she was also permanently knackered, seemed to endlessly be making packed lunches and never seemed to have a minute to herself. Add in the fact that her husband worked all the hours God sends, that she worked part-time and that they rarely saw each other during the week – and it did not seem like the kind of life Maggie wanted. Children were just not on the agenda; she had enough trouble looking after her husband who was doing a fantastic impression of being a Victorian Dad.

Derek gave a defeated sigh. "I'm working from home today." He turned and walked into the kitchen without giving her a kiss.

"Right, well, I'm meeting Isabel for coffee and then I have a meeting in Holywood with Lizzie about the NSPCC ball, so I'll see you later," Maggie said to his departing back.

Derek made no response.

She slung her black Epi leather Louis Vuitton bag over her shoulder, picked up her car keys from the hall table and left the house. The cold October morning was a pleasant shock after the suffocating heat of the house. She bleeped her Mercedes SLK unlocked and slid into the driver's seat, instantly calmed by the dark interior and the smell of the leather seats. Derek had bought the car three weeks ago for her. It had been a fabulous surprise, but now she wondered if it was a bribe because he wanted children and she did not.

Reversing out of the driveway, she could see him at the kitchen window, already on the telephone. Whoever he was talking to was making him laugh.

"What has happened to us?" she asked herself as she drove down the Malone Road, her Macy Gray CD filling the silence and making her tap her glossy fingernails on the steering wheel in time to the rhythm. She and Derek had been married for six years. When they had got engaged all her friends had been so jealous. Derek was a career man with a good job, on the fast track in the management system. Well-liked and hard-working, he provided her with everything she could ever have wanted: a big house in Malone, undoubtedly one of the most desirable addresses in Belfast, all the clothes she could ever want and, best of all, she didn't need to work any more. Goodbye, beauty salon! Hello, ladies who lunch! Their first couple of years had been blissful. So what if they didn't really have sex that much? They were a good team, they loved each other and that was what mattered. Maggie didn't think either of them had really noticed the lack of a strong physical relationship at the start. But recently it was pushing them apart, love or no love. Maggie had a deep niggling feeling that something was fundamentally wrong with her marriage, but was terrified that if she looked too hard she would see the cracks she knew were there. A baby was Derek's way of cementing over those cracks, but Maggie didn't feel it was the right answer. She wanted to leave the lid on this Pandora's box.

Pulling up outside Isabel's house in Derryvolgie Avenue, she put those thoughts out of her mind, and put on a smile as Isabel shot out of the front door like a bullet out of a gun, shoving her arms into her coat as she pulled the door closed behind her.

"Thank Christ you're here! Joanne is driving me insane with her constant gossiping about her neighbours and all the various ways they scam the dole office."

Joanne was Isabel's cleaner, who spent more time reading *Hello!* and imparting local gossip than polishing the silver.

"Well, if you weren't such a soft touch, you should tell her to smarten up – or she'll be joining them in the queue."

"Maggs! Don't be such a bitch! Joanne is a real find! It's hard to get someone you really trust," Isabel said indignantly, her chestnut curls bouncing round her pretty face.

"Hard to get someone who actually cleans too."

Isabel glared at her then started to giggle, colour flushing her pale cheeks. "Sorry to start off by moaning, but the twins didn't want to go to school this morning – it was a bit of a battle of wills."

Maggie put the car into gear and pulled out of the driveway.

Isabel's children, Amy and Henry, already started school at age five, had to continuously come up with ingenious reasons why they should not go.

"This morning Amy had covered both her face and Henry's in talc, claiming they were too ill to get up. Only she had forgotten to cover their necks and they just looked like a couple of mini Geisha girls in Harry Potter jammies." Isabel grinned at the memory.

"I take it you eventually coaxed them to go?"

"On the understanding that there would be sweets waiting for them on their return – remind me to buy a bag of Jelly Babies before you drop me home." She snuggled into the heated leather seat. "God, I love your new car!" she cooed.

Maggie smiled. "Bribe. Derek is on about kids again."

"Oh." Isabel stopped at that.

"Not you bloody too! That's all I need! My best mate ganging up on me with my husband!"

"No-one is ganging up on you! Jeez, are you paranoid or what this morning? Anything I say on this matter you will misconstrue so I had much better remain mute on the subject and thus avoid you bollocking me. And anyway, I didn't say anything."

"You gave me your look."

"What look? I don't have a look."

Isabel grinned and they continued the rest of the car journey in companionable silence until they reached the coffee shop.

This was their weekly event. In order that they saw each other at least once a week, they had formed a habit of going out for a coffee and a chat every Thursday morning. Expressive Expresso on the Lisburn Road was their favourite haunt. It had the best sticky danishes, enormous scones and they did every kind of flavoured latte you could think of.

Plonking herself down on one of the lovely squashy sofas, Isabel could feel the hassle of her early-morning tussle with her beloved monsters begin to evaporate. Lifting her hazelnut latte up to her lips with both hands, she sipped and then said, "So, running the risk of you going berserk on me – Derek was on about you two having kids again?"

Maggie nodded, her mouth full of custard danish.

"God, I hate you!" said Isabel. "You can eat what you like and you never put on any bloody weight!"

"Mum said it would all pile on when I turned thirty." Maggie spat danish crumbs all over her polo-neck.

"You're thirty-six and it's still like being friends with a golf club!"

Maggie laughed, spraying more crumbs over herself. Wiping them away, she said, "Lay off the compliments. I can't take any more. At least you have boobs."

Isabel tugged at the front of her top – it was a little strained over the chest and she wondered if she had put on any weight recently without noticing. Well, she had managed to jump from a size 14 to an 18 in a year and a half so what were a few more pounds? "I've got enough boobs for two people," she sighed. "It's a wonder I don't fall over sometimes. I'm like a Weeble – remember those plastic toys you couldn't push over? They just kept bouncing back up again?"

They both laughed at the idea and Maggie steered the conversation smoothly from weight to the '10% off' sale at Debenhams.

"They have an excellent make-up department. You should go and have your make-up done one afternoon when you aren't busy. I'll go with you, it would be fun," Maggie enthused.

"God, I'd love to," Isabel sighed, looking in her handbag and fishing out a furry-looking Lipsyl and a Max Factor bronzer whose remnants were only just clinging on to the sides of the compact.

"Yuck, you need new make-up! Let's go tomorrow." Maggie wrinkled her nose in disgust, thinking of her own well-stocked make-up drawer at home and her Prada mini-make-up pouch sitting in her handbag.

"Can't tomorrow. I'm working in the morning in the office and then the kids have to go to their elocution lessons in the afternoon."

"Elocution lessons? You never mentioned that before! My word, aren't they a bit young?"

"I know, but their teacher said they should start young and then it would all come naturally. Charles is very keen that they don't have strong accents."

"What! Their accents aren't strong at all!"

Isabel shrugged. "Well, they don't seem to mind going. To be honest, their teacher is a lovely big woman who spends most of the time feeding them buns and juice – they never want their tea after an afternoon with her. They haven't even managed to learn a poem yet."

"Well worth the money then."

"God, don't! Everything seems to be about money. The kids are costing a fortune, but then they always do. Charles is keen that we go skiing next year. I don't know how we're going to afford it."

"You've never skied before."

"Another of Charles' ideas. Apparently all the men and their wives at work ski, so Charles thinks it would integrate us into the social scene more. I mean these guys mostly work in London – what do they care whether we can ski or not?"

"What a load of shit! Before you know it, it will be Club Med holidays and getting ponies for the children. Has he settled into his new job?"

"I don't know, Maggs. He was so pleased when he got the job – he had worked so hard for it. But now that he has it, all he wants to do are things the guys in London do – he works all the hours that God sends and he still isn't content."

Isabel looked into her empty coffee cup and swirled the remaining foam round the bottom. As she looked up, Maggie saw she had tears in her eyes.

"Oh Maggs, he still loves me and the kids as much as he ever did, but now he's caught up in some horrible career race with these other guys who by the sounds of it would sell their own granny if it meant they made their targets! I feel that I'm not glamorous enough any more."

Maggie bit her tongue; she knew the pressure of trying to fit in.

"I really don't mean to moan but the new job means lots more travelling over to London, to Head Office, and whenever he comes home he's so wiped out he can hardly climb into bed. I couldn't tell you the last time we went out, just the two of us, for a romantic dinner, or even a flipping pizza."

"How is your job going?"

"Same as ever. I'm like a third-class citizen in there because I have kids and I'm not interested in world domination. Jesus – I'm just a part-time receptionist! Do I have to have ambition as well? All the women are dead set to prove to the men that they're every bit as good if not better, which I totally agree with – but everyone is entitled to a life outside work."

Isabel worked as a receptionist three mornings a week for a large firm of insurance brokers.

"Can't you leave?"

"Not at the moment. The money isn't great but it pays for the food shopping and new clothes for Amy and Henry. Most of Charles' salary now goes on our bloody mortgage. I sound like such an ungrateful old cow, but we don't need such a big house. It's just another status symbol as far as I'm concerned."

Maggie moved over beside Isabel on the sofa and gave her a massive hug. "Can you talk to Charles about it?"

"He just looks at me like I'm mad. We have to keep moving forward, onwards and upwards and all that, bugger the consequences." Isabel's eyes filled with tears again.

"Anyway, enough about my marvellous life – what about you?" She smiled brightly, a little too brightly to be convincing.

"Oh everything is fine! Derek hopefully will forget

about children for another six months, giving me a temporary reprieve."

"Jesus! Listen to the pair of us! Do you think they sell gin?"

* * *

After dropping Isabel back to her house, Maggie couldn't shake the gloomy feeling that had descended on her since Isabel had revealed how unhappy she was – she and her husband were still totally in love and committed to each other, but somehow they had let his career take control of their lives.

Her mobile rang as she drove through the centre of Belfast.

"Hello?" She didn't immediately recognise the number.

"Maggie, glad I caught you, it's Lizzie here."

"Lizzie, hi!"

"Listen, I've had to cancel the meeting, Matty has come down with measles, so it's not a good idea that anyone comes round to the house."

"God, I'm sorry, is he OK?"

"Well, not the happiest little chicken at the moment – he's currently Spots 'R' Us, but he'll be fine. We'll rearrange the meeting for next week, OK?"

"Sure, fine, thanks for letting me know. Give him a big kiss from me." Maggie hung up. She drove round the City Hall – no need to drive all the way to Holywood now. Would she go shopping? She considered her options. Nah, nothing she wanted. Would she go to the gym? God no, too much like hard work. Those trainer blokes at the gym always made her feel guilty for not going more. Maybe she would just go home and try and avoid her husband.

Pulling into her driveway, Maggie nearly hit a dark-green Saab that was parked behind Derek's BMW. It forced her to park out on the road. The car looked like Cliff Cameron's from next door, but why he would drive instead of just walking she didn't know. Cliff should be at work. Couldn't be him. Probably someone from Derek's work, she thought, as she let herself into the house.

She was aware that music was playing somewhere in the house, but it wasn't coming from the kitchen or living-room. Maybe Derek's study which was on the first floor.

"Another one of his bloody presentations," she said aloud.

Walking past the hall mirror she caught sight of her reflection. "Ugh, I'm as pale as anything," she thought to herself.

There were no visitors in the living-room. She did a quick tour of the rest of the ground floor. Finding no-one around, she decided that there was no time like the present – she would go upstairs and have a St Tropez session which would make her feel more like Posh Spice and less like the Ghost of Christmas Past.

She had kicked off her shoes in the kitchen so her feet made no noise on the carpeted stairs as she climbed them. Reaching the landing, she listened for noise from the study. She couldn't hear voices, as the music was louder up here.

As she pushed open the bedroom door, she realised the music was coming from inside – but why would Derek have the stereo on in the bedroom? The alarm-radio must have set itself off again.

Maggie dropped her handbag and her jaw. In front of her she could see her husband's naked back rising and falling in time to the music and he wasn't doing aerobics. Maggie took a huge intake of breath. She felt like she was suffocating. Derek must have heard her behind him. He stopped his rhythmical movement and turned round, his face scarlet and sweating, the body beneath him hidden.

"Maggie!" He paled instantly.

Maggie backed out of the bedroom, unable to believe her own eyes. She could hear Derek calling her from inside as, almost in slow motion, she descended the stairs, shock stopping her tears.

In the kitchen she held onto the worktop at the kitchen sink, trying to get her thoughts in order.

"You stupid fool, you knew something was wrong, but you refused to admit it. An affair, an affair, why didn't I see it?" She was finding it hard to breathe, her chest hurt and her head was spinning.

"Maggie?"

Derek's voice was right behind her. She spun round to see him standing in the dressing-gown she had bought him last Christmas, his hair still tousled from his sex romp with some slut in their marital bed.

"Look, I'm so sorry, I really, really am, sweetheart. I have wanted to tell you for so long, but never knew how." Derek looked absolutely gutted.

"Sorry? Sorry! Listen, you miserable fucker! I leave the house for an hour and the minute I go, you're shagging someone else. The bed was probably still warm! How long has this been going on?"

"Just over two years," Derek said softly.

Maggie stared at him in disbelief. Her husband, her Derek, had been having an affair for two years and she hadn't even noticed? Not read any of the signs?

She suddenly felt quite faint and grabbed hold of the granite island-unit for support. Derek pulled out a kitchen chair and she sat down without any argument.

"But what about the kids you wanted?" she asked in a small voice, her anger suddenly gone. She felt deflated, uncomprehending.

"I promised myself if you got pregnant I would stop this immediately. But the more you resisted the idea, the harder it became."

"Quite literally," Maggie said sadly, thinking of the Mercedes guilt-present parked on the road

"Maggs, I'm so sorry. I really didn't want it to turn out like this. I still love you."

"Only you don't want to sleep with me, do you? Derek, if kids are so important to you then we'll have as many as you like! I love you!" The tears came, like the opening of floodgates.

Derek said nothing. He put the kettle on and sat

down beside her. Maggie couldn't speak, her chest heaving with grief. When he got up to make the tea, her eyes followed him and it was then she saw the figure in the doorway: the same dishevelled hair, look of guilt and clothes askew, a sign of dressing in a hurry.

It took Maggie a few moments to work out why Cliff Cameron was standing in their kitchen at a time like this. Then the penny dropped and her rage came back with terrifying force.

"You fucker!" She hurled the tea that Derek had just set down in front of her right back in his face.

"Maggie! Stop it!" Derek's hands were up at his face, wiping away the boiling liquid. Cliff moved to help him.

"You stay away, you fucking bastard!" Maggie hissed, her green eyes narrow and cold. "You must have found it funny, fucking my husband behind my back. Well, let me tell you, Cliff, you revolting creature, Claudia isn't going to like it much either!"

"Maggie, please, I want to tell her myself. I owe her. Screaming won't help. Derek and I are both desperately upset about what this is doing to our marriages." Cliff looked like he might cry.

"What bloody marriage? I go out for coffee, come home to find my husband in bed with a *man*! I think you can presume your marriage is over. Get out of my house, *get out*!" Maggie ran at Cliff, fuelled by anger, her fists beating down on him.

She turned round and grabbed the first thing she could lay her hands on – the fruit bowl – and threw it at him. He deflected it with his hands and it shattered onto the polished marble floor. She grabbed the mugs off the mug-tree and hurled them at him as he made a quick exit out of the kitchen, the Bridgewater pottery exploding behind him.

Running after him she threw the portable phone, a bin, a vase full of irises, all the while screaming abuse at him at the top of her voice. She couldn't think of enough hateful things to scream at him.

"Bastard! Fruit! Bastard! Baaaaastard!" Her eyes were hard and narrowed as she spat out the words.

"Maggie! Stop this." Derek caught up with her at the front door, preventing her from hurling the terracotta pots filled with herbs on the front doorstep.

"Fucker!" she screamed at Cliff as he got into his car.

Derek pulled her back into the house, her arms flailing as she tried to wrench free from his grip.

"I'll speak to you later," he called to Cliff, who nodded white-faced.

"No, you won't! You won't ever speak to that fruit again! Do you hear me!"

"Maggie! Shut up for one second, would you!" Derek closed the front door and stood with his back to it, blocking her way to pursuing the rapidly retreating Cliff.

She glared at him, silent temporarily.

"It's not Cliff's fault."

"Ha."

"Maggie!"

"You're gay, for Christ's sake! I married a gay man!

Ha! How on earth did I let this happen to me?" She smacked the palm of her hand off her forehead.

"I think I may be bisexual."

"Oh great! That makes it all better then, does it? When my friends ask why my marriage broke down I can tell them my husband was a closet bisexual who was riding one of our neighbours." Maggie was virtually snarling now.

Derek winced, listening to the expletives tumble out of her mouth. Maggie was no saint when it came to swearing, but she would have done a docker proud this afternoon.

"Listen, you need time to calm down." Derek attempted to be rational.

"If you leave this house now, do not expect it to be still standing when you get back!"

"Maggs, this is not getting us anywhere."

"I have just caught you in flagrante with Cliff! Our bloody next-door neighbour who we see around twice a bloody year for crappy drinks parties and I didn't even think you liked him – or his sodding wife! Do you seriously expect me to be reasonable?" The anger had subsided marginally, from a boiling hot lava of hate to a slightly less volatile river of sarcasm.

Crumpled irises were strewn everywhere, water trickled across the solid oak floor in the hall from the smashed vase, and was soaking into the antique oriental rug.

"I'd better wipe that up before anything gets ruined," said Derek.

"Jesus, you're so camp! I can't believe I never saw the signs." Maggie slumped onto the floor beside the door – her legs had given way beneath her.

"Bitching at me is not helping. I realise that this is a massive and unpleasant shock, but please let us talk like rational adults," Derek pleaded.

Had Maggie been of Romany origin, they would have called the look she shot her husband the Evil Eye.

Chapter 6

Standing at the kitchen sink, Isabel felt a sinking sensation as she gazed across the highly polished tiled floor. Amy and Henry were painting about three feet away from her and had spilt cerise-pink paint all over the floor. The pale grouting that Charles had insisted upon would surely stain and he would be raging when he came home. She sighed, took off her soapy rubber gloves and picked up the kitchen roll to mop the mess up. The two blonde little heads bobbed happily as they created the chaos.

"Come on, kids, you'll have to stop painting if you're going to keep spilling it on the floor." Not to mention slipping on it and cracking your heads open, she thought wryly.

"Mummy, I made this for you." Amy pointed at her picture proudly.

"Wow! Amy, it's lovely!" Isabel opened her eyes wide to show her approval.

Amy beamed at the high praise. "It's you and Daddy with some lovely flowers," she offered by way of explanation.

It really looked like a large pink blob sliding off the paper.

"What have you done, Henry?" Isabel turned her attention to Amy's twin brother.

"Mummy, it's a tractor of course," Henry replied without looking up. He was engrossed in a pink tractor that looked remarkably similar to Amy's Mummy and Daddy with some lovely flowers.

"When they're dry, will we put them on the fridge for Daddy to see when he comes home?" Isabel asked.

The children were delighted. Isabel did a deal with them. If they were good she would put their pictures on the fridge with their alphabet magnets and then Daddy could admire them when he got home – usually well after they had gone to bed.

Amy tried to help Isabel clear up the painting mess, while Isabel tried to prevent Henry from rolling in the spilled paint. She was behind in the washing and didn't want to send her son to school in a pink jumper in the morning.

The twins ate their Marks & Spencer mini-pizzas with baked beans without any of the usual arguments. Nothing was thrown, no tears were shed and afterwards both settled down quietly in front of a Disney video.

She watched them from the door into the kitchen, the two little heads side by side, engrossed in Balloo the Bear and Mowgli. The nice thing about the twins being five was that she could take her eyes off them for a few minutes and they were generally OK. Before, when they were younger, she couldn't take her eyes off them at all or one would be drinking bleach while the other tried to put the cat down the toilet. Returning to the washing-up she stared out the window above the sink. It was dark outside and she couldn't see the garden, just the reflection of herself and the living-room behind.

Looking at herself, she sighed with disappointment. Mostly she didn't notice, or tried not to, but recently all she could see was a woman she hardly recognised. When she was younger she had prided herself on her appearance. Never naturally slim, she had worked hard to maintain her size 14 figure. After she got married her clothes gradually became a little bit tighter, almost imperceptibly she started to buy size 16, then she fell pregnant and never really got back down from an 18. Charles didn't seem to notice. She was so busy with work or the twins that she never had time to go to a gym and if Charles was away on business she ate with the children, and usually hoovered up anything they left behind.

Now, instead of the well-groomed, fashion-conscious twenty-something with too many shoes for her own good, she was a thirty-five-year-old, plump, slightly rosy, unthreatening Mum type. The sort of woman you would hug rather than admire. Gone were the well-tailored trousers, replaced with wide-legged jersey-cotton ones with elasticated waists. The saucy heels she used to trip about in had been retired, while trainers and comfy loafers littered the bottom of her wardrobe. The only thing to remind her of how she used to look was her glossy mane of chestnut hair, which was now scraped back in a ponytail rather than falling about her shoulders as it used to.

Her eyes fell down to the suds in the sink and she sighed.

The dishes all done, she let the water out of the sink and went into the living-room to see what Amy and Henry were up to. They were sound asleep, Henry with his thumb in his mouth.

Sliding the patio door open, Isabel stepped outside as quietly as she could, not wanting to wake them up. She slid the door closed behind her, checking there was no movement on the sofa. Sitting down on the cold step outside she took the illicit packet of Silk Cut out of her apron pocket, removed one cigarette, placed it in her mouth, lit it and inhaled. Exhaling and sighing with pleasure as she did so, she leaned back against the glass door.

It was October, the nights were getting darker much sooner, the temperature had noticeably dropped and it wouldn't be too long before it was getting frosty. But tonight it was a clear night and the stars were just starting to appear. The birds were silent and there was no noise from the road outside.

She thought about work the next morning. She worked three mornings a week and hated it. She didn't hate the work – she just strongly disliked the people she worked with. The men in the office pretended she didn't exist – all except Mr Anderson the boss, who despite being possibly the next busiest man in the world to her husband always took the time to say "Good Morning" or "Good afternoon". The women were even worse than the men: some looked like they had been up most of the night applying make-up, others were far too busy with their careers to bother with make-up or nice clothes. None spoke to Isabel at her desk at the front of the building. She job-shared with an older woman called Muriel who seemed to have been with Mathers Smithson since the year dot and thought all the men were great and the women were bitches. Isabel never really got to chat to Muriel but something told her she was not missing out on much. Muriel was as sour as eight-day-old milk.

The cigarette finished, she ground it out on the underside of the step and threw it over her hedge into her next-door neighbour's garden, giggling to herself at the thought of Mr McNeill finding it the next morning. He was so precious about his bloody garden, always giving out if Henry's ball fell onto his rockery or flower-beds. It gave Isabel a kick to throw the odd fag-butt onto his grass.

Sliding the glass door open again, she stepped back into the living-room and locked the door behind her. Then, popping an extra-strong mint into her mouth, she woke the twins to give them their bath.

* * *

"Good morning – Mathers Smithson," Isabel answered

brightly. She transferred the call to the Claims Department and quickly answered another.

The whole morning was a blur of ringing phones and couriers arriving delivering official documents and Next Directory orders for the girls in the travel-insurance department. By one thirty Isabel still had not managed to have a cup of coffee and she felt as if all her make-up had slid off her face, which it had.

Muriel arrived swathed in smiles. Her son living in Australia had sent her a bunch of flowers for her birthday and she was delighted – she had also brought them with her to flash at Isabel.

"Isn't he great!" She conveniently seemed to forget that the same son hadn't bothered to contact her since her birthday last year.

Isabel nodded without much gusto as the flowers were thrust in her face.

"So generous! He sent these all the way from Australia!"

"Well, all the way from the Lisburn Road," Isabel joked, stepping back out of the way of the proffered foliage.

Muriel's eyes narrowed momentarily, but, without skipping a beat, she smiled generously at Isabel like she was a child who didn't know what she was talking about.

"Well, it's the thought that counts."

"It certainly is, Muriel." Isabel was quick to make amends. "I have a card for you."

"Oh Isabel, thank you," Muriel crooned as she opened the envelope.

Isabel was taken aback at such a display of appreciation, until she noticed Mr Anderson crossing the reception.

"Happy Birthday, Muriel," he said as he pushed open the door.

"Thank you," she beamed. "So kind," she mouthed to Isabel in a conspiratorial way as the door swung shut behind him.

Muriel propped the card up on top of the reception desk so anyone passing would see – she had the flowers in a vase beside her. With her cardie over her shoulders, her half-moon glasses balanced on the end of her nose, her collar turned up and a bucket of L'Air du Temps emanating from her, she was ready for the afternoon.

She waved goodbye to Isabel, who always felt like she was being dismissed, and started to answer the phones.

* * *

Isabel opened the driver's door of her Mercedes A-class and flung her large skip-sized handbag onto the passenger seat. Settling herself into the driver's seat, she put on her seatbelt and started the engine. Nothing happened. She tried again. The engine whined and then stopped.

"Arse!" she muttered to herself

She tried again. Same thing, some chuntering under the bonnet and then the awful sound of silence.

"Shit." Isabel got out of the car, popped the bonnet

and wedged it open to have a look inside. If she was totally honest with herself she knew the car was well overdue for a service, but she hadn't had the time or the money to get it done. An acrid blue smoke seemed to be rising off the engine. Dropping the bonnet back down again, she rummaged round her bag and pulled out her mobile. The car wasn't under warranty any longer, but she was sure they were members of the RAC. She rang the number on the back of the tax disc sellotaped to the windscreen.

After a brief conversation with a most helpful man called Andrew on the other end, she was able to ascertain that she was no longer a member of the Royal Automobile Association as she had not paid the reminder bill they sent out to her three months ago.

"So if I pay my membership fee now, will you come out?"

"We will need to receive the payment first, madam."

"Isn't there anything you can do?"

"If you give me your card details now, I can process your payment and then send someone out."

"Great, hang on while I get my purse."

A bit more rummaging and the purse was located. She pulled out her and Charles' joint-account bank card and read the details to Andrew.

"I'm afraid that card has been declined," he told her a few moments later.

"Are you sure?"

"Yes, madam."

"Oh, right." She tried to sound calm. "How about this one?" She called out the number of her Visa card and the payment went through. Declined? Why ever would the other card be declined? The last time she had checked their joint account there had been well over three thousand pounds in it.

"Mrs Adams, we will have someone on their way to you very soon – can you stay with your vehicle?"

She concurred; Andrew took down her location details and then hung up.

Isabel sat in her car, in the company car park, wondering why the card had been declined. Surely it must be a mistake? Or had Charles taken out all that money for some reason – without telling her?

"I'm totally sure there was at least three thousand pounds a month ago," she thought to herself. She must check it as soon as she got home. Both she and Charles put part of their salaries into that account, which was mainly used to pay the mortgage and bills. They had also been saving into it to take the children to Disney World Florida. She didn't remember Charles mentioning paying any big bills recently.

She had only been sitting there for about ten minutes when the RAC van arrived to get her started. A flat battery was to blame and she was on the road again, though pounds lighter than she had been. Sadly it was sterling and not weight.

"I could be a rich man or a superstar," she sang along to the radio, nipping through the busy lunch-time traffic.

She made her way back to Derryvolgie Avenue to try and tidy before Charles came back from London and freaked out at the state of the house.

She stopped off at the Mace on the Malone Road and ran in to pick up some tea bags and milk. The same song was playing as she entered the shop and she hummed her way round the aisles searching for Nambarrie tea bags. By the time she had found the tea bags she had managed to accumulate nearly a full basket of stuff she had forgotten she needed. Spare candles in case there was a power cut, a jar of pesto sauce (she loved it, the children hated it), two light bulbs, a loaf of white bread, Marmite, butter, three packets of sugar-free chewing-gum, crisps for the kids' lunches and a giant-sized Mars bar. Plus the tea bags and milk she had come in for. As she reached for the twenty-pound note in her purse she again made a mental note to check the balance of that joint account immediately – lucky for her Charles had signed up for the telephone banking. She wouldn't even need to go into the bank and queue; she could just ring and speak to some anonymous stranger who would give her all the details she needed. Dropping the change into her purse she took her carrier bag and headed out to the car.

Back at the house Joanne was vacuuming upstairs as Isabel let herself in the front door, tucking the empty Mars Bar wrapper into her handbag. One of the nice things Charles had let her do since they moved to the big house was get a cleaner for a few mornings a week. It had been a nightmare getting one who was any good.

Joanne was great, though it was true she had an awful habit of drawing Isabel into a conversation and talking non-stop until Isabel realised they had been gabbing for half an hour. In order to combat this, Isabel arranged for her to come on mornings when she knew she would be at work. She did come on Thursdays but thankfully Isabel and Maggie usually met for a coffee on a Thursday morning so at least she had a couple of hours away from Jo who was more informed than the editor of *Hello!*.

Isabel dumped her bag down on the island-unit in the kitchen and flicked on the kettle. She had an hour before she had to pick up the twins from school and she and Joanne would normally have lunch together before Joanne caught her bus back to North Belfast and Isabel rushed out to get Amy and Henry.

Getting the lunch things out of the fridge, she jumped when she heard a voice behind her.

"You're back?"

"Jesus, Joanne! I didn't hear you."

"Sorry, Isabel." Joanne was standing behind her, wearing her rather decrepit housecoat. She told Isabel she cleaned better with it on. Isabel didn't care if she wore a bikini as long as both the bathroom and the en suite were toothpaste-smear free and the toilets didn't look frightening.

"Salad and cheese sandwiches OK?" Isabel asked.

"Great, whatever you're having."

"Make the tea, would you? I just bought some – it's in the plastic bag over there."

"How was work?" Joanne asked conversationally as she rummaged through the bag.

"Oh fine, the usual. It was Muriel's birthday so she was slightly less caustic than normal. The morning flew in. Though my car refused to start and I had to rejoin the RAC to get them to come out."

"God, I hate when that happens," Joanne nodded, though she had never owned a car nor even knew how to drive.

Isabel put the sandwiches together while Joanne brought her up-to-date on what was happening in the world of the celebrity.

"Such a shame about Tom and Nicole."

"But I thought they split ages ago!"

Joanne nodded. "But still a shame. The divorce has come through. They had assets of over 200 million dollars."

"Gosh," Isabel commented, head deep within the fridge, looking for the salad cream, thinking two hundred quid would be nice.

"Nice to see Prince Gustaf is getting married."

"Really? I had no idea there was a Prince Gustaf."

"Austrian, very close to the Spanish royals, but he has opted for Lady Snorniz from Switzerland."

"Joanne, how you remember all these names is beyond me!"

"Well, you never know when it might come in handy."

"Hum . . ." Isabel couldn't think of any situation which would require the listing of the Euro royals from memory.

They sat at the kitchen table, Isabel still in her work jacket and Joanne still in her housecoat. They ate in a companionable silence, albeit a brief one.

"Is Charles back tonight?" Joanne still had her mouth full of sandwich.

Isabel nodded, swallowing. "He's on the six o'clock flight into the city airport. His car is there so I don't have to pick him up, which is great."

"He works very hard, doesn't he?"

"Very," Isabel agreed.

"Do you know, I have never met him."

"Really?" Isabel was surprised. "You've been working for us for nearly three months and you've never met him?"

"Never."

"Well, I suppose he's away so much at the minute. His firm was bought over by a bigger firm in London, so he's there two or three nights a week."

"Must be lonely though, eh? All that time in hotels?"

"Yes, I suppose it must be. Though he never complains."

Now that she thought about it, Charles never seemed to mind that he was away from his family so much.

"Must really love his job."

"Yeah, he does," Isabel agreed, though to be honest she had no idea – Charles just didn't talk about it. All he seemed to be interested in was what his London colleagues did, and how 'small town' they themselves were living in Belfast.

"I'd better get this stuff put away," Joanne indicated

the box of cleaning stuff she carried round the house, "or I'll miss my bus."

"Don't bother – leave it and I'll put it away."

"Thanks, Isabel." Joanne folded her housecoat and put it in the cupboard where the Hoover and the ironing board lived. She took out a fleecy jacket and pulled it on over her jeans.

"See you," said Isabel. "Thanks."

"Bye." Joanne closed the door loudly behind her and left Isabel stacking the dishwasher.

Chapter 7

Sitting outside Malone Primary School waiting for the twins twenty minutes later, Isabel was lost in a daydream. She was three stone lighter, with a fabulous wardrobe, angelic children and a husband who adored her and wasn't bothered by what other people had.

In reality she knew that Charles loved her, but it was just that his job seemed to have taken over, pushing his family into the background. The twins didn't really seem to notice – maybe they were too young? But at five years old they didn't miss much. Isabel longed for the nights when she was just married. Six years ago when they were both happier in their own company rather than that of work colleagues, they would have laughed at the idea of useful networking dinners. Charles was happier with a bottle of red wine and Isabel's home-made shepherd's pie than he would have been in some posh restaurant where everything was served with a 'jus' or in a 'timbale'. These days she couldn't remember the last time he had eaten something she had cooked for him. He was either on his way to the airport or had just got home and was too tired. He seemed to have his hands permanently glued to his laptop as if it was some sort of vital lifeline he couldn't disconnect from. It drove her nuts.

Charles never used to bother about *things* or what other people thought of them. They used to live in a beautiful old cottage on the edge of Belfast near parks and lots of woodland. It had three bedrooms and an old range Isabel had loved cooking on. The children had masses of room to play and they had two cats that roamed the woods at night and slept all day by the Aga. Charles liked nothing better than pulling on his wellies and taking the whole family for a walk or an 'adventure', as he liked to tell the twins. But when his company had been taken over by the London firm, he had been exposed to the wealth and excess of the London traders and the way they conducted their lives – their amazing homes, wives and mistresses. Right from the start he had been overwhelmed by what he saw. Coming home from business trips, he started to criticise the cottage for being too ordinary, too small, too far out of town. Then he started bringing property brochures home and spending long hours looking up property sites on the Internet. Saturday mornings became a ritual of dropping Amy to ballet, Henry to mini-rugby and then attending the string of appointments Charles had made to view houses in the more salubrious areas of Belfast. He didn't seem to hear Isabel when she told him she didn't want to move, that she and the twins loved their cottage. Instead he bought a huge barrack-style semi-detached red-brick six-bedroom house in Malone with a much smaller garden and a big parking space to the front. He didn't see the tears in Isabel's eyes as she packed away all their belongings, as he had gone back to London for another bloody meeting. But they couldn't sell the cottage. It had been on the market for months without a single viewer – what it must be costing she shuddered to think.

Since the move, Amy had nightmares about monsters in the roof space and she didn't sleep all the way through the night. Henry had started to develop a stutter. One of the cats had been run over on the busy road outside the house, the other had run away – the twins had been inconsolable. Isabel refused to get any more cats, as she couldn't bear the thought of them getting run over too.

They had been in the house for three months when Charles decided to employ a well-known interior designer to come in and do the house up from top to bottom.

"You're far too busy with the kids, love," he had offered by way of explanation, while busily flicking through the day's post. Isabel had been horrified at the idea of a stranger deciding on her paint colours.

"You'll love this girl. She comes highly recommended. Apparently her taste is superb."

Isabel had been furious and tried arguing with him, but he just went to bed in a huff, left for work the next day without discussing it further and organised the interior designer anyway.

Shirley Maxwell was the name of the interior designer

who turned up a week later. She was impossibly tall and incredibly thin, dressed head to toe in flowing black. She looked more like the Grim Reaper than a super-successful designer. She was definitely not a 'girl'– she was in her mid-fifties, Isabel was sure. She also suspected a talented surgeon's knife had had a role to play in her unlined face, but the neck gave it away. Shirley picked her way round the boxes Isabel hadn't quite finished unpacking, looking each room up and down without making any comment. Isabel felt as if she was being assessed along with her home and didn't really like it very much.

"There is a very dark feeling about this house," Shirley finally said bluntly, after wandering for over half an hour with Isabel trailing round after her with a smile plastered onto her face.

"Yes, well, we would never have picked purple velvet curtains ourselves," Isabel joked, fingering their inherited drawing-room curtains, trying to remain jovial.

"Of course you wouldn't, dear, how perfectly ghastly." The humour going right over her head.

"We need light and bright. Yes, light and bright," the designer muttered to herself

"Do bear in mind we have two five-year-olds," said Isabel.

Shirley seemed lost in thought and did not respond.

She arrived several days later when Isabel was at work, apparently with a key that Charles had had cut for her. She brought with her swathes of "fabulous material, just perfect for that London pied-à-terre".

"Oh. Will it do for plain old Derryvolgie Avenue then?" Isabel was singularly unimpressed: it just looked like very expensive crinkled cream material and certainly did not look overly child-friendly.

The next day Isabel had arrived home at lunch-time to find Shirley there with wallpaper samples – the same cream colour as the curtain material.

"Isabel, this will transform your home," Shirley told her knowledgeably.

"Think of the Ribena stains," Isabel replied, equally knowledgeably.

Shirley waved her concerns away as if they were nothing more than a few annoying gnats.

The next few weeks, Isabel would come home and the house would be in various states of decoration. It was pointless getting cross with Shirley. The woman simply didn't get it. She was entirely unaware that she was irritating the hell out of Isabel and probably wouldn't have cared less had someone taken the time to point it out.

Isabel lost the cream wallpaper and curtain argument. The large spacious hall retained its parquet flooring but Shirley had her team of decorators paper it in a deep midnight blue with white cornicing. The effect was very dramatic but it wasn't very Isabel. She felt it was like walking into a nightclub.

The drawing-room was papered in a heart-stoppingly-expensive very pale green with tiny gold squares on and a deeper green carpet. The pale colours made the room look absolutely enormous and all their furniture seemed lost in its vastness. Isabel felt sick when she thought about what this must be costing, but Charles kept signing cheques and Shirley kept coming back.

The kitchen now had a polished marble floor, and neutral walls – thank God, Charles had drawn the line at a new kitchen, so Shirley had to 'work round' the solid-wood country-style kitchen, which Isabel secretly loved. Isabel privately thought the polished floor was a death-trap for the kids, but since she only found out what was being laid when the tiler was halfway through the job, there was little she could do about it.

Their bedroom looked like a boudoir that Vivienne Westwood had got her hands on. 'Sensual and relaxing' was how Shirley described it; 'bloody awful' was how Isabel described it. She felt that she was walking into Barbara Cartland's bedroom every time she opened the door. Charles, however, loved (or at least claimed to) all the changes Shirley had made, right down to the huge fake orange lilies in a giant vase in the drawing-room.

"Feng shui is all-important – you're lucky your house is south-facing," Shirley explained, mistaking Isabel's shocked silence for wonderment. She was trying to take in the lack of curtains which had been replaced by rice-paper screens. Isabel had gone out for coffee with Maggie and come home to discover that her once cosy, homely living-room had been transformed into a 'feng-shui-correct' haven of calm.

"Shirley, um, where has all the furniture gone?" Isabel bit her lip to stop herself from crying.

"The sofa and chairs?"

Isabel nodded, wondering how the hell this woman managed to work so quickly once she left the house.

"I'm having them re-covered to match – that chintzy pattern was just awful."

"Oh, right." Isabel was experiencing a range of emotions, from wanting to cry to wanting to scream abuse at this bloody woman. "What are we going to sit on?"

"They'll be back in a few weeks, you won't even notice they're gone. Now don't you love this material? Weren't you right to trust me?" Shirley breezed on with self-congratulation.

"I had no bloody choice," Isabel muttered to herself, wishing she had let Maggie come home with her for moral support.

"I feel like I'm living in a show house!" she had protested to Charles that evening as they lay in the midst of the pink and leopard-print bed watching the *News at Ten*. "Every time I open the front door I think I've got the wrong house."

"Darling, the house looks fabulous! You'll get used to it. We'll be able to have the chaps over from London soon."

Isabel took a deep breath to stop herself from beating him to death. "I'm terrified to let the twins out of the kitchen in case they ruin anything with their sticky hands."

"Henry and Amy love the house – they'll get used to it too."

"Charles, they don't. Amy is having nightmares and Henry's stutter is getting worse."

"Now, Isabel, don't be a bitch, the children are fine. I haven't noticed Henry's stutter – you must be imagining it."

"How the hell would you know? You're never sodding-well here!" She glared at him.

"Take the children to elocution or whatever to sort Henry out then," said Charles. "We're not moving back to that bloody damp old cottage, so stop even thinking about it and make a bloody effort for me. I'm trying to impress the London office and you aren't helping. All the other wives and girlfriends go out to dinner – you haven't even been over to London once." He delivered his diatribe without taking his eyes off the television screen.

"It wasn't damp," was all Isabel could say. There was absolutely no chance of her going over to London to meet the tossers who had turned her husband into a virtual stranger.

Charles did not reply.

Isabel turned over on her side and shut her eyes to stop herself from crying. She seemed to be teary all the time. She desperately wanted to wring her husband's neck for being so bloody stupid, but she didn't want to ruin the first evening that he hadn't taken his papers to bed, even if he was glued to the news.

Chapter 8

"Mummy! Let us in!"

The twins knocking on her window, wanting to be let into the car, shook Isabel out of her reverie. She hadn't even noticed all the children getting out of school, she had been so deeply involved in her thoughts.

"So how was your day?" she asked, as she put Henry into his seat.

"Henry ate his crayon and Miss Turner was really cross with him," Amy reported.

"Oh, Henry, why did you eat your crayon?"

"It smelt nice, Mummy." Henry still had little bits of blue wax round his mouth. Isabel wiped them away with one of the baby-wipes she always kept in the car. More for her than the twins – nothing got stains out of clothes quite so well.

"Now, you know eating crayons will make you sick."

Henry nodded, looking suitably repentant.

"You don't want to make Miss Turner and Mummy cross, do you?"

"No," he replied though he didn't look entirely convinced.

"OK, that's you both strapped in. Now sit quietly and you can have crisps when you get home."

The children chatted all the way home. It was a short drive and Isabel pulled into their driveway just after two thirty. Maggie's car was parked in the driveway at an odd angle as if she had driven in at speed.

"Now, be good, your Auntie Maggie is here," Isabel told the twins as she lifted them one at a time out of the car. They both shot off round the side of the house to the back garden. Isabel lifted their school-bags out of the boot and locked the car. She followed them round the house wondering what on earth Maggie was doing in her back garden in the middle of the afternoon.

"Pooh! Mummy, Auntie Maggie is smoking!" Amy held her fingers over her nose in an exaggerated display of distaste.

Indeed Maggie was smoking, furiously in fact, as she sat on the back steps. Her mascara had run all over her face as if she had been crying heavily.

"Maggie? What on earth is the matter?" Isabel rushed over to her friend.

Maggie promptly burst into tears again and buried her head in her hands.

"OK, kids, let's get Auntie Maggie inside. Amy, you

take her bag and, Henry, will you carry her car keys and her coat?"

The children did as they were told and Isabel put her arm round Maggie and walked her back to the front door.

Letting them all in, she instructed the children to set Maggie's things down in the hall. They both stood quietly, not sure what to do. They had never seen their Auntie Maggie cry before and they found it unsettling. Isabel took Maggie straight into the kitchen and sat her in one of the kitchen chairs. The twins were each given a packet of crisps and a juice box and told to go and play, preferably in their rooms. Once they were dispatched Isabel made a big pot of tea and got an ashtray out from one of her kitchen cupboards. She set the ashtray and a mug of steaming tea in front of her friend.

Maggie looked at the tea and laughed. "I seem to have drunk a lot of tea in the last day."

"Maggs, what on earth has happened? Are you OK? Is Derek OK? You seemed fine yesterday."

"Derek? Derek is bloody fine, I don't think he has ever felt better." Her voice rose sharply.

Isabel put a hand on her friend's shoulder. "What is it then? You're in a right state."

"I found my husband in bed with someone else."

"Oh my god, Maggs, I'm so sorry! I had no idea."

"You had no idea?" Maggie laughed again. "It was Cliff Cameron, our sodding neighbour, how's that for a surprise?

92

Isabel set her tea down as her hands were shaking so much.

"You're joking, aren't you?" She couldn't take it in. Maggie must be imagining it. Derek in bed with a *man*?

Maggie shook her head and dug another cigarette out of the crumpled packet. Isabel lit it for her and then lit one for herself.

"Tell me about it, Maggs."

"After I left you yesterday morning I was on my way to an NSPCC meeting."

"Yes, you mentioned it." Isabel nodded.

"Well, I got a phone call from Lizzie when I was on my way, to let me know that her son had measles and the whole family were in quarantine so the meeting was obviously cancelled."

"So you went home," Isabel prompted.

"When I got back there was a car I didn't really recognise in the driveway, though it was a Saab like Cliff Cameron's, and I thought it must be some work-related visit for Derek. So I went into the house and assumed that Derek must be in the study with whoever it was." Maggie's voice started to crack at the memory. "I walked into the bedroom and there they were, only I couldn't see Cliff, just Derek. I ran downstairs and he followed me. I thought it was a woman."

Maggie's eyes were shining with tears. Isabel was rapt with morbid fascination, gobsmacked at what Maggie was telling her.

"We were standing shouting at each other in the

kitchen when Cliff appeared at the door. You know, it took a minute for me to realise exactly what had been going on. Then I just started chucking everything I could get my hands on."

Maggie took a drag on her cigarette and flicked the ash in the general direction of the ashtray. She exhaled slowly and took a slug of her tea.

"Anyway, Derek couldn't deny it. Cliff scarpered like a scared rabbit and Derek and I have been talking, shouting and crying ever since – with him trying to stop me breaking things."

"Jesus. Maggs, I have absolutely no idea what to say. You look wretched – have you slept?"

Maggie shook her head. "I can't. My brain is whizzing at a hundred miles an hour, though I feel knackered now. I'm all cried out."

"Where is Derek?"

"Packing probably."

"He's leaving then?"

"Isabel, he's bloody well gay! My husband prefers *men*!" Maggie shouted, stubbing her cigarette out angrily. "I think we can safely assume my marriage is over."

"I'm sorry, I'm sorry. I just didn't know what you were going to do."

"I don't know," Maggie said quietly, reaching for another cigarette.

Isabel put her hand over Maggie's. "Listen, you have just had an enormous traumatic shock. Why don't you lie down here for a few hours? You can even stay here for a while – you maybe don't feel like going back there straight away."

Maggie nodded and put the cigarettes down. She looked totally defeated. Isabel hugged her tightly.

"Now, you know we're here. I'm your best friend and I will help you in any way I can."

"Thanks, Isabel."

Isabel took Maggie upstairs to the guestroom which Shirley had redecorated in pale coffee colours – she hoped the effect was as calming on the nerves as Shirley had claimed. She drew the curtains on the grey afternoon and sat with Maggie until her friend's eyes closed and she drifted off to sleep. Then she rounded the twins up and took them downstairs so they wouldn't wake Maggie. In an effort to keep them downstairs and relatively quiet, and to keep her mind off what Maggie had just told her, she got them to help her make fairy cakes and Rice Krispie buns. They particularly liked when they got to stick their hands into the melted chocolate. By the time the buns were ready to go into the oven the kitchen was a bomb-site: dirty bowls, spatulas, flour, butter, eggs, chocolate, icing sugar, hundreds and thousands littered every work surface and most of the floor. Giving them both a still slightly runny Rice Krispie bun each, she let them play in the garden where Amy was a pony and Henry was a racing car.

"They'll probably not want any tea," she thought to herself as she cleared the mess away. She now had fifteen fairy cakes covered in a very generous amount of hundred and thousands – that had been Henry's task. The Rice Krispie buns were in varying degrees of size, from a quite large tennis-ball size right down to a mini-bun made from the remaining chocolate and about four Rice Krispies. The fairy cakes were left out on a cooling tray and the Krispie buns went straight into the fridge, still on their baking sheet.

Maggie reappeared a couple of hours later when the children had had their tea and Isabel had made a sizeable dent in the fairy cakes. Maggie still looked wretched but seemed a little more rational than she had been earlier on in the afternoon. The twins, sensing it was alright, hurled themselves at her. Once she had finished hugging the pair of them, Isabel gave her a glass of red wine.

"So how are you feeling?" she asked.

"Just exhausted. But thanks for the loan of your spare room. Shirley may have ridden over you roughshod but your spare room is glorious, very peaceful. Not so sure about your bedroom though." Maggie giggled

Isabel sat down with a glass of wine, delighted to see a smile on Maggie's face.

"You were right about the boudoir look. Does Charles seriously like it?"

"Well, he claims to." Isabel shrugged. "It's bloody horrible, isn't it?"

"Like sleeping in Hugh Heffner's pad."

"God, I thought it was like Barbara Cartland's bedroom!"

"Both totally disgusting thoughts!" Maggie dissolved

into giggles. "Anyway, look, it's nearly six – I should go home."

"Why don't you stay and have a small bowl of the spaghetti bolognese? I made it for the twins earlier but there's enough for us."

"Well, I suppose there is only me now, nothing to rush home for." Maggie looked like she might cry again, but managed to recover her composure.

They ate and chatted, both side-stepping any references to Derek or what had happened.

"You're more than welcome to stay tonight if you like," Isabel said at last. "Though Charles will be here, if you can bear it."

"Don't be silly, he doesn't annoy me. Have things got any better?"

"After he let us be Shirlified? Are you serious? He'll be lucky if I ever speak to him again! No, things are much as they were."

"Have you tried talking to him?"

"At the moment if I could get him to lift his head out of the paper, television or laptop, I'd be doing well. But you had to listen to me moan yesterday. The very least I can do is listen if you want to talk."

"Thanks, I suppose it's times like these that remind you who your real friends are. I'm really dreading the neighbours all finding out. I know it sounds really pathetic, but I'm going to be so embarrassed. All those people who thought we had it all – they'll just be laughing at us."

"Who gives a shit what they think? They were jealous

to start off with, now they'll feel like they've exacted some sort of revenge on you or something. I'd say most of those women are in miserable marriages and you're just a bit of light relief – something else more interesting will happen next week and you'll be yesterday's news."

"I hope you're right."

"Of course I am. Do you want a top-up?"

She refilled their wine glasses, cleared away the dinner dishes and got out the cigarettes. Somehow when Maggie was here, it was OK for her to smoke inside the house.

Once they had finished the wine, Maggie got up to go.

"No point in putting off the inevitable."

"Are you absolutely sure?"

"Nope, but I'm going to do it." Maggie squared her shoulders in a mock show of defiance.

"This is going to be really hard, you know," said Isabel.

"God, don't I know it!"

As Maggie pulled out of the driveway she waved and beeped and then she was gone, back to her big house, all on her own. Isabel's heart hurt for her. She could not imagine a worse scenario.

Chapter 9

"You presumably know about Derek Morris then?" Charles asked while he ate his late supper at the kitchen table. He had arrived home shortly after Maggie had left. Isabel was relieved Maggie hadn't had to face him.

"How do you know about it?" She was finishing off the washing-up from the spaghetti bolognese.

"Jim McMartin rang me on my mobile on my way home from the airport."

"Oh, I see the old grapevine is alive and well then?"

"Everyone is talking about it, Isabel. That man is a bloody fool – he's thrown away a perfectly good career."

"Not to mention his marriage and the last six years of his life!" Isabel stared at her husband as if he was a stranger. How could he be so heartless?

"Of course, Maggie must be upset."

"Gutted, devastated, confused."

"OK, OK, Isabel, I get the bloody picture. The man is

99

stupider than I thought: I hear he and the boyfriend are going to run away. Set up a love-nest abroad."

Charles said the last comment with childish sneer on his face, exaggerating the word 'boyfriend' as if it were something funny. Isabel suddenly realised what her friend was going to have to deal with. People were going to be shocked. Maggie and Derek would become an urban myth, embellished and embroidered. Talk at dinner parties would suddenly revolve around the unfortunate couple that not one of them knew well enough to discuss with any authority. But, Isabel thought angrily as Charles retreated behind *The Times*, still with his stupid smirk on his face, when had that stopped the gossips before?

"I expected a little more sympathy from you," she snapped at the back of the sports section.

Charles just grunted as she took his empty dinner plate away and finished loading the dishwasher. He seemed unaware that he had annoyed her but Isabel was wholly aware that he was perfecting his selective hearing: he had tuned her out. That pissed her off even more.

* * *

"Ooh!" she sighed with pleasure as she slipped into a steaming hot bath with some of the Jo Malone Amber and Lavender bath oil Maggie had given her for Christmas last year. The wonderful smell seemed to infiltrate her bad humour and relax her tense muscles, which had only seized when Charles had come home. She had left him sitting in the living-room, still firmly wedged behind his beloved paper.

"I wonder if the kids and I left, would he actually notice until he had read his whole way through it?" she asked herself as she sank under the oily water right up to her neck.

In the water she felt light and weightless, a sensation that she adored. Her frumpy, pale, lumpy body gleamed pale gold under the recessed low-voltage light. If only she could feel like this all of the time, maybe Charles would view her as his wife again rather than his personal chef, maid, ironer-of-shirts.

The house was quiet; the children were sound asleep and all that she could hear was *The Best of Gabrielle* that she had playing at a very low volume on the bedroom stereo. She listened to the gentle voice singing, closed her eyes and slipped back into her earlier daydream – her perfect life with perfect children, perfect husband and her perfect body. She only opened her eyes when she realised that the TV had replaced Gabrielle. Charles had come into the bedroom and was watching some news programme about the Euro and the public's reaction to the new currency. The water was cold and she wanted to get out, but Charles came into their bathroom and started unpacking his wash-bag. Suddenly she stopped gleaming gold and returned to her pale lumpy self under his gaze.

"You'll turn into a prune if you stay in there any longer."

He wasn't even looking at her as he said it, but his presence had ruined her lovely daydream and she felt self-conscious.

She climbed as gracefully as she could out of the bath,

as quickly as she could, wrapping herself speedily in a bath-towel. She pulled out the plug and watched as the bath water created a mini-vortex in its haste to get down the plughole. She dried herself off, still smelling divine from the gorgeous oil, and got straight into her jammies. She was in bed with her light off before Charles had even come out of the bathroom. She needn't have worried: he wasn't paying any attention to her. He was talking to the TV.

"Well, that's total bullshit!" he said in reference to the point the presenter was trying to make.

"Oh, for God's sake!" muttered Isabel.

"This man has no idea what he's talking about. Isabel, are you listening to this? What a load of crap! The guys at work and I were talking about it and we totally disagree."

Isabel tried to remember when Charles stopped being an individual and started talking in 'we' terms. If the 'boys' at work thought something then he automatically thought it too.

She considered asking him about the joint bank account, but that probably wasn't a good idea in his belligerent mood.

Lying there, she allowed herself to think about the problem again. No point warding it off any longer with daydreams. Might as well admit to herself that she was terrified. She had rung the 24-hour telephone banking service just before Charles got home and confirmed her worst fears: their joint account had a deficit of £200, they were not covered for an overdraft in that account and they had already accrued a £40 fine as they had been overdrawn for over two weeks.

"What had he done with the money?" she worried as she lay on her side, turned away from him.

Six months ago they had paid a deposit for Disney World Florida and they would have to make an interim payment: they were going in July and it was already nearly November. She knew the interior designer had cost a fortune, but Charles had told her he was paying that out of his own account. They would leave their little nest-egg safe for the summer holidays and the mortgage and bills as usual. She felt sick, just wishing she could ask him where it had all gone. When he had arrived home, something had stopped her from just turning round and asking him straight out. She felt emotionally drained after Maggie's visit – and she was terrified of what he might have spent the money on. He had never been much of a gambler, but she knew there were lots of casinos in London. There were also lots of topless dancer bars – what did they call them? Lap-dancing clubs. She had seen the programmes on TV – she knew that men could pay to have a naked woman cavort virtually on top of them. She didn't even want to think about the escort services she had read about. She felt physical pain imagining her husband with another woman, someone he had paid for. Her mind whirred. Did he have a mistress? Some dolly-bird he wined and dined when he told her he was having boring business dinners? Someone he spent three thousand pounds on, buying her jewellery when his wife and kids were at home believing he was working all the hours God sends? She hoped she was being unfair to him, but he was so different – harder, meaner somehow.

And then there was their savings account . . . what if he had been taking money from that too?

She took a deep breath and forced herself to get a grip. Think about Maggie, she told herself, imagine the pain that she's going through. At least my husband is still here and I have two beautiful angels whom I love and adore. Her breathing slowed and began to return to normal. The TV and then Charles' light clicked off. She wondered if had he any idea what she was thinking about? She thought not. She felt him move around his side of the bed trying to get himself comfortable.

He kissed her shoulder and whispered, "Good night, love."

Tears sprung into her eyes.

Why did she always assume the worst of him? She hadn't always done this. Maybe it was her and not him after all? She squeezed her eyes shut to stop the tears.

"Sleep well," she whispered in reply.

Seconds later his breathing deepened and she knew he was in a deep sleep. The gentle snores started minutes later and she knew he would sleep soundly until morning, unaware of all the bad things she had been thinking about him. She made up her mind to confront him about the money in the morning and then she would go and check on Maggie.

Comforted by her plan, Isabel drifted off into sleep.

Chapter 10

Early morning light seeped in under her eyelids. Rubbing her eyes, Isabel glanced at her alarm clock: five minutes to eight.

"Good." She stretched out. "Time to get the twins up and dressed and have their breakfast."

Her feet felt cold as she moved them over to Charles' side of the bed. She turned and sat up sharply, but there was an empty space where he had slept. She must talk to him before he left for work. She got up and went into the en suite. The window was open to let the condensation out – Charles did this after his morning shower.

"Shit," she muttered to herself. He hadn't woken her. She ran downstairs but it was as quiet as a church. He had left for work.

Shit, she repeated to herself. There goes another opportunity missed. She really had wanted to speak to him about the money.

There's always the phone – he'd be in his office now, she told herself. No, I want to speak to him face to face.

Her conscience told her she was just procrastinating. She admitted hating herself for being so easily deflected from her course.

She busied herself getting the twins ready for school. Henry really didn't want to get up and she had to use all her powers of persuasion, not to mention a bit of brute force, to get him going.

On the way out the door she noticed another letter addressed to Charles from the building society. That was two this month. Though she knew little about the mortgage and was even vague about how much they paid every month, she knew that too much correspondence was not a good thing. She made a mental note to steam the letter open when she got home and had more time.

Having delivered Amy and Henry to school on time, she decided that she would go straight round to Maggie's house, have a coffee with her and see how she was feeling. The thought of the letter on the hall table irked her. Concentrating on someone else would take her mind off things. Maggie's car was parked in the driveway as she pulled up and parked. She got out and noticed a couple of the pots on the doorstep had been knocked over. She righted them and then rang the doorbell. She waited. No answer. She rang again. Still no sign of Maggie. She was quietly repeating, "I'm not an ostrich," to herself almost like a little mantra.

She rang again. Now she was getting worried. The car

was there. Maggie must be inside. Still asleep? She knew where Maggie hid her emergency key in case she ever locked herself out of the house: in the left wellie just inside the door of the garage. The key fell into Isabel's palm as she shook the wellie upside down. She returned the wellie to its place and closed the garage door.

She let herself in the front door.

"Hello?" she called out as she closed the door behind her.

"Maggs, are you in?" she called again in the quiet house.

No response. Isabel did a quick tour of the downstairs and finding no evidence of her friend she proceeded to the first floor and headed straight to the master bedroom.

"Maggie?" She gently pushed the bedroom door open.

She gasped as she viewed the trashed bedroom, the mirrored doors on the sliderobes smashed, bits of broken glass littering the cream carpet. The bedclothes were strewn across the floor. The bedside tables had both been knocked over, one of the bedside lights still on. Clothes were everywhere; the whole room stank of urine. She clapped a hand over her mouth and nose to block the stench.

What in God's name had happened here? Maggs was such a tidy-freak, this would usually send her into orbit. She turned the upended light off and continued her search.

She looked into each of the four remaining bedrooms. Three were untouched as if they were primed for a photographer. In the last and smallest room she found Maggie.

"Maggie!" Isabel rushed forward. Her friend was curled up in the single bed, an empty bottle of Black Bush on the beside-table sharing space with a huge tub of paracetamol. Isabel caught her breath as she checked for a pulse in Maggie's slender neck. She found it immediately and breathed a sigh of relief. Maggie stirred beneath the bedclothes.

"Maggie, how many paracetamol did you take?" Isabel yelled.

Maggie groaned back some gibberish and tried to roll over in the bed, but Isabel was blocking her.

"Maggie!" Isabel grabbed her skinny arm and pulled her up into a sitting position. Maggie's head lolled frighteningly forward.

"Maggie!" Isabel screamed right into her face.

"What?" Maggie replied crossly, looking up for the first time.

"How many did you take?" Isabel shook the tub out for Maggie to see.

"Two," she replied sullenly.

Maggie's eyes were bloodshot and she looked worse than Isabel had ever seen her. Her hair looked as if she had spent most of last night back-combing it.

"Two? Don't play games with me, this is serious!" Isabel really thought her heart might stop, she was so scared.

"I'm serious. I took two."

Isabel looked at her, uncomprehending.

"I drank all the whiskey in the bottle and it gave me such a headache I took two tablets and then I fell asleep."

Isabel could have cried with relief. She had had images of ambulances, stomach pumps, and permanent liver damage.

"Jesus, you stupid bitch, I thought you'd topped yourself. I nearly had a heart attack." Isabel hugged her fiercely, tears flowing freely down her cheeks.

"Kill myself over that fruit?" Maggie murmured into Isabel's chest. "Oh, my head hurts like hell!" She pulled away from Isabel, putting both hands up to her temples as if to hold her head together.

Isabel started to laugh.

"Serves you bloody right, you scared the shit out of me! What the hell are you doing in here anyway?"

"Couldn't face our bedroom, especially after I went on the rampage last night."

"The place is a mess and it stinks – what the hell happened?"

"I peed on his clothes," Maggie said sheepishly, looking down at her hands.

"You peed on his clothes?" Isabel repeated.

"I got home last night and I was so angry I smashed a few doors and then as my grand finale I pulled some of his good suits out of the wardrobe and peed on them."

"That is totally disgusting!"

Maggie started to giggle. Isabel stared at her wondering if she was in her right mind, then she started laughing too.

109

They stayed like that, hugging each other and laughing until Isabel's head hurt too.

After helping Maggie throw Derek's suits out, which was such a huge waste it saddened her, Isabel tidied up the broken glass from the floor in the bedroom while Maggie had a shower and straightened herself out. After coffee and some toast, Maggie went back to bed and Isabel went home to face her own problems – after she had returned the emergency key to the wellie.

Chapter 11

Initially Maggie and Cliff's equally surprised, dumbfounded, heartbroken wife, Claudia, supported each other. Claudia would come round to Maggie's house and scream and shout obscenities about her husband.

Maggie was now a little more controlled, but she tolerated Claudia as she felt for some reason that they both had to stick together – women scorned and all that. Funny, prior to the 'incident', as Maggie now referred to it, she and Claudia had never really got on.

Derek had left the afternoon that Maggie had found him in bed with Cliff. She had only seen him once after that, three days later when he called round in the evening to collect some of the clothes that Maggie hadn't thrown out, pee-soaked, in the rubbish.

"I wanted to tell you myself. Cliff and I are leaving." Derek wasn't taking the time to pack a suitcase. He hurriedly threw his clothes into black bin-liners.

Maggie didn't say anything. She stood at the end of the bed with her hands on her hips.

"Maggs, did you hear me?"

"Yes," she replied dully.

"We're going to live in Ibiza."

Maggie had laughed hard when she had heard that.

"Can't face the shame, eh?" She wouldn't let him see how devastated she was. It took all her willpower not to try and talk him out of it.

"The house is yours, of course. My solicitor will be in touch regarding a monthly allowance for you and the divorce. You won't want for anything, I promise."

"Just a husband." Her expression was deadpan.

"I could contact you every month if you would prefer?"

"Your solicitor will be fine." She bit her lip.

Derek had searched her face for some small sign that she didn't hate him. Finding none in her dead eyes, he finished packing his bags.

"Leave your key on the hall table," she said as coldly as she could muster.

She followed him out of the bedroom they had shared for so many years, down the stairs and into the hall. Without a word Derek removed his house key from his key-fob and set it on the small silver tray on the hall table. He left. Getting into his car and pulling out of the drive, he offered a small wave. Maggie did not return it. Giving up, Derek drove away and Maggie cried herself to sleep for the third night in a row.

After a couple of weeks Claudia, a native of Germany,

returned to Hamburg and her family, unable to deal with life in south Belfast without her beloved La Perla underwear (Cliff had taken it to Ibiza) and probably a tad embarrassed that she, who came from a long line of Arian blonde beauties, had been duped into marrying a gay Irishman. Maggie drove her to the airport, promised to oversee the sale of the house, and hugged her goodbye.

With Derek gone the house seemed huge, empty and hollow. All the expensive furniture and furnishing, meant nothing. Maggie retreated from her life. She moved all her things into the small back bedroom. She went to bed early, hadn't shopped in a month and had virtually stopped eating. The noise of the wind in the trees outside that used to thrill her with how private they made the house, now terrified her on her own. She had never felt more alone in her life.

Chapter 12

"Miss Watson, you have been with us for four years."

Alice nodded. She had no idea where this was going, but Balfour using her surname was surely not a good sign. She was sitting in front of his enormous walnut desk; he seemed about a mile away, the thing was so huge.

"Yes, Mr Balfour."

"How do you think you have performed for us over the past four years?"

Oh fuck, what had she done? Was he mad at her taking off for a week? She swallowed the lump which had just appeared in her throat.

"Well, I believe I have performed to the best of my abilities and I have been a credit to the company." Holy shite, she couldn't believe she had added the last bit on.

She virtually held her breath while she waited for his response.

"Do you indeed?" was all he said.

"Yes, sir, I believe I work hard for Balfour & Mayley. I have a well-established client base now and I have had a lot of repeat business for those clients."

Fuck him, how dare he question her professionalism! She glared at him, only Mr Balfour was looking down at a sheaf of notes on his desk and missed the whole thing.

"You're probably wondering why I have asked to see you."

"Well, yes, sir." She looked down at her feet and cringed to see two different-coloured socks peeking out the top of her boots. She tried to pull the legs of her trousers down so he wouldn't see.

Mr Balfour was not remotely interested in her socks.

"We have had several reports about you, Miss Watson." He did not lift his eyes from the papers he was reading.

Alice couldn't believe her ears. Suddenly, she exploded. "Mr Balfour, I work bloody hard. I appreciate the opportunity it gave me to work for a well-respected firm and I feel I have given my best, worked extremely long hours without any praise from the partners. Quite frankly, I don't give a damn what reports you have heard. Perhaps if you bothered to ask me yourself you would know what I do and how I do it. My success rate is consistently high and I earn my money, Mr Balfour. So if you have a problem with me, let me make this a little easier – *I quit!* I'm handing in my notice today. I will work my four weeks' notice and then I shall be out of your hair. Thank you."

Alice got up, leaving Mr Balfour sitting open-mouthed.

She slammed his door behind her and angrily strode past an equally surprised Bettye back to her office.

"Bloody hell, Alice, what happened?" Louise asked as she saw the anger in Alice's face.

"I need to dictate a letter to you," Alice said sharply.

Louise got out her diction pad without another word.

"Dear Sirs," Alice began.

Louise started scribbling.

"I wish to hand in my letter of resignation which will be effective from four weeks from this date blah, blah, blah. You can finish the rest, can't you?" Alice looked up to see that Louise hadn't written any of the last bits down.

"You're doing what?" Louise was incredulous.

"I basically told the boss to go and rub himself up the rough side of a pineapple."

"You did what?"

"I resigned, Lou. I'm going to go and run a hardware shop in County Down for six months. Who knows what the future brings?" Alice felt almost triumphant. She had absolutely no idea what made her lose her cool. Up until ten minutes ago she had no intention of doing anything drastic, but something inside her just told her to go for it. London wasn't going anywhere. If it didn't work out she could always come back. There would be other solicitor's jobs – mind you, it was unlikely that after the last half-hour she would get a reference from Balfour & Mayley, fuck'em.

All that Louise could say was, "Bloody hell! I thought he was going to offer you a promotion!"

Alice stared at her, gobsmacked. "A promotion?"

"Yes!"

"Shit, I hope not! I didn't give him a chance to say anything." She was appalled.

A little later, when Louise went out to get them both an expresso from the coffee-shop round the corner from the office, there was a tap on Alice's door and Bettye came in.

Alice was sitting at her desk, wedged between the radiator and the filing cabinet.

"Alice, Mr Balfour asked me to give you this." Bettye sounded almost apologetic as she proffered an envelope.

Alice took the envelope. "Thanks."

Bettye nodded and closed the door quietly as she exited.

Alice opened the envelope and read the letter inside.

Dear Miss Watson,

After careful consideration, Balfour & Mayley accept your resignation. We will honour the four-week notice and your salary will be paid until then. However, we do not require you to work the notice and would ask that you leave the offices at your earliest convenience. May we wish you every success for your future,

Yours sincerely
Gerald Balfour.

Alice felt slightly sick. It was done now: she had managed to talk herself out of her job.

Louise came back in with the coffees and handed one to Alice. Alice showed her the letter.

"That didn't take too long," said Louise. "What on earth did you say to him?"

"Can't really remember. I was very cross though. I think I managed to get that across."

"Now would not be a good time to tell you that he actually was going to offer you a promotion."

Alice slumped in her chair. She could feel her leg burning against the radiator again, but she didn't move.

"Oh God."

"I caught Bettye on her way back to the office. Mr Balfour may have a strange way of approaching it, but he was actually going to praise you."

Alice rested her forehead on her desk.

"Louise, I'm possibly the most stupid person you will ever meet."

"Possibly. You realise that now I have to work for May Bishop?"

"Sorry, Lou." Alice genuinely was.

May Bishop was the expert in martial settlements – to say she was the human version of a shark was the understatement of the century. The woman ate errant husbands or wives for breakfast. She viewed everyone with the same suspicion that she gave to rich husbands with a penchant for exotic dancers. If you wanted to empty your ex-spouse's Swiss bank account, strip their assets or take away their yacht or Aston Martin, then this was the lady to do it for you. Louise was going to have a hell of a job working for her: she had a team of secretaries and all lived in abject fear of her and her acerbic tongue.

* * *

Alice was surprised at how little she had managed to accumulate in the four years she had worked in that little office. She barely had enough to fill a smallish cardboard box. She had a box of tissues, a tester of Clarins *Eau Dynamisante,* a mini-filing cabinet for business cards someone had given her as a joke a few years ago, a couple of legal books that she had bought herself, a jar of freeze-dried coffee and four nail-files which had been at the back of drawer. Everything else belonged to the company. There had been a tearful goodbye from Louise, but other than that no-one else was really interested that she was leaving. As the revolving door swished behind her and she was popped out onto the street, she felt an overwhelming feeling of freedom. She took a deep, polluted breath of air and made her way purposefully through the throngs of shoppers and crowds watching the street performers in Covent Garden, to catch her last ever bus home from work.

She had spent a bit of the afternoon setting up an appointment for a estate agent to come round and have a look at her flat. If she was only going to have a couple more months of salary she would need the rental income from the flat to keep her going in Ireland. She had no idea how the shop was going to do. Mike from Alderly

Estates, the chap she had spoken with, had sounded optimistic about getting it rented quickly as Hammersmith was always popular.

"I'll come round tomorrow to measure the place up, get a feel for it and give you a bit of advice on how much we think we could get for you. We take 15 per cent of the total rental value – don't want to give you a nasty surprise tomorrow."

"Oh."

"We will manage the property for you – it's all included within the 15 per cent. We credit-check any potential tenants of course and keep you advised on who is moving in. It's a standard fee – you're welcome to ring a few other agents if you're not sure."

Alice had agreed to see Mike at ten thirty the following morning.

Back at the flat, Gary looked almost surprised to see her already home when he delicately climbed through his magnetic cat-flap in the front door.

"We're moving to Northern Ireland," Alice informed him. "Actually, that's a point – I'm going to have to get you a cat-carrier. Oh, and hire a car to get all my stuff over."

Alice was quite excited by the prospect of their move. Taking her message pad out of the cardboard box she had put on the kitchen table, she checked it and dialled Ted Dunbar's office number.

The call was answered after three rings.

"Good afternoon, Dunbar O'Toole," a pleasant female voice answered.

"May I speak to Mr Dunbar, please?"

"Who is the client?" the voice asked in reply.

"This is Alice Watson regarding Jean Maguire."

"One moment, please."

She was on hold for less than ten seconds before she heard Mr Dunbar on the line.

"Alice, good to hear from you so soon. I take it that you have made a decision regarding the will?"

"I have indeed."

"Good, good."

"I accept the terms of Auntie Jean's bequest and I'm making arrangements to move to Donaghadee as soon as I can get a few loose ends tied up over here."

"Excellent news. I know your aunt would be pleased."

They were both silent for a moment as they mutually considered Jean.

"I will process the paperwork. There will be a few things for you to sign when you come over. Keep me advised about your arrival."

"I will indeed, Mr Dunbar, and thank you for taking care of all Auntie Jean's affairs so well."

"As I mentioned to you before, Alice, Jean was a friend as well as a client and it was a pleasure. I'll be glad that I still have somewhere to get my household bits and pieces!"

Alice laughed at the idea of the elderly solicitor coming into the shop to buy washers for a dripping tap or those essential curtain hooks.

Chapter 13

Dave, the guy who was manning the desk at Eurocar, handed over the keys to the Ford Mondeo estate that Alice had hired for two days. She was going to drive it to Stranraer and from there she would take the Seacat fast ferry to Belfast Harbour. Her boat sailed at 6am the following morning so she planned to leave that evening at around nine or ten pm and drive straight there, her theory being that the traffic would be significantly lighter if she drove through the night. She had never driven the route before, but Dave assured her it was a straightforward run – once she was out of London she could by-pass all other major cities and towns. It should take her around eight hours if the traffic was light.

Mike from Alderly Estates had managed to get her flat let for six months to a visiting dermatology consultant working in several hospitals in the city. The location of Alice's flat suited him down to the ground. The rent would cover the mortgage and give her a little spending money but not enough to get excited about.

Back at the flat, Bernie and Susie helped her pack up the car. She wasn't taking much other than her clothes and her video player. She had to leave her furniture, beds, and a couple of sets of bed linen and the kitchen utensils for the new tenant. Still, there was not a lot of room in the back of the large estate car when Bernie finally closed the boot. Gary was ensconced in his new cat-carrier complete with a furry bed Susie had purloined from the pet department at work. He had settled down onto his bed but he didn't look too pleased with the arrangement. Alice hoped he would be OK in the car for eight hours. She had no idea how she would let him out to stretch his legs without him disappearing on her. He was on the passenger seat with the seatbelt pulled round the cat-carrier to secure it.

"Well, my dears, thank you for helping me make up my mind and helping me pack."

Susie gave her a huge hug and tried not to cry. "Here, this is for you." She handed Alice a large Harvey Nicols carrier bag.

"What is it?"

"You can't open it until you get to your new house." Susie sniffed, losing the battle against the tears

Alice hugged her again. "Thank you so much."

Bernie was next and he gave her a massive bear-hug, lifting her feet off the ground as he did so. "Now you drive safely and call us if you're lost, nervous, homesick or anything else at all. In fact, just call us and let us know how you're getting on, OK?"

"Yes, sir!" Alice nodded.

"Now, you have our number and both our mobiles, don't you?"

"I do, and you have mine?"

"We do, and we have your address in Donaghadee and a number for Mike at Alderly Estates in case we need to get in touch and for some reason can't."

"I hope you're going to get yourself email, young lady," Susie said severely.

"Of course. As soon as I'm organised I will email you both. Now promise that some time between now and the end of May you will come and visit me. I should know all the good places to go out by then."

"You try and stop us!" Bernie laughed. "Now get going, and don't get lost trying to get out of bloody London!"

"OK, love you guys – bye, bloody London." Alice climbed into the driver's seat, pulled her seat-belt across her shoulder and clicked it into place. She started the engine, put the car into gear and indicated left.

"Drive safely and good luck!" Bernie and Susie chorused as she pulled away from the kerb.

In her rear-view mirror, Alice could see Susie passing Bernie a tissue to dab his eyes. She waved all the way round the corner until her building was out of site.

"It's you and me, babe," she told Gary as she pulled up to traffic-lights.

Forty-five minutes later, a wrong turn at Brent Cross, and Alice was on the outskirts of London. She found the M1 and was on her way. She felt a little sad at leaving the place that had been her home for so many years, but she was sure she was doing the right thing. The road stretched out before her and she turned on the car radio, flicked the CD command and let Jill Scott keep her company until Birmingham. She passed signs for Coventry, Leicester, and Stoke-on-Trent and kept going. Little towns she had never heard of, they all passed in a blur. The traffic was light – it seemed to be just her and long-distance lorry-drivers keeping each other company. She saw signs for Liverpool and knew she was making good time.

She stopped at a service station to fill up on petrol, and buy some chocolate and water to keep herself going. Gary had been relatively well-behaved; he had stopped mewing by the time they had reached Finchley Road, back in London. Alice opened the cage-like door of his carrier and put a little bowl of dried food and some of the water from her bottle in beside him to see if she could tempt him. He took a little water but turned his nose up at the dried offerings. Alice set the water and food dishes down on the floor of the passenger side – they were travelling bowls, which promised on the box not to spill all over the car. She decided to leave the carrier door open in case Gary needed to stretch his legs.

Once they were back on the road she lit a cigarette and opened her window a little to let the smoke out and the fresh air in. Gary came out of his carrier slowly, mewed a little bit and then jumped into the back seat. Alice knew that he would probably find a comfy pile of clothes and would settle down there, which is exactly what he did.

After Carlisle it wasn't too far to the Scottish border. She arrived exhausted but happy to be there at the Seacat terminal around four thirty in the morning. It was still pitch dark, but lights were on inside the terminal building. Alice was able to check herself and the car in, but the café was shut and she couldn't buy a coffee to keep herself awake. Back out at the car she reclined the car seat as far as it would go. Gary appeared from his hidey-hole and climbed back into the furry warmth of the cat-carrier. Alice locked all the doors and decided to try and sleep for a couple of hours – her eyes were burning with tiredness. All the time spent concentrating on the road had wiped her out.

"Let's not do that again for a very long time," she whispered to the cat in the darkness.

Headlights from other cars woke her just over an hour later and she joined the early-morning passengers as they lined their cars up ready to get onto the ferry as soon as it arrived in from Belfast.

She dozed for most of the sailing. She was vaguely aware of the other passengers but she couldn't keep her eyes open. The journey was relatively short, docking in Belfast in ninety minutes. After what felt like five minutes she was back down in her car waiting for the bow door to open so that she could drive out into the early-morning traffic in Belfast.

* * *

It was drizzling as she sped out of Belfast, grey and distinctly unwelcoming. Alice refused to be depressed.

"Not the best impression for you," she said to Gary who had reappeared from his sleep and was now trying to climb onto her knee.

She knew the road to Donaghadee well enough, though she had never driven it. All the traffic was heading into Belfast and she was driving against the rush hour so it was easy. She drove past Holywood, with the pub where she had attended Jean's wake. She bypassed Bangor, once a small town, which in the last ten or fifteen years had become a suburban sprawl of new homes, past Groomsport where Jean had been a member of the church and the minister had said so many lovely things about her during the funeral.

"Next stop is Donaghadee, Alice informed Gary, who had resumed his back-seat wandering and was very much looking like he would dearly love to get out of the car which they had been in for nearly twelve hours.

Ten minutes later Alice pulled up outside 20 Shore Street, Donaghadee, County Down. The sleepy French-style fishing village was definitely not looking its most picturesque.

"Welcome to your new home," Alice grandly announced as she carried Gary into the house. She set the cat-carrier down in the back room and opened the door for her cat to explore his new surroundings.

While Gary sniffed strange furniture Alice lugged her various bags and clothes on hangers into the house from the boot. There didn't seem to be much life on Shore Street at eight fifteen in the morning, no sign of Emlyn lurking in the shop – of course, he had no idea she was coming back or when.

Then she nearly jumped out of her skin when she heard his voice behind her as she stretched for an awkwardly positioned box in the far reaches of the boot.

"Emlyn! Bloody hell! I didn't hear you! God, you gave me such a shock."

Emlyn was looking very dapper in a cord waistcoat, spotted cravat and his hair Brylcremed to perfection.

"Need a hand?"

"Yes, please."

"Will you be coming in to the shop today?" he asked as he carried a suitcase up the stairs and into Jean's old bedroom.

"Not sure. I want to get sorted in here. I'll try and come in later on." She paused and looked him in the eye. "You don't look surprised to see me."

He shrugged as he set the suitcase down on the floor beside the others. "I'm not."

Ten minutes later the car was totally empty. She had the car until the following morning so she locked it and went back inside. Emlyn was sitting in the living-room, stroking a slightly nervous Gary.

"Nice cat. What happened to his eye?"

"He had to have it removed. I found him at the side of the road in London – road accident, the vet thought."

"Hum." Emlyn scratched Gary's chin, finding one of the feline's weaknesses. Despite being unsettled, Gary started to purr automatically. "I'll go and open the shop. Come through once you've got yourself a bit more organised." He stood up, letting Gary down gently, and brushed imaginary cat-hair off his waistcoat.

Alice nodded and Emlyn went off, closing the front door behind him.

"Right, let's get organised," said Alice to Gary who had retreated under the sofa.

* * *

Once she had got unpacked and hung her clothes in Jean's wardrobe she decided she needed to do a serious shop: washing powder, cat food, human food, and cleaning stuff. She re-inspected the cupboards, which obviously hadn't changed since she had been there a week ago. But now that it was her home temporarily, she intended to make it as cosy as her flat had been. She set out all her little bits and pieces: her silver candlesticks, her scented Jo Malone candles which had cost a king's ransom, her good John Rocha crystal wineglasses Bernie and Susie had given her last Christmas.

Susie's leaving present! She had nearly forgotten about it – it was behind the driver's seat out in the car.

Bringing the Harvey Nic's bag into the house, she

peeped inside and was excited to see that Susie had made up a very posh survival kit. There were fresh-ground coffee beans from the food hall, Earl Grey tea bags (her favourite), a bottle of vodka, two more of the John Rocha glasses, a bottle of red wine and a gorgeous soft black cashmere cardigan from DKNY, just like one of Susie's she was always admiring. Alice burst into tears at the generosity of her friend. She rang Susie's mobile and left a teary message on her answering service thanking her and letting her know that both she and Gary had arrived safely and were settling in.

She was very tempted to go straight for the vodka, but instead she boiled the kettle and spent fifteen minutes hunting for her cafetière. She located a mug in a kitchen cupboard and then she sat in the front room in Jean's uncomfortable chair looking out over Donaghadee harbour in the rain, sipping the delicious coffee.

She had arrived.

* * *

A week later and Alice was starting to find her feet. She spent a few mornings in the shop getting to know the basics from Emlyn. He had actually surprised her by taking his time and not totally patronising her. Their relationship was starting to improve.

She had made a list of things she hated about the house and changes she intended to make. The first thing on her list was to redecorate. She also wanted a new kitchen, but it was one thing at a time. She couldn't afford decorators so she was going to do the whole thing herself. She had borrowed Emlyn's fifteen-year-old Mini and had driven to B&Q in Belfast to buy some decent paint. One of the advantages to owning a hardware shop was that she didn't have to buy paintbrushes, rollers or white spirit: it all lived next door.

The shop was closed on a Wednesday afternoon so she and Emlyn made a start. Alice had already moved all the bedroom furniture out of her room into the smallest spare room. She had decided on a very pale green, thinking that it would be calming while still a warmish colour. Thankfully the garish wallpaper disappeared quickly as they applied the one-coat paint.

"I think you may need two coats just to be on the safe side?" Emlyn said as he stood back to admire their handiwork.

"Thanks for doing this, Emlyn."

"Not a problem. The only thing I ever have to do on a Wednesday afternoon is to buy my lottery ticket." He looked at his watch. "But I have plenty of time – the shop is open until six."

Alice grinned. She had forgotten about Emlyn's love of the lottery: he even had a friend in Dublin who bought him a Lotto ticket there every week. Amazing! Despite only marginal success, he remained optimistic that one day his luck would change and he would be the millionaire he had always dreamt of being.

They had been at the painting for a couple of hours and had just finished the first coat when Bill, the

American guy she had met the day of Jean's funeral, rang the door bell to see how she was getting on. Instead of the coffee he was probably expecting, Alice handed him a paintbrush.

"Well, you look like you're settling in well. This is a lovely colour. Good thing I didn't come round in my Sunday best!" He eyed the paint on the end of his brush.

"I love green. You don't mind, do you?"

"About the green? Nope, it's a favourite of mine too."

"No, I meant about helping."

"As long as we get a coffee break at some stage, otherwise I may have to go and have a word with my union rep!"

Alice laughed.

"I was hoping that you would still stock the goose eggs for me," Bill said as he started the careful job of painting round the light-switch.

Alice looked at Emlyn who nodded his consent.

"Doesn't look like it would be a problem. What do you do with them?"

"I eat them, of course."

"Oh, do they taste like normal eggs?"

"Normal eggs? You mean chicken eggs?"

Alice nodded.

"They're a little different to normal eggs – they're also a little bigger than your standard egg."

"Oh."

"You sound disappointed."

"No, not at all."

"Would it have been more exciting if I said I used them in a bizarre ritual involving the eggs and a dead goat?"

Alice wrinkled up her nose. "No, better you just eat them, I think."

* * *

Alice did a couple of hours painting every day. After she finished her bedroom, she did the two spare rooms in apple white, then moved onto the first-floor landing and stair which she painted a very pale barley cream. She painted the spindles in the staircase a gloss white and left the handrail varnished. Moving downstairs, she painted the front room a pale lilac colour which looked gorgeous with the sunlight pouring in;. the back room, which had been Jean's living-room, she painted a pale coffee colour. The kitchen was painted the same barley cream as the hall. Lifting a bit of the carpet in the hall and downstairs rooms revealed fairly good wooden floorboards which she sanded and varnished with more than a little help from Emlyn and her new-found friend, Bill.

With the decorating done, Alice turned her attention to the furniture. The front room had a really dated suite of furniture, which went straight into the skip she had hired. She went to a nice furniture shop in Bangor and bought a fairly inexpensive (but comfy) sofa and armchair for the front room, and a nice comfy sofa for the living-room. She couldn't bear to part with Jean's favourite TV chair so instead she had it re-upholstered in a chocolate-brown faux suede fabric to match the sofa and tie in with the pale coffee walls. The framed tea towels came down from the walls and her few good paintings, which had belonged to her mother and father, adorned the freshly painted walls, along with some carefully selected prints in nice frames. The ornaments sitting on their doilies were wrapped in newspaper and stored in cardboard boxes, which went up into the attic. With all the surfaces cleared and the carpets lifted, the hallway and the two downstairs reception rooms looked virtually twice the size.

* * *

Alice looked at the kitchen cupboards glumly. They were on their last legs and she promised herself that she would get a new kitchen as soon as she could afford it. The little gas cooker was on its way out: only one of the rings worked and half the grill, though thankfully the oven worked. The twin-tub washing machine was a pain in the arse: it took nearly three hours to complete a cycle and her clothes looked as though they had been beaten up rather than washed when they came out.

She decided to go and see her aunt's accountant, Mr Saunders. He was surprisingly upbeat. He told her the business was in good shape; Jean had given it a cash injection fairly recently and she could afford to take out a loan to have the kitchen re-done.

Once the loan was in place, she went to have a look at what a kitchen company had to offer. She chose some pale beech Shaker-style doors and the company designer agreed to call out to the house so she could mock up a couple of designs. Once they had agreed on a price and a design, the kitchen company ordered everything she would need including a new washing machine, tumble-dryer and an American style fridge/freezer which was the most expensive she could have chosen, but which she insisted on squeezing into her galley kitchen.

The house was unbearably dusty for the best part of two weeks and Alice had almost considered moving in with Emlyn, who seemed upset about her changing the kitchen. Was he annoyed because he thought she was trying to get rid of Jean? The end result transformed the once poky and depressingly dated little kitchen into a space where she wanted to spend time. Her new built-in gas hob was stainless steel, as was the double oven, and the fridge/freezer was almost big enough for her to climb inside! The designer had even managed to fit a small breakfast bar on the end of one work-surface with a couple of stools fitted underneath.

Alice was really starting to like her new house. It was beginning to look less like a museum and more like a home. She decided to use a bit more of her dwindling resources to finish off the job by getting the exterior re-painted. Just in time for Christmas.

* * *

Christmas was always a funny time for Alice. It was usually just her and Gary, but this year Emlyn came round and had Christmas lunch. She got two presents, one from Emlyn and one from Bill, both of which Emlyn brought with him.

"Oh, thank you!" Alice unwrapped a rather unwieldy cardigan from Emlyn.

"Well, you're always complaining about the shop being so cold, I thought that would keep you warm."

"It certainly will." She nodded appreciatively.

"It's from Arran, in Scotland."

"Great." She put the cardie on to keep Emlyn happy and discovered it was in fact very warm indeed. She wouldn't win any fashion awards in it, but it was certainly the cosiest thing she now owned.

She unwrapped a cookery book from Bill. There was a blue post-it note sticking out of the middle. She flipped the book open and found the post-it marked a recipe for goose egg, onion and bacon quiche.

"Oh, how thoughtful!"

Emlyn gave her one of his knowing smiles. She handed him his present.

"Oh, fantastic!" he cried as he opened the drill set he had wanted for ages. Inside were five lottery tickets for the following Saturday. He gave her a big hug.

"Brilliant present, Alice, thanks." He blushed at his little display of affection.

He made Alice blush too.

Lunch was straight out of Marks & Spencer. They had a little turkey breast for two (and a bit for Gary who was salivating at the side of the table), roast potatoes, carrot and parsnip mash, stuffing, chipolatas and gravy, sitting in the front room looking out over the stormy harbour. Afterwards they watched TV in the back living-room: the usual Christmas films and a couple of TV-blooper programmes, which weren't terribly funny, but passed the time.

"Fancy a walk?" Alice asked Emlyn.

"Now?"

"Yeah, why not? I feel stuffed to bursting and could really do with the exercise."

"It's dark."

"Come on, I'll protect you!"

They walked along the deserted pier and as they came back through the town it started to snow, gentle little flakes spinning wildly and then disappearing as soon as they hit the ground.

"Gosh, do you think it will lie?" asked Alice.

"Sky looks like it's full of snow. I'd say it'll get heavier and it'll lie."

Despite his protests, Alice walked Emlyn back to his house, which was about half a mile from hers. As they walked the thought occurred to her to tackle him again about his strange theory on Jean's death. But what was the use? She had tried on and off to get him back on the subject but he always shied away like a frightened rabbit. Besides, Christmas wasn't an appropriate time to stir up those bad feelings. Especially not now in this peaceful lovely snowfall.

She said goodnight to him at his door and wished him

a Merry Christmas and then she walked slowly back to her house, snowflakes whirling onto her face and coat. The snow started to come in bigger flakes and faster. Alice was always fascinated by the deadening effect snow had – it made everything silent – all she could hear were her own muted footfalls on the pavement. When she let herself back into the house her whole front was covered in snow as if she had had to battle through it. She sat for a while looking at the snow falling into the sea before she pulled the curtains and lit the fire.

"Merry Christmas," she said to Gary who was purring quietly tucked up on his favourite cushion on the sofa. It had been a lovely day she decided as she picked up her cookery book and flicked through the recipes.

Chapter 14

Christmas had been almost unbearable. Charles was virtually monosyllabic on Christmas Day. Isabel had to force a smile on her face when she watched the twins opening their pressies and shouting with delight. She would be lying if she didn't admit that the thought of leaving Charles was more than a fleeting one. As she looked at her husband, who was engrossed in some film on TV, she felt something she had not felt before – she was starting to despise him. This feeling was fuelled by the fact that nothing had been clarified about their financial situation. She hadn't confronted him, she hadn't steamed open any letters – she hadn't checked their savings account. She was afraid of the truth, whatever it might be.

She cleared all the wrapping paper away and tried to pretend that she wasn't upset that Charles had not bought her anything.

"I wasn't sure what you wanted. We'll get you

something you really want in January, yeah?" he had told her by way of explanation.

His indifference towards her was the most upsetting thing she had ever had to deal with. If the twins had not been there she thought she would have packed a bag and moved in with Maggie.

Isabel served up Christmas lunch to Charles and his mother and father and the twins. Charles' mum, Ursula, complained the whole way through lunch.

"Oh, that's far too much for me, dear!" she had admonished Isabel when she set the plate in front of her. She patted her stomach, which was virtually concave and whispered, "One can't let oneself go."

Isabel had stared at her in amazement: the older this old bitch got, the less tact she bothered to use. She had always used thinly disguised insults against Isabel, even before she had put on her weight. Isabel looked to Charles for a bit of support, but he was smiling indulgently towards his mother. So Isabel just smiled and gritted her teeth. She was half-tempted to tip the plate into the bin.

"Just leave what you can't manage," she said.

Charles' father was already three-quarters of the way through a bottle of wine and his nose was starting to resemble Rudolf's. He made no comment as she set his plate down other than, "We look a bit short on the old vino."

Isabel looked over at Charles again, but he made no move to go and get another bottle of white out of the fridge. She served the children and Charles and then went to the fridge, got the wine, opened it and poured a large glass for her father-in-law, secretly wishing he would choke on it.

"Isabel, would you pass the wine up?" Charles asked, his mouth full of Brussels sprouts and roast potatoes.

"Let me pour myself a glass, OK?" she said sharply, on the verge of tears.

"Calm down, I only asked for the wine." Charles looked a little humpy.

Isabel dug into her turkey – at least it didn't complain. She thought she had done a good job: the turkey wasn't all dried out, the roasties were crispy on the outside and fluffy on the inside, the sprouts weren't mushy and the carrot and parsnip mash was lovely and buttery.

She had made it all herself and even stuffed the sodding turkey and not one of these bastards round the table said a word of thanks. Amy and Henry grinned away like mad and cleared their plates, which was all the thanks she needed from them. She also noticed with great satisfaction that Ursula had cleared her plate – in fact Isabel wondered if she hadn't had a go at the pattern as well. The woman looked like a crow, only less friendly. Steely grey hair cut in a short severe crop; a dark suit which hung off her; stick-thin legs poking out the bottom of the woollen skirt; patent black shoes with huge velvet bows; pearls at her neck, wrists and ears. Isabel saw the look of mild distaste she gave the twins – the woman had never once, in the five years since the twins had been born, offered to baby-sit them, not once.

There was no conversation round the table. Isabel stayed silent – she was buggered if she was going to do all the work and then make all the conversation. She kept half an eye on the twins and reached for another roast potato – she could virtually feel Ursula's eyes burning onto her hand. She popped the small potato into her mouth and smiled at Ursula who didn't return it.

It's Christmas, for Christ's sake, she thought, looking into the cheerless face of her mother-in-law and wishing her own mother hadn't gone over to England for Christmas. Sophie, her younger sister, had got married back in January and was having a big family Christmas in Bristol where she and her husband, Steven, lived. Isabel and Charles had been invited but Charles had said no – what would his parents do? Now, looking round the table she could only think – fuck his parents! Next year wild horses wouldn't keep her and the twins away from Bristol.

She was glad Maggie had gone to her brother Michael's for Christmas. Michael and his girlfriend Lucinda lived in Fermanagh beside Lough Erne. They ran a fantastic guesthouse where the rooms had four-poster beds and views over the stunning lough. However, there weren't any guests over the Christmas period – just Michael, Lucinda, Maggie and Lucinda's sister Harriet who came over from Glasgow for three days. By the sounds of it, they all just got terribly drunk and ate like mad. Thinking of Maggie's tiny frame, Isabel hoped she had actually eaten something and not just drunk.

After Christmas, Maggie had flown out to Malaga. She had decided that a fortnight away from Malone Park was what she needed more than anything.

New Year had been a disaster for Isabel. Charles and she had such a bad argument before they were due to go out over what they should pay the baby-sitter, she had actually thought for one terrible minute that he might have hit her. But he didn't. He just left without her and went to the party alone. She could have followed him, but all the arguing had upset the twins so she ended up paying the baby-sitter anyway and sending her home. She sat in, still in her evening trousers and glittery top, with the twins either side of her and they watched movies. She put them to bed around ten, then opened a bottle of wine she found at the back of the fridge and toasted the New Year in by herself.

Chapter 15

The wind was rushing round Maggie's head, making her hair stick to her lipstick. She prised the sticky strands away from her face and laughed. José smiled at her and returned his focus to the road, rubbing his hand on her slim brown thigh.

They were on the coast road, on their way to Malaga from Marbella where Maggie had just spent two weeks – shopping, having sex with a much younger man and eating well for the first time in months. José had a convertible Golf and Maggie had had a wonderful time whizzing up and down the Costa del Sol with him.

By the time they arrived at the airport her hair was standing on end and far from attractive. While José was paying for petrol she frantically dug through her vanity case looking for a product that would return her hair to normal rather than the 'dragged through a hedge backwards' look she was currently sporting.

Standing at the drop-off point while José got her bags from the car, she felt a little miserable at the thought of having to go back to Belfast in January – she could have quite happily holidayed permanently. Traipsing into the terminal building with José, following the herd of tracksuit-clad tourists to her check-in desk, she felt an almost uncontrollable desire to grab José and drag him back out into the sunshine away from the screaming children and exhausted parents who had all but given up on trying to control them. But she didn't. She stood quietly in line and passed her ticket and passport to the unsmiling Spanish girl at the check-in desk.

"How many bags?"

"Four," José replied, smiling at her

"These are over the allowance for one person," the check-in girl announced with an expression that could freeze water.

Even though Maggie had the height advantage, the seated Spanish girl still managed to look down her nose at her.

"Oh, I didn't have any problem on the way out." Maggie tried to win her over with a smile.

José muttered something to the girl in Spanish. She then ignored Maggie and smiled at José while she stared at the computer screen in front of her, tapping a few keys. The baggage labels spewed out of the printer beside her on the desk. Without saying another word she tagged Maggie's four bags and they disappeared down the baggage conveyor-belt.

They moved away from the desk.

"Your hand luggage is too big to take on board!" the bitch called after Maggie.

José blew her a kiss and she blushed but still indicated that Maggie should return to the desk.

"OK bitch-features, that's enough of your crap!" Maggie turned on her heel and, before José could say another persuasive word, marched back to the desk, leant over and in her most threatening voice hissed at the girl.

"Listen, I realise that you're bored out of your mind, and nothing gives you greater pleasure that making innocent travellers' lives a misery. In this hand luggage is a state-of-the-art computer and if you have a problem with that then I suggest you get the person in charge out here right now, and you had better organise to have my plane held."

How was 'Miss Customer Service' to know that the bag was in fact packed with the overflow from a very extensive shopping trip which had resulted in both Maggie and José having to sit together on the cases trying to get them shut?

The girl shrugged and returned to her computer screen.

"I thought so," Maggie said under her breath and walked away without looking back, trying not to do a little triumphant dance on the way.

José was standing with his mouth open. "Maggie, I had no idea you could be so frightening!"

Maggie mock-snarled at him and then burst out

laughing, his surprise lightening her mood. "Sorry, but I really could not be arsed with any carry-on from someone like her."

"I see this."

"I have to go through now."

"I will miss you. Can I see you again?"

"Maybe the next time I'm in Marbella," Maggie responded noncommittally, but quietly delighted he liked her so much.

He waved all the way until Maggie had disappeared out of sight.

Maggie eyed the Duty Free shop as she passed on her way to the Priority Passenger lounge.

"A quick look wouldn't do any harm," she thought.

The doors opened into the VIP lounge and Maggie plonked herself down into a suede sofa and dumped her vanity case and handbag beside her.

"May I get you a drink, madam?" A waiter had appeared silently beside her.

"Oh, um, an expresso would be great – thanks."

The waiter vanished as quietly as he had appeared.

Draining her tiny cup of the super-strength caffeine, Maggie picked up her bag and boarding pass and made her way back out into the main terminal to the Duty Free shop. Outside, the departure lounge was heaving with people queuing for sandwiches, pushing trolleys into each other's ankles and generally getting hot and cross. Ten different languages assailed her ears as she made a beeline for the perfume and skin-care section. She spent the next ten minutes spraying herself with a selection of perfumes, until she couldn't tell which was what and she stank to high heaven. Next she made her way to the Elizabeth Arden counter and sniffed creams and tried nail varnishes until she got a few dirty looks from the girls behind the counter. She settled for some eight-hour cream she had heard good reports about and walked over to the cashier, picking up some Toblerone for Isabel and the twins on the way.

* * *

Landing in Belfast Maggie could feel her new-found strength ebbing away. Thank God she had asked Isabel to collect her from the airport. Pushing her trolley out of the arrivals hall into the wintry afternoon, she considered turning back into the airport and booking herself onto the next available flight to anywhere else. But she didn't. She pulled her cardigan round her shoulders and tried to find Isabel's car. She didn't have to look too hard, as Isabel was just pulling into the car park in a car that sounded like a tractor idling in a field.

"You're home safe and sound!" Isabel exclaimed as she hugged her friend, delighted to see Maggie looking almost back to her old self.

"Thank you so much for coming for me."

"Always a pleasure. How was Spain?"

"Fantastic! The weather was warm and I had a ball."

"God, I'm jealous – it has either snowed or peed out of the heavens since the day and hour you left." Isabel had started loading Maggie's luggage into the boot.

"Where are the kids?"

"At home."

"With Charles?" Maggie was surprised.

"No, with Mum. Charles is in London, just for a change."

"Oh, well, all the better as I bought you this." Maggie produced the bag with the Toblerone and the eight-hour cream.

"Wow, Elizabeth Arden! Maggs, you shouldn't have! And Toblerone too – God, am I spoilt or what?"

Though the cream had actually been for Maggie herself she couldn't do anything but smile at her friend, who hadn't had a treat of any description in ages.

"Because you're worth it."

"Isn't that L'Oreal?"

"Who cares, you are."

Maggie was rewarded by another massive bear-hug.

"So, tell me all your biz," Isabel demanded, her mouth full of an Alp she had broken off.

"Well, I met a man." She shook her head at the chocolate that was offered to her.

"No!" Isabel nearly drove into a hedge.

"He's twenty-eight and called José."

"Seriously?" Isabel's eyebrows nearly vanished into her hairline with surprise.

"And was he great in bed or what!" Maggie laughed as her friend nearly choked.

"I'm still attractive, you know," she added in mock indignation.

"Shit, sorry, that wasn't what I meant! I mean, I just thought . . ."

"You thought I would go and sit in my apartment for a week and wallow in the self-pity that I have been wallowing in for months?"

"Well, now that you put it like that."

"Isabel!"

"Only messing. I'm delighted, if not a tiny bit jealous. Was he sexy?"

"Was he what? Isabel, he would have made your hair curl!"

"My hair already is curly."

The two women roared with laughter as they whizzed down the M2 into Belfast.

Chapter 16

All Jean's things had been carefully packed away, the family photos had been wrapped up alongside the ornaments, and Alice had managed to get rid of any painful memories.

Now that the house was more to Alice's liking she had to get to grips with the shop, so she could start paying the loan back. She had been living in Donaghadee for almost three months now and the time had flown. Gary had adjusted to life by the sea and he seemed to enjoy having his own garden to play in. Mind you, the garden was something Alice still hadn't quite come to terms with. It was very neglected – Jean would have been upset to see it so uncared-for. Still, at least it would give her a place where she could go and sit outside when the weather improved. It was January now and the weather was still fairly grim.

One afternoon while she and Emlyn were changing

the window display in the shop, she was pondering on whether she should take in a lodger. It was great having her own space, but a little lonely. Maybe if she could rent one of her bedrooms out to a girl, they would be company for each other.

"Emlyn. What would you think about me advertising for a lodger?"

"I think it's a great idea – be good for you to have someone your own age around. I think going to the local pub with me is starting to lose its appeal."

"Oh I didn't mean –"

"Alice, I know what you mean. I think it's a great idea."

"I wonder about advertising?"

"Well, there is the *Spectator*, but it could be a bit local. Why don't you try for the *Belfast Telegraph*? That way you'll reach more people. Give them a ring and find out how much it would cost."

Alice nodded. "Good idea, I'll ring them tomorrow."

"Ring them now – the phone book's beside the phone – it won't take a minute."

She left Emlyn, who was trying to construct a figure out of scrubbing brushes, cord and broom handles. He had made the hair out of a brush-head, put a small washing-up basin for the face and was now adding scrubbing-brush hands to broom-handle arms.

After getting through to the classifieds, Alice was told that the property advertising night was on a Thursday and a lot of people felt advertising alongside the sales advertising gave them better results than if they just advertised in the main paper. You paid per word so obviously the shorter the advert, the cheaper it was. Alice came off the phone eager to compose her ad, which still had time to run in that week's paper.

In no time at all, she produced: *Housemate wanted, female, to share 3bd house in Donaghadee, all mod cons, OFCH, etc. £250 per month Tel: 91885967*

"Does that sound inviting enough?" she asked Emlyn, as he was putting the finishing touches to his broom-handle and washing-up-bowl man.

"Well, you don't want a load of weirdos turning up, do you? You have been specific and yet described your house adequately – that's pretty good going. Now go and ring them back. I can't wait to see who applies."

"Maybe I shouldn't have said where it is – maybe no-one will want to live with me."

"Ring them." Emlyn pointed sternly in the direction of the phone.

After placing her ad, Alice wondered when she would get the first enquiry.

"Well, not until Thursday night I would imagine," Emlyn commented helpfully.

"That's two days away," Alice complained.

"Here, help me attach this scrubbing-brush to his foot." Emlyn handed Alice a length of cord and she bent down to help him.

Chapter 17

Watching January turning into February, with memories of her Spanish holiday fading, Maggie had to fight hard to keep her resolve to stay on top of things. Isabel had been great and she had no idea where she would be if it weren't for her friend – probably in some horrid institution somewhere.

She realised that she would have to take drastic action as she no longer needed her huge house in Malone Park. She was virtually a laughing-stock – not that she ever actually saw any of her neighbours, tucked away as they were down their tree-lined driveways, but she heard the rumours. She didn't think she even wanted to live in Belfast any more. She had made enquiries from a couple of estate agents that she had heard were good. Both had come out to her house and had explained what they could offer, measured every room, the amount of money she should expect to get for her house, how people would view etc. She didn't want to be around when people came to visit so when she finally decided on an estate agent she did so on the condition they did all the viewing, which was no problem for the agents. They prepared a brochure, got a spare key from her and put a sale board in her garden.

The same night her house was advertised, the agents conducted open viewing from 7 to 8pm so Maggie went round to Isabel's.

"So Derek gave you the go-ahead to sell it?"

"Yeah, he had to consent as part of our separation agreement and he agreed to me getting all of the sale proceeds."

"That was kind."

Maggie nodded. "I know, but he's still racked with so much guilt and rightly so. I think he'd give me the shirt off his back if I asked him right now."

"Must be hard for him," Isabel commented.

"I really don't care." Maggie flicked through a copy of the *Belfast Telegraph* that was sitting on the kitchen table. "It's weird to see your own house on the market."

"I know it is. Isn't it an odd feeling knowing that, while you're out, there could be loads of strange people walking round your house?"

"It is, but I tidied so much and I even got contract cleaners in for half a day so the place looks more like a shoot for *OK* than my bloody house. If I can sell it quickly I'll be pleased."

"I still can't believe your house is worth so much money."

"I know – it's madness, isn't it? I mean we bought it less than seven years ago and it has virtually doubled value since then."

"What will you do with a million quid?"

"If I get it!"

"If you get it."

"Well, I'm sure there are loads of taxes to pay, but after that I don't know."

"Buy somewhere smaller?"

"It sounds ridiculous but I don't think I even want to be that tied down. I may even rent for while. My allowance from Derek will more than cover it. I don't even know if I want to live on my own – I might share with someone."

"You mean like a student, a flatmate?"

"Yeah, that sort of thing, could be a good laugh."

"Maggs, I think you should seriously consider your options before you do anything. You're used to a certain standard of living – moving in with someone else is something you're not used to."

"Pass the paper back."

Isabel slid the paper back, filled their glasses with some more red wine, and went to check on the dinner. "I still can't believe Charles took the kids to the cinema without a major argument."

"Mmm," Maggie nodded her agreement from behind the paper. "Look – in the rental section there's an advert for a female housemate to share a three-bedroom house in Donaghadee! What's OFCH?"

"Oil-fired central heating."

"How did you know that?"

"Have you any idea how many bloody property sections I had to read before we got this place?" Isabel waved her wooden spoon around the kitchen.

"Moving is a pain in the arse, isn't it?"

"Totally. They say next to a death or divorce it's the next most traumatic thing."

"Two out of three ain't bad!"

"Oh shit, Maggs! I didn't realise, I didn't mean . . ." Isabel went bright red realising what she had just said.

"Forget it, don't tiptoe round me – just because we don't talk about it doesn't mean it isn't happening."

"Still, pretty tactless of me."

"Forget it. I haven't been to Donaghadee since I was little. Mum used to take Grandpa to that wee restaurant. Oh, what's it called?" She tapped her lacquered nails on the wooden kitchen table, trying to recall the name. "Something Bell, I think."

"Never heard of it." Isabel looked blankly at Maggs who was now staring into space.

"You're not serious about this, are you? I mean, where would you put all your stuff?"

"Maybe the other woman would let me bring some with me. The rest I'll either sell or put in storage."

"How do you know it's a woman? It could be a pervy old man looking for a good time."

"Well, we'll know after I give the number a ring. Do you mind if I use your phone?"

"Maggs, I really think you should think about this more."

"Oh, Isabel, one phone call isn't going to hurt, is it?"

"I think you're mad." Isabel passed the cordless phone to her and turned back to the oven.

A couple of minutes later, Maggie hung up. "She sounds nice. Doesn't sound like an old perv, I'm sorry to say."

"So you're really going to go down and meet with her?"

"Yep, tomorrow morning. She owns the hardware shop next door so she said if she wasn't in when I rang the bell I should just go next door. Bow Bells!"

"Sorry?"

"The name of the restaurant I used to go to with my grandpa: 'Bow Bells'. Glad I remembered that – starting to worry about old age setting in."

"I think you're safe enough at thirty-six. Mind you, not for too much longer. What do you fancy doing for your birthday?"

"Bugger all – let's pretend it isn't really happening, shall we?"

"Maggs, you have to do something! Come on, tell me, it's only a few weeks away."

"The 18th of April, what day is that?"

"Look on the wall calendar."

Maggie turned in her seat and studied the calendar on the corkboard behind her head.

"Thursday. Fancy dinner in Cinnamon?"

"Won't that be a bit of a drive if you're living down the country?"

"Ha ha, smart-arse. Fancy it or not?"

"Dinner sounds good, but only if it's my treat."

"No chance – this little celebration is on Derek. I also feel a trip to Leonard's coming on."

"I like your style," Isabel giggled, "but you must let me come too."

Leonard's was a very expensive jeweller in town and the owner used to do a lot of business with Derek at Christmas and for Maggie's birthday. Why change tradition? Maggie reasoned.

"This year, I think I fancy a diamond bracelet. You know, one with lots and lots of diamonds!"

"I know exactly what you're talking about!"

Isabel served up her chicken and broccoli bake and Maggie attacked it with more enthusiasm than Isabel had seen since she came back from Spain.

"I was just thinking." Maggie spoke with her mouth full of food.

"Maggie, if you were one if my kids I'd tell you off for speaking with your mouth full."

"Ah shut up! I was just thinking, how do you fancy a week in Spain with me this summer?"

"You're serious?" Isabel stopped eating.

"Of course I am, fancy it?"

"Bloody hell, of course I do. But what about the kids?"

"Couldn't your mum take them?"

"She might, but I couldn't ask her for the whole week."

"That's what husbands are for. Ask Charles."

"Now you're just being funny,"

"Ask him, you're not a single-parent family. He has taken them to the cinema for goodness sake."

"Yeah, and he'll think that's his duty done as a father for the next six months."

"Promise you'll ask?"

"OK, I promise."

"Here's to our summer holiday!" Maggie raised her glass and Isabel did the same.

"And to you selling your house for a million quid!"

Chapter 18

The estate agent had left Maggie a note when she got home from Isabel's the previous night. They had twenty-seven parties through the house and of those twenty-seven, five were seriously interested. The agents were delighted that they had taken an offer of eight hundred and seventy-five thousand cash on the house, but their advice when they rang her that morning was to wait. The house had only just gone on the market and they felt there were more bids to come in.

Buoyed by the good news, Maggie hummed as she got ready. She was back sleeping in the master bedroom again. Of course she had had a sacrificial burning of the bedsheets that Derek and Cliff had been using when she caught them. She felt almost like a new person. Selling the house was definitely the right thing to do. She drove down Malone Park and almost felt like doing the fingers to the passing houses.

She drove to Donaghadee, singing all the way to the

radio. As she arrived in the little town, she slowed down so she could read the numbers on the doors. She saw the sign for Maguire's Hardware and pulled in to the kerb. The shop was at one end of a pretty terrace overlooking the harbour. The sign looked freshly painted, as did the whole building. Next door was the house from the advert. It too had been freshly painted a very pretty duck-egg blue, while the shop was a creamy colour and they looked very appealing. It all looked promising. Locking her car she walked over to Number 20 and rang the bell. No reply. She tried to peer in the front room but she couldn't see in as there were pretty muslin blinds – probably for privacy, she thought. She followed the instructions the girl on the phone had given her and went into the hardware shop. It was much darker inside than it had been outside on the pavement.

"Hello?" she called into the gloom.

"Hi. You must be Maggie?"

An attractive blonde girl appeared from the back somewhere. She was wearing jeans and a polo neck with her long hair tied back in a swingy ponytail. Maggie's first impression was that she liked this girl.

"Yes, I am, and you are?"

"God, sorry. So rude of me. I'm Alice."

The pretty blonde extended her hand and Maggie shook it.

"Very pleased to meet you, Maggie. Sorry I was in here – we had a delivery of terracotta pots and they weigh a ton so I wanted to make sure the delivery man put them in the right place."

Maggie nodded, as if she had to deal with terracotta-pot deliverymen all the time.

"Righto, follow me – you will probably want to see the house?"

"That would be the general idea." Maggie laughed.

She followed Alice out of the shop.

"You don't sound local," Maggie commented as Alice unlocked the front door of the house.

"I'm originally from Belfast, but I lived in London for eleven years, so I worked hard at losing the accent."

"Why did you come back?"

"I inherited this place."

"Did you work in hardware in London?" Maggie was intrigued.

"No!" Alice laughed as if Maggie had said the most hilarious thing. "I'm a solicitor and this is my six-month sabbatical."

"Ah right. So will you be going back to London then?"

"Actually, I thought I'd go back like a shot, but I'm kind of enjoying myself here."

Maggie felt something rub against her ankles as she walked into the hallway and nearly jumped out of her skin.

"Holy fuck!" she exclaimed in fright.

"Sorry, don't mind Gary." Alice pointed down to where a cat with seemingly only one eye was purring up at her.

"Sorry, didn't mean to swear, he just took me by surprise. I'm not that used to cats."

"More of a dog person?"

"Actually, to be honest, I'm not really used to animals at all."

"Oh. Right. Well, he won't hurt you or anything."

Maggie felt really stupid for overreacting – the cat after all looked totally harmless.

"This was my aunt's house – she died a few months ago and she left me the house and the shop in her will. I've painted all the rooms and got rid of and replaced all the furniture I could afford. The kitchen's brand new. The only thing I haven't touched is the garden. It's quite a good size and I'll have it in order for the summer."

"You've done a great job," Maggie said most sincerely. The house was a lot smaller than she was used to and the furniture was mostly dated. But the rooms were pleasant and the kitchen was lovely.

"Would you like a look upstairs?" Alice offered.

"Yes, please."

They climbed the stairs, Alice leading the way.

The two bedrooms were significantly smaller than Maggie's huge bedroom at home with its marble en suite, but they were freshly painted. The beds were terrible – if she was going to seriously think about moving in here, she would bring a bed from home to sleep on – in fact, she would bring a double from one of the guest rooms.

"You're thinking how uncomfortable the beds look?"

Maggie nodded.

"Well, unfortunately, I can confirm that they're appalling, I kind of ran out of money after I took the headstaggers and painted the house and the shop."

"I have a bed I would bring with me," Maggie said before she had even realised what she had said.

"You like it then?" Alice sounded surprised.

"Well, yes, I do, but I'd need to –"

"Say no more, I have a few more people to see, but if you're serious give me a ring in the next couple of days and we'll see how we both feel."

Alice was so nice and laid-back about it; Maggie didn't feel any pressure and she wandered round the house again on her own, getting a feel for the place. It actually had a nice vibe about it and she imagined living with Alice would be rather enjoyable. Though perhaps at her age it was a ridiculous thing to be doing – house-sharing?

"Would you mind if I asked you a personal question?" asked Alice.

They were standing in the front room looking over the harbour. It was very peaceful. Maggie shook her head. "No, not at all."

"Well, it's none of my business of course, but you arrived in a beautiful sports car, you're well dressed and, well, I hadn't expected anyone so well, um, groomed to apply."

Alice was clearly trying to be diplomatic.

"I don't look like the sort of person who answers house-share ads out of the classifieds?" Maggie tried to help her out.

"Well, to be honest, I wouldn't really know – this is my first time advertising for someone. I lived on my own in London – but I had really good friends who lived in the flat below me. I miss the company. It can be lonely on your own."

"Tell me about it." Maggie nodded her head in agreement. "I'm on my own for the first time in six or seven years and it certainly takes some getting used to."

"Would you like a coffee or tea?"

"I'd love a coffee if you're having one."

Alice disappeared into the kitchen. Maggie surveyed the room. It had a new-looking sofa and a bureau in one corner and a rather awful sideboard, which had a faded, blotchy top as if it had had lots of things sitting on it for a long time in the sun. Maggie guessed that Alice had inherited most of the furniture apart from the comfy- looking loose-covered cream sofa. The view was spectacular from here – she could see the Copeland Islands quite clearly and she imagined on a clear day you could see Scotland, which was only a few miles away. Her cabinet would fit perfectly into the space where the sideboard was currently residing. She sat down on the sofa – it was one of those ones where you wanted to curl your feet up beneath you and never get up again.

"Here we are." Alice came back into the room with a tray. She set it down on the sideboard.

"Ugly, isn't it?"

"Sorry?"

"The sideboard."

Maggie grinned.

Alice passed her a mug with some delicious-smelling coffee and offered a biscuit out of the Belgian selection tin from Marks & Spencer. Maggie took one and dunked it into her coffee. The chocolate melted off and disappeared into the steaming mug.

"Gorgeous coffee."

"Thanks. Susie, one of my friends, made me a survival pack when I left – this was in it."

"Nice friend."

"One of the best. I miss her."

"How are you finding it being back?"

"Initially very odd. But I spent my youth here and it's growing on me. As I mentioned to you, I was only going to stay for the six months but I'm considering a more long-term approach now."

Time slipped by as Alice explained about her aunt and the conditions of her inheritance. Maggie was rapt; she curled up on the sofa quite unselfconsciously and took a cigarette when it was offered to her.

"Now, how about you?" Alice asked once she had filled Maggie in on her life to date.

"God, where do I start?" Maggie rolled her eyes, and then without quite knowing why she opened up to Alice and gave her a breakdown of the last six months, right up to her Spanish trip and José. Alice listened without interrupting. Maggie found it quite cathartic, like talking to her therapist only cheaper.

Talking about your life to someone who has not previously known you is quite a liberating feeling, Maggie decided on her way back to Belfast. She was almost reluctant to leave. She reckoned they could have talked all day if Emlyn had not come in and asked Alice to come back into the shop as they were getting busy.

* * *

167

"I think I might just move in, if she'll have me," Maggie told Isabel on the phone later that night.

"Seriously?" Isabel had been amazed when Maggie had told how well she had got on with Alice.

"Most seriously."

Over the next few days the bidding continued on her house. Maggie couldn't believe that so many people could want to live in it. However, she was totally delighted. The bidding had gone from eight hundred and seventy-five thousand to nine hundred and fifty thousand in three days and the estate agents were as delighted as she was.

"Hang in there," Seb, the chap who was dealing on her behalf, advised her. "It's important to get the maximum for your house without letting the bidding go crazy. That way, if the person you agree to pulls out, the underbidder will reinstate their offer without reconsidering in the cold light of day. Bidding wars are great as long the sale actually completes. Remember, your house has been on the market less than a week. There's nothing more disappointing for a vendor than to get caught up in the bidding between different parties, only for those bidders to both get cold feet and the house go for thousands less than expected."

Maggie told him that she would follow his advice since it was in his interest that the sale was completed as smoothly and as soon as possible. What she didn't tell him was that all that mattered to her now was to get shot of the place.

On Monday evening Maggie answered the phone. It was Alice.

"Hi, is that Maggie?"

"Yes, hi, Alice."

"Sorry to ring you. I don't want to hassle you – have I caught you at a bad time?"

"No, not at all."

"Well, I know it's pretty unusual for me to call you rather than the other way round but I have had a weekend of interviewing total maniacs and I just wanted to see if you had any further thoughts about the matter?"

Maggie laughed, glad that Alice had rung her.

"As matter of fact, I have. I would be interested, but I was wondering if I would be able to bring some furniture with me?"

"God! I'd be delighted!" Alice exclaimed.

Maggie smiled with relief. "Do you want to come up to my house and see what you think would fit in?" she asked on impluse.

"I'd love to, but it's really entirely up to you. Let's face it, anything is better than what's there at the moment. But only if you're sure?

"I'm totally sure – save me having to store or sell everything."

They chatted on, discussing how the rental would work. Alice said she would set up a rental lease for Maggie to sign for six months and then after that they would see how things went. Maggie agreed that this was fine and they arranged to meet the following morning.

Chapter 19

"She's going to take it!" Alice danced into the shop the next day.

Emlyn popped his head out from the watering cans he was trying to hang from hooks in the ceiling. They were venturing into some garden equipment to see how it sold before they thought about actually stocking any plants or flowers.

"That's great news – are you pleased?"

"Really pleased. Maggie is so much nicer than any of those other eejits who applied."

Maggie had been the first person Alice had shown round. Over the weekend she had had a lesbian couple who wanted to retire to the sea. No, thank you very much. A rough girl in her early twenties with a tattooed neck who seemed to eat Regal cigarettes since she smoked copious amounts in the short while she was in the house. She had produced a huge wad of notes to try and bribe Alice into giving her the room – thank God Emlyn had been with her otherwise she would have seriously been shitting herself. Then there had been three or four totally nondescript girls who would've bored her to death. Yep – Maggie was by far and away the most entertaining though the most unlikely candidate. Alice was overjoyed that she was going to take the room and bring some decent furniture with her into the bargain.

"She wants me to go up to her house to have a look a look at what furniture would suit my place here! How great is that?"

"You'll want to borrow the car again?"

"Do you mind?"

"No, not at all, it would be a pleasure as always. When are you going to have a look?"

"Tomorrow afternoon, if that's OK?"

"No problem, I'll mind the shop."

Alice looked sideways at him.

"Now, where should we put the garden parasols?" he said.

* * *

The next afternoon, Alice drove through Belfast trying to get her bearings. Her old house had been in the east of the city, but Maggie lived in South Belfast. She followed signs for Malone as she headed through the city centre. She drove up the Malone Road past Methodist College and The Bot and The Egg, two pubs which were very popular amongst students, or so she had been reliably

171

informed. She knew she was on the right track when she passed the Ulster Clinic on her left and she moved into the outside lane to turn right into Malone Park. Maggie's directions had been good so far. She counted the turnings on the right, Osborne Park, Myrtlefield Park and then Maggie's turning. She drove through the stone pillars that indicated that this was a private park. She had never been here before and was impressed with the huge tree-lined avenue. The road was much wider here than in the other parks. The houses were huge; some you could hardly see from the road. She was the only car on the road so she was able to crawl along in Emlyn's ancient Mini looking for the house. Maggie had told her there was a *For Sale* board attached to the gatepost. There it was. She turned into the driveway and the sight of the house took her breath away – it was absolutely huge! A vast expanse of red-brick and sandstone stood before her.

"Wow!" she said to herself. She recognised Maggie's Mercedes from her visit to Donaghadee.

"Why on earth would anyone want to leave this place, gay husband or not?" she wondered as she rang the bell.

It took Maggie a couple of minutes to come to the door, but she opened it and her smile widened when she saw Alice.

"Come in, come in!"

Alice walked into the hall a little awkwardly, not really sure where to put herself in such grand surroundings.

"Do you want the grand tour first or shall we have coffee?"

"Coffee, please."

Maggie led the way into an enormous kitchen, with marbled floor and granite worktops. The kitchen units were solid wood and screamed money. It didn't look like Maggie cooked much. The copper saucepans on display had never been used; the chrome blender looked brand new. There wasn't a speck of dirt on the hob – either she didn't cook or she had amazing cleaners.

"I don't think my coffee will be up the standards yours was – it's Nescafé!"

"That's fine. I like instant – actually I prefer it to fresh ground."

Maggie burst out laughing. "So do I!"

They ended up walking round the house, drinking their coffee as they went. Maggie had a couple of favourite pieces of furniture that Alice loved and was only too happy for Maggie to bring with her. She was also going to bring a double bed, not the super king-size one in the master bedroom, but a smaller one from one of the guest-rooms. It was a white hand-painted French country-style bed with matching bedside tables and Alice thought it was perfect – in fact it was gorgeous and she was a little jealous.

"God, your stuff is fabulous! I'm envious."

"Why don't you take some bedside tables too? You said you hated yours, that they're all faded and old-fashioned. How about these?" She pointed to some pretty pale wooden ones with three drawers in each.

"Gosh, they're lovely but I can't take your stuff."

"You're not taking – I'm loaning them to you – long-term of course. If you don't I'll either sell them or they'll end up in storage."

"Well, how about I buy them off you then?"

"OK." Maggie nodded.

"How much?"

"A tenner for the pair."

"Maggie, be serious."

"I'm serious. Derek paid for all this stuff, it didn't cost me a penny."

"Doesn't mean that you should just give it away!"

"I'm not – they're ten pounds. Now pay up!"

"OK, OK. My purse is downstairs."

By the end of the visit they had managed to visualise quite a lot of Maggie's furniture in Alice's house and Alice was the proud owner of the cheapest and loveliest bedside tables she had ever seen. She had tried to pay Maggie more, but she wouldn't hear of it.

Chapter 20

The removal van pulled up in front of the house. Maggie had moved her car in front of the garage to keep it out of the way. She ran down to let the men in. Her whole life was boxed in various parts of the house.

"Ready?" Isabel asked. She had come round to lend a hand – it could be quite traumatic for Maggie on her own.

"Ready," Maggie replied, pulling back the front door.

The two removal men worked quickly and efficiently. They had dropped round lots of flat-pack boxes a week beforehand and Maggie and Isabel had packed away all the clothes, furniture, kitchen utensils, books, rugs etc that Maggie could take with her. Some stuff had already gone into storage – bigger pieces of furniture. The rest she had given away to charity and she had drastically downsized her wardrobe.

"But only to build it up again," she had giggled conspiratorially to Isabel.

Bags, shoes, jackets, skirts, trousers, coats, ski stuff and any last vestiges of Derek's stuff were all bagged and delivered to a most delighted charity shop on the Lisburn Road.

Maggie had thought about selling her stuff in Déjà Vu, a second-hand clothes shop that only dealt with designer goods. She'd decided however that she didn't want to make a profit on anything Derek had paid for. That included the chocolate-brown Dolce and Gabbana trousers Derek had bought her for her birthday along with a Chanel jacket and skirt, two Gucci handbags (which Isabel swiftly grabbed) and several pairs of Prada strappy sandals.

"Oh, I wish I was the same size as you!" Isabel moaned, looking longingly at the trousers.

"Isabel, it doesn't matter how hard you try to squeeze in – they're too small for you." Maggie laughed, watching her friend hopping round the bedroom.

Isabel could have wept.

"And damn me for having such big clodhoppers!" Now she was attempting to squeeze her size 7s into Maggie's size 5 sandals without any success.

The men finished packing in under an hour. They were to go directly to Donaghadee where Alice was waiting for them. Maggie and Isabel would follow in Maggie's car.

"How do you feel about leaving it?" Isabel asked as Maggie took one final look round to make sure she hadn't left anything behind.

"Strangely, I feel like a weight has been lifted. Sure,

I'll miss the big house, but I'm excited about where I'm going next." She hugged Isabel and the pair of them walked out the front door and pulled it closed behind them.

They drove to the estate agent's.

"There you are." Maggie handed the keys of her house over. The new owners were calling in at lunch-time to collect the keys – her solicitor had the money and the sale had completed.

"Good luck, Maggie." Seb, the estate agent, shook her hand. "Good luck in your new house."

"Thanks, Seb!" She grinned as she swept out the door.

She jumped back into the Mercedes and started the engine. "Right, here we go!" "Done and dusted?" asked Isabel.

"I am no longer a property owner."

"How do you feel?"

"Like I'm sixteen going for my first flat-share – dead excited."

Isabel had never seen Alice's house and was keen to know what it was like.

Maggie described the pale duck-egg blue exterior right through to the Shaker kitchen and the small bedroom that would soon be hers.

"My God, I just can't imagine you living in someone else's house! What will you do without your en suite?" Isabel joked.

"This is the new Maggie – this Maggie can cope with any and all situations!"

"Well, as long as this isn't the new Maggie who can't

stop moaning about not having enough space, or someone borrowing her shoes," Isabel teased.

"Alice's feet are clodhoppers like yours, and anyway she seems to have plenty of shoes so at least we won't have that problem." Maggie did the fingers at Isabel.

Pulling up outside the house, Isabel was taken by surprise at how pretty it was.

"God, I had no idea it was so cute. The window-boxes are sweet."

Maggie nodded as she turned off the engine. The removal van was parked in front of them. The front door was open and they had started taking the boxes into the house. As they approached the front door, Alice appeared.

"Hi, Maggie." She gave a little wave.

"Hi, Alice – this is Isabel. Bestest friend in the entire world. She has been giving me a hand packing and getting out of Malone Park."

"Nice to meet you." Alice put her hand out and Isabel shook it.

"Good to meet you too."

They followed Alice back inside, staying out of the way of the men carrying boxes.

"You had labelled each box so the guys are putting them either in the front room or up in your room."

"Great, I hoped they would."

"Oh God." The front room was already full of boxes; there was hardly any room to move. "Sorry, Alice, I hadn't realised I had so much stuff!"

"No probs, we'll get it all sorted. It's got to be better than Auntie Jean's stuff anyway."

The next two hours Alice and Isabel spent unpacking the boxes downstairs while Maggie dealt with the boxes upstairs.

"Bloody hell, I'd forgotten how much I hate moving!" Maggie called down from upstairs.

They stopped for a sandwich at lunch-time and Alice showed Isabel round the shop and introduced her to Emlyn who was nearly bursting with nosiness. Alice knew it had taken all his restraint to stop him from galloping next door to find out if he was missing any gossip.

"Delighted to meet you." Emlyn was clearly as taken with Isabel as he had been with Maggie and he kissed her hand in what he thought was a bit of a Cary Grant move. It made Isabel giggle and made Alice want to hit him on the nose.

By late afternoon Maggie was officially a resident of Donaghadee and the house looked superb with all her stuff in residence – well, she certainly thought so.

They all collapsed on the sofa in the living-room.

"Hang on, one thing I forgot." Maggie jumped to her feet and lifted her car keys.

"Back in a mo."

"Maggs, what could you have possibly forgotten? You've brought every conceivable thing with you! God bless Alice is all I can say!"

"It's only a small thing," Maggie called as she opened the front door.

Alice and Isabel looked at each other, but neither had a clue what she was talking about and were frankly too tired to care.

"Voila!" Maggie announced coming back in.

Both girls turned to look at her waving a bottle of champagne.

"Let's celebrate!"

Alice got her John Rocha crystal out of the cupboard.

"Lovely glasses," Isabel commented, studying hers before Maggie filled it with bubbles.

"What shall we toast to?" Alice asked

"To new friends and new beginnings!" Isabel raised her glass.

"To new friends and new beginnings!" Maggie and Alice chorused and they all clinked their glasses together and took a slug of the champagne.

Chapter 21

March – Isabel

It had been a pretty awful few months for Isabel. Since Maggie had sold her house and moved down to Donaghadee she had felt lonelier than ever.

Walking into her hallway, she was thinking of how this house always depressed her. Closing the front door behind her, she bent to pick up the post and there it was, sitting there virtually flashing at her. Another letter from the building society, this one in red. Isabel dropped her handbag on the floor, picked up the letter and held it with both hands. It was daring her to open it and read the contents. But she felt sick at the thought. She set it back down on the hall table and walked into the kitchen.

"Jesus, if I drink any more bloody coffee I'll turn into a cup," she thought to herself as she switched on the kettle.

She frogmarched herself back into the hall and picked up the letter, then walked back into the kitchen. She held the letter up to the sun to see if she could see through the envelope, but it was too thick.

"Stop being so pathetic," she told herself sternly. "This is your home too and therefore your mortgage." She let the kettle boil and then held the flap of the envelope over the steam. Easing her index finger under the flap, she opened the envelope and slid the letter out.

She read the letter slowly, only understanding half of what was written. Payments now appeared to be three months in arrears – could Charles please contact them informing them when they would receive payment or if there was a problem with the payments that had been negotiated? There was a number at the bottom of the letter just above the signature. Isabel sat down heavily at the kitchen table.

Charles hadn't being paying the mortgage. She was also horrified to see that he had been paying two thousand pounds per month. She thought about the missing three thousand pounds – maybe that was where the money had gone, she thought hopefully?

She slumped in her chair, unsure of what to do next. Putting the letter back into the envelope, she tried to reseal it – it didn't look too convincing. Maybe Charles wouldn't notice when he came home – but she knew that he would.

Sitting on her own in the kitchen, she felt flashes of anger as she thought of the wild spending, the Shirley Maxwell Experience he had put the whole family through –

at what cost? All the talk about skiing holidays, boarding schools for the twins when they were older. She laughed out loud in the empty kitchen.

Who the hell did he think they were? They couldn't even pay the mortgage! She clenched her fists and paced around the kitchen. She decided there and then that she would confront him that evening when he got home.

She spent the rest of the afternoon working out how much money she had in her account and what they owed the building society, and checking that all the other bills like electricity and gas were up to date. She was relieved to find out that they were.

She collected the twins as usual and ferried them home. Half-listening to their chatter she wondered about the car payments. Charles had taken out a loan from the bank to pay for his BMW and her A-Class. Now that his company had taken over the payments for his car, it should only be hers they were paying.

The afternoon dragged as she tried to keep herself busy. She and the twins did some painting and played in the garden – she was goalie while Henry tried to kick a football between two garden chairs. It was a beautiful afternoon – it was hard to believe that on a day like this they were in so much trouble. She half-hoped she was imagining it all, but in her heart she knew it was real. The way her husband had been acting, his constant moods, hiding out behind the paper, constantly comparing himself to work colleagues. For all she knew it was probably the done thing in London to be up shit creek.

She was at the front door as soon as she heard his car on the gravel driveway.

"Hi, Isabel," he said brightly as he opened the front door, setting his briefcase and laptop case down by the hall table.

She didn't say a word, just held up the envelope.

His smile faded on his lips.

He played dumb. "What's that?"

"You know what it is. This is a letter letting us know that the mortgage hasn't been paid for three months, Charles."

"Give me that." He stepped towards her, his face set in angry lines.

She side-stepped him. "Where the fuck is all the money in our joint account?"

"What the – ? Having you been checking up on me?"

"No, Charles, I had to rejoin the RAC because my car broke down back in October and guess what? I tried to pay the membership with our joint-account card. Imagine my surprise to discover the card was declined. I rang the telephone banking service and, would you believe it, our account was empty? And it's still empty. I wonder where all the money has gone?"

"What are you trying to say?" Charles stood completely still

"Women? Have you got an expensive mistress in London, darling?"

"What!" he exploded.

His reaction suggested that perhaps she was wrong. Isabel was relieved but she didn't let up.

"Or like the horses, do you?"

"Isabel! For Christ's sake! Have you gone mad?"

"You tell me, Charles – have I imagined three thousand pounds gone?"

"Fucking hell! I work hard all day and I come home to this!"

"I haven't had the courage to check our savings account. But by God, Charles, if I find out that you've spent all our savings I'll break your bloody neck!" she vowed, her voice rising higher and higher.

They stood facing each other, both seething with anger: Isabel for letting herself and her children be put in this position; Charles, because he had been found out.

"I want to know everything, Charles – don't even consider leaving anything out. Your marriage could depend on it." She stood defiantly in front of him, hands on hips, a force to be reckoned with though shaking like a jelly inside.

Charles couldn't remember a time when his wife had stood up to him like this. Normally if he got aggressive, she backed down, not wanting to cause a fight. But this evening she was really mad – he had threatened her family, her equilibrium and she was not going to be fobbed off with bull-shit excuses. He felt for one short moment that he could deny everything. Tell her to shut up and go on as things were. But things were bad. He dearly wanted to tell her everything, how much trouble he had got them into, how much he loved her and the kids and how sorry he was – but something was holding him back. She would be so let down, so disappointed – he couldn't tell her. What would she think of him? Already she knew some of what he had done, but not really the half of it. Could he turn round and tell her the truth? Then suddenly, seeing the look of desperation in her eyes, he blurted it all out, all the feelings and thoughts he had bottled up for the last few months.

"Darling, I'm so sorry – I have lost everything, I put our family at risk and I lost. I re-mortgaged our financially crippling home, and used up all our savings and the money we had saved for the holiday to Disney World. It's all gone. I went in with the guys in London and we bought shares in an e-commerce company that was all set to go through the roof. I was going to make us millionaires. You wouldn't have had to work at all. You could stop worrying about how much everything cost, we could get rid of this place and its hideous décor. I was going to buy us a villa in France so the kids could learn French, you could take cookery courses like you always wanted to and I could maybe do a little consultancy work a few days a month. But instead of making us millionaires, I have left us virtually destitute. I can't pay our mortgage and I don't know what to do. I've no-one to talk to and I'm spiralling out of control." It all came out in a garbled heap. He had never felt so weak, vulnerable and relieved in his whole life.

She was staring at him, silent.

He slumped down onto the floor, his strength sapped from the constant pretence and the shame of confession.

"Say something," he pleaded.

"How long has this been going on?" She stood, back against the opposite wall, her eyes never leaving his face.

"A few months. The company was suspended from trading; it was supposed to re-list on the stock exchange, but instead it advised its investors that it has gone into liquidation."

"You reduced our marriage to a shell." She stared at him hard. She had wanted to know, she had demanded to know. This was as bad as it could get. "Neither Maggie nor I made very smart choices." She could see the pain in his eyes as she said it and she was glad – she wanted to hurt him, hurt him for all the hurt he had caused the children and her. Why? All for a stupid fucking dream, the chance to make it really big.

"Isabel, I never –"

"Don't say any more, you've said quite enough. What do you intend to do about this mess you have created?"

He shook his head. "I don't know."

Charles had always been in charge in their lives; now here he was sitting on the floor like a little boy. She was shocked at how he had crumbled in front of her.

"How much do you owe?" She held her voice steady.

"Four hundred thousand."

"Pounds?"

He nodded, tears rolling down his cheeks.

"How much is this house worth?"

"Possibly four hundred and fifty thousand."

"If we sell it, does it get us out of this nightmare?"

187

"The Mortgage Company will repossess it if we don't make next month's payment."

"You didn't answer my question."

Charles had never seen his wife so hard and business-like; it was a new side to her.

He nodded. "It should do, if we can sell it quickly."

"The market is strong at the minute, at least it was whenever Maggie sold her house – spring is a good time to sell, isn't it?"

"Wouldn't you mind?" he asked.

"Are you joking? I never liked this place. We'll move back to the cottage. I presume you still have a job?"

"Yes, the company doesn't know anything about it – we've kept it quiet."

"We'll have to get the house on the market and soon. I have enough money in my account to cover this month's payment, and possibly the bridging loan on the cottage after that. Well, we'd better sell this place fast."

"Isabel, I'm so sorry."

"So you keep saying, Charles, but sorry isn't going to get us out of this mess, is it?"

She turned on her heel and walked up the stairs, leaving him sitting on the floor alone.

"What the hell have I done?" Charles sobbed. If he had had a knife in his hand he would have plunged it into his own chest.

Upstairs, Isabel burst out laughing as she walked into their bedroom and took a look around.

This fucking house, she thought, so important to

Charles and the life he was trying to create and then he admits he hates as much as I do! Oh God, the irony of the whole thing! It would be funny if it wasn't so fucking serious!

Cold steely reserve kept her together as she took a pen and notepad from beside her bed and went back downstairs.

Charles hadn't moved from his position on the floor. He looked ridiculous with his tear-stained face and crumpled business suit. She was suddenly aware of the strain he must have been under these past few months, and was tempted to take him in her arms and hug him and tell him that as long as they had each other everything would be OK. But she hardened her heart. She didn't know if things would be OK. He had taken his family to the edge; now was the time for damage limitation, not hugs and kisses.

"Get up, we have some work to do."

Charles followed her into the kitchen, wiping his face on the sleeve of his suit jacket.

Isabel was sitting at the kitchen table. There was a calculator, pen and paper in front of her.

"Now let's work out how we get out of this mess."

He pulled out the chair opposite her and they went to work.

Isabel listed all their outgoings and estimated how much they were currently and how much, with some serious belt-tightening, they could reduce it to.

"If we were seriously frugal for a few months we could live on your salary," he said at last. "We could renegotiate with the building society and, with my salary, we could start paying them back. We could start building our savings back up – maybe we could even still go to Disney."

"Let's not run before we can walk." Isabel stared at the figures in front of her. "Remember, you re-mortgaged the house."

Charles nodded. "But, Isabel, we can get out of this mess, I know we can." Light was starting to come back into his eyes.

"Let's get one thing straight right now. We have been married for seven years and for the past six months you have been keeping a very serious thing secret from me. I have been through hell; I nearly left you at Christmas. This does not exactly inspire trust, Charles. If we're going to survive both financially and within our marriage we need trust."

"I understand." He nodded, trying not to dwell on the fact she had considered leaving him

"You have to stop trying to keep up with those city boys you call your colleagues. Maybe they can afford to take a hit like this but we can't – look what it's done to you. Jesus, Charles! I thought you were having an affair, or had a gambling problem."

"Isabel, I love you, I would never have an affair."

As Isabel looked at her husband, attempting to make a comeback after his defeat, she was strangely proud of him after all. He had admitted he had cocked up and got them into trouble, but here he was sitting down with her discussing how together they could get out of this situation.

"Will we ring the building society and see if we can renegotiate our mortgage?" she asked.

He agreed and they discussed who would do what the next day.

When Isabel climbed into bed that night she felt more relaxed than she had done in months. Charles and she lay close like spoons and she slept soundly, only waking when the alarm went off.

Charles shuffled off sleepily to the shower and she lay back on her pillow, thinking about the previous evening. She made the decision not to tell a soul about their money worries. She had a feeling that everything would work out – it would be bloody hard, but they would get there. After watching what happened to Maggie and Derek, she didn't want to become the next talking-point for BT9 dinner parties. When Charles came out of the shower, she followed him downstairs in her dressing-gown and made them a cup of tea.

Charles, who hadn't eaten at all in the last two days, had a couple of slices of wheaten toast with marmalade. Worry lines were still etched on his face, but the stress of keeping secrets was already starting to lift.

Sitting beside his wife in their kitchen, he wondered for about the seventieth time since last night why he hadn't told her in the first place. He had no idea how close he had come to losing her and the twins. The idea made him nauseous. He was completely aware of what a bastard he had become and was deeply ashamed of himself. He had not liked the man he nearly was.

He kissed and hugged his wife goodbye and left for work feeling human for the first time in a long time. He could not believe that Isabel was standing by him. She had been hard on him last night, but had the shoe been on the other foot, he probably would have been exactly the same. They had spent time together for the first time in ages and he had enjoyed it, even though he wished it had been for a different reason. He drove to work and actually hummed along to the radio.

He knew that with a little wrangling he could cut down his travelling substantially and spend more time with his family rather than trying to be a city trader. Initially it had all seemed so exciting, those guys on their fantastical salaries and huge bonuses. They had money to burn. He suspected that for most of his London colleagues the fall of 'E-dock', the company they had all invested in, was little more than an annoyance. He really had let himself be taken for a ride. From now on he would need to get his priorities right.

Chapter 22

One month on and sometimes Alice couldn't believe Maggie had answered her advert for a housemate. It seemed so removed from everything she was used to. Yet they seemed to have so much in common, apart from the fact that Maggie was six years older than Alice, had a habit of referring to "When I lived in Malone Park", and was addicted to buying make-up. Maggie maintained that she couldn't walk through Boots without at least stopping to test a nail varnish or purchase a new lip-gloss. These compulsions had worsened since her break-up and the bathroom now looked like Space NK while Alice's rather pathetic make-up bag, relegated to a corner of Maggie's chrome trolley, looked like somewhere mascara-wands go to die. Alice could go into the bathroom, open the cabinet and spend a happy hour twisting up lipsticks and trying the colours, checking to make sure that she still didn't suit electric-blue eyeliner and if Touché Eclat really got rid of bags. Maggie of course sympathised with this fascination and was happy to lend any of her copious amounts of make-up products to Alice. When Alice questioned the amount of make-up she owned, Maggie explained that she was an advertiser's dream: she could not resist the sexy advertising. Besides, with her dark hair and swarthy (a word she hated) complexion, without carefully made-up eyes she would just end up looking like a small Italian man. Alice knew this was total crap – she had seen Maggs without any make-up and she looked just as lovely without a bucket of slap on.

When she had turned up at Alice's door, Alice was surprised as she had half-expected a trendy young thing wearing the latest in Topshop standard issue. Well, Maggie was still relatively young, of course, and did wear the latest Topshop standard issue – and, as it transpired, she was as easy-going as she had first appeared to be.

Maggie started to help in the shop soon after she moved in. Sometimes she came into the shop and annoyed Emlyn by trying to move things about to make them look better on the shelves.

"Just because it's a tin of varnish and not a pair of Gucci loafers doesn't mean it doesn't deserve to be displayed properly," she would tell an exasperated Emlyn and Alice just stood back and let her get on with it. Customers also seemed to warm to her and the glamour she added to the dark little shop.

She also worked for charity, or charities to be exact. Living off the very satisfactory sale of her marital home and a generous monthly payment from Derek, she didn't need to work but felt that she needed to do something, so she did two mornings a week in the Action Cancer shop and one in Oxfam.

Alice still could not really fathom why Maggie had sold her beautiful old house in Malone and moved to Alice's much less salubrious home miles from the city. Maggie had explained that after Claudia's departure she had felt very alone and the joy had gone out of owning that big house with all its expensive furnishings – especially since the neighbours looked on her with a mixture of sympathy and amusement.

"I hated knowing I was being talked about. Derek did what he did and there's nothing I can do about it, but I'll be damned if I'll spend the rest of my life as a laughing-stock. Besides, the house was far too big with just me rattling round in it. There's a lovely couple there now with a huge family so the whole place gets used as it should, as a home."

She explained that the only way she could deal with what had happened to her was to move – either to move country or move to a different part of the city. Since she wanted time to think about a new direction, she had decided a move fifteen miles east would suffice for the moment. Oh, and she had the apartment just outside Marbella where she could go whenever she felt like it, alone or with friends – to sunbathe, shop and have it away with the local talent.

Alice would have given her eye-teeth for a week in the

sun. She couldn't remember the last time she had gone abroad – in fact, her passport was so out of date, in the photo she was still in braces, a bad perm and iridescent lipstick – immigration officials always tried not to laugh when she had handed it over the few times she had ever had need for it.

Maggie now viewed men with a suspicious eye. Being slim and very attractive, she was not going to be short of suitors for long, but she could not have been less interested.

"I'm taking a swim in Lake Me," she would joke, putting on a phoney American accent.

In the six months since her break-up, she had started to come to terms with Derek and his infidelity. She told Alice she "never wanted to clap eyes on the wee fruit again".

It had taken her a few weeks to get used to the pace of life in Donaghadee, which was definitely more relaxed than Belfast – not that she had ever worked in the rat-race. She liked Donaghadee as a town. The people were friendly – it really wasn't much more than a large village and she quickly found her way around. It was fifteen miles to Belfast which didn't take too long in the car when she went to meet Isabel.

Though Isabel had now increased her working hours, they still met for coffee. Sometimes Isabel would met her halfway, in Bangor, but most of the time they met in town – Maggie loved her weekly trip as it gave her a chance to pop into the shops she loved on the Lisburn Road.

Maggie knew something had happened between Charles and Isabel, though nothing was mentioned. One minute Isabel was complaining that Charles was turning into a moron obsessed with all the things he used to despise – the next she stopped talking about him altogether and started smiling a lot more, around the same time as she started working a lot more. Which was distinctly odd, Maggie thought, as presumably she was working more because of financial pressures.

Maggie loved the shop. She loved all the strange things that it sold and wondered when people ever used things like rawlplugs or brass curtain hooks.

"Maggie, I don't think I have ever met someone less useful than yourself!" Alice laughed as Maggie stared at a red plastic rawlplug in her hand.

"What's it for?"

"For holding heavy things in the wall, like pictures or shelves."

Maggie looked at her blankly.

"God! OK, say you wanted to hang a painting on the wall and you knew it was too heavy for ordinary nails or picture hooks." Alice held a small nail in her hand to demonstrate her point.

"OK, I understand so far."

"Yeah, OK – so the painting would pull the nail out of the plaster, yeah?"

Maggie nodded.

"So what you do is drill a hole in the place you would have put your nail, then you hammer in the rawlplug. It expands inside the hole and you put your nail inside it and voila! It holds the picture or whatever firmly in place."

"Expands inside the hole? How?"

"Like a tampon!" Alice exclaimed, just as two middle-aged women walked in. They gave her a very strange look.

Alice went red and Maggie burst out laughing and had to go into the back until she calmed down.

"Well, that's a lesson I won't forget in a hurry!" Maggie said, grinning, as she handed Alice a cup of tea later.

The two women had paid for a mop-head and left in a great hurry as soon as Alice handed them their change.

"Oh shit! How embarrassing it was! Do you think they heard?"

"Unless they had turned their ears off I would have to say yes!"

"Oh well, rawlplugs, eh? Just a fact of life."

They were sitting side by side behind the counter sipping their tea when the door opened and a rough-looking man walked in. He looked around the shop and then walked straight back out the door again.

"Odd?"

"Very."

Emlyn came back after lunch, in a great mood and unusually chatty. Maggie was helping set up some garden furniture that Alice was thinking of stocking. The shop had a nice back garden, not as big as the house's one – more of a courtyard/patio type thing, a perfect place to put a couple of recliner chairs and a table and chairs.

Maggie was wrestling with a parasol when the little bell in the back room rang to signal that someone had walked into the shop. Maggie didn't leave her post, knowing that Alice and Emlyn were both inside, having a discussion on the new window display Emlyn wanted to try out. Alice wasn't convinced that hanging hammers with fishing wire at different lengths was the most effective display and Emlyn was trying to convince her otherwise.

"May I help you?" Maggie heard Alice ask the unseen customer.

"I'm lookin' for Jean, is she here?" a gruff voice asked.

Maggie gasped, put her parasol down and peeked in. It looked like the same rough-looking man who had put in an appearance that morning.

"I'm afraid Miss Maguire is no longer with us," said Alice.

"I thought it was her shop," he continued in the same gruff manner.

Alice, who was trying to be diplomatic without embarrassing the man, tried a different tack.

"Maybe there is something I could help you with?"

"I was told to speak to Jean."

"She's dead, for Christ's sake!" shrieked Emlyn, slamming down the handful of hammers he had been holding and marching into the back.

Maggie almost went into the shop to lend support but then heard Alice responding calmly.

"Miss Maguire passed away last October. I run the shop now. Can I help?"

"Do you deal with the antiques then?" He didn't sound in the least bit embarrassed for the upset he had caused.

"Antiques? No, I'm sorry, we're a hardware shop." She indicated the shelves containing rubber plungers, screwdrivers, lengths of washing-line and weedkiller.

"So who deals with them now if she's not here?"

"Jesus! Is this guy the missing link?" Maggie thought to herself. Again she was just about to go to Alice's rescue when Emlyn shot out of the back room like he'd been fired out of a cannon.

"I'm going to have to ask you to leave." He rushed over to the door and held it wide open. Daylight flooded into the shop.

The strange man didn't move. He just looked at Alice waiting for her answer.

"I'm sorry but I don't know what you're talking about. I'm sorry. There is an antique dealer further down the road, I think he's open today. His name is Mr Farmer." She was still smiling but Maggie could hear a tremor in her voice.

"I'll come back then, shall I?"

"Sir, I –" Alice was just about to say something when he left as abruptly as he had arrived.

Maggie came in the back door.

"Who the fuck was that?"

"Haven't a clue?" Alice sat down behind the counter again. "Freaked me out a bit. Emlyn, are you OK?"

Emlyn, who was still standing over by the door, had gone as white as a sheet. He didn't reply to Alice.

"Emlyn, are you still with us?" Maggie asked.

"That's outrageous, you can't just come into a shop and start offending people like that – we should call the police," he babbled.

"Emlyn, are you sure you're OK? Sit down." Alice offered him her stool.

Emlyn seemed oblivious to her and Maggie and walked round the shop like a whirling dervish.

"Emlyn, do you want to go home?" Alice asked him after witnessing five minutes of this bizarre behaviour.

"No, no, I'm fine now."

But he clearly wasn't.

"Emlyn, go home, would you!" Alice was getting tired of this.

"I can't go out there . . . alone."

Alice and Maggie looked at each other in amazement. Emlyn's Mini was parked right outside the door.

"Here, Emlyn, I'll walk you to your car," Maggie offered.

He collected his car keys and his jacket from their hooks and he left without a backward glance at Alice, who was sitting staring at him wondering what on earth had just happened.

Maggie walked back in two minutes later.

"What flicked his switch?"

"Must have been the mention of Jean's name. He's still having trouble coming to terms with her death, I guess. He has the notion she didn't fall. He thinks she was pushed."

"Seriously?"

Alice nodded.

"Why would he think that? You've never really given me any details. God! Sorry, didn't mean to sound macabre."

"Not at all. I don't know what to think. If you had known Jean, you would know that it's a really weird thing for her to have been out collecting blackberries – and at the side of a road! And so late in the year – it was October. If it had been sloes I could have believed it. Jean wasn't past making a little home-made gin, but what the hell would she do with blackberries?"

"Jam?"

"She was a dreadful cook, the first to admit that if she could buy it in Tesco's why bother attempting to cock it up herself? She was definitely not a jam-maker. But at the same time Emlyn has no theory or won't admit to having a theory to explain why someone would have killed a women in her mid-sixties who ran a moderately successful hardware shop in a seaside town. What possible reason could there be for pushing her in front of some ropy old coach?"

"What about what that guy said? You know, about the antiques?"

"Do you think that had something to do with it?"

"Don't have a clue. But from where I'm standing it seems strange that a man you've never met before comes in asking for her nearly six months after she died, asks for her by her first name, but then wasn't in the least put out to find out she had passed away. It's clear he was only interested in these antiques and someone had told him to ask for her."

"Maggie, what connection to antiques could she have had? I mean, most of the stuff in her house was total crap – nice enough, but had no real value. There aren't any antiques hidden in the shop – mind you, that stockroom is a bloody shambles. She never talked about antiques or showed any interest in them. Was it antique furniture? Antique china, mirrors, what?"

"Maybe we're over-analysing it. He seemed rough enough – maybe he just got the wrong end of the stick and thought she sold furniture, instead of just furniture polish."

"You're probably right, but he certainly freaked Emlyn out."

"Do you think he'll be OK?"

"Yeah, I'm sure he'll be fine."

"Maybe he can shed some light on the whole thing?"

"Possibly. Anyway, let's see this display you've been working on. Are we going to have to branch out into garden consultants?"

"I like the sound of that."

They went outside to consider Maggie's handiwork.

Ten minutes later the bell jangled again and Bill appeared before Alice went inside.

"How did I know you pair would be out here having a sneaky cigarette?" he said, grinning.

"Hey, I like that table and chairs!"

"What are you up to on this fine day?" Alice asked him. "It's not egg day."

"Can't a friend just call in to say hi?" Bill put on a fake frown.

Maggie watched the repartee and smiled. When would they ever get it together? It was almost painful. In the month that she had been living here, Bill kept 'just popping in'. She wished fervently he would ask Alice out soon or she would bang their heads together.

"Actually, there's a weird guy standing across the street," said Bill. "He was staring in this direction. I wondered if everything was OK in here?"

"We're grand, but that sounds like the guy who was in here earlier."

"He asked for Jean by name and kept insisting she dealt in antiques!" Maggie added for maximum dramatic effect.

"Curious," Bill commented.

"Mean anything to you?" Alice asked.

Bill shook his head. "Not a thing, sorry."

"We reckoned he had just got mixed up," said Alice, "but Emlyn got himself into such state afterwards we had to send him home."

"Doesn't sound like Emlyn either."

"I wonder if the guy is still there?" said Maggie.

The three of them went to the shop window and peeked out, trying not to be seen. The man was sitting on the wall across the road with his back to the sea, talking to another man. Bill didn't recognise either of them.

"Perhaps they've got the wrong Jean?" said Maggie.

The second man moved on after a few minutes, but the other stayed exactly where he was for over half an hour.

"Should I go and have a word?" Bill suggested at last.

"No. There isn't a law against sitting on a wall. I don't want him to know that he has worried us."

Without any warning, nearly as soon at the words were out of Alice's mouth, the man jumped off the wall, headed off down the street and disappeared round the corner.

"Problem solved," Alice said.

"Well, if you're sure?" Bill was reluctant to leave.

Alice nodded. "We'll be fine – thanks for your concern though."

Ask her out, go on, ask her out for crying out loud, Maggie thought.

"OK then, I'll be off."

"See you soon, Bill."

Bloody hell! Maggie was exasperated – how long was this man going to take?

"Fancy closing early?" Alice suggested.

"It's your shop, I don't mind!"

"Come on, let's go and get a drink."

Alice locked the shop and Maggie looked up the street, but there was no sign of the strange man.

"All clear!" she joked.

They walked up the main street and turned up the hill to Grace Neil's where they both had a gin and tonic and definitely felt the benefit of it. The pub was warm and cheerful, there was a band about to start and the atmosphere sure beat the hell out of the shop. In fact it was so good they stayed and had a further three gins followed by a huge chicken Caesar salad each and a shared banoffee pie.

Walking home later they were both a bit tiddly, chatting and laughing to each other.

Suddenly, Maggie grabbed Alice and pulled her into the doorway of the shoe shop.

"Don't say a word, that guy is down the street, looking in the travel agent's window."

Alice peered round the doorway and pulled back in again.

"Maggs! Are you nuts? What if he just saw you do that? What do we do now?"

"Do you think he saw us?"

"Not sure, but if he did he probably thinks we're just a couple of drunks." Alice gave a lopsided grin.

"OK, so I overreacted – let's go home the back way," Maggie whispered.

They both sobered up as they walked briskly all the way home. Maggie had her key in her hand as they reached the front door.

"Turn off the hall light so he doesn't think we're home," Maggie instructed.

"Maggs, he didn't follow us," Alice complained, her feet stinging from the brisk walk. She rolled her eyes, but turned off the hall light. They closed the back living-room door so from the front of the house you couldn't see any light.

"He wouldn't go round the back, would he?" Maggie peeked into the dark kitchen.

"I'm hoping he was just really keen on Tenerife for two hundred and fifty quid," Alice giggled. "Why on earth would he be round the back? And why are we in virtual darkness?"

"Shh, he might hear us." Maggie held her finger up to her lips.

"Standing at the side of the house with a glass against the wall? Maggs, these houses are over a hundred years old, solid stone. If we fired a shot in here probably no-one would hear us."

Nonetheless they both sat on the sofa, the television on softly, and with half an ear listening out to hear the front door-handle turn or the doorbell ring. After half an hour Maggie relaxed sufficiently to allow Alice to put Gary out the front door and turn the TV up so they could at least hear it.

Chapter 23

Two days later Alice opened her front door and the same man was standing right in front of her house, but on the other side of the street. The urge to slam the door and turn back inside was incredibly strong.

Stay calm, don't look like you're scared, she told herself calmly as she went next door to open up. If you run he'll be suspicious – don't make him suspicious! But as soon as she was inside she locked the door again and stood waiting for Emlyn to arrive before she could relax.

"Bloody hell, you look like you're hiding out in here," Emlyn joked once Alice had unlocked the shop and yanked him in off the street.

"Did you see him?" she demanded.

"Bill? No, it's too early for him – he'll be doing something technical at this time of the morning, getting his e-whatsits."

"Emails. No, not Bill, the guy! Remember? From a couple of days ago?"

"Oh my God, the guy!" Emlyn's hand fluttered up to his chest. He looked out the front window. "Where?"

"Right across the street."

"Nope, there's no-one there now. Are you sure you saw him?"

"Yes. I'm officially going mad. I see a bloke twice in one week and suddenly I feel like I'm being hunted. I should probably be flattered."

"Nah, I wouldn't fancy being the object of that ogre's affections." Emlyn shuddered.

"Here, what about Saturday?" demanded Alice. "Why did you go off the deep end and start with the *Rain Man* impressions?"

"No reason." Emlyn looked down without catching her eye.

"Emlyn, whenever you stare at your shoes you look unbearably like a bad five-year-old and it always means you're lying your head off. What is making you so jumpy?"

"You're quite bossy when you want to be."

"Emlyn! Stop trying to change the subject, it won't work. I want to know!"

"OK, OK. Let me put the kettle on. Do you want a tea or coffee?"

"I feel like I'm about to turn into a cup of tea – but yeah, tea, very little milk." Alice went back to nervously peering out the window.

"Is Maggie coming in today?" came Emlyn's voice from the kitchen.

"Not sure, think so. She was still in the bathroom when I left."

"Long walk to work," Emlyn joked, reappearing with two mugs of tea.

"I gotta tell you, Emlyn – this sure beats the rush hour in London."

"Hi there." Maggie opened the front door making both Alice and Emlyn jump.

"Sorry, Maggie, Alice saw the man again."

"Oh God, seriously?"

"Yep, but he disappeared pretty quickly."

"Can't fathom it at all." Maggie took the tea Emlyn offered her.

"Actually, Emlyn was just about to tell me something." Alice looked over at him as he disappeared to make another mug of tea.

"Tell you what?"

"What was making him so jumpy on Saturday."

They were both standing waiting for him when he re-appeared with the tea.

"I'm not sure if it's appropriate now." Emlyn looked uncertainly at Maggie.

"Go on, Emlyn, I won't tell a soul."

"Well, it's about Jean, but if Alice doesn't mind?"

"I don't, go on."

"Well . . ." Emlyn cleared his throat. "It all kind of happened by accident."

"What did?" said Alice.

"If you want to know the whole thing please don't interrupt or I may lose my nerve."

"Sorry."

"About two years – was it two years? No matter, it was roughly two years ago. There was a guy who had come in and out of here for quite a long time so both Jean and I knew him. He asked Jean if she would have room to store a couple of pieces of furniture for him – he said he didn't have any room at home."

Alice and Maggie were silent; he had their full attention.

"Jean, being Jean, said no problem and later on that week the furniture arrived and we duly put it in the stockroom and covered it with sheets to stop anything damaging it. The guy came back and the stuff was taken away. He gave Jean two hundred pounds for letting him store the stuff. She of course didn't want to take the money, but he insisted. Anyway about a week later he was back with more stuff. By now both Jean and myself thought this was pretty suspicious, but she said OK, although this would have to be the last time as we were getting a big delivery and there wouldn't be any more room for furniture. Anyway the guy came back again, but this time it was small bags of stuff. Jean took them, but later we had a look at what was inside the bags – they were stuffed full of jewellery. Well, you can imagine, Jean didn't want to get involved any further so when the guy came back she explained all this to him, (except for the bit that we had looked in the bags). He said he understood and left it at

211

that. Or so we thought. About two weeks after that, a man neither of us had met came into the shop. He was rough, from Belfast, and he basically threatened Jean that if she didn't continue to store the stuff, bad things would happen to her and her shop. She was terrified."

"Oh my God, why didn't she say something to me?" said Alice.

"Why didn't she go to the police?" Maggie asked.

"The man, the rough character, told her that the place was being watched and so was she. If she went to the police he would find out and –" Emlyn made a slicing action across his throat.

Alice felt nauseous.

"I don't think Jean really believed that – she told me she thought they were just trying to scare her. But she did think something else bad could happen – like they could set fire to the shop or something. So anyway Jean and I continued to harbour stolen goods against our will. After a while, though she really didn't like it, she kind of got used to the comings and goings. Sometimes they were in here two or three times a day. And the money kept coming in. She was convinced that she was under surveillance. But then instead of just storing and collecting the stuff, they started to sell it on the premises and then they got Jean to do it for them."

"What!" both Alice and Maggie chorused.

"Yes, I'm totally serious. Jean was basically fencing stolen goods! At least I think that's the term. They thought she had a trustworthy face – a well-known local and all that. God love her, she was up the bloody walls. She thought about telling you, Alice, or the police so many times but she was heart-scared. This went on for over a year. Then, about four or five months before she died, some of the 'antiques' went missing from the stock room. The heavies were brought round as they thought Jean had sold them and not let on. They thought she was trying to take a cut of the profits."

Emlyn took a sip of his now-cold tea. Making a face he put the cup down.

"Anyway, they harassed Jean and threatened her, but she stood fast. She told them she wasn't stupid – why would she do a thing like that when she would be the first one they would suspect? She also made up a story about the shop being broken into, to deflect suspicion from us, and even showed them where the intruders had supposedly smashed a window and done some damage in the storeroom."

Alice and Maggie both nodded as if it all made perfect sense.

"Anyway, where was I? Oh yes, the missing diamonds."

"Diamonds!" Maggie exclaimed as if the story had just got a lot more interesting.

"That's what went missing – twenty cut diamonds – don't ask me where they came from." Emlyn put both hands up to his chest and rested them on his patterned tank-top.

"So what happened, who had taken them?" Alice asked, unable to bear any more suspense.

"Jean, of course," Emlyn said as if the answer was perfectly obvious.

"What?"

"Well, I didn't know right off – she didn't tell me – didn't want me to talk her out of it. But she got fed up pandering to these thugs, bossing her around, turning her shop into a burglary showroom so she decided to do a couple of side-deals herself. It was insane and I tried to tell her so when I eventually found out. But it did all go extremely well – I must say, Alice, Jean had a bit of a talent." Emlyn looked wistful for a moment, before he got back to the point. "She told me she had only sold some of them though and hidden the rest."

"Emlyn, if I didn't know you better I would swear that you're making this up."

"Scout's honour." Emlyn did something vague with three fingers and his forehead.

"Anyway, twenty diamonds were a big hit for any gangster to take. Seeing that their threats didn't scare Jean – or me – into coughing up the diamonds, they believed that the shop had been broken into and that the diamonds had been stolen by their rivals and they went to war."

"Bloody hell, you and Jean sitting in the middle of a mobster war!" Maggie was impressed.

Alice felt ill again. This was not quite how she had imagined Jean.

"Anyway, while all this was going on, Jean was trying to extricate herself from the situation." He paused.

"So then what?" Maggie nearly fell off her perch on the counter in her eagerness to hear more.

"Maggie, this is my Auntie Jean we're talking about, not a bloody episode of *The Sopranos*!"

"Sorry." Maggie tried to look contrite, but failed.

"Anyway, finally they came to see Jean and took all the stuff she had been storing. They told her she would not be seeing them again."

"That's good, right?"

"Good-ish. Northern Ireland is a small place and Jean had sold the diamonds to someone in Dublin, but it appears that they talked and either the original gang or the rival gang who had been blamed found out and came looking for Jean. I've thought about it a lot – day and night, you can imagine – and I figure she must have confessed but told them she had sold *all* of the diamonds, not just some of them."

"Yes," said Maggie excitedly. "Exactly. Otherwise they would have kept her alive until she told them where the rest were."

"But," said Alice, "what if she *did* tell them? Maybe thinking that way she'd be rid of the problem?"

"But then why would they kill her?" asked Maggie.

"Revenge?" suggested Alice.

"Look," said Emlyn, "we talked about it on the morning of the day she died and she swore she wouldn't hand the remaining diamonds over, no matter what. I know how stubborn Jean could be – she did *not* tell them where the diamonds were."

215

"But, Emlyn, why haven't you told the police?" said Alice.

"I tried. They thought I was talking a load of poppycock. It didn't sound very convincing – you see, I could only tell them I suspected all this. I couldn't actually tell them I was in the know, that I was an accomplice! They told me it was a criminal offence to waste police time." Emlyn's voice wavered and he looked like he might cry. "I also thought it might be better to let things die down. If Jean's death was an act of revenge, that should be the end of it. But if I drew the police on them, they'd have been sure to come after me."

"Well, the fact they're back now looking for them means you're right," said Maggie. "They didn't get them!"

"So where are they?" asked Alice.

"I have absolutely no idea – she wouldn't tell me."

"How many were left?"

"Don't know that either."

"Bloody hell, Emlyn, do you mean to tell me that there could be an undisclosed number of diamonds in this shop?" Alice trembled as she asked him.

"Or the house." Emlyn nodded miserably. "I've looked everywhere. I tell you, if I found them I'd just hand them over to the next person that came and asked for them!"

Alice felt faint.

Maggie looked excited. "So this is the reason for the weird guy's sudden appearance."

Emlyn nodded again. "Though I've never seen him before. I had so hoped it was over. Somehow they must

216

have found out that Jean only sold some of the diamonds."

"Christ, what a bloody mess." Alice had her head in her hands.

The doorbell jangled and they all looked up like startled rabbits as the first customer of the day walked into the shop.

"Sorry, the door was open – you're open, aren't you?"

"Of course, come in," Emlyn encouraged.

It was a young mother with a little girl – she wanted a couple of keys cut. Emlyn got to work.

Alice splashed cold water on her face while Maggie made strong coffee for three with a touch of Emlyn's whiskey that he kept hidden in a cupboard in the back office and that he thought neither Alice or Maggie knew about. She had a good look about when she returned the whiskey to make sure there wasn't a bag of diamonds hidden there too.

Chapter 24

Isabel had been able to negotiate another morning a week, and when Muriel fell and broke her collar bone she got to work three of the afternoons too while Muriel was off recuperating. Though sorry for Muriel's misery, it was more money for her and all rather timely. She had also started taking typing home with her. She put a small home-made advert in the Mace on the Malone Road and was amazed with the work she got. She had work nearly every evening; Charles showed her the way round the computer in his home office and she was off. Both she and Charles were working like mad, saving everything they could. They'd had a meeting with the building society and then the bank. Neither were thrilled about the situation but the building society agreed that, since the couple had addressed the problem, they would renegotiate the monthly charge and give them permission to put the house on the market. They also came to an agreement with the bank that Charles' salary was channelled into a separate account which covered the mortgage and bridging loan and they could not access it for the time being. Isabel's account was for everything else. Things had never been so tough financially, but if the house sold they should be in a stronger position in a few months.

The sale-board for the house went up the first week in April with the same agent Maggie had used. Isabel and Charles found Seb the valuer to be every bit as good as Maggie had said.

Isabel actually grinned the first time she drove into the drive and saw the board up. Unlike Maggie, she didn't mind showing people through her house as she liked to see their reactions to each room. She was amazed that the vast majority of people appeared to like it. The house didn't hold any special memories for her: there was no love lost between her and Derryvolgie Avenue. The bids didn't come as thick and fast as they had for Maggie, but there were a lot of viewers. The agent showed the house during the day and Isabel and Charles showed in the evenings. Seb was confident that they would get four hundred and fifty at least. She had her fingers and toes crossed that he was right.

"Jesus, it's tiring always having to have the house clean and presentable. Especially as we had to let Joanne go."

Joanne had been tearful saying goodbye to Isabel, who had felt like a total heel, but she had told Joanne the truth: they couldn't afford her any longer and she was so sorry.

She still hadn't explained to Maggie why they were selling.

"It's none of my business," Maggie had said, when Isabel had apologised for being so silent on the matter.

"Thank you." Isabel was glad not to have to explain to her friend.

"But if you want anything you only need to ask."

Isabel nodded, grateful for the offer, but with no intention of asking for anything from anyone.

Maggie and Isabel were having their weekly coffee ritual, but in the afternoon, as Maggie had surprised Isabel at home and insisted she leave the bloody typing and come out for a latte with her. It was a sunny April day, but not so warm that you could sit outside so the two women chose a window table.

Maggie had been growing increasingly anxious about Isabel. She wasn't at all convinced that her friend was OK. She knew the house was on the market, but obviously Isabel wasn't telling her the whole story. Maggie also knew that when you were going through something as traumatic as a house-sale it might help to have the sympathetic ear of one who had just been through it, but had gone through a marriage break-up at the same time.

Actually, though, the last few times Maggie had phoned, Isabel had sounded fine – even when she was in work she sounded remarkably chipper, although normally she would sound totally pissed off to be there. Odd. Distinctly odd. And now, sitting in the sunlit café, she had to admit that, though she had thought Isabel and Charles were heading for trouble, instead they seemed closer. She was delighted to see her friend so together.

"Whatever is happening in your life has certainly put a smile back on your face," she said to Isabel.

"We're working through everything. He has cut his London trips right back and is doing well at work. I've managed to get quite a lot of typing work and I'm really enjoying it as it's getting me used to a computer. I felt like such an old fart not being able to use one! But last week I managed to get on the Internet at work! Do you know we have a computer at reception, but neither Muriel nor I knew how to use it! But now that I do, I was able to check my bank balance on screen – and nearly all the big shops are online, you know."

"Really? Doesn't that kind of take the fun out of shopping?"

"Well, I haven't bought anything online, just looked. But you can have it delivered anywhere in the UK so it's pretty handy if it's raining and you can't be bothered to go out!"

"You'll have to show me how to use this machine – I'm an old fart too."

"I can't wait – Muriel is going to come back into the office in a couple of weeks and be so pissed off that I'm whizzing round the computer."

"Isabel –" Maggie hesitated. "How is everything – really?"

"Really, Maggs, we're good, better than ever in fact. I'm sure you've worked out we've hit a bit of a brick wall financially, but we really will be fine. Getting Christmas out of the way was a relief. There is a solution and we're working towards it. Funny that it took something pretty drastic to bring Charles and me back together. Did I tell you we're sleeping together again – as in, you know . . .?"

"I thought those cheeks looked a bit unnaturally rosy!"

"I'm so happy." Isabel nearly hugged herself, then clapped her hand over her mouth. "God, Maggs! I didn't mean to be insensitive!"

"Don't be stupid. I'm getting back on my feet too."

"And still enjoying living with Alice?"

"Absolutely! I really like helping out in the shop and Emlyn and I are getting on really well now. I've discovered he's actually a pretty good laugh and – did I tell you? – we've started to do the lottery together. We haven't won anything yet, but it's fun."

"Sounds interesting."

"I really like it, Isabel – though Alice is a little worried at the moment. I didn't mention it last time I saw you, but there's this guy who has started hanging round."

"That guy Bill you were telling me about?"

"No, Bill's a cutie! I think he has the hots for Alice, but she hasn't noticed yet."

"So who is the guy?"

"No idea. Sometimes he's sitting on the wall opposite the shop. Alice nearly has heart failure when she sees him."

"Maybe he's just a local oddball."

"Emlyn says he has never seen him before. He looks

like a type who could be involved with organised crime. He has a Belfast accent."

"How the hell would you know? You've got a Belfast accent! You'd better watch yourself, Maggs, you'll be twitching the net curtains next!"

Maggie laughed. "Piss off, you!" She sat back in her seat and took a big sip of the steaming Americano she had in front of her.

"Seriously, explain to me how having a Belfast accent means he's involved in organised crime?"

Maggie hesitated. "Thing is, there's more to it than that. The first day, he came into the shop and asked for Jean."

"Oh God, did that upset Alice?"

"A bit. Emlyn got very emotional though. But the weird thing about this guy – he didn't seem to care at all that Jean was dead and that he had upset them both."

"Were you there?"

"Yes, I was out the back. Alice is starting to supply garden furniture and nice pots and things. I was setting up a display out there. But I peeped in and could hear everything he was saying. He wanted to know if Alice was dealing with the antiques instead of Jean!"

"Antiques?" Isabel had been in the shop and the oldest thing in it was the cash register.

"Yeah, what was that all about? Anyway, Alice said no she wasn't, it was a hardware shop. He said he heard Jean dealt in antiques and then Emlyn lost it and the guy disappeared."

"That is really odd."

"Emlyn was really freaked out afterwards so Alice told him to go home, but he wouldn't walk on his own out to the car. Most unlike him. I think him carrying on was more unnerving than the weird guy."

"But have you spoken to the police?"

"And told them what exactly? 'There's a guy we don't like the look of, can you move him on?' Hardly."

"So did Emlyn say why he was so freaked?"

"Well, yeah, Alice made him spill the beans. It sounded wildly far-fetched and if the pieces didn't kind of fit I'd think he was being melodramatic.

"So what's the story? If you're at liberty to tell?"

"Well, only because you know Alice and you won't whisper a word of it to Charles." Maggie smiled. It had been a long time since she had needed to say that. She had come here today ready to hear about Isabel's plans for a trial separation – not to hear that they had some money worries but the sex was great!

She gave Isabel a quick summary of Emlyn's confession.

"Bloody hell!" was all Isabel could say when Maggie had finished. "It sounds more like a film than real life."

"Tell me about it. Alice nearly fainted when Emlyn told her he had no idea where the missing diamonds were."

"So you think this guy hanging round is one of the rival gang?"

"We don't know. But somehow he knows or guesses that the diamonds weren't all sold and that they're still around somewhere. We don't know whether he believed Alice or not when she said she knew nothing about it. When he asked she genuinely had no idea what he was talking about. But the fact that he's still around is definitely unnerving."

"Too right. Do you want to come and stay with us for a while?"

"No way. Miss all the excitement? Anyway, I wouldn't want to leave Alice on her own in the house – she's a bit edgy at the moment."

Chapter 25

For the next couple of weeks the strange guy was nowhere to be seen and Alice hoped like hell this would be the end of the trouble. Maggie wasn't so sure – she didn't know who was looking for the diamonds, but she was pretty sure, if it were her, she wouldn't give up until she had them. The trouble was, what extremes would they go to? Had they really killed Jean, as Emlyn thought? Maggie was sure that if Alice knew where the diamonds were she would hand them over to the police. But would that provoke another revenge killing? Maggie shuddered. Auntie Jean sounded like a bit of raker in Maggie's opinion and she was sorry she had never met her.

One morning Maggie walked next door after a leisurely breakfast to find Alice lying on her back behind the counter, her head in one of the cupboards.

"What on earth are you doing?" she asked.

"I've decided to do a proper systematic search for any mystery packages." Alice wriggled out of the cupboard and nearly blinded Maggie when she shone the flashlight she had in her hand straight into her eyes.

Of course, there had been regular *un*-systematic searches ever since Emlyn's confession.

"Where's Emlyn?"

"Out the back talking to a *friend* on the phone."

"Really? Do we know if this friend is a male friend or a female friend?"

"No, we don't know, but he did make sure the door was closed before he made the call."

Maggie walked over to the door, but only heard muffled sounds. "Bugger! Can't hear a word."

"Maggs, you're an awful bitch."

"I know. Can I ask you something?"

"Sure." Alice moved down to the next cupboard and stuck her head in.

"Do you miss being a solicitor in London?"

Alice considered the question. "Do you know, I don't think I do. It's funny, I thought about London for a bit when I moved over. I still miss Bernie and Susie, but other than that I haven't thought about it for ages. The legal world must be losing its appeal."

"So you don't think you'll go back then?"

"Not right now. I'm actually finding the shop quite therapeutic. Apart from Emlyn's recent revelations, I like the pace of life, the customers, the lack of traffic jams. Why, is there a problem?"

"No, quite the opposite actually. I'm enjoying myself down here a lot more than I thought I would."

"That's good, isn't it?"

"Yeah, it definitely is. I kind of like the freedom of not owning a house."

"Tell me about it!"

"Well, I was thinking about where I would go if you decided to sell up and go back to London."

"What did you decide?"

"Well, I hadn't really got that far."

"Well, I've no immediate plans," said Alice.

"Good."

"Glad you're pleased."

"Now, do you want a hand to find these elusive diamonds?"

"That would be great," came the voice from the cupboard.

"What are you girls doing *now*?" Emlyn asked, finally emerging from the back office looking pleased with himself.

"Who were you on the phone to?" Maggie sidled up beside him.

"I've got a date!" he beamed.

"With who?"

"Try not to sound so shocked, Maggie. I'm a great catch and don't you forget it."

"Sorry, but with who?"

"Brenda."

"Brenda?" both Alice and Maggie repeated.

"Yup."

"Where is *she* from?" Maggie asked, thinking surely it should be Brendan.

"She works in the bank on the High Street."

"When did you meet her?" Alice got to her feet, covered in a liberal coating of dust.

"About two weeks ago, when I went to Bangor on business." Emlyn helped her wipe some of the dust off.

"But you said she worked in Donaghadee."

"No, I said she worked on the High Street. I didn't say which one."

"Oh, so we wouldn't have met her then?"

"Don't think so."

"So where are you going to take her?"

"When?"

"On your date, Romeo."

"I thought I would cook her dinner at my place."

"You like this girl, right?" Alice was still trying to grasp the concept that it was a girl and not a guy.

"Yes, so what?"

"Well, I'd take her out somewhere nice."

"Are you saying my flat isn't nice?"

"That is exactly what she's trying to say," Maggie jumped in.

"I'm not! But if you take her there she'll be worried about your collection of Doris Day memorabilia. Definitely take her somewhere that isn't your flat."

"Ladies, I have to tell you I'm a little more than offended." Emlyn looked quite put out.

"Emlyn, if we didn't love you so much we wouldn't

say a thing, but this little romance should be nurtured and taken gently, not fall flat on its face at the first hurdle."

"Is my place really so bad?"

"Emlyn, you have framed pictures of nearly all the well-known gay icons of the twentieth century! Definitely a concern for any lady in your life."

"Kylie is a gay icon?" Emlyn looked perturbed.

Alice rolled her eyes. "Emlyn, I don't think I'll ever work you out."

Emlyn looked confused.

Alice and Maggie spent most of the day taking the shop apart, searching, while Emlyn took care of customers. Every time one of them found an envelope or a small bag fallen down behind a shelf she would shriek and the other would come running, but all were false alarms.

"God, I think all we've found so far are a lot of dead spiders and twenty years' worth of rubbish," Alice said at last, sitting on an upturned plastic bucket.

Maggie was picking cobwebs out of her hair. "What time is it?"

Alice looked at her watch. "Twenty past three."

"We haven't even had any lunch." They had been so engrossed in the task in hand that the time had flown past. "Come on, I'll buy you a late lunch, in Belfast."

"Where?" Alice was interested.

"We'll grab something on the Lisburn Road, then have a quick look in the shops."

"You're on. But first I think we should change."

Maggie looked down at her dusty jeans and agreed. "Yes, we look like couple of tramps."

"Unfair to tramps," Emlyn commented as he watched them leave. "Don't worry, I'll lock up."

"Thanks, Emlyn." Alice deliberately ignored his tone.

* * *

"Should we call in to Isabel?" Alice asked as they drove to Belfast.

"I think she's working this afternoon. She's doing a lot of typing for a professor at Queen's – he doesn't want his secretary to read it."

"Is she temping too?"

"No, he drops work in to her and she types it, he calls back a day or so later and pays her."

"Sounds unusual."

"Don't knock it, she's earning a fortune."

Alice loved Maggie's car. You felt like you were going no speed at all even when you were flying along. She saw the longing glances from other drivers when they pulled up to lights. Women in their little Nissan Micras with back seats full of children, wishing they could put their roofs down and speed off. Businessmen in their standard company cars, looking at the smart little sports car and dreaming of driving to Donegal to play golf and forget about the worries of work.

Alice rested her head on the plush leather headrest and closed her eyes. They were in Belfast in no time at all. Maggie parked the car on the Lisburn Road in a space Alice would have thought was too small. She calmly reversed the car into the space, ignoring the angry beeping from the van-driver behind her. Turning to face front as she took the car out of gear, she flicked the bird at the van-driver who dropped the B&H he had clenched between his teeth. Alice saw him disappear as he desperately searched for the burning cigarette. Maggie laughed as the traffic built up behind him and the horns started blaring. They had already vanished into a nearby coffee shop by the time he had managed to locate the cigarette and toss it out the window. He drove off cursing the lady in the sports car, who by that time was deciding on lentil and bacon soup with wheaten bread.

Alice ordered a toasted bagel with sun-dried tomato and cream cheese and a coffee.

"This is lovely," she said, looking round the little coffee shop. The next-door gallery used the café walls to exhibit some of its paintings and the one above their heads was a watercolour of somewhere in Dublin. The painting was lovely – though, priced at seven hundred and fifty pounds, the person who bought it would need to think so too.

"Isabel and I come in here from time to time. The food is great."

Alice nodded, taking a bite of her bagel, now slathered in cream cheese. "Delicious," she agreed.

After their lunch Maggie led the way to a little boutique which sold fabulous shoes, then to another which had beautiful clothes. Alice tried on a neutral leather jacket, which was as soft as butter.

"Suits you."

"Hmmm." Alice looked at the price and hung the jacket back on its hanger.

The women in the shop seemed to know Maggie and they were chatty without getting in their way. An hour later and Alice was exhausted. She had watched Maggie shop, and boy could she shop!

Maggie was on a roll. She particularly loved Élan – she said the clothes always fitted her and the girls were remarkably honest.

Alice thought Maggie looked dazzling in everything she tried on. It was a great afternoon's shopping.

They had a reviving coffee before heading home, Maggie nine hundred pounds lighter.

* * *

"I was just thinking, Alice."

"Yes?"

Alice was running a bath and Maggie was standing in the doorway.

"If that guy turns up again."

"Yes?" Alice turned with a questioning look on her face.

"I think we should follow him."

"Really? You think we should follow a potentially dangerous criminal? For what purpose, do you suppose?"

"Well, to find out where he goes."

"Right, and once we know where he goes, what should we do then?"

"Watch him."

"Right." Alice stirred the bath water, making sure it wasn't too hot. She closed the door to get undressed, pushing Maggie out onto the landing.

"It makes perfect sense." Maggie pushed open the door as Alice prepared to lower herself into the bath.

"Maggs!"

"Well, it does!"

"Not about that! I'm having a bath."

"Oh, big deal! Anyway, if we knew where this bloke went, we could keep an eye on him and possibly even find out what he wants."

"Maggie, he never came back. You could be making a mountain out of a mole-hill."

"He hasn't come back *yet*."

Alice lay back in the water and tried to relax, a bit difficult when Maggie was hovering inches from her head.

"But I think he will."

"OK, if he comes back, we'll do a Nancy Drew routine, OK?"

"Yes!" Maggie was delighted.

"Now, may I please bathe in peace?"

"Yes, master." Maggie laughed and closed the bathroom door leaving Alice to soak.

Chapter 26

Isabel and Charles got their first bid two weeks after the house went on the market. They danced round the kitchen, with the twins clapping and laughing as they watched them. The first bid had come in at four hundred and twenty-five thousand. It wasn't enough, but it was a good opening offer. They had shown round what seemed like a hundred people. Everyone had *oohed* and *aahed* at the house, but the agent had advised them that most people did this whether they were interested in a house or not. They had only one couple who were a complete nightmare. God wouldn't have pleased them, as Isabel's mother would say.

The couple had been very insistent about the time that would suit them to view the house. Isabel had the day off work so she told the agent that she would show them round. The girl at the agency who made the appointment said in her most diplomatic manner that the couple were very exacting – they had shown them properties before. Isabel assured her that she would be able to cope. But just to be on the safe side both she and her mum had done a major tidy and clean in the house the morning before the viewing. Floors had been vacuumed, washed and polished. All the toys and colouring-in books had been put away in the twins' bedrooms and clothes neatly hung in the wardrobes as Isabel had been amazed to discover how many people actually looked in wardrobes and kitchen cupboards. Isabel lit a few scented candles around the place to create a comfortable ambience.

At one thirty her doorbell rang: they were on the dot. Isabel straightened her skirt and opened the front door with a welcoming smile on her face.

"Good afternoon! Isabel Adams, pleased to meet you, do come in."

"Ernest and Aoiffe McLean." The man shook her hand, but didn't return her smile. Mrs McLean didn't say anything, nor did she smile. She was clutching the estate-agency brochure in her hand.

"Well, this is the hall!" Isabel laughed and walked down the hall to show them the drawing-room.

The McLeans didn't follow her; she turned round to see Mrs McLean turn off the hall light.

"Um, dark, isn't it?" she said to her husband. He nodded and wrote a note in the margin of the brochure.

"Would you call that parquet flooring?" Mrs McLean asked her husband again.

"Not sure." Another scribble in the brochure.

Isabel took a deep breath and tried to tell herself these people could be the ones to buy the house. Her smile firmly in place, she tried again.

"The drawing-room."

This time they followed her into the room. Mr McLean immediately started tapping all the walls, as if he was expecting to find a hidden doorway or a wall that hadn't been built correctly. Dull thuds were all they heard.

"Solid walls," he grunted.

Neither made comment on the delicate colours Shirley had raved so much about.

"This door opens through to the dining-room." She led them through the adjoining door into the deep red dining-room. The silver was polished and a bunch of roses were arranged in her favourite Galway crystal vase.

Again no comment and more wall-tapping.

Back out into the hall and into the kitchen.

Mr McLean went straight to the patio doors and checked the seals in the double-glazing.

"We put it in six months ago, so it's still under warranty," Isabel said helpfully.

Mr McLean didn't turn round; he unlocked the door and walked out into the garden. Mrs McLean was opening all the cupboards; Isabel was so glad her mum had tidied them earlier.

"It's a good kitchen to work in." Isabel attempted to start a conversation with Mrs McLean as Mr McLean was outside seemingly inspecting the plants. "Lots of room to put in a table."

Mrs McLean looked over at the table and nodded.

"Just through here is our living-room, where we probably spend most of our time." She felt like adding, "In Zen-like bliss," but didn't – she thought it would go right over this humourless woman's head. She then led her into the living-room which was benefiting from fresh tulips in a blue-and-white painted vase that Isabel had bought at a French market years before.

"Nice enough garden." Mr McLean suddenly re-appeared at the doorway. Isabel looked down and saw that he hadn't bothered to wipe his feet and had walked dirt all over the tiled floor. Neither he nor his wife seemed to notice this and Isabel suddenly felt too embarrassed to point it out.

They tramped up the stairs behind Isabel who was now fighting to keep smiling and stay civil.

She showed them the first floor with the children's two bedrooms, the main bathroom and a guest room at the back overlooking the garden. No comment. Taking them to the second floor, she showed the second guestroom and then the master bedroom with its en suite. She was quite looking forward to shocking this pair – usually someone had a comment for their most unusual bedroom. Silence. They just peered around the room as if they had both just arrived on the planet. She walked them through into the en suite. The first sign that Mrs McLean might have actually liked anything was when she ran her hand over the marble-tiled walls. Even then Isabel couldn't be sure if she liked it or thought it repellent.

The third-floor bedroom was currently being used as Charles' home office and it was full of suitcases, a clothes-rail with their summer clothes, Charles' big desk and his flat-screen computer. It was tidy for once.

"Access to the roof space is from in here?"

"Um, yes," Isabel replied, never having actually looked in the roof space.

"Mind if I take a look?"

Isabel shook her head.

Both McLeans looked at her, waiting for her to do something.

Isabel finally realised they were waiting for her to get the ladder down. "Right, I'll get the pole."

She hooked the pole through the metal catch which held the door shut, pulled and the little trap-door yawned open. It was an old slingsby ladder affair, so as the door opened the old wooden ladder was weighted to come down. Once the door was fully opened the ladder had to be extended – this Isabel did inexpertly, wishing she had just let the estate agents do this. With the ladder now fully extended she stood back, pleased with her first attempt.

"Light up there?" Mr McLean asked.

Isabel nodded, not having a clue.

He disappeared up the ladder like a ferret up a trouser leg.

"Come up, Aoiffe!" he called once the light clicked on.

Mrs McLean climbed up the ladder still without having said one word to Isabel since her arrival.

Five minutes later and Mr McLean's tweed legs came back into view as he descended.

"Good storage." He scribbled another note on his brochure, not helping his wife down the ladder after him.

"Possibly you would like another look round by yourselves?" Isabel asked when they got back down to ground level.

"No, that's all we needed to see. Thanks for your time."

With that Isabel opened the front door and the McLeans strode purposefully off down the short driveway, turning left towards the Malone Road. Mrs McLean had not said one word to her the whole of her visit. Isabel was sure they were not in the slightest bit interested.

"I wouldn't bother even ringing them to be honest," she told Cathy, the girl in the office, when she rang the estate agent to let them know the McLeans had kept their appointment.

"We'll ring them as a matter of courtesy anyway," Cathy told her. "You can never tell with people. An exacting couple, wouldn't you say?"

"Well, that's one way of putting it!" Isabe laughed.

Amazingly, two days later the McLeans made the offer on the house.

Chapter 27

"Alice?" Maggie whispered through the bedroom door. "Alice, wake up!" She pushed Alice's bedroom door open and peered round. Alice was sound asleep. "Alice!" Maggie shook her shoulder gently.

"What the – Maggie, what on earth are you doing? It's . . ." she glanced at the alarm clock, "it's four thirty in the morning!"

Gary jumped down off the end of the bed, shooting Maggie a dirty look for disturbing his sleep, and padded off to the airing cupboard to get some peace and quiet.

"Shhh, keep your voice down!" Maggie held her finger up to her lips. "He's in the backyard at the shop."

"Who?"

"The gangster bloke!"

"Holy shit!" Alice sat bolt upright in bed. "What do we do?" She climbed out of bed, reaching for her dressing-gown and shoving her feet into her animal-claw slippers.

"I'm not sure, but keep quiet."

"Maggs, the house is double-glazed, he won't hear us." Though her heart was beating so loud she thought they would be able to hear her at the other end of the street.

They both padded silently back into Maggie's bedroom and moved the curtain almost imperceptibly so they could see out, but the weird guy wouldn't see them. Sure enough, there was a dark figure moving around in the yard at the back of the shop.

"Are you sure it's him? Did you get a look at his face?"

Maggie shook her head. "He was in the shadows and I thought if I shone a light in his eyes it would be too obvious."

Alice gave her a dig in the arm.

"Ouch!"

"Well, stop being such a cat! I was only asking a simple question."

"Well, it's him alright."

There was a muffled sound in the yard and immediately their attention was diverted back to the external nocturnal activity. A flashlight clicked on and it revealed that there were two men, not one, in the yard and they were trying to break into the shop.

"Shit, what do we do now?" Alice jumped off Maggie's bed and went to get the phone.

"Hang on! Do you think if we turned the lights on it would scare them off?"

"I'll try the bathroom." Alice tugged the cord light-pull in the bathroom and light shone into the yard.

The men flattened themselves against the wall.

"I think it's working," Maggie stage-whispered from next door.

"Are they leaving?"

"No. I think they're hiding."

"Well, it's not working then, is it? I'm calling the police."

"What about turning on some lights downstairs, make like we're up or something?"

Alice ran downstairs turning lights on as she went and wondering why she wasn't calling the police.

"Well?" she called as quietly as she could up the stairs.

"They're still hiding, I think we've trapped them."

"Great, trapped baddies in the yard! What do we do with them now?"

"Hang on, I think they're making a move. Yes, they're trying to escape. Bloody hell, they're climbing over into this garden!"

"Doesn't sound like a great escape plan." Alice hotfooted it back upstairs.

"S'OK. They climbed onto the oil tank and out into the street." Maggie let the curtain fall back over the window.

Alice trudged back downstairs again and switched off all the lights. Climbing the stairs again, she said goodnight to a still-excited Maggie and got back into her bed. She had been up for less than twenty minutes, but already she was cold and wanted to pull the duvet up over her.

"Alice, are you awake?" Maggie opened Alice's door.

"No!" came the muffled reply from the lump under the duvet.

"Sorry, I couldn't hear you." Maggie pulled back the covers.

"Maggie, I'm cold and tired. We've managed to foil the baddies, let me go back to sleep!"

"Well, I'm too excited to go to sleep." Maggie climbed in beside Alice and pulled the duvet back up. "Why do you think they climbed in the back? They were looking for the diamonds, weren't they?"

"Maggie, I'm going to ring the police about this later on. It's not right us being harassed in our home. For a flippin' crime we didn't even commit."

"But if you found the diamonds would you give them back?"

"Give them back to who? I'd hand them over to the police and that would be that."

"Oh." Maggie looked very disappointed. "We don't know how many diamonds Jean sold. There could be ten or more left."

"Maggie, Emlyn also told us – the same time as he was giving you notions about the diamonds – that he believes that Auntie Jean was killed for those bloody stones. Whether it's true or not, they haven't brought any luck and I want nothing to do with them. If we do ever find them." She was very awake now – there wasn't any point in going back to sleep.

"What if they were really big?"

"Big or small, they're not ours."

"Doesn't it freak you out that there were two men trying to break into your shop?"

"Right now nothing is surprising me. It was weird but I actually wasn't scared – they just seemed really amateurish somehow. Anyway, apart from forgetting to thank you for narrowly averting a burglary, I forgot to ask – how come you were awake anyway?"

"I was trying out a new yoga video I had sent away for, and I heard them talking."

"Yoga video?"

"Well, when I say 'trying', it was more like watching. I was in bed. I quite like watching the exercises – I just can't be bothered to do them."

Alice shook her head. "At four thirty in the morning?"

"I've never been a great sleeper." Maggie shrugged as if this explained it all. "Do you think we should have followed them?"

"Where to? At this time in the morning? In our pyjamas? I think they would have noticed."

"True, but we definitely should next time."

"God, I hope there isn't a next time!"

* * *

Nothing much happened for the next few weeks – nevertheless, Maggie still took the odd look outside her bedroom window at night. Alice got Emlyn to enlist the help of Bill to rig up a sensor light in the backyard of the shop so anyone going near the door or the back storage shed would set it off. The light would more than likely scare off anyone prowling around and would wake Maggie at any rate.

Three nights after the light was installed it went off. This time it was two in the morning. Maggie woke immediately. She listened closely, but she couldn't hear a thing. She sat up in bed and, pulling the curtain back the smallest millimetre, peeked out the window. She had to clasp her hand over her mouth to stop herself from squealing out loud. There was a man right outside the bathroom window. He had his back to her and was crouching over in the direction of the backyard. She got a brief look at his face in profile. It was not the man who had been hanging round outside the shop. She dropped the curtain and virtually slid out of bed in her haste to get into Alice's front bedroom.

"Holy fuck, holy fuck!"

Alice nearly wet herself on being woken by Maggie jumping into bed beside her swearing like a Tourette's Syndrome sufferer on speed. This time Gary disappeared under Alice's bed in protest at the interruption of his beauty sleep.

"Are they there again?"

Maggie nodded her head frantically. "At the bathroom window! Not the same guy – definitely – I saw his face. Oh God, Alice, he was really scary, right up against the window."

Maggie hugged Alice, shaking uncontrollably.

Trembling, they crept back into Maggie's room where, to their horror, they could hear scuffling outside. Just then the sensor light was shut off.

The girls scuttled, shaking, back to the other bedroom where Alice phoned emergency. Her voice was wobbling and the dispatcher told her to keep calm – they would contact Donaghadee immediately.

It seemed an age until they saw the blue flashing lights as they came up the High Street, but with the siren off. Alice pulled on a pair of track-suit bottoms and Emlyn's Christmas cardigan and went downstairs to let the police in. There were three officers.

Alice explained and one policeman went round the back while the other two went into the dark shop. Alice retreated into her dark front room and hugged herself as she circled around looking out the window for signs of the police coming back out.

"You OK?"

She turned. Maggie was at the door wearing her jogging bottoms and a fleece that had been hanging over the banisters.

"Yeah, the police are in the shop now."

There were a few shouts and the sound of scuffling. They heard the police call out and the lights went on in the shop. They both stood stock-still listening.

"Should we go and have a look?" Maggie had regained her composure and was ready to go again.

"I don't know, maybe we should just stay here and wait for the police to come back."

Ten minutes later a policeman rang the doorbell.

"Miss Watson?"

"Yes?"

"You did have intruders. Unfortunately they made off before we were able to apprehend them. They've damaged the back door to the shop. We will need you to take a look to see if anything has been taken. My colleagues are making the door secure, though you will need to get a glazier first thing in the morning."

Alice nodded.

"Do you have any idea who these intruders may have been?" he asked.

Both Alice and Maggie shook their heads.

Maggie looked at Alice to see if she was going to tell about the missing diamonds, but Alice remained silent.

Chapter 28

"Oh my God! That's awful!"

Isabel was on the phone to Maggie who was recounting the story of the men breaking into the shop, the visit from the police and the several sleepless nights she and Alice had had subsequently.

"Do you still feel safe enough to stay there?"

"Of course! I couldn't leave just when it's getting exciting. Anyhow, as I said before, I couldn't leave Alice to deal with this on her own."

"It's not your problem," Isabel gently reminded her.

"I feel I'm in it with her. Alice found out about this the same time I did. She can't believe her aunt could have let herself get involved with that kind of people, let alone start selling the stuff on the sly."

"Maybe we shouldn't talk about this on the phone?"

"Come on, Isabel. The Donaghadee police are not the FBI, I don't think they listen in on land-line calls."

"Even so, you can never be too careful." Isabel looked over her shoulder into the garden. She was making herself a cup of tea, taking a break from typing Professor Offenstein's research paper on the effects suffered by plants growing in a city environment. Hardly riveting stuff – Isabel could have told him the answer: the plants didn't like it much.

Muriel had recovered sufficiently from her collar-bone injury to return to work. Isabel had been on hand with a get-well card and was trying not to mind her hours being cut. But Muriel returned the same old snotty bitch she had been before her accident, only now she had something genuine to moan about. If Isabel hadn't been so busy she would have been jealous of Maggie, with all the mysterious and exciting goings-on in Donaghadee.

"How are things with you? Still typing Professor Whathisname's study on dandelions?"

"Yes. Actually, things couldn't be better. We've had the first bid on our house."

"Yippee! Isn't it a great feeling?"

Isabel agreed. "Charles is down to one trip to London a month. I can't get over how his relationship with the kids has improved. He has taken to reading them bedtime stories and both Henry and Amy are getting fewer and fewer bad dreams."

"Talk about turning over a new leaf! Charles has turned over a new chapter! I'm so pleased things are better."

"Jeez, you and me both. It's like being newly married

again. We talk all the time and go for walks along the Lagan towpath with the twins and they run around and play and we just chat and make plans. I have to tell you I'm really looking forward to getting back to the cottage."

"Right enough, have you been back recently?"

"Well, you know we rented it for a few months to that doctor who had just split up from his wife?"

"Yeah, I remember – Leamington, wasn't it?"

"Yes. Well, I think I know why his wife left him – he's the dirtiest, most untidy article I have ever come across. And I thought my children were messy. He has the place nearly destroyed."

"I don't believe you!"

"Well, he moved out a couple of weeks ago. Now, I know he's a man, and generally speaking they tend not to be overly concerned with cleanliness. But, Maggie, there were plates lying on the living-room floor with dried tomato sauce on them – still with chips sticking out of it."

"Yuck, that's disgusting!"

"I'll not even tell you what the bathroom was like. Pubes everywhere. I wouldn't be surprised if the man is bald – I think he left every conceivable body-hair in the sink, loo or shower."

"Enough! No more! I can't bear it."

"I need hardly tell you, if we could afford it we would burn the bed and all the bedclothes! It's going to take a mammoth clean-up before I'll let the twins in the front door even! I think Charles has been traumatised by seeing our wee house in such a state, but that's tenants for you."

"Well, you'd need to speak to Alice about that," Maggie joked.

"Seriously though, Maggs, what is she going to do about everything?"

"I don't know. She's going to have an alarm fitted to the shop and possibly one to the house. I think we would both feel more secure knowing one was there."

"Still no plans to buy a place for yourself?"

"Haven't thought about it. I'm enjoying the time I spend in the shop. I don't know how Emlyn and Alice find anything in there, but it's fun being surrounded by all this weird DIY stuff. Talent isn't bad at all either."

"I thought you were off men for a while."

"I'm only joking. I think the average age of our customers is about sixty-five, with a liking for rubber plungers!"

"Ooh! Now I'm really envious."

* * *

After finishing her chat with Maggie, Isabel typed a few more pages of the research paper and then decided that, with her mum collecting the twins from school, she would go and have a bit of a clean in the cottage. If the bidding started getting close to what they were looking for, they would need to be able to move fairly quickly.

Driving up the slightly overgrown driveway to the cottage. Isabel smiled to herself. She couldn't wait to move back in. The cottage was an old stone barn, which they had converted as soon as they had got married. It had been a labour of love and Isabel had always been secretly pleased that they hadn't been able to sell it. They hadn't told the children about the move yet – they didn't want to get them over-excited. But she knew Amy and Henry would be pleased. They loved to play in the garden here, ever since Charles had made them a swing out of an old tractor tyre and rope procured from a neighbouring farmer.

Opening the slightly faded and peeling yellow front door, Isabel stepped inside. There was a bit of a musty smell, but the house hadn't been aired for a few weeks. The heating was still on a timer that came on for a couple of hours a day, so it didn't feel damp, just a little neglected. The house was still a total tip after the tenant but she didn't care. It was home and she was glad to be back. She turned the heating on as it was freezing inside though outside it was a relatively mild day. Setting her cleaning stuff down, she took off her coat and hung it on the hook on the back door. She hated the furniture in here now – they had left a lot of old stuff here for the tenant to use, but she didn't want to keep it. She hoped they would bring most of the furniture from Derryvolgie with them, especially their bed. The one upstairs was going straight into the skip.

Rubber gloves on and spray-bleach in hand, she set about returning the cottage to an acceptable level of hygiene. She put the radio on and hummed to herself as she worked. Isabel was one of those strange souls who find cleaning a peaceful pastime. As she washed the kitchen floor, she thought about her family and where they would go from here. She was pleased and relieved that Charles had finally admitted what was causing him to be such an utter bastard. Though horrified that he could fritter away their savings on some stocks and shares, she was so relieved it hadn't been another woman. She had to work hard not to get angry when she thought about the lost money, but there was nothing that could be done about it and working herself up would not solve anything. She loaded all the dirty plates, cups, glasses and ashtrays that littered the house and put them into the sink full of hot water and washing-up liquid to soak. Once the welded tomato sauce and mould had started to come off, she put everything into the dishwasher.

After the kitchen had been returned to a state of normality, she started on the living-room, vacuuming as if her life depended on it. Now she was mentally redecorating, and not the Shirley Maxwell way! Each room needed a lick of paint and the sofa and chairs in the living-room had had it. All the furniture seemed to sag in the middle – Isabel couldn't begin to imagine what the doctor had been up to. He had quite a reputation as a lady's man – though she couldn't imagine any woman wanting to stay in the place when he was clearly trying to grow a cure for cancer in his coffee mugs. She worked her way upstairs. Of the three bedrooms, the two smaller ones were relatively untouched. The doctor had used one as a makeshift study and the other he had used as a wardrobe. Their old bedroom however was a different story. There were a few cigarette burns in the bedside tables. Isabel could just imagine the big burly hairy man lying back in bed cigarette in hand thinking he was God's gift to women – she shuddered. Thankfully the bedside tables had been picked up cheaply in Ikea on a trip to Edinburgh a few years back so they were no great loss and Isabel would happily drop them in the nearest dump. There were a few unidentified stains on the carpet throughout the house – Isabel was sure some were coffee or red wine but others looked like ink stains. Thank God the agent hadn't returned the doctor's deposit after he left! The carpet would need to be replaced. She vacuumed up hundreds of toenail clippings in the bathroom and tried not to baulk as she stuck the vacuum in the bath and vacuumed up the hair that was lying in the bottom. The shower was another disaster. The nozzle of the vacuum was pointed in there to get rid of as much hair as possible. After scrubbing the bath, shower, loo and sink with the strongest cleaner she had, she put bleach down the plugholes to try and melt the grot she couldn't reach. As she cleaned away the evidence of the man who had lived there, Isabel felt that the cottage was really starting to feel like hers again. She remembered the first time she had met him to show him the cottage.

"Just call me Graham," he had smiled.

Isabel had thought he was just a little pathetic and wrote his behaviour off as low self-esteem after his separation. But the more she got to know him or of him, the more she realised that this man actually thought he was the most talented surgeon in the country and utterly irresistible to women. The fact that he enjoyed a modicum of success baffled her even more. Isabel thought he took delight in trying to make her nervous, though she knew he was not in the slightest bit interested – he seemingly only went for blonde dolly-birds.

At last, packing her cleaning stuff back into the boot of her car, she locked the cottage up and drove back into Belfast, her mind now focused on paint colours. She would call into Alice's shop and pick up new paintbrushes and some bits and bobs that she would need for the job.

She mused on Maggie as she drove. She was proud of her friend – proud of her having the courage to tell her errant husband to bugger off and still manage to maintain her dignity and her lifestyle. Though she didn't understand why Maggie had moved in with Alice, when she could have bought a perfectly lovely home nearer to Belfast, she had definitely felt a little jealous at the time when she was left in her big house, with the twins to deal with, and a husband who was never at home as he was either in London or entertaining clients in Dublin. But now the house was on the market, Charles had cut his trips right down and things were looking rosier. She, Maggie and Alice had late-night chats over hot chocolate and Rich Tea biscuits, poker nights with Emlyn and Bill which usually involved lots of beer and pizza and very little money changing hands – or 'chick flick' video marathons, watching two or three romantic comedies in a row without anyone complaining.

When her mum took the twins, Maggie and Isabel

would sit out in the back garden on the bench slugging a nice Rioja Isabel had brought with her, puffing away. They would chat about the latest happenings in their lives. Isabel; her latest diet, Maggie; her latest purchase, or who was having it off with the personal trainer at the gym. Not that either of them could remember what the inside of the place actually looked like. In fact, Isabel couldn't be sure she was still a member.

Chapter 29

"What is it?" Maggie asked, standing with her hands on her hips and her head tilted to one side.

It was a sunny afternoon in May and they had decided to defrost the freezer and had gone outside to dig out Jean's old barbecue from the garden shed.

Maggie had finally insisted they employ the help of professionals and the landscape gardeners that they had engaged were halfway through turning the jungle back into a pretty seaside garden.

Maggie and Alice hadn't got far on their quest for the barbecue before something caught their eye.

"What do you think?" Alice shrieked, recoiling in horror, forcing herself not to run a mile.

They were staring at what looked impossibly like a foot sticking out of a pile of cut-back branches, dead plants and mown grass the gardeners had left in the middle of the lawn. Maggie bent down to take a closer look.

"Get away from it!" Alice grabbed her arm and tried to pull her back, away from the protruding limb.

"Oh, come on, Alice, it's hardly likely to really be a bloody great foot sticking out of a pile of leaves at the bottom of your bloody garden, now is it?" Maggie reasoned.

Alice flinched at the thought.

"I mean really, when was the last time you found a foot lying round your property? I for one have never seen one."

Alice turned a greyish green. "OK, so I'm a drama queen," she said, moving away from the heap and back towards the house.

"I'm going to grab it and prove to you that it isn't a foot at all – it's probably just some dirty old shoe that has been lying here for ages and that the gardeners raked up without noticing." She leaned towards the dirty foot/ shoe-like thing, grabbed hold and tugged.

Their faces were a picture when they discovered there was a leg attached to the foot. Alice turned away and threw up.

"Alice, I think we may have just discovered our first dead body. It felt like there was definitely more attached." Maggie took a step back as if trying to work out how to unearth the rest of the body – then *she* threw up.

Alice threw up again.

"Oh my God, oh my God," she kept repeating.

Maggie, who had clearly been watching too much of *The Bill* on telly, started to move a few of the leaves and twigs away from the leg. "It's fairly hairy so I reckon it must be a man."

Alice was appalled. "Listen, isn't there something about leaving a crime scene untouched or something? Shouldn't we like ring the police?" She wiped the side of her mouth with a crumpled and undoubtedly snotty tissue from her pocket. She felt hot and queasy and needed to lie down.

"Yes, absolutely, go and ring them." Maggie's attention was not deflected. She seemed to have fully recovered from her bout of vomiting in record time.

"I'm not going on my own – come with me."

They went into the house together and rang 999. The voice on the end of the phone sounded less than convinced about the grisly discovery.

"You have found a leg sticking out of pile of rubbish in your garden?"

"Yes, for God's sake, that's what I said! Jesus! There is a dead person in my garden. We thought it was an old shoe and when my friend pulled it, there was a leg attached, so we think there is a whole body in there."

She was starting to get a bit fraught. She would have thought they'd have been round in seconds with hundreds of squad cars, but the woman on the other end just thought she was taking the piss.

Maggie took the receiver off Alice who was going to pieces and gave the police-operator her name and address and asked her to please send someone round immediately.

Her distressed tone must have convinced the operator that she wasn't just having a laugh. She instructed Maggie not to touch anything outside.

"Stay calm until someone arrives to check it out – a car will be dispatched immediately."

"Thank you." Maggie put the phone down. "She didn't sound very convinced. OK, so what now?"

"Jesus, I don't know – when was the last time you rang the police about something like this?" Alice paced up and down the tiny kitchen, not really sure what to do but desperately wanting to put a bit of distance between herself and the garden. Maggie was washing her hands with the strongest antibacterial product she could find in the kitchen.

"Let's go back out and have another look," she suggested.

It was like seeing a crash on the road: you knew it was bad of you to look as you passed it, but you couldn't tear your eyes away.

"Maggie, Vim isn't terribly good for your hands – would soap not have done?"

Maggie ignored her and dried her hands on the curtain, dismissing the tea towel in this moment of crisis.

"I don't know that that is such a good idea, going out there – the woman told us not to touch the body." Alice watched Maggie rummaging in a cupboard under the sink.

"Don't you want to know who it is?" Pulling on a pair of Marigolds, Maggie opened the back door.

"For Christ's sake, do you actually think we would know who it was? What are you looking for?"

"Alice, the body is in your garden for a reason. We won't know unless we go and look. Have you anything long and pointed?"

"Pointed, no – would a brush do?"

"Yes, good idea, go and get a broom-handle from next door."

Alice ran through the house and into the shop.

Emlyn was surprised to see her crashing through the door.

"Couldn't stay away?"

"Emlyn! There's a body in the garden!"

Emlyn slumped over the counter in a mock faint. "Ha, very good, Alice, but you're a bit late. April Fool's Day was a month ago!"

"I'm deadly serious," she said as she grabbed a broom-handle out of a galvanised bin and headed back out the door.

"Alice!" Emlyn shouted after her, but she was already opening the door of the house.

Maggie was looking out the kitchen window, bouncing on her heels as if she was about to start a race. Alice handed her the broom-handle.

"Long enough?"

"Perfect."

But thankfully the police arrived before Maggie had the chance to play forensic examiner and expose the rest of John Doe. A police car pulled up outside the house and two extremely young police constables came to the front door. They were very pleasant, but didn't seem convinced when Alice tried to explain calmly about the suspected body in the leaves.

"Officers, I'm well aware that wasting police time is a criminal offence. Please come through."

Emlyn was locking the shop as she ushered them into the hall. He followed closely behind, determined not to be left out. Alice took them out through the kitchen to the back garden were Maggie was standing staring at the leg, still wearing her rubber gloves, broom in hand. They didn't stray too far into the garden, having been taught that they could contaminate evidence. One look at the pile of dying plant-life was enough to get them on their radios back to control, reporting that it looked like a suspicious death and requesting a scene-of-crime team from Newtownards. Maggie and Alice were ushered back inside and the policemen retraced their steps so as not to confuse evidence at a later date, and to secure the crime scene.

Less than half an hour later the garden was full of police trained in dealing with violent-crime scenes: the police photographer, a forensic medical officer, who had to pronounce the body dead, and two scene-of-crime officers who sectioned the garden off. One drew a map of the scene and the other collected evidence. What seemed like hundreds of photographs and a video were taken before they were able to carefully remove the leaves and twigs from the leg and unearth the rest of a very naked, very dead man. Alice, Maggie and Emlyn watched with an inexplicable morbid fascination from the kitchen window.

"I expected to be more grossed out," Maggie commented, "having never seen a dead body before."

Alice was silent, clutching a glass of whiskey as if her life depended on it, wondering why someone had chosen her garden.

The dead man looked really porcelain-white, but as more of him was exposed they could see the purple pinkish tinge to his skin on his right side. This was what was referred to as postmortem staining, as Alice heard the scene-of-crime guys say to each other. He almost looked as if he were asleep – apart from the bullet-hole in the right side of his skull.

Detective Inspector Henderson arrived. He was the Senior Investigating Officer. Detective Sergeant McIlroy, a policewoman, and Detective Constables Murphy and Kane accompanied the Detective Inspector. They would form the murder squad responsible for solving this particular crime.

Detective Inspector Henderson warned the girls that, though the entry wound looked almost neat, the exit wound would be significantly more gory. The body didn't appear to be anyone they knew which was a huge relief, though it was hard to tell as they could only see the right side of the face.

"This is what we refer to as a 'fresh' body which would indicate that it hasn't been dead for long," DI Henderson told the three wide-eyed faces.

Alice tried not to look at the body, but her eyes were inextricably drawn to him. He was a big man with blonde hair; he had probably been quite handsome. There was a look of shock on the dead face as if he had been taken by surprise. There wasn't much blood or gore, just his wet hair stuck to his face and the pale almost translucent skin which thankfully hadn't started to bloat or whatever it is that dead bodies do. The body was laid out on a clean plastic sheet; plastic bags were secured around the head, hands and feet. DS McIlroy, who was standing beside Alice, told her the plastic was to prevent any trace evidence that might have adhered to the body from being lost. As Alice watched them ease the body into a large plastic body-bag she wondered where his clothes were. After a series of complicated procedures he was eventually removed from the garden and driven away, for identification and a post-mortem.

Then they were questioned by DS McIlroy and DC Kane in the back living-room.

DS McIlroy had a kindly face. She was keen to know if the girls had any contact with the body prior to the police arriving. Maggie admitted that she had touched the foot initially, but after that neither she nor Alice had touched anything. On being asked if they recognised the body, they said they had never seen the man before that day.

She then asked if they had heard any strange noise outside in the garden at any time. They racked their brains, but drew a blank – they explained, however, that they had been out of the house shopping at Tesco's around lunch-time. Alice also mentioned their previous nocturnal visitors, but explained that that had happened weeks before. She said nothing about the diamonds, so Maggie took her cue from that. Nor did Emlyn mention the diamonds, though he kept offering the officers other wild theories until they had to ask him to leave. Reluctantly he went back next door.

The police were quite decent about the whole thing. Seeing that the girls were so shaken, DC Murphy told them that, in his experience, and from what the SOCOs (Scene of Crime Officers) were saying, initial evidence suggested that the man had been killed elsewhere and moved to the garden. There was little evident blood on the leaves and the way the blood had settled in the body suggested he had been killed elsewhere and had lain there on his right side for some time. There was no sign of his clothes or any obvious signs to indicate a struggle. These facts, combined with the fact that the body was fresh, indicated that it was probable he had been dumped the night before, though possibly he had been dumped around lunch-time while they were out shopping.

It occurred to Alice to wonder whether, until the police had further evidence, she and Maggie were suspects. However, she kept that thought to herself.

Meanwhile, the garden had been sealed off as a crime scene, as was the alley the back gate opened out onto and the footpath at the side of the house. The two scene of crime officers combed the garden looking for any forensic evidence, but nothing obvious was found. Photographs of everything were taken and at every conceivable angle. They took away most of the pile of rotting plants and twigs and different samples from around the garden. The garden gate was meticulously checked for fibres, fingerprints or any other foreign body that could point to the murderer or the victim. The back gate and fence, the windowsills and back door were all covered in fingerprint powder.

The girls were fascinated to hear that hundreds of prints had shown up on the back door and windowsill.

DI Henderson and his team left shortly after the body had been taken away to the mortuary. One of the officers would now have to attend the postmortem along with the scene of crime technicians. DS McIlroy told the girls that they would be back to ask further questions. Maggie and Alice both nodded like dumb animals.

As soon as Emlyn saw the last of the police and technicians leave, he was back round like a shot.

"I know what this is about," he kept telling them, nodding as he sat nursing a whiskey in the front room.

Neither Alice or Maggie paid him much attention – they were wrapped up in their own thoughts and ideas.

After half-listening to him for an hour Maggie asked him to leave. They were sickened by the afternoon's events and Alice was talking about going to sleep in a hotel.

Chapter 30

Laura, Isabel's Mum, was sitting with the twins in the kitchen watching them colour in. There was a shepherd's pie in the oven and the kitchen smelt of home cooking.

"Oh, thanks, Mum, you're such a lifesaver!" Isabel kissed both twins on the head, but they hardly glanced up from their colouring-in.

"Were the twins OK?"

"Good as gold."

"Really?"

Laura was one of the most capable women Isabel knew. The twins had probably been a couple of nightmares, but Laura never stood for any nonsense and no matter what they did she never snitched on them to their mum.

"No trouble, darling. Now I hope you're not cross, but I made dinner for you all."

"Cross? I'm bloody delighted. My God, that cottage was such a wreck! I thought I'd never get the tidemarks off the bath, to say nothing of vacuuming up all the toenail clippings and trying to coax mould out of mugs. I'm onto the painting now." Laura wrinkled her nose. "What sort of revolting person doesn't clean before they leave somewhere? Mr Graham Leamington. That's who."

"Oh yes, the surgeon, wasn't it?"

Isabel nodded.

"I've heard of him. I think Siobhan O'Neill had a bit of a thing with him for a while."

"Well, Siobhan must be nuts – the guy's a creep."

"Didn't last," Laura agreed. "Now, two things before I forget. The estate agent called – something about another offer." Laura smiled as she said it.

"What, Mum? Did he say what the offer was?"

"Four hundred and thirty-five thousand."

"Yes! We're getting there."

The magic figure of four hundred and fifty was getting closer.

"And the other thing was, Maggie rang just about five minutes ago. She sounded really over-excited. You had your mobile off as usual so she told me to get you to ring her as soon as you got in the front door."

Isabel picked up the phone and wandered into the living-room and over to the patio door, looking out over the garden as she dialled the Donaghadee number. She was nibbling on the corner of a digestive biscuit.

The phone rang at the other end, but it took several rings before it was answered.

"Maggie? It's Isabel – sorry I was out when you called – what's up?"

"Isabel, we found a body in the garden a couple of hours ago!" Maggie sounded breathless as if she had been running.

Isabel did a double take – surely she had heard incorrectly.

"Sorry, Maggs, must be a bad line – I thought you said you found a body in the garden."

"I did! There was a dead body lying in a pile of leaves and stuff."

"A body?" Isabel sat down heavily on a chair, the digestive forgotten. Laura looked over at her hearing the change of tone in her voice.

"Alice and I were out in the garden – we were going to defrost the freezer, get the barbecue out of the shed and stuff – and we both saw something sticking out of the pile of leaves. It was a man! A dead man in our garden!"

"Who was he?"

"Dunno, I've never seen him before."

"Maggie! Are you telling me that there was a dead body in your garden and you don't know how it got there?"

"Yes."

"Bloody hell. God, it must be something to do with the diamonds!"

"I know! Listen, come down, would you? Alice really hasn't taken this well at all and Emlyn is all skittery."

"OK, I'm on my way."

Isabel hung up the phone and called her mother out of the kitchen. "Mum," she said in a low voice, not wanting the kids to hear, "something dreadful has happened. Maggie and Alice found a dead body in the garden."

"Oh, my good God! Whose?"

"Well, they don't know who it is, but Maggie says that Alice isn't at all well and asked if I'd go down. Would you mind looking after the kids for a couple more hours?" Isabel thought about the typing she should be doing, but it wasn't every day your best friend discovered a dead body and requested your assistance.

"I'll stay the night," her mum nodded. "Then you don't have to rush back."

"Thanks Mum, really appreciate it." Taking a long last look at the shepherd's pie bubbling away in the oven she kissed the twins again, pulled on her coat and headed off to the murder scene.

On the way down in the car she had plenty of time to think. What does a dead body look like, she wondered as she turned onto the ring road at Bangor. Why would someone have dumped a body in that particular garden? Was it a random attack? Maybe it was a warning to Alice to find the diamonds before she suffered the same fate as her aunt did. That is, if her aunt really was pushed and didn't fall. But then, it didn't make sense to frighten someone who, as far as the thugs knew, didn't know any of the history or who were they dealing with. And why would they want to draw attention to Alice's house, if they had really killed Jean and got away with it?

Isabel's mind continued to whirr as she sped on to Donaghadee.

Chapter 31

Maggie was amazed to see Isabel – it seemed like only minutes since she had spoken to her. She must have driven like the wind.

"Oh, good! Thank God you're here! And you didn't have to bring the twins."

"Mum is staying. My God, it's so horrific!" shrieked Isabel excitedly. "Tell me exactly what happened!"

Maggie ushered her into the kitchen so she could admire the yellow police-tape which adorned the trees round the garden with its decimated pile of leaves.

"Wow, so the body was just there!" Her voice was a mixture of repulsion and amazement.

"Yes, we were out to get the barbecue when Alice noticed the foot."

"The foot!" Isabel looked at Alice.

Alice shuddered and nodded.

"What did you do then?"

Isabel lapped up the dramatic retelling Maggie embarked on.

Alice boiled the kettle for tea, to try and revive herself after the very strong whiskeys that Maggie had been pressing on her since the police invasion.

"And you didn't recognise him?" Isabel asked once Maggie had finished her Jackanory bit.

"No, thank God!" Alice shuddered at the memory.

"Well, to be honest, one dead body looks very similar to another," Maggie said sagely.

"Maggs, have you have ever seen a dead body until today?" Alice asked her, handing her a cup of Earl Grey.

"What I don't understand is," said Isabel, "if they wanted you to find the body, to frighten you, why would they have bothered trying to bury it in leaves? And if they didn't want it discovered why hide it so badly?"

"Oh, for God's sake, guys, you've no idea what you're talking about!" Alice's colour was still pale green and she felt a little bit wobbly again.

"Why don't you go and have a hot bath?" Maggie suggested, pouring her tea down the sink and getting a couple of wine glasses out of the cupboard. "Then we could order a Chinese or something."

Isabel looked positively delighted – suddenly, missing the home-made shepherd's pie didn't seem quite so bad. "I really shouldn't. You know, I was telling Charles about three weeks ago that there is more to life than looking like Jennifer Lopez. I was trying to make myself feel better for skiving off Weight Watchers for three weeks in a row. He nodded in agreement and said, 'There's also more to life than looking like Ann Widecombe!'"

She laughed as she told the story, but both Maggie and Alice knew it must have hurt her. Poor Isabel! Even when she tried to be the picture of controlled abstinence, whenever she came round to visit the chocolate biscuits got the shock of their lives.

"You haven't eaten anything today," Maggie reminded Alice.

"I know, I really don't think I could eat. I haven't felt this queasy since I watched Hannibal in the cinema and nearly retched over the man in the seat in front of me. I . . ."

Isabel saw her sway and ran to catch her before she fell.

"Out cold," she said.

When Alice came to, she was lying on the sofa covered with a blanket with Isabel peering anxiously at her. She felt cold and clammy.

Next thing there was Maggie holding out a mug of tea.

"Can't stand sweet tea, but everyone swears by it to bring you round." She proffered the tea as if it were the elixir of life.

Alice took the tea and sipped at it, pulling a face, not being a fan of sweet tea either.

"Thanks. How long have I been asleep?"

"You mean how since you fainted on the kitchen floor and nearly cracked your head open? Only for about ten minutes."

"Sorry." Alice felt rotten.

"Nothing to apologise for. You saw a dead body in your garden this afternoon," Isabel said matter of factly. "But I do think you should try and eat something,"

"OK. But please promise you won't mention 'it' again."

"We've ordered Chinese. We're going to collect it en route to Isabel's house – should be ready in half an hour – I thought you would prefer not to stay here tonight."

Alice nodded gratefully.

* * *

"Would you mind if I go and have that bath?" Alice was lying on the sofa in Isabel's house, feeling slightly better.

"Good idea," said Maggie. "You stay there and I'll run it for you, with lots of bubbles."

"Thanks, Maggs." Alice lay back on the sofa, cradling her head in her arms, still seeing the unidentified dead man in her mind's eye.

"TV?" Isabel asked

"Sure – I don't mind – whatever you want to watch."

Isabel flicked on the TV and channel-surfed, moving swiftly past an episode of *Casualty*.

"Ah, I love that film." She stopped at Channel 4 which was showing *French Kiss*.

"Me too."

Together they watched Kevin Kline schmooze Meg Ryan for ten minutes until Maggie called down that the bath was ready.

Maggie who was a great believer in 'more is good'

when it came to bath products appeared to have dumped half the bottle of Isabel's coveted Jo Malone bath oil into the steamy water. Alice could hardly see through the steam.

"Thanks, Maggs, this is great. Beautiful bathroom." Alice looked at the floor-to-ceiling marble tiles.

"Isn't it, not sure about the china ducks though!" Pointing at the little family of porcelain ducklings which were positioned in a group by the door, almost as if they wanted out.

"Wait one minute." Maggie produced a lighter out of her pocket, leant forward and lit a grapefruit-scented candle beside the bath. She turned the light off as she exited and left Alice standing in the soft glow of the candle.

Alice slipped out of her clothes and dumped them all in the corner of the room – she wanted to burn or at least boil-wash the clothes she had been wearing today. The scented steam seemed to cleanse her and as she inhaled she felt the unpleasantness of the day leave her. The nausea gone, she was just left with a few questions she couldn't answer. But she wasn't going to think about them tonight. Right now she was going to stay in the bath until she wrinkled like a prune.

* * *

After a heavy-duty sweet-and-sour pork with fried rice, a glass of red wine and a healthy dose of romantic films Alice felt one hundred per cent better. Isabel showed her into one of the guestrooms. Alice gratefully slipped under the thick goose-down duvet and buried her head in the downy pillows. She fell into a dreamless sleep.

Maggie and Isabel remained on the sofa chatting about the day's events, surrounded by the debris of the Chinese.

"Why the garden? Why not the yard at the shop?" Isabel wondered.

"Maybe it was more personal to leave the body where Alice lives rather than next door."

Isabel considered Maggie's idea. "Maybe the guy was drunk, came into the garden through the gate and passed out and died from natural causes."

"Mysteriously opening a padlocked gate, hiding his clothes and burying himself in mulch head first? Nice way to go. And there is the small matter of the bullet in his brain."

"Oh! Yes – I think it must be past my bedtime. Wait, wait, wait! Oh, God!"

"What?"

Isabel was staring at her, wide-eyed. "What if it's a plant? To put Alice under suspicion! To get her arrested?"

"What good would that do? They must be hoping she has the diamonds, that she'll hand them over."

"Oh, yes – God, I don't know!"

"But," said Maggie, "I'm sure we *are* under suspicion. I'm not at all sure DS McIlroy believed us earlier on."

Chapter 32

"What the . . ." Alice sat straight up in bed. She looked around the room, unsure where she was. Then she realised she was in Isabel's house and relaxed back onto her pillows.

The door pushed open and a shaft of light fell across the bed. A little figure was standing the doorway.

"Hi," a little voice whispered.

"Hi," Alice whispered back. It must still be early, for them to be whispering.

"My name is Amy."

"Really?" Alice smiled.

"I'm five and I have a gerbil called Fluffy."

Amy shuffled into the dark room in her huge slippers.

"Where is he?" Alice asked, glad of a bit of company.

"He's in his bed – it's too early for him to get up." She shuffled closer to the bed.

"What time is it?"

"It's half past six." Amy sat down on the end of Alice's bed

"Gosh, that is early. Aren't you tired?"

"Nope. But Mummy gets cross if we wake her up too early." Amy sidled up towards Alice.

Alice was amazed this little girl wasn't nervous of a stranger in her house.

"Well, I'm sure she does. Mummy doesn't get too many lie-ins, does she?" It was Saturday after all.

Amy shook her head and climbed up beside Alice. They chatted for a little while. Amy told her all about her brother Henry, her mummy who was the nicest lady in the world and would Alice like Amy to make her breakfast?

"Maybe we should do it together?"

Amy nodded her head vigorously in approval. Taking Alice's hand, Amy led the way down to the kitchen through the silent house. Alice had no idea where Maggie or Isabel were, but she was sure they would not appreciate the early-morning alarm call.

"Well, what would you like?" Alice asked the little girl, turning on the light.

"Coco Pops."

"Do you know where they are?"

Amy shuffled in her pink Barbie slippers to the corner cupboard, pulled the cereal out and handed it to Alice, who opened a few cupboard doors before finding where the bowls lived. She filled two small ones while Amy hauled the fridge door open and got the milk. Alice boiled the kettle and made herself a strong coffee. Amy handed her a spoon as she sat down.

"*So chocolately they turn the milk brown!*" Alice sang as she had seen on the television adverts.

Amy giggled as she scooped a spoonful into her mouth. Alice couldn't remember ever having Coco Pops before but she had to admit they were bloody lovely. After breakfast Amy showed her that she could work the television and they sat down to watch some awful early-morning programme for kids.

"I don't like this," Amy said to Alice as they sat side by side on the cream sofa.

"Me neither," Alice replied. "Have you got anything better?"

Amy nodded, climbed off the sofa and went to the blanket box beside the TV. It was full of videos. She thought for a moment before picking one.

"Do you know how to put it on?" Alice asked.

Amy nodded and loaded the video correctly. Alice was impressed. The music from *Beauty and the Beast* flooded into the room and Alice turned the sound down so as not to wake everyone. Amy appeared to know all the songs and she sang along and rocked in time to the music . . .

"Alice?"

"Hmm?"

"Alice, are you OK?"

Alice opened her eyes to see Isabel bending over her. She was still on the sofa, with Amy tucked under one arm. Amy was fast asleep and the TV screen was showing a snowstorm.

"God, what time is it?"

"It's nine," Isabel said softly. "Did Madam wake you?" She indicated Amy.

"No, I was awake anyway. We had breakfast."

"So I saw." Isabel was smiling. "Do you want a coffee? Maggie is still asleep."

"Yeah, that would be great. I can't believe I fell asleep in the middle of the Beast wooing Belle," she said, disentangling herself from the sleeping child.

Isabel covered the still dozing little girl with a throw from the back of the sofa.

"How are you feeling this morning?" she asked a still pale Alice.

"Much better. Thank you. It was good not to have to stay at home last night. Do you think the house will be OK?"

"I'm sure it will be fine. Once we have the kids organised I'll take you and Maggie home if you feel up to it."

"Absolutely. Thank you so much."

Alice gave Isabel a big hug. The woman's warmth did Alice's heart good. Isabel opened the patio doors and the kitchen was filled with the sounds of early summer.

"Will you miss this place? You know, now that you and Charles are on a more even keel?"

"Not really. This house represents the bad times for me. I know it has great rooms, high ceilings and plenty of room, but when I was back at the cottage the other day it felt right. We were good there and I think we'll be good again."

"Well, at least you won't miss it. It would be terrible to have to leave and not want to."

"Yes, you're right. I'm looking forward to the cottage. I'm going to paint the whole place myself before we move back, as a surprise to Charles. He still feels bad that we have to leave and, no matter how much I tell him that it's what I want, he blames himself."

Alice didn't know the ins and outs of what was happening in Isabel's life, but was glad it was heading in the right direction.

"I wish I was heading in the right direction," she said out loud.

"The body freaking you out?"

"Yeah, totally."

"Well, it is scary. I think we all know it's unlikely to have ended up in your garden purely by fluke – chances are it was planted. But, don't let them scare you. One way of dealing with what has happened is to try to solve the mystery."

"Sorry?"

"OK, it might sound a bit strange but . . . well, if there's one thing my recent experiences have taught me it's that if something is freaking you out then you should face up to it and try and understand it. Not play ostrich – which is what I'm inclined to do. Does that make sense to you?"

"Actually, yes, I need to do something. It feels a bit mad to be a suspect in the murder. The police didn't say so, but it was pretty obvious."

"Well, do a bit of investigating. Try to find out – or guess – what Jean did with the diamonds that are missing."

"But I've searched and searched and there's no sign of the diamonds."

"Yes, but you knew Jean better than anyone – bar Emlyn of course. What would Jean do with the diamonds? Put yourself in her position – try to understand her thought processes. They were taking advantage of her and she didn't know how to get out. And somehow she hit on a plan which she thought was reasonably safe."

"Except she didn't realise the seriousness of the situation – the ruthlessness of the people she was dealing with."

"Yes, I think that's the most useful thing you can do right now: try to think like Jean."

Isabel was right. Alice needed a game plan, one that wouldn't put her or her friends in any danger. She needed to get her life, her home and her shop back. Living in fear of the unknown enemy was not her style, it never had been. She put the image of the inside of an easy jet-plane escape out of her mind. She wasn't going to run back to London just yet.

Maggie came down the stairs as they were in mid-discussion.

"Morning!" she said, stretching her hands over her head to loosen tense shoulder muscles.

She sat down at the kitchen table and poured herself a mug of coffee from the cafetiere, which was still hot.

"What's our plan?" she demanded.

"Think like Jean," Isabel told her.

"Good plan," said Maggie.

* * *

Laura took the twins for a walk after they had both had time to show Alice their bedrooms and their favourite teddies, books and plastic action figures.

Isabel then dropped Alice and Maggie back to Shore Street after a further coffee session round her kitchen table.

It would have been perfect to sit out in the garden, but that was out of the question until the police told her it would be OK to have the remnants of the pile of rubbish moved. Instead, she and Maggie sat on the sea wall opposite the shop, which Emlyn had insisted on opening, and ate ice cream. There were quite a few walkers out today striding out in earnest stretching their limbs after a cold and damp winter. Alice was happy to sit and watch them pass and wondered idly what each one did. She had never been able to fathom why some women went for a walk in pleated skirts, court shoes and anoraks. Surely it couldn't be comfortable?

Watching seagulls soaring and diving round the fishing boats and the normal everyday goings-on in the town, it was hard to believe they had discovered a dead body the previous afternoon.

And then, as they were sitting, the strange man from weeks ago walked up to the shop. He peered in the window, hands in his pockets. Alice and Maggie were afraid to move a muscle. He wasn't looking around – he just stared in the window, making no move to take his hands out of his pockets or open the front door. Then he straightened up and walked on.

Maggie jumped down off the wall, still licking her ice cream.

"Come on, now's our chance!"

"Maggs, I'm not sure about this. That man could have actually killed someone."

"It's the middle of the day, loads of people about, bring your ice cream as cover. That way, if he spots us, we just chat and eat our ice cream like we're out on a jaunt."

Alice jumped down off the wall and they jogged across the road.

Emlyn flung open the door of the shop. He was nearly puce with excitement.

"Did you see him? Did you see how he just walked up and looked in the window, bold as bloody brass!"

"We saw him, and we're going to follow him," said Maggie.

"Jesus! Can I come?"

"No, Emlyn, stay and keep the shop open. That way if someone is watching the shop they won't know what we're doing," said Alice.

"So they're still carrying out surveillance on us?" Emlyn's eyes were as big as saucers.

"You can bet your life on it," Maggie said, keeping her face straight.

Emlyn popped back into the shop, alarmed at the idea of being on view out on the street.

Alice and Maggie rounded the corner; no sign of the man.

"Shit, were did he go?"

They ran up the street. The road forked, as it was a one-way system. Alice looked left and Maggie looked right.

"There he is!" Maggie spotted him. He was heading out of town, still on foot.

Ice cream into the nearest bin, they raced to keep him in sight. They saw him disappear into a garage. They had almost drawn level with the garage when they saw him emerge in a white Ford Escort. They ducked behind a parked lorry and watched him drive away in the direction of Bangor.

"Shit, we've lost him!" said Alice.

"I could run back and get the car?"

"He'll be miles away by then. We'd never find him."

"Did you get the number plate?" said Maggie.

"Nope, did you?"

"Do you reckon he saw us?"

"Luckily, no. He was concentrating on the traffic."

Glumly they walked back to the shop. A white Escort was a pretty common car, but at least they knew what to look out for now and where he parked it.

"I think we should call him Jimmy," Maggie said as they wandered back down the High Street.

"Why?"

"Well, we can't keep calling him 'the weird guy' – it takes too long. As we don't know his name, I vote we call him Jimmy."

"Why not call him Jimmy the Murderer?"

"Very funny, Alice. Jimmy is easier to remember. So are we agreed?"

"Suppose so." Alice was feeling very disheartened about her first time following a suspect and losing him within minutes.

* * *

The following Monday morning Alice was on her own, as Emlyn had taken the day off. She was putting change in the till from her float when the bell jangled. She shut the cash-register drawer and turned to find herself looking straight at Jimmy the Murderer.

"Any more news on the antiques?"

"Look, I'm sorry, I really don't know what you're talking about."

Suddenly his name didn't seem quite so hard to remember.

"Any strange night-time visitors?"

"Pardon?"

"Don't expect to sleep well until our antiques show up. Terry says he's starting to lose his patience with you. You don't want to end up like old Malcolm, now do you?" He grinned, displaying teeth not overly familiar with a toothbrush.

Alice tried to think of something to say, but instead

stood looking like a stunned mullet. Finally she found her voice, though it didn't sound like her.

"Who's Malcolm?" she squeaked.

"You really are badly informed, aren't you? Why don't you ask that ponce that works here? I'd say he'd know about old Malcolm. Terry is giving you until next week to find the diamonds. Don't think about calling the police – we'll know if you do."

"You'll get your diamonds!" Alice blurted out.

"Good girl, learning fast." He slapped the counter with a huge hairy hand and left, leaving a faint smell of body odour and bad breath behind him.

Alice locked the shop and set the alarm that Bill had fitted for her. She opened her front door and went into the living-room where Maggie was experimenting with different nail varnishes on her toes.

"I've just seen him again!"

"Who? Rare Hair? I mean Jimmy?" Maggie nearly dropped her bottle of silver sparkle on the sofa. "Where?"

"He was in the shop about fifteen seconds ago," gabbled Alice. "He told me Terry –" She paused to get her breath back.

"Who is Terry?"

"I don't know, but he said Terry was giving me until next week to find the diamonds – and this time he actually said 'diamonds' – or I'd end up like Malcolm!"

"Who's Malcolm?"

"I don't know that either. Are you going to let me finish? If I didn't come up with the diamonds in a week,

I'd end up like Malcolm and I should ask the wee ponce, that's Emlyn, who Malcolm was!"

"Jesus! Does Emlyn know?"

"What the hell am I going to do?"

"I'm going to ring Isabel – she'll know what to do."

Maggie grabbed the cordless phone and dialled in Isabel's number.

"Hi there – oh yeah sure, it's urgent, but ten minutes is no problem." She hung up again. "She's showing someone round the house, she'll ring us back."

Alice sat down on the sofa and put her head between her knees. She felt light-headed, and the last time that had happened she had fainted.

The phone rang and Maggie pounced on it.

"Isabel? Thanks for ringing back. The guy was back! He threatened Alice and openly talked about the diamonds."

"Oh my God!" Isabel couldn't believe they were being so blatant.

"We have no idea what to do now." Maggie recounted the story Alice had told her.

"Contact the police straight away," said Isabel.

"But this guy Jimmy said they would know if we had!"

"He could just be trying to frighten you. He as good as admitted to murdering Malcolm, whoever he was, in your garden. You or the forensics don't have any evidence as yet, but now at least you could point out the prime suspect to the police."

"What if they don't believe us?"

"You have nothing to lose by telling them."

"That would be your advice then?"

"Definitely. I also think it would be a good idea to keep note of as much as you can so that you don't forget anything in the heat of the moment."

"What are you doing tonight?"

"Nothing, why?"

"Is Charles at home?"

"Yes, should be."

"Would he look after the twins for a few hours?"

"Yes, I'm sure he would if I asked him."

"Do you fancy coming round tonight for a pizza or something and we could talk about it?"

"OK, I'll check with Charles and call you back."

* * *

That same evening the doorbell rang and, thinking it was Isabel, Maggie answered it. It was DS McIlroy and DC Murphy.

"Do you mind if we come in?" said DS McIlroy.

"No, not at all." Maggie led them into the front room and they sat down. "Can I get you tea or coffee?"

"No, thanks, we'll not stay too long," the DS assured her.

Alice came downstairs on hearing Maggie talking to the police and perched on the arm of the Maggie's chair.

"Does the name Malcolm Hewitt mean anything to either of you?" the DS began, her face gentle, but her eyes totally focused on the girls. "I see from the looks on your face that the name isn't entirely unfamiliar?"

DC Murphy was taking notes today and his head hardly lifted from his notebook.

"Well, um, it does sound a bit familiar," said Alice, to her horror feeling herself blush. "But I can't think where I've heard it. What about you, Maggie?"

"It does sound familiar," said Maggie coolly.

After a pause, the DS continued. "Well, the body we recovered yesterday from your back garden was Mr Malcolm Hewitt, an antique dealer from Hillsborough. Any idea why he turned up dead in your back garden?"

Both girls shook their heads. Truthfully, they had no idea of any connection between Jean and Malcolm Hewitt.

"Did your aunt know him?"

"Well, I wouldn't know," said Alice. "I'll ask Emlyn tomorrow. He might know."

"Fine. If he does or if you remember anything useful, please contact me or the other officers – we're based in Newtownards." She passed Alice a card with the Incident Room's direct line. We won't take up any more of your evening then."

Alice escorted them to the front door.

"Thank you, DS McIlroy."

Alice shut the door and heaved a sigh of relief.

* * *

Later that night they all sat round a 14-inch Ham and Mushroom Special and discussed the best way forward.

"Obviously these guys, whoever they are, want their diamonds back, so they must be the original guys that brought stuff to Jean in the first place." Isabel reasoned as she picked up a slice of pizza.

"No! They could also be the rival gang who now know about the diamonds and want them for themselves," said Maggie, pulling a huge bit of stringy cheese off the centre of the pizza and popping it into her mouth

"Or it could be the people from Dublin wanting more diamonds – we don't know what Jean's deal was with them," Alice reasoned. "And he didn't seem to know that Jean was dead."

"The guy didn't have a southern accent."

"Doesn't mean that they won't have people working for them in the north though, does it?"

"Good point. So we really have three scenarios here then." Alice was taking notes.

"Well, three different groups, one scenario. Unfortunately, we don't know which one we're dealing with, but we can be pretty sure whoever they are they're gangsters."

"But we know where he leaves his car and what it is," said Maggie, "so if we left one of our cars at the garage we could follow him the next time."

"He seems to be around in the morning – so it's more likely we'll see him between nine and eleven," said Alice.

"So we need to be ready. Whoever is going to follow him needs to be in position at the garage, but not actually in the car – in case they're seen."

"And they'd need a mobile to ring in to say where they're headed," said Isabel.

"Would it be a good idea to have a back-up car?" Alice asked.

"So if I follow him initially from the garage, I ring in and someone else follows behind as back-up, right?" said Maggie.

"It could work – he wouldn't be expecting two cars to follow him." Isabel was struck by the idea.

"With a bit of luck he won't be expecting any cars to follow him," said Alice. "I looked like such a big Jessie in the shop I'm sure he thinks he has us frightened half to death."

"He's not that far from the truth," said Maggie.

"So are we ready to go then?" asked Isabel.

"Isabel, are you sure you want to get involved?" Alice was concerned that she was dragging people into this nightmare.

"Definitely, you can't follow the guy and keep the shop open pretending everything is normal if there aren't three of us. I'm the unknown so it will be easier for me to go unnoticed. We have the advantage that he isn't expecting us to follow him so he won't be too careful. With a bit of luck we can find out whose side he's on."

"But aren't you working some mornings, Isabel?" asked Maggie.

"Look, I have Wednesday morning off for a dental appointment. I'll cancel it and let's hope we'll be lucky and he turns up on Wednesday."

"Quite likely he'll skip a day," said Maggie. "We could be lucky on Wednesday."

"All we need to do now is tackle Emlyn about this

Malcolm's connection to Jean. Hey, no time like the present." Alice picked up the phone from the arm of the sofa and rang Emlyn's flat.

He answered on the first ring, as if he had been waiting.

"Oh Alice, hi." He sounded a bit flat and dejected.

"Waiting for Brenda to call?"

"No, no, just glad you're not a double-glazing salesman."

Alice could hear the false bravado in his voice.

"You really like her, don't you?"

"Yeah. I thought our date went so well, I don't understand why she hasn't called."

"Emlyn, can I ask you a question?"

"Yes."

"Who was Malcolm?"

"How do you know about Malcolm?"

"Never mind, who was he?"

"He was, um, he was Jean's kind of business partner – he helped her move the-you-know-whats."

"The diamonds?"

"Alice! Shhhh!"

"That's who we found in the garden."

"Malcolm? That was Malcolm in the garden? I didn't recognise him! Are you serious?"

"Completely. The police were round earlier on to see if either Maggie or I knew him."

"Oh my goodness, I feel faint."

"Well, sit down then. There's more. Emlyn, the guy came back today and threatened us – well, he threatened me to be exact – he mentioned Malcolm as a threat."

There was a sort of muffled wail from the receiver.

"We need to find those bloody diamonds and fast. He's given us a week. Add that to the fact we're suspected of murdering a bloke we don't even know . . ."

There was a noise that sounded as if Emlyn had dropped the phone.

"Great, now he goes to pieces," Alice said to Isabel and Maggie while she waited for Emlyn to gather himself off the floor. "Emlyn, help me please!"

"OK. There's a key sellotaped to the underside of the cash register. I think it's the key to a safety-deposit box at a bank in Belfast."

"You mean you knew the whole bloody time and you never said?"

"I don't know for sure if the diamonds are there! I just know that Jean only got the box after the diamonds were left in the shop."

"Which bank?"

"Bank of Ireland, Donegall Place."

Alice hung up on him. "Give me strength, he's only gone and told me that Jean has a safety-deposit box up in town."

"Where is the key? We never found it?"

"Under the sodding cash register."

"No!"

"I'm not joking. I'm going to wring Emlyn's neck tomorrow – he sat and watched us dig our way round that shop looking for the diamonds for days!"

"Don't be too hard on him," said Maggie. "He probably

295

had no idea what to do. Was it safer to say nothing – you know what they say about 'ignorance is bliss' and all that? Maybe he thought this Terry bloke couldn't touch you if you had genuinely no idea where the diamonds were. Now that you've been directly threatened and this bloke Malcolm turns up in your garden as stiff as a board he doesn't have any option but to tell you."

"So you think Emlyn was just trying to protect us?"

"The only way he knew how."

"Funny way of going about it."

"It's just a theory, mind – don't go breaking your heart over it."

"So what do we do about the key? Go and get it now?"

"Well, it's been safe so far. I think we should leave it until the morning and go up to the bank to have a look."

"Your Aunt Jean gets curiouser and curiouser."

"Tell me about it! I wish she had never left me this bloody shop."

"Maybe she thought your life was boring, and in any case if it hadn't been for Aunt Jean you would never have met Isabel and myself! Now what a tragedy that would have been!" Maggie beamed, trying to lighten the sombre mood.

Chapter 33

They drove into Belfast in Maggie's car. Maggie was totally overexcited and Alice felt like a criminal. They had found the key as Emlyn had said, stuck to the base of the heavy register, and it had taken both of them to tip it on its side. Alice had phoned the bank as soon as it had opened and she had the prerequisite forms of identification to open the box.

The assistant manager of the branch led her to a private room and returned a few minutes later with the box. He set it down on the table and withdrew to let Alice and Maggie inspect the contents. They could hardly breathe as Alice slid the key into the lock. She turned it anticlockwise and the lock clicked open. She lifted the lid.

"Ohmigod, ohmigod!" Maggie whispered as they both peered inside.

There was a brown padded envelope sitting inside.

Alice took the envelope out and shook it to release the contents. Two envelopes were inside and one was addressed to her. She ran her index finger along the flap, tearing the envelope open. Jean had written a letter to her. They read the letter simultaneously in total silence.

21 September
Dear Alice,

If I am not with you when you are reading this letter then I am unfortunately in trouble or perhaps even dead. Emlyn will have no doubt told you by now, but if he has managed to keep the secret I should tell you that for some time I have been storing certain items of stolen furniture, antiques and paintings. Emlyn will tell you that it was against our will to harbour stolen goods, but we were given no choice. He is telling the truth.

The other envelope contains diamonds. There are sixteen. These were stolen from a jeweller in Hamburg, I believe, several months before they were given to me for safe-keeping. My death is a direct result of my decision to sell four of the diamonds without the permission of the men who left them in my possession. It was an unwise thing to have done as these diamonds tenuously belong to Terry Lomax. Please ensure that he never gets them back. His intentions were to trade the diamonds for heroin to sell in Ireland. I want no part of this any more. The value of the enclosed stones is approximately half a million pounds.

The jeweller's name is Herr Henkel and his shop is of the same name. Please return these to him and my death will not have been in vain.

Please contact Malcolm Hewitt (Emlyn knows who he is) and he will help you return these stones to their rightful owner. I do not need to take the opportunity to tell you that you are dealing with ruthless men and they cannot be allowed to make money through other peoples' suffering.

Emlyn, if you have found the key and are reading this letter, make sure that Alice is safe, I don't want her in any danger. You are a good man and I trust you. Take care of her and the shop.

Alice, finally, I must ask your forgiveness for involving you in this terrible business.

God bless and good luck
Jean Maguire

Tears ran down Alice's cheeks. Maggie was speechless. Alice re-read the letter and then setting it to one side she opened the second envelope. The girls caught their breath at the beautiful, perfect stones that lay in the bottom of the vanilla-coloured envelope.

"Half a million pounds," Maggie whispered.

Alice didn't say a word; she just stared at the twinkling diamonds.

Maggie tipped the diamonds out of the envelope into the palm of her hand; she had never seen so many large diamonds in her life. "Wow!" She rolled them around her hand, admiring the way each tiny facet caught the light. She tipped them onto the table and they counted sixteen.

"Some jeweller in Hamburg must be very pissed off right now."

"How the hell do we get these back to him, now we don't have Malcolm to help us?"

"If we tell the police do they end up as evidence?" Maggie asked, unable to take her eyes off the stones that lay in a glittery pile.

"I'm not sure."

"I wish we could keep them and say nothing." Maggie sighed, thinking of all the fabulous jewellery she could have had made out of these.

"Maggs, it's drugs money. Two people have died so far because of these. I don't want us to be next."

"Me neither." Maggie was brought back to earth with a bump.

Alice put the stones back in the envelope.

"Should we put these back in the safety-deposit box? For safe keeping?"

Maggie nodded. "Then we should somehow contact Herr Henkel and tell him we have his diamonds."

* * *

The first thing to figure out was how to contact Herr

Henkel. The answer came in the unanticipated form of Bill. He came into the shop to collect his eggs and generally have a chat with Alice. It was the afternoon following the diamond discovery and Alice needed a sympathetic ear, a shoulder to cry on and anything else she could get her hands on. Bill had this easy American way about him which made conversation natural; he was the kind of person you wanted to tell things to and he had a knack for being in the right place at the right time. In the seven months that Alice had known him he had come to be a good friend – though a slightly evasive one any time she asked him why he would have left Chicago to come and live in a backwater like Donaghadee. It was a backwater that she loved, but Bill had no obvious history with the place and it just seemed a weird place to choose. He managed to evade her questions by cleverly turning them into questions which *she* always ended up answering and that is how she accidentally divulged the secret of the diamonds to him.

"So this guy, Jimmy, the one who was acting strangely and asking about Jean came back, only this time he threatened you?"

Alice nodded miserably. "He even told me the identity of the body in the garden. But I didn't tell the police that."

"He told you?" Bill seemed really surprised.

"Yes, he said if we didn't recover the missing diamonds within a week I could end up sharing the same fate as Malcolm Hewitt."

"Who is this guy Malcolm?"

301

Alice explained all that Emlyn had divulged in his most recent confessions, right up to the discovery of the safety-deposit box and Jean's letter.

"So Jean actually knew she was in danger?" Bill was incredulous.

"Seems so. But Emlyn says she was fairly confident she could deal with the situation, that she didn't really understand how ruthless the gangsters were. She was over-confident and that was her downfall. Oh, she also managed to trace the jeweller that the diamonds had been stolen from – a Herr Henkel from Hamburg."

"Well-known jeweller," he murmured.

"You've heard of him?" Alice was surprised.

"Well, yeah, my mom was originally from Germany. I think she had some Henkel jewellery."

"Oh right." Alice had forgotten how Americans never say they're just American – they're always Polish, German, Scottish, Irish or Italian.

"So what are you going to do?" Bill steered the conversation back to the diamonds and away from his family tree.

"Bill, I really don't know. I want to contact Herr Henkel and tell him I have sixteen of his missing diamonds. I know I could maybe just get his number from international directory enquiries or something, but then how do I know that I have the right guy? Or if I do find him and arrange to meet him, what if another one of Terry's henchmen with a convincing German accent comes round and bludgeons Emlyn and me to death?"

Bill nodded, considering her predicament.

"In any case, if I get the diamonds back to their rightful owner, what then? Terry's lot come round and bludgeon me to death anyway, scare me out of the country, burn my house down or something!"

"You need to set up a sting, that's what you need." Seeing Alice's expression, he went on hurriedly. "Seriously, in order for you to return the diamonds and remain un-bludgeoned I think you need a certain amount of police involvement."

"But Jimmy intimated that they would know if I contacted the police. I have no idea how big Terry's gang is, presumably fairly big if he's trading stolen diamonds for drugs – I mean, he may have police in his pocket."

"How did you know he was dealing in drugs?"

"Jean's letter, that is why she was so keen for the diamonds to get back to their rightful owner. She said Terry's gang would sell the diamonds in return for drugs and then they would sell the drugs to people – children in Ireland. Cause misery to loads of families and make a huge profit in the process."

"Your stopping Terry selling the diamonds won't cause the illegal drug industry to collapse, you know."

"Yeah, I know, but it meant a lot to Jean."

Bill shrugged. "Well, I guess if you don't give the diamonds back and don't take any other action, they will continue to threaten and harass you until they get them back. As I said, you're going to need some sort of a sting. The police have to be on hand to capture Terry and his compadres before they get you once they discover that you do know where their diamonds are and that you have returned them to their rightful owner. Otherwise you're leaving yourself vulnerable to some sort of retribution."

Alice looked at Bill with a new respect. He really wasn't just the chirpy smiley American she had thought he was.

"But who do I contact?"

"I know a guy, a policeman who specialises in this sort of international crime."

"In America?"

"Nope, right here in Belfast."

"Would he help us?"

"Sure. You have the diamonds, so you know that Emlyn was telling the truth and it looks increasingly like Jean didn't lose her footing and fall in front of an oncoming bus. You said earlier that this hardman of Terry's basically admitted that they had killed Malcolm. So one would automatically assume that they were involved in Jean's death."

"But then why would Jimmy have come into the shop and asked about Jean if Terry knew she was already dead?"

"Good point. Things are often not that straightforward."

"The rival gang?" Alice suggested

"The ones who were going to sell Terry the drugs?"

"Or someone who was trying to stop him?"

"Listen, let me ring this guy I know. He's on the level and if this Terry guy has policemen in his pocket, which I very much doubt, Liam won't be one of them."

"How can you be so sure?"

"He's my cousin."

"But I thought your family were German."

"Mother's side – Dad was Irish. Liam Donnelly is my aunt's eldest son. He's in CID – they work with Interpol and other agencies. He'll probably know Terry Lomax. I owe him a pint anyway."

"OK, thanks, if you're sure?"

"Totally. I'll also check out this Herr Henkel guy, the jeweller – make sure he's legit."

"How will you do that?" Alice was amazed that Bill, who never seemed to have much of an opinion on anything, could suddenly have all the answers.

"Internet. If they're as big a jewellers as we think, they're bound to have a Web site."

"Oh." That was a good idea. She wished she had thought of that. "What do I do?" she asked, suddenly not sure of her own role.

"Make sure you and Maggie are secure in the house, maybe go and stay with your friend Isabel for a couple of nights. I'll ring you when I have had a chat with Liam."

"What about the shop? Wouldn't it be too obvious if we just closed and disappeared?"

"I think at this point no-one is really fooling anyone else. They know you know exactly what they're talking about. You agreed to get the diamonds back for them. I'd stay out of the way."

"Isabel has a family – I don't want them involved. Anyway, how will Lomax get in touch with me so we can arrange some kind of sting, if I'm not here?"

"True."

"Oh, God, what if they come looking for them before we can set anything up?"

"Don't worry. I'll get on it right away. If you won't go away, then try and stay out of any more trouble!" Bill smiled affectionately at Alice, then added, "Seriously, Alice, be careful. This is not a joke."

His face was serious, but he broke the expression with another warm smile. Alice decided, though the timing wasn't great, he was much more attractive than she had previously given him credit for. Maybe she was getting over his American twang.

"Yes, sir!" She grinned, selectively forgetting to mention to him that she, Maggie and Isabel had a surveillance exercise planned for first thing the following morning.

"I'll call you when I have news," he said as he left.

"Bill, you forgot your eggs!" she called after him, but the door had closed and he couldn't hear her. Alice picked the box from the counter and ran after him.

"Bill!"

He stopped and turned.

"Thanks." He took the eggs and smiled again.

Alice's heart did a little flip. She watched him walk away from her, half-admiring his bum in his cords and half wondering what the hell she thought she was doing.

* * *

At nine the following morning, Alice wasn't sure they were doing the right thing at all. After talking to Bill she felt reassured and thought they really should leave it up to the professionals. But their plan was in motion. Maggie was sitting up at the garage behind this month's issue of *Marie Claire,* waiting for the white Ford Escort to appear with Jimmy in it ready for a bit of mid-morning intimidation. Alice was in the shop pretending that she was working in the back office and not climbing the walls. Emlyn was out at the front with customers. He had sold quite a lot of the new teak garden furniture and now thought he was salesman numero uno. He had no idea what they were up to, so was in ignorant bliss.

Isabel was in her car just a bit down from the shop, ready for action with her mobile beside her on the passenger seat. She had daubed her number-plates in mud – in fact she had covered the whole car in mud – so that if they noticed her they wouldn't get her identification She unwrapped a chocolate-mint humbug and popped it in her mouth. She was keeping an eye on her rear-view mirror in case Jimmy decided not to park at the garage and just park straight in front of the house.

They had been sitting for about an hour, with nothing happening, and Maggie had resorted to ringing both Alice and Isabel and reading their horoscope to them down the phone when a white Escort pulled into the far side of the forecourt. Maggie, who was talking to Isabel at the time, nearly dropped the phone.

"Looks like there are two of them. The one I don't recognise is going into the garage. He's inside! I can't see what he's buying."

"I'm sure it's not that important," Isabel said on the other end.

"He's coming back out now, heading back to the car. They're both in the car. *They're not going to park! They're heading in your direction!*"

"OK, now stay where you are." Isabel hung up and rang Alice.

"Hello?" Alice was on the phone on the first ring.

"There are two of them, heading our way. Maggie is at the garage. I'm outside. Stay in touch." Isabel hung up before Alice had a chance to say one word.

"Oh fuck!" Alice said to the dead line, replacing the handset.

Should she go out or should she just wait here until Emlyn came to get her? She walked outside and greeted Mrs O'Neill with a bit too much enthusiasm. Emlyn gave her an odd look. She ignored him and helped Mrs O'Neill put her new washing-up basin and brush into a plastic bag.

"Thanks now, see you soon!" Alice called after the woman's departing back.

"Are you OK? You seem a touch out of sorts."

"I'm grand. How's Brenda?" Alice asked abruptly.

"She's OK – we're meeting for a drink at the end of the week. Alice, are you sure you're all right? You've gone a bit green round the gills."

The door jangled and Emlyn's attention was drawn away from Alice's green pallor. His matched hers very quickly. Jimmy and a new guy neither of them had seen before walked straight up to the counter. There were a man and wife over in the corner looking at eggcup holders and a young man was going through the different sizes of plugs looking for the right one. Neither Alice nor Emlyn moved to assist him.

Alice smelt the familiar stale smell from Jimmy and fought not to put her hand up to her mouth.

"Alright, ladies?" Jimmy grinned at Emlyn as he said it as if he was daring Emlyn to retort.

"Good morning. I think you're a bit early. I seem to remember we were given until next week," Alice said with a confidence she did not feel. In fact, her confidence was sinking into her shoes.

"Just thought we'd check up on you. You know how it is – Terry likes to protect his investments."

The other guy, who was equally repugnant, gave Alice a lascivious look.

"I wouldn't mind doing a bit of investing myself." His voice was gravelly, like a very heavy smoker, and he had a country accent. He raised his eyebrows by way of an invitation.

Jimmy laughed and they nudged each other. Emlyn and Alice were standing so close to one another that they were practically touching.

"Well, we're fine, thanks for asking," said Alice coolly.

"We can see that," the gravel-voiced Casanova tried again.

Alice kept her expression blank; she didn't want to give the wrong signals either way.

"Wanted to make sure yous hadn't planned any city-breaks this weekend." Jimmy and his pal laughed at the joke.

"We have an arrangement for next week. We'll be here." Alice didn't specify what the arrangement was or with whom, but she wasn't lying, she would be here.

"Good, glad to see you girls are behaving yourselves."

Jimmy looked around and picked up a box of candles from the dump-bin beside him.

"Handy," he said and pocketed the candles. His mate took a box too.

"See you soon, ladies!"

They laughed as they went out the door.

Alice hit speed-dial on the phone before the door was even closed.

"Can you see them?"

"Yes," Isabel replied.

"I'll ring Maggs."

Emlyn was opening and shutting his mouth like an oversized goldfish.

The call disconnected. Alice hit another speed-dial and Maggie picked up.

"They've left the shop, Isabel is following."

Maggie's phone rang almost immediately she cut off from Alice.

"We'll be passing you in about thirty seconds." Isabel hung up.

Maggie turned the key in the ignition and put the car in gear. She saw the Escort pass the garage, with Isabel one car behind. Maggie pulled out so she was directly behind Isabel's car. She hoped Isabel had remembered to note the Escort's number down while they were in the shop.

Maggie, unlike Isabel in her mud-spattered car, had taken full advantage of the special offer in the garage while she waited: her car was washed, alloys polished and the oil topped up. Unfortunately this made her a little more obvious. While Isabel did a great impression of a harassed mother, because she was, Maggie looked more like a film star who had got lost. Thankfully, the men two cars ahead from Isabel were deep in conversation and unaware that two amateur sleuths were following them.

They followed the Escort into East Belfast, Isabel making sure they were always a few cars behind. Maggie was having a little more trouble – people kept trying to cut in front of her and she had to drop back a couple of cars not to look like she was trying too hard. The Escort pulled up down a dead-end street. Isabel saw the sign and drove past the entrance, pulling in and jumping out of the car. She peered down the street just in time to see the Escort driving into a lock-up garage and the roller-shutter doors coming down behind it. Maggie pulled up behind Isabel's car. Isabel went back to her car and indicated for Maggie to follow her. They parked in the next street, parallel to the dead end, and walked back, trying to look as casual as two well-dressed women out for a walk in a rundown part of town could.

"What do we do now?" Maggie whispered.

"Get the name of the street and get out of here. We don't want to arouse suspicion."

Maggie dropped into the newsagents on the next block and bought a packet of cigarettes and a scratch-card. She walked back to her car, got in and drove off. As soon as she was far enough away she pulled in and rang Isabel's mobile number.

"I'm going back home," said Isabel. "Mum can't look after the twins this afternoon and I've loads of typing to do."

"No problem, what was the name of the street?"

"Charleville Street."

"OK, I'll speak to you later."

Maggie rang Alice.

"They drove into a lock-up garage in Charleville Street. I'm on my way back."

Maggie was so busy fiddling with her CD player that she didn't notice that Bill was three cars behind her.

Chapter 34

Bill arrived round to Alice's house two days later with a man she had never seen before.

"This is Liam Donnelly – Liam, this is Alice Watson, Emlyn Gordon and Maggie Sullivan."

"Hi there, pleased to meet you." Liam shook hands with each of them.

He was bigger than Bill, dark-haired with piercing blue eyes. Alice could see Maggie was unable to take her eyes off him. Nor could she wipe the grin off her face. Bill noticed it too. He shot Alice a sideways look and she smiled.

"OK, the good news is we have been able to track down Herr Henkel," said Liam. "It wasn't too hard – he is one of the largest jewellers in Hamburg and we have spoken to him. He's delighted that you've managed to recover some of his diamonds. Bill tells me that you think four are missing."

"Um, yeah." Alice was glad that Bill hadn't dropped Jean in it.

"No matter, he's delighted that he hasn't lost the other half a million pounds worth!"

Liam seemed to be searching Alice's face for something. Then he continued. "He's sending his son, Frank, to Belfast to collect them. A couple of German police officers will accompany him, for protection."

Alice nodded. Maggie was still behaving like a love-struck teenager so she was being bugger all help.

"They'll be arriving on Monday afternoon. Now, the bad news is that in order to take down Terry Lomax and his Merry Men we're kind of going to need you as, well, as bait."

"Bait?" The word wiped the grin off Maggie's face. Emlyn turned pale.

"What do we have to do?" asked Alice.

"We're working on the assumption that Terry will have someone watching you, coming up to the time he expects to collect the diamonds from you. This man is known to the police, so going on our experience we take the threat he had Darren make to you very seriously."

"Darren?" Three blank faces.

"The guy you called Jimmy," Bill clarified for them.

Three heads nodded their understanding.

"Now, I realise that this is a very stressful time for you all and we really appreciate your coming forward. We've been after this bastard for a long time and if we can take down Alfie Nailor, his partner in crime, we can all retire." Liam broke into a smile. His eyes twinkled just like Bill's.

"What about the murder investigation?" Alice asked.

"That's on-going, but I think we can safely say you've been discounted as serious suspects. Though DI Henderson thinks you're hiding something."

"Yeah, stolen diamonds," Maggie blurted out; desperate to get this man's attention.

Alice thought Maggie might faint.

"We'll arrange for you to meet Frank Henkel under armed guard at the airport hotel. You'll bring the diamonds with you which you'll have collected from the bank on Monday morning. Frank will take the diamonds and make a bit of a show checking them. Terry will have had someone follow you to the airport so they will immediately report in what they have seen. Then Frank will return on the next flight to Heathrow and on to Hamburg, armed guards all the way. There will also be some undercover SSU officers along for the ride in case Terry sends any heavies to accompany them. Are you clear so far?"

"So far. But what are SSU officers?" Maggie asked before Alice had a chance to say anything.

"Specialist Support Unit. They're our crack unit which we will have in place."

Maggie nodded, impressed.

"Then you'll drive back to Donaghadee and resume your normal working day. We'll need all three of you in the shop. Unless Ms Sullivan has a safe place in Belfast where she can go – she wouldn't be needed if she doesn't want to be involved."

"I'm involved," Maggie said quickly. She wasn't going to let this god of a man out of her sight if she could help it. Who knew when she might need to be rescued?

"OK, so the three of you come back here. We'll have officers on the stairs and in the stockroom on the first floor above you. Next door, in the house and in the backyard. We'll have other people watching the roads into Donaghadee. As soon as one of Lomax's men is spotted, they will alert the officers in the building that you can expect company. You will not be more than fifteen seconds away from us at any time."

"What if they don't come straight away? What if they come in the night?"

"Bearing in mind Terry Lomax is legendary for unleashing his temper at an exchange that goes wrong, we can expect fairly immediate retaliation. But if he holds off until later, there will be officers with you at all times."

There was little more to say. Liam left, telling them he would be back to go over the plan with them before the meeting at the airport. It was Friday now, so they had two days to pretend to carry on as normal while the final arrangements were made.

"One thing, Liam."

"Yes, Alice?"

"Jimmy, sorry, I mean Darren told me that if we involved the police Terry would know. How can you guarantee that one of the others involved won't leak your plans? We could be face up in leaves before Sunday."

"It may surprise you to know that corruption is pretty rare in our force. The SSU will be deployed especially for this take-down – the local police won't be informed. Your friend Terry is wanted in several countries. I cannot reinforce how important this is for us. My partner is Detective Inspector Patrick Macauley. His brother was killed a number of years ago by Terry Lomax, a case of wrong place at wrong time. There is no love lost between him and Lomax."

Liam was so intense, after he and Bill left Alice felt exhausted just thinking about Monday.

"What a dream-boat!" Maggie mock-swooned as she watched him climb into an unmarked police car.

"Hardly the most humorous man I have ever met," Alice countered.

"I thought he was gorgeous! Do you think he fancied me?"

"Hard to tell, between telling us that he was going to stick us straight in the firing-line, with you volunteering your services, and about his fucked-up partner!"

"Should we ring the bank to let them know that we want to see the security box again?" Emlyn asked, ignoring the differing opinions of Detective Inspector Donnelly.

Alice was surprised by the idea; the most unlikely candidates were astonishing her recently.

"Good idea, Emlyn."

"What do we do now?" Maggie picked a bit of nail polish off her index finger with another talon.

"I guess we wait for further instructions," Emlyn said most calmly.

Both Maggie and Alice looked at him.

"Did you have a bowl of steely reserve for breakfast today?" Maggie asked him.

Emlyn laughed and shrugged his shoulders.

Just like Bill had on Tuesday, Alice thought. She looked at him to see if anything was different about his appearance, but he looked exactly the same. Spotted cravat, jeans, every hair in position. Must be Brenda, she thought to herself.

"Well, in that case I'm going shopping – maybe call in and see Isabel, bring her up to speed on the latest developments. Oh, I nearly forgot, she agreed her house yesterday."

"Thank God, at long last! What was the final bid?"

"Four hundred and eighty-five thousand pounds!"

"Hurrah for them! I'll bet they're both delighted."

"Relieved. Funnily enough, it was that strange couple the McLeans that got it in the end. Mrs McLean had never seen such a beautiful house apparently."

"Go Shirley Maxwell!" cried Alice.

"Indeed," Maggie laughed. "Shows how much we know. Tell her bloody well done from me."

Alice and Emlyn spent the rest of a busy Friday in the shop doing a roaring trade in their garden furniture.

"Just as well this stuff is selling so quickly, gives our visitors somewhere to sit in the stockroom on Monday," Emlyn commented as a young couple carried out the last of the teak tables and four matching chairs.

"Don't remind me. I'll have to order some more of

those quickly. With the warm weather it seems to be Barbecue Central round here. We're selling the stock faster than we can get it in."

"It's the first of June tomorrow, summertime."

"When this is all over do you think you'll go on holiday?" Alice asked.

"Well," Emlyn blushed slightly, "I don't want to jump the gun with Brenda but I thought I might ask her to go for a long weekend to the Lake District or something."

"Things must be going well."

"Well, from her not ringing at all, now we speak nearly every night. I'm taking her to Pier 36 for dinner tonight."

"Good for you, Emlyn! Everyone needs a little love in their life."

Emlyn looked up from the stock catalogue he was flicking through. "Indeed? And what would you be doing this evening?"

"Nothing so far." Alice smiled at the memory of Bill's bum in his baggy cords as he walked down the street. Maybe she would ring him later on and see if he fancied dinner or a drink.

* * *

Later on that same Friday Alice was slightly annoyed. She had rung Bill several times and hadn't got an answer. He was probably out with his heavy-going cousin, she thought to herself.

Then the phone rang, beside her on the sofa.

"Hi, Alice."

It was Maggie.

"Hi, where are you?"

"I'm going out for dinner with Isabel and Charles. They want to know if you'd like to come."

Alice looked down at her track-suit bottoms and knackered old tee-shirt. Suddenly she couldn't be bothered to go out, especially drive all the way to Belfast.

"Thanks but I've already eaten, I'm just going to have a bath and an early night."

"OK, well, I'll probably stay the night in that case. If you don't mind?"

"Course not, have a great evening."

Alice threw the phone down on the sofa. What was she going to do now? Emlyn was out on a date. Maggie was away for the night. She hadn't eaten yet at all. She was waiting for bloody Bill to return her call.

"Oh, sod him!" she said and got up off the sofa, poured herself a generous glass of red wine and went upstairs to run a huge bubble bath.

Sitting up to her waist in hot water she applied a face-mask – the stress of the last couple of days had brought her skin out in a few reddish pimply-type spots. The mask was a pale green colour and promised to draw all the impurities from her skin, leaving it totally cleansed and refreshed. It was one of those hardening masks. After five minutes her face felt like it had solidified.

Then the doorbell rang downstairs.

"Bugger!" She didn't move, enjoying the cocoon-like feeling.

The door rang again. Alice got a little anxious. Could it be Darren come round to hassle her again? She dipped her hands into the bath water and bent forward, scooping the warm water up to rinse her face. The mask melted off. She climbed out of the bath and pulled her dressing-gown round her, bubbles still clinging to her legs. She descended the stairs fearfully. There was a figure at the front door, but she couldn't make out who it was through the frosted pane. Too tall to be Emlyn, not broad enough to be Darren, too male to be Maggie.

"Hello?" She didn't stand too close to the door. Her heart beat a little quicker as adrenaline started to pump round her system.

"Alice?" Bill's American twang replied.

She almost clapped in relief. "Hang on a sec, I was just in the bath!"

She opened the door with a huge smile on her face. Bill was standing with a bottle of wine in his hand; that was good; he also had Liam over his shoulder, which was not. Alice tried not to show her disappointment. The last thing she wanted was Liam bloody Donnelly running through their movements on Monday again.

"Sorry to have disturbed you." Bill looked a little unsure of himself.

Alice told herself not to be an old bitch. "Come in, come in!" She stood back and let the two men in.

"Just let me run up and change." She ran up the stairs as the men shrugged off their jackets in the hall.

"Buggeration!" Not the sort of Friday night she had

planned at all. She scanned her bedroom looking for her clean jeans – they were nowhere to be seen and she didn't want them to think she was spending ages in deciding what to wear. She pulled on her grubby jeans from earlier and a clean black v-neck figure-hugging jumper. It gave her figure shape without looking like she was trying too hard, which she definitely was not. Catching sight of herself in the mirror she was aghast to see a ring of pale green face-mask round her chin and into her hairline.

"Bloody marvellous," she muttered as she washed her face in the bathroom sink. Rubbing in some moisturiser, she added a bit of bronzer for colour, though her cheeks were probably red enough after her bath. A touch of lip-gloss and a sweep or two of Maggie's Chanel Drama Lash mascara. Reluctantly she let her bath water out and jogged downstairs to see Bill and Liam.

They were sitting a little uneasily in the back living-room.

"I'll just get a corkscrew." Alice breezed past them on the way to the kitchen.

When she came out with the corkscrew in hand Liam was sitting ramrod straight on the sofa. She handed them each a glass and Bill opened the wine.

"It's difficult to try and think about anything else but the sting right now," Alice commented.

"Actually," said Bill, "one of the reasons we came round was I wanted to give you something as a kind of good-luck token for Monday." He handed her a small box. She blushed a little as she took the box from him.

"Gosh, that is really kind, you shouldn't have." She really wished that Liam wasn't there – she would have liked to have leant over and given Bill a kiss to say thank you. Opening the box she saw a silver bracelet inside with a little cat charm attached to it. It was a little tacky, but he meant well so what the hell!

"Thank you! It's really lovely!" She thought she might keep it in her beside table drawer.

"Let me help you put it on. I thought it would remind you of Gary."

Bill was obviously keen that she wore it straight away.

"OK." She sat forward in her seat and held her wrist out so that Bill could fasten the bracelet on.

"There you go!"

It actually didn't look too bad once she was wearing it. She made a mental note to point desirable items out when they next passed a jewellers' window together, just in case.

"Promise me you'll wear it on Monday," he said earnestly, gazing into her eyes. "For luck."

Alice could only say, "I promise" like a child as she returned his gaze.

Suddenly Liam got up from the sofa and went out into the hall. When he came back in he gave Bill an almost imperceptible nod. Alice saw the exchange, but had no idea what it meant. But she was tired and relaxed after her bath so she didn't dwell on it. She sat back in her seat and sipped her wine, the little silver cat swinging from her wrist.

"Where is Gary by the way?" asked Bill. "I haven't seen him in ages."

"Oh, after the incident in the garden he took to sleeping in the airing cupboard – it's all too much excitement for him."

The two men stayed for an hour. Liam became increasingly fidgety and Alice wished he would just go.

"Shame you're not more like your cousin," she thought, wondering how on earth Maggie could fancy such a dull, impolite man. Though she supposed he was under pressure, organising this operation.

Bill was his usual self, though he took great pains not to talk about Monday, focusing instead on Saturday and asking Alice if she would like to go for a walk then.

"We could go to Crawfordsburn Country Park for a bit of a change of scenery?" she said eagerly.

"That sounds good. Liam, will you be joining us?"

"No, I have plans tomorrow."

Thank God, said Alice, but only to herself.

They left shortly afterwards, not even staying to finish the bottle. After they had gone Alice finished the rest off accompanied by a Chicken Tikka Masala that she microwaved in a few minutes.

"What a disappointing evening," she commented to Gary when he reappeared from his new nest in the airing cupboard, roused by the smell of food.

She squeezed a sachet of tuna in jelly out into his bowl and sat at the breakfast bar in the kitchen forking up the tasteless chicken, watching Gary scoff his dinner in record time. She lost interest in the bland meal about halfway through, the remnants went into the bin and she decided to finish her dinner by eating two walnut whips in quick succession.

"I'm walking tomorrow," she told Gary, thinking she could see him gave her an accusatory feline stare as he climbed onto the sofa beside her. She folded the wrappers into tiny triangles and pushed them down the neck of the empty wine bottle.

"See? Now no-one knows."

The cat curled up beside her, resting his large head on her leg, and purred contentedly with his eyes half-closed. Alice channel-surfed: there was absolutely nothing on at all.

"Why do I pay my cable subscription to get hundreds of stations with nothing on?" she asked her snoozing cat. Finally she settled on Sky One which was showing a programme on Ibiza. Alice thought she had seen this one before, a few months ago when she was still in London. As she listened to the narrator she realised she had seen the programme and now she knew who two of the main characters were. She wondered if she should tape it to show Maggie when she came home. It was the episode about the two gay men from Belfast setting up their bar in San Antonio: it was Maggie's ex, Derek, and his partner Cliff. Alice couldn't tear her eyes away and she watched, cringing as she thought of her friend married to the character on the television in his linen suit and George Hamilton suntan. Maybe Liam wasn't so bad after all.

Climbing into bed that night Alice looked sleepily at the bracelet on her wrist. She thought about taking it off, but smiled at the memory of Bill being so keen to see her wearing it. If she was going to meet him for a walk she'd better still wear it so as not to offend him. She was asleep before her head hit the pillow, but her dreams were confused images of being chased by a man in the shadows that she couldn't see, but she knew was there and the little silver charm, in her dream, sounded like a little silver bell.

Chapter 35

Maggie woke at six. She lay in bed and tried to get back to sleep, but it was no good – she was too nervous about the day ahead. She kept telling herself that they were in the hands of professionals and all would be well, but she couldn't help feeling that today was based on a lot of assumptions: everyone hoping Terry Lomax behaved in his usual impetuous way and got himself caught by the short and curlys. She heard Alice in the bathroom – the shower was running.

Alice had had trouble sleeping too. She had given up trying to read a book, flicked through all Maggie's copies of *Heat* magazine and now she just had to busy herself with the procedure of getting ready. She took a shower and then slathered herself in one of Maggie's numerous expensive body creams. She took her time, making sure she got cream rubbed in all over. She washed her face, moisturised and even put on foundation and full make-up, something she rarely bothered to do unless she was going out for the evening. Now made-up, moisturised and scented from head to toe she went through a lengthy process of deciding what she should wear. Should she wear trainers in case she needed a quick get-away from Terry? Should she wear something smart to meet Frank Henkel? Should she wear something sexy because of Bill? Finally, she settled on a pair of olive green trousers and a camel boat-neck top, both smart and comfortable enough to run in should the situation require it. She was still faffing about with different necklaces when Maggie came in and sat on her bed.

"Morning, couldn't sleep either?" said Alice.

Maggie, still in her satin Agent Provocateur nightdress, shook her head.

"Have a shower and I'll make coffee."

"OK. You smell nice. Dolce and Gabbana?"

Alice nodded. "You don't mind me borrowing it?"

"Jesus no! I haven't worn it in ages, nice though."

Maggie got off the bed and went into the bathroom, which was still a bit steamy and warm after Alice's shower. She slipped her nightie over her head and hung it on the back of the door. She climbed into the shower and closed her eyes as the jets of water bounced off her head and back.

Downstairs Alice poured the last of Susie's survival-pack coffee into the cafetiere. She felt guilty, as she hadn't spoken to either Bernie or Susie in a couple of months. The kettle boiled and she poured the hot water over the coffee grounds and watched as they sunk slowly to the bottom of the glass container. Alice was too nervous to eat so instead she had a cigarette, normally something she hated doing. The nicotine hit her system and she relaxed a little, but not much. Maggie came down a few minutes later and even with her make- up on she still looked pale.

They sipped their coffee in relative silence. Maggie lit a cigarette too; she had nervous knots in her stomach that she couldn't shift.

"What time are we going to leave?"

"Around nine, I think. Bill will ring to let us know."

Maggie looked at her watch: it was seven thirty. "He's got awfully involved, hasn't he?"

"Suppose it's just because Liam is his cousin."

"Yeah, probably right. Do you want to watch breakfast TV for a while?"

"Anything for a distraction."

They both tramped into the next room and flicked on the television. Eamon Holmes on ITV had some painful woman on, hideously dressed. She was explaining the important necklines of the season and what people should be wearing.

"Nothing that you've got on," Maggie said as she flicked to Channel 4 to see some poor man being harangued on his front-door step by someone from the *Big Breakfast* wanting to know if he put his shoes on before or after his trousers.

At eight thirty-four, Bill rang.

"Alice?"

"Yes?"

"Ready to go?"

"The bank doesn't open until nine thirty."

"But you and Maggie are both sitting fully dressed, with your coats on ready to go?"

"Well, we don't have coats on."

Bill laughed. "OK, you go to the bank as planned. Liam and his partner will follow you."

"How will we know who to look out for?"

"You won't, that's the whole idea. We just want you to know that they're close."

Bill sounded very business-like as if he dealt with this sort of thing every day.

"OK, then what?" Alice wanted to make sure she had every conceivable detail in her head before she closed the front door behind her.

"Next drive straight to Aldergrove, park in the hotel car park and walk into the lobby. Frank Henkel will already be there – his flight is landing about now. He will be with another man, from the insurance company, and two members of the German police. Other policemen will be in lobby, but you won't recognise them. Hand the diamonds over to Frank as Liam discussed with you – then he will leave with the other men. You and Maggie stay, make time to have a coffee, look a bit pleased with yourselves, don't look as if you're worried. If Terry has men watching you, we want them to think you're on your own and you're relaxed. Then get back in the car and drive straight back here. With a bit of luck we shouldn't have to wait too long."

"OK, I think I have committed every move to memory."

"Good luck, Alice. Piece of cake. Now – most important – remember to go and unlock the back door of the shop so that the SSU team can get in."

"OK, Bill."

"And Alice –?"

She held her breath – it sounded as if he was about to make some kind of declaration.

"Are you wearing your good-luck charm for me?"

"Oh – yes, I am." God, he was obsessed about the bracelet!

"Are you sure?"

What! "Sure I'm sure!" She shook it close to the receiver. "Can you hear it tinkle?"

Bill laughed. "Good!"

"Well, bye," she said.

"See you soon."

They disconnected.

"OK, Maggs, let's go."

Maggie was pulling her jacket on as she walked into the hall. "God, I'm so nervous I don't think I can drive."

"Of course you can. Come on, Maggie Sullivan, this is the adventure you so wanted to be involved in."

"Well, in hindsight I think I really wanted to be involved in Mr Donnelly, preferably with very little on."

"Tart!" Alice laughed and the mood lightened considerably.

They left the house making sure they didn't look like they were looking out for Liam or any of Terry's men.

They went into the shop, turning off the alarm. Alice unlocked the back of the shop and nearly passed out when a man in civvies gave her the thumbs-up from the backyard.

She jumped back in fright. "Where the hell did he appear from?"

Leaving the shop they walked purposefully out to Maggie's car, which was parked at the back of the house. Maggie obeyed the speed limit all the way to Bangor, then they hit the ring road and the morning rush-hour.

"If this keeps up we should arrive right on time."

They stop-started all the way to the Sydenham by-pass, where a lot of traffic turned off for the city airport. The traffic thinned as they took the slip-road for the city centre. They drove over the Queen's Bridge onto Oxford Street, then turning right onto May Street they followed the road round the back of the City Hall turning right again onto Great Victoria Street. Maggie pulled over opposite the front of the City Hall outside Marks & Spencer.

"OK, you wait for me here and I'll be back as quickly as I can." Alice climbed out of the Mercedes and headed through Marks & Spencer. She side-stepped the early-morning shoppers and came out through the Donegall Place exit onto the main shopping thoroughfare. Hundreds of people were on their way to work, heads down, on this Monday morning. Alice turned left and was outside the Bank of Ireland in a matter of seconds. She took a deep breath and pushed the front door open. She met with the same assistant manager that she had seen the previous week. He led her back to the private room and left her alone with the box. Alice removed the single envelope from the box, shut the lid and locked it. She slipped the envelope into her inside jacket pocket and left the room. She thanked the bank manager who had no idea whether she had put something in or taken something out of the box. She hurried back down through the bank and back out onto the street.

This time instead of heading through the shops she walked round the corner back onto Chichester Street. She looked up at the clock above Karen Millen and the hands told her it was nine forty-five. She was making good time.

Maggie saw Alice heading towards her. She started the engine, but didn't unlock the passenger door until Alice had her hand on the door handle. She had seen too many films where the bad guys climbed in the back and put a gun to your head. In this situation with the car only having two seats the gunman would have to get in beside her, but this was all perfectly feasible if the rumours about Mr Lomax were to be believed.

"Get them?"

Alice pulled the door shut as she slid into the passenger seat. Maggie locked the doors again. "Yeah."

"Good, let's get out of here before that snotty little traffic warden gives me a ticket." She pointed at a beady-eyed man who was eyeing Maggie's car. He looked like he might have a itchy ticket-finger so Maggie pulled away from the kerb and they were back in the main flow of traffic in the centre. They drove past the law courts, past the Albert Clock. They stopped at the lights at the old Co-op, turning left to join the bottom of the M2. As they reached the motorway the traffic thinned out, most of it heading into town rather than out.

"Well, let's see them," Maggie asked once they were well clear of the city.

Alice took the envelope out of her pocket and held it open so Maggie could see inside.

"Bloody hell. They're so gorgeous!"

"I know," Alice said, "but they will be out of our hands forever in fifteen minutes."

"I could miss the turn-off for the airport, you know," Maggie said hopefully.

"With Liam and pals following us and God knows who else?"

"Good point, well presented," Maggie said as she took the Templepatrick turn-off. They drove through the village of Templepatrick quickly and soon were on the final straight up to the Airport.

"I know I shouldn't be, but I'm so nervous I think I could be sick."

"I'm busy trying to look like I'm not nervous too."

They giggled uneasily and stopped abruptly. Up ahead of them was construction work. Temporary lights had been set up and only one lane of traffic was free to move at any one time.

"Shit, I've seen this on television before. These road-works are a hoax – we pull up and stop then the baddies reach in and pull us out of the car." Maggie's knuckles were white as she gripped the steering wheel. She felt queasy and wanted to go home.

"Firstly you have the doors all locked and secondly the lights are changing," said Alice.

And so they glided by the workmen who stopped to admire the attractive beauty driving her car like her life depended on it.

"Maggs, calm down before you put us both into the back of that van."

Maggie slowed up behind a blue transit van. She flicked on the radio and tapped her nails impatiently on the steering wheel. The van turned off left at the roundabout and Maggie pointed her car straight on. The airport was less than half a mile now. Minutes later they pulled into the car park of the Fitzwilliam Hotel. Alice had slipped the envelope back into her pocket. They climbed out making sure they didn't look around too much. They both had been totally unaware of Liam on the road behind them.

"Either they're very good, or they aren't there at all," Maggie stage-whispered to Alice as they crossed the car park towards reception.

Alice kept waiting for Terry Lomax to jump out of the bushes as they passed, but nothing happened. So far everything was going according to plan.

The lobby was typical of a three-star hotel: a tiled reception area with seats dotted around low tables, all in warm welcoming shades of terracotta. They couldn't miss

Frank Henkel and his entourage as they were the only ones in the reception area, their table covered in coffee cups and milk jugs. It was ten minutes past ten.

The men stood up to greet them.

"Hello, Miss Watson, Ms Sullivan, thank you for meeting us. I'm Frank Henkel and this is Mr Schol from Monde Insurance."

He wasn't at all good-looking which Maggie thought was a real shame for a jewellery heir. He was unimpressive, to say the least. His suit looked as if it had been tailored for someone else: it hung off his skinny frame. His hair was smoothed over to one side, a bit like Terry Wogan's, and his skin was pock-marked, a testimony to teenage acne, or perhaps glue-sniffing. Maggie grinned at the improbability. Mr Schol was an older man, well-dressed and grey-haired. The two policemen on the other hand would both get it. Maggie looked them both up and down surreptitiously. Both tall and well-built with striking Germanic features.

Frank didn't bother introducing the two policemen who had also stood up. They nodded and smiled at the girls, but didn't say a word.

Alice and Maggie shook all the hands that were offered and sat down in the two spare seats. Alice took out the envelope and handed it to Frank. He took the envelope from her and peered inside. He muttered something in German to the other men and then took out an eyeglass. He began to check the stones, smiling as he did so.

"I believe you know my cousin, Ms Sullivan." He looked at Maggie through thick lenses.

336

"I do?" Maggie looked blank, wondering how she could know a relation of his.

"Claudia Cameron? Well, Claudia Henkel as she is now."

"Gosh, I didn't know she was your cousin. How is she?" Maggie was really taken aback. This was Claudia's cousin!

"Very sad business, but she's well." His face reddened slightly.

"Well, please send her my regards."

"I will."

The conversation ended as brusquely as it had begun. He returned the diamonds to the envelope and placed it into a sophisticated briefcase.

"I thank you for returning my father's property to us. All seems to be in order. If you will excuse us, we're booked on the eleven o'clock flight back to Heathrow." Everyone stood again and shook hands. Then the entourage left with the diamonds. It was sixteen minutes past ten.

"Bloody hell!" Maggie slumped back down into her seat once the Germans had disappeared from view.

Alice sat down too. "Shame it's too early for a drink." She looked longingly at the closed bar.

"Ha, would you believe that was Claudia's cousin? She was more of a man than he was!"

A waiter walked over to the table. In Northern Ireland there are two sorts of waiting staff, thought Maggie, the extremely good well-trained ones and those who work in hotels. This particular chap seemed to have had a fight

with a bottle of tomato sauce and he appeared to have lost
– he was wearing most of the contents over his straining
waistcoat, which seemed to be intended for a slimmer
man. They ordered two coffees and he shambled off to
get them.

"I thought that went rather well."

"Me too." Maggie pulled a packet of cigarettes out of
her Celine handbag and offered Alice one; she then lit
both and sat back to wait for her coffee. The coffee was
lukewarm and bitter. They didn't finish it.

"Do you think we've waited long enough?" Alice asked
Maggie.

"I should think so. There's no bugger here. What was all
that guff about Interpol agents mingling in the lobby?"

"Maybe they had no-one to mingle among and are
hiding." Alice looked left and right quickly. All she could
see were two receptionists who were not paying them the
slightest bit of attention.

"Let's get out of here." Maggie threw down three
pounds to pay for the coffee and a five-pence tip for the
waiter of the year, who had vanished without a trace.

They stood up and walked back out of the hotel.

"Remember to smile," Alice hissed as they walked out
into the fresh air.

"Why? There is absolutely no-one here." Maggie smiled
anyway as if Alice had said something funny.

They got into the car and headed for home. It was a
very quiet morning and there were not many cars on the
road – a couple of cars in front of them and nothing behind.

"Well, I don't know whether to be relieved or disappointed," Maggie said brightly.

"It's not over yet – we still have Terry Lomax and his thugs to deal with."

"Yeah, but that's what the SSU are wedged in your shop for, isn't it? I can't see Liam anywhere – I bet he's not here at all." Maggie craned her neck in the rear-view mirror to try and spot him.

"*Maggie!*" Alice screamed.

Maggie whipped her head round, eyes back on the road. The cars in front of her had slammed on their brakes and the front car had pulled into the oncoming traffic lane blocking any chance of Maggie pulling round them. The tyres on the Mercedes screamed as Maggie slammed her Russell and Bromley-clad foot to the brake – blue smoke billowed out from the back as the car went into an emergency stop.

"Holy fuck!" Alice screamed as she braced herself for impact.

As they hit the car in front, both girls were thrown forward and their airbags took the impact of the crash.

Alice was aware of men's voices. She was a little dazed from the stop, but she felt no injuries. Her car door opened – one of the men was cutting her seat beat with a Stanley knife. Then, a rough hand was pulling her out of the car.

"Get those bitches into the back," a gruff male Belfast voice shouted.

Before she could see who they were, some sort of rough material was tied round her head – she glimpsed the same happening to Maggie. The coarse hands bundled them into the back of the car which had pulled into the oncoming traffic lane and the driver took off, wheels spinning as he did so. The entire exercise had taken less than a minute.

* * *

By the time Liam pulled up behind the SLK, its engine still running, all he could see were skid-marks from the lead car. They had fallen a bit behind Maggie and had been unable to reach the Mercedes in time.

"Fucking hell!" He smacked the palm of his hand off his forehead. Slowing down, he pulled round the car and then slammed his foot down on the accelerator. "Get on the radio and let Bill know what has happened. Pull those SSU guys out of Donaghadee – they aren't going there now."

Patrick Macauley, his partner, had seen this kind of ambush before and he didn't need to be told twice. Within seconds he had alerted the SSU that the targets had ambushed the bait and the operation had gone seriously wrong.

Liam radioed into control and gave a description of the two cars that had been involved.

"I hope like hell she's wearing that bloody bracelet," Patrick said to his partner as they took off after the cars.

"She is," said Liam.

Police were called in all over the local area, but the getaway cars appeared to have vanished into thin air.

* * *

Alice and Maggie were whimpering in the back seat of the car, both with their heads pushed between their knees.

Alice was aware that one of the voices had a foreign accent, but she couldn't place it. She was aware that Maggie was beside her. There was a heavy arm leaning on her back so there was no way she could straighten up. She could feel her charm bracelet slide down her wrist and sit just above her hand; she clasped the silver cat for comfort. She was sure they were both going to be killed, but she tried to focus to get her bearings. She knew she was in the back of a blue car; she had seen it as it screeched to a halt, but she had no idea what make the car was. It sounded like a diesel tractor so it couldn't be too new. She was also aware of the smell of petrol. It was coming from the rag they had tied round her head and it was making her nauseous. She fought to keep her consciousness.

After what seemed like an age the car came to a halt and the men started speaking – they had been silent for most of the journey.

Alice and Maggie were hauled out of the back of the car. The blindfolds were pulled off and they both gasped for fresh air after the heady fumes of the rags. They were standing in a half-built room, wiring hanging out of the ceiling while scaffolding and plastic sheeting covered one wall. They must be on a building site, Alice concluded. There were no windows, only the plastic sheeting. Water dripped down one wall making a green slimy trail as it dripped onto the concrete floor. She glanced over at

Maggie who was standing beside her – one of the heels of her stiletto boots had come off in the fracas meaning she was left standing at an awkward angle. Her face was streaked with make-up. Alice knew she must look equally dishevelled. Two plastic chairs were brought in and they were pushed into them and their wrists were tied with rope.

Maggie was taking a good look at their captors. Darren, the man who had been in and out of the shop, was there. The men who had ambushed them she had never seen before. Two of them didn't look Irish – this was confirmed when they spoke to each other in an unfamiliar language which sounded eastern European to her. They glared at her when they saw her staring at them. She faced front immediately.

What happened to Liam and Patrick, she wondered angrily. What about this so-called amazing crack team of policemen supposed to be protecting them?

Her body was starting to ache from the impact of the crash earlier and the fumes had given her a headache. She wished she were in Isabel's living-room having coffee and discussing the merits of her American Express Platinum card rather than sitting here shivering with Alice and a group of thugs. She was of the same opinion as Alice: she was sure they were going to die. She fought to keep her panic under control, but almost wet herself when she heard a voice from behind.

"Do you mean to tell me that it's this pair of fucking women who have been causing me all the problems?"

The voice was English, male and mean.

Footsteps sounded on the bare concrete floor behind them.

A small man walked into their field of vision. He was so pale he was almost albino apart from his very dark and demonic-looking eyes.

If Maggie hadn't been so utterly terrified she would have laughed: this man was no taller than a twelve-year-old boy! He looked as if he couldn't weigh more than about seven stone. Was this Terry Lomax?

"So, darlin'," he walked up to Alice and grabbed her chin and cheeks in his pale little hand, "what have you got to say for yourself?" He cocked his head to one side.

Alice couldn't speak. He was crushing her jaw with his unexpectedly strong grip. She just looked at him with wide frightened eyes.

"You've just lost me a lot of money, darlin'." He let go of her face and walked to the other side of the room, a menacing little figure in a black leather coat and jeans.

"What am I going to do with the pair of you?" He turned on his heel to face them again, his face devoid of expression. "Your aunt had us fooled, you know. We believed she had got rid of all the diamonds – and we weren't the only ones she fooled. But then we got information that she still had the diamonds when she met that bit of a surprise accident." He smiled as if it was some sort of a joke. "But where were they? That ponce didn't know. So it was a bit of luck when you turned up, darlin', to inherit the family fortune. We thought, wait up, we'll just wait for this little lady to lead us to the diamonds and hey presto we're back in action. We were puzzled when you made no move. But I'm a patient man. So it was deeply disappointing when you met with the Germans and returned the gems to them. An unexpected and unwise move on your part." His eyes narrowed, hard and glittery like two polished jets. "And who are you, love?" Maggie had diverted his attention. "I think I could have a little bit of fun with you." He grinned malevolently and grabbed his crotch.

Maggie tried not to shudder at the thought.

There was a growl over Alice's left shoulder, the sound of nails as they scraped on the ground. A huge Scandinavian-looking man, also dressed in a black coat and dirty jeans, came into view with two huge Rottweilers straining on their leashes. He yanked them to come to heel; both slunk back and sat at his feet.

"Now these are what I call my ladies," the small man said, crooning as he spoke to them. The dogs lay down on the cold floor and their tongues lolled out the sides of their mouths.

Alice thought she and Maggie had become trapped in some horrible television nightmare.

"What do you want?" she asked.

"Did you hear that, fellas? The little girl has found her voice."

The men all grinned inanely at the little man.

"Allow me to introduce myself properly." He stood in front of them – not exactly towering over them, but the presence of his dogs and their equally huge handler created a suitably terrifying scenario. "I'm Terry Lomax and these are my associates." He waved his arms round to include all the men in the room. "We're a rather surprising bunch, I think you'll find. Pedro there is Spanish, Raj from London same as myself and that's Jurgen from Holland," he pointed to the dog-handler, "and then there is Darren, a local lad, who I think you have met before, and Jock from Scotland. We're quite European in this day and age. I find being able to speak many languages makes for an easier life." He laughed again and his men joined in as if on cue.

Alice didn't think it was a good sign that he was introducing everyone to them. Normally if you were meant to survive they wouldn't be so keen to be named.

"Now let me tell you what I want." He stopped laughing, pulled out another chair and sat with his elbows over the back. He would have looked ominous if hadn't been for the fact that his feet just touched the ground and no more. "I want me money back, that's what I want. But more important than that, I won't be made a fool of. If I don't sort you pair out then that sends out all the wrong signals to my competitors, doesn't it?"

Pedro the Spaniard fingered a black pistol in his left hand. Maggie saw this and nearly slid off her seat in fright. A helpful hand from Raj behind her pulled her back upright. She looked at Alice, fear written all over her face.

"Now I have been thinking how I can make you repay your debts to me." Terry rubbed his chin with his right hand as if lost in thought. He eyed Maggie lasciviously again. "I think you should be made an example of. That way I sent a clear message to everyone. Terry Lomax is not to be messed with." He stood up, pushing back his chair. The dogs got to their feet, growling again. "Now I thought about letting my ladies maul you, but that's just messy and I can't be doing with a big cleaning bill, so I thought a nice clean shot to the back of the head would do it. You won't feel a thing." He laughed a high forced laugh.

Raj and Darren pulled a large piece of the plastic sheeting down off the walls and laid it on the ground in front of the chairs.

This is it. We're going to die. Alice looked wildly around for something to distract the men with, to give her and Maggie time to make a run for it. She knew it was a fruitless exercise. They were both in pain, their joints sore from the accident and being pushed around. She also had no idea where they were. She looked down at her little charm bracelet from Bill and thought it hadn't brought her much luck. The silver cat swung about her wrist, which was bloody from the rope. She couldn't feel any pain in her wrists any more.

Darren and Pedro pulled Maggie to her feet and brought her over to the plastic sheet which was flapping on the ground – the wind was blowing in through the place where it had been removed. Maggie whimpered as they forced her to her knees, hands in front of her. Alice was positioned in exactly the same way, her blonde hair hanging over her face so that she couldn't see her friend.

"I'm so sorry, Maggie," she whispered.

She could hear soft sobs beside her and knew that Maggie had heard her.

"Right, lads, let's get this over and done with quickly and don't make a mess of me building. I gotta have the amusements in here in a fortnight. Gotta get all the money out of them kids, ain't that right?"

Alice was aware that Terry was moving away from them: his voice was receding. She heard the click of the pistol that Pedro had been holding and guessed that he was taking the safety-catch off and cocking it, ready to fire.

"Police! Put down your weapons!" Bill's voice filled the empty concrete shell. *"Alice, Maggie, hit the floor!"*

Alice and Maggie fell forward, more out of surprise than in accordance with Bill's orders. Suddenly the room was filled with the sound of gunfire and the smell of smoke. Both girls were lying face down and couldn't see what was going on. The gunfire seemed to last forever, but when it finally stopped Alice felt a hand on her shoulder and elbow, pulling her up. A hand pushed the hair from her face and she found herself looking at Bill who was wearing a bullet-proof vest and a ski cap with chequered markings on it.

She opened her mouth to speak, but nothing came out. Then she started crying, unable to stop the torrent that flooded forth. Liam was helping Maggie to her feet; in fact, he actually lifted her right off her feet and into his arms. He was dressed in the same vest and cap as Bill. Alice looked uncomprehendingly round the room. Four of the five men who had moments ago been their captors were lying

347

dead on the floor. Another man in the same bullet-proof vest as Bill and Liam was holding the two Rottweilers who were now whimpering in fear.

"Where's Terry?" Alice whispered.

"He got away, but Paddy has gone after him with the rest of the team," Liam answered as he untied the knot of Maggie's wrist bindings. She collapsed against him and he caught her again in his arms – she passed out cold, her arms falling limply like a rag-doll's.

"Let's get you out of these," Bill said as he went to work on Alice's own home-made handcuffs. "Looks sore," he commented as he threw the ropes down on the floor and examined her bleeding wrists.

Alice found her voice. "What are you doing here?" She still couldn't believe she was alive and the men from Lomax's gang were lying at her feet dead. She picked her way through the bodies and the empty shells.

"Come on, let's you out of here." Liam led the way with Maggie still in his arms.

Out on the street Alice couldn't believe her eyes: they were in the centre of Belfast. They had been held in a partially completed building – the large board said it was due to be Ireland's biggest amusement centre.

"How did you find us?" Alice asked as Bill led her gently to a waiting van with blacked-out windows.

He lifted her wrist and shook the little charm bracelet.

"Homing device," he said simply. "We use them in the CIA."

Chapter 36

Isabel hung up the phone and turned to her husband who was elbow-deep in packing boxes.

"You're never going to believe what just happened to Maggie and Alice!"

"Don't tell me that pair were off amateur-sleuthing again." Charles smiled as he wrapped a bedside lamp in newspaper.

"Nope, this is a million times better!"

Charles was still shaking his head in disbelief when the removal lorry pulled up in the driveway. The twins were with Isabel's mum who had taken them out to buy ice cream down the Lisburn Road.

The next couple of hours were spent loading the lorry and their respective cars until they were full to bursting. Then Charles followed the lorry out of the driveway and down Derryvolgie Avenue back to their cottage. Isabel stayed behind doing some last-minute cleaning. There was no way she was going to leave her house a tip like Doctor Leamington had done for them. She washed the floors and vacuumed the carpets, finally loading the vacuum cleaner into the back of her car. She smiled as she turned off all the lights. In the back garden she found Henry's football lying by the greenhouse and she picked it up. He would be playing a lot more football where they were going. She looked at the back steps with their little tell-tale signs of hastily stubbed-out elicit cigarettes and grinned as she thought of her next-door neighbour's torment as mysterious cigarette butts kept appearing in his azaleas. The house cleaned and empty, Isabel set the alarm for the last time. She closed the front door on their midnight-blue hallway and walked out to her car. Nothing gave her more satisfaction as she pulled out of the driveway, spinning the wheels a little making the gravel spray up behind her, than the SOLD sign on the gate-post. She headed down Derryvolgie Avenue with a light heart. She pulled out onto the Malone Road and headed for the outer ring and their cottage. Things could only get better, she decided. That chapter of her life was now closed and she hoped things would now get better for both Alice and Maggie too.

Turning the radio up loud she rolled down the windows and sang along to the song the DJ played. At the traffic-lights a van full of workmen pulled up alongside her. Gone were the days when she would have kept her eyes front and hoped they wouldn't notice her. She sang even louder and gave them all the benefit of her sunshine smile. When the lights turned to green she got a round of applause as she pulled away from them, making her smile grow even more.

While Isabel was in the cottage unpacking, Charles took the lawnmower out of the garage and cut the grass in the front garden, which was secluded from the road by trees and bushes. She unpacked the kitchen things from the box marked 'kitchen' and made sandwiches and drinks for them all. She put them all onto a tray and took them out into the garden which was now sporting a freshly mown look. It was a bit of a makeshift picnic, but Henry was in his element, playing commando in the undergrowth and coming back for bites of sandwich, while Amy tried to force-feed some of her teddies sandwiches, but only ending up getting butter on their fur.

Isabel lay back on the rug that Charles had produced out of the boot of his car. The garden was filled with the noise of birds chirping and Henry's pretend gunfire. The sun was shining and even though she had mountains of unpacking and loads of re-organising to do Isabel felt totally relaxed. It was good to be home.

"Right, let's go for a walk." Charles stood up after he had finished off the last of the sandwiches.

"Honey, I have loads of unpacking to do." Isabel looked back at the house – she could see the boxes left by the removal men piled up in the windows.

"They can wait, come with us for our first walk and I'll help you later."

351

Isabel knew this would be highly unlikely, but the twins both whined so she agreed – anything for a quiet life.

"I'll go and get the wellies." Charles walked round the back of the house.

"The wellies are all in the back of my car!" Isabel called after him, but he had already disappeared.

Moments later he reappeared with something very small and furry in his arms, no wellies in sight.

"A puppy!" Amy registered first and dropped big Ted on his head as she ran over to her Dad.

"Wow!" Henry appeared from under the apple-tree and joined her.

"What the – ?" Isabel was completely taken by surprise; he hadn't asked her if they could get a dog.

"It's a girl, so you'll both have to think up names so we can choose one for her."

The puppy squirmed to get down. Charles set her down and she immediately rolled onto her back for the twins to tickle her tummy. They were used to the cats, so were not strange with the dog, but Charles had to show them how to stroke her tummy gently and not hurt her.

Charles looked up at Isabel with what he hoped was a seriously winning smile.

"Oh what the hell! She's gorgeous." Isabel dropped to one knee as the tiny dog came crashing towards her in an adorably uncoordinated way.

The puppy was silky soft with little black buttons eyes and a little wet button nose.

"Can we call her Amelia?" Amy asked her mum as

Isabel got her hand chewed by some very small yet sharp little teeth.

"No, sweetheart – you have two dolls and a teddy called Amelia. You'll have to call her something else." Isabel was glad that there were no good carpets to ruin here – she had visions of many little accidents occurring round the house.

Charles gave the puppy a little chewy stick to play with and she immediately crunched it to pieces, very loudly.

"Crunchie!" Henry said. "She's sounds like a Crunchie and she's the same colour as the middle of one!"

Charles looked at Isabel who nodded in agreement.

"Crunchie she is then."

Henry clapped his hands, delighted that his name was chosen. Amy looked a little put out.

"Shall we take her for a walk?" Charles asked.

"Is she old enough?" Isabel asked.

"Well, we could take her round the garden."

Isabel sat back down on the rug and sipped the glass of wine she had been enjoying with the sandwiches and watched her family try and coax Crunchie to follow them round the garden. Crunchie, who had never been in such an exciting place, was running everywhere she wasn't supposed to and the twins squealed with laughter, as they had to keep running after her. Charles was red in the face, running round after them all. The puppy was very much a surprise, but a welcome one. Isabel hoped that she wouldn't end up being the one that fed her and walked her, but then she thought of the exercise the dog would give her – and she would be good company in the house when the twins were at school and Charles was at work.

Isabel had kept on with her typing and was now a sort of PA to Professor Offenstein whose position had been made permanent after his ground-breaking report on the inner-city plant life. She was pretty much able to run his office from her house, and emailed all his work to him. But once a week she went into Queen's and worked in his office there. She enjoyed the work and the professor was so grateful for her organisation that he was a peach to work for. She liked the university and the bustle of the students milling around with huge textbooks bearing unpronounceable things on the covers and she hoped that one day her two would go there.

She was also going to take up a bit of painting – there were courses she could attend and Maggie had already promised to buy some of her stuff, on the strict understanding that it had to be good.

* * *

A week later Alice and Maggie were recovering nicely. They had both hurt their wrists quite badly from the rough handcuffs that Terry Lomax's men had made out of dirty rope – but other than being very frightened, they had sustained no other injuries from their ordeal, except for a few repairs to Maggie's car. They had had a constant stream of visitors anxious to hear the whole story. Journalists had been on the phone wanting exclusives. Maggie had taken great delight in saying "No comment!" before hanging up on them. In fact, Maggie had recovered to such an extent that she had considered a career in private investigation.

"Maggie, you fainted at the sound of gunfire."

"Well, I don't mean 'heavy' detective work. You know, we could find old ladies' cats and stuff like that."

"Thrill a minute stuff, you mean. Oh, why didn't you say? Let's get business cards printed straight away."

"I suppose you're right. I just don't want my life to be boring again."

"Well, with the way you and Liam are getting on I think there's a fair chance that won't happen."

Maggie grinned like a Cheshire cat. They were both lying on the sofa covered in Alice's duvet watching some old crappy war movie that was on Channel 4.

The doorbell went and Alice and Maggie looked at each other, each willing the other one to answer it.

"I'll give you a fiver if you get up," Alice offered.

"I'll give you a tenner if you go," Maggie counter-offered.

"OK, you get the Indian takeaway tonight." Alice shuffled down the hall in her slippers, feeling the cold now that she was in the dark hall.

"Hi, just thought I'd call in and see how the invalids are getting on." Isabel was standing on the door with a huge box of Thornton's continental selection under one arm and her first really good painting in the other.

"That's a rather heavy box you're carrying, let me help you with that," Alice giggled as Isabel handed over the chocolates and followed her through into the living-room.

355

"Maggie, you lazy bugger," Isabel grinned as Maggie put her face up to get a kiss on the cheek, but made no effort to actually stand up, which meant that Isabel had to lean right over to get to her.

"Wow!" Maggie spied the chocolates.

"I just thought, fuck it! We're back in the cottage, you're both safe and well and romance looks like it could be on the horizon for the pair of you with a couple of law-enforcement officers!"

"Well, I don't know about that." Maggie went bright red.

After Liam had carried her out of the building following the gunfight, he had been about to put her in the back of the police van to take her to hospital. She had opened her eyes and the first thing she could focus on were a pair of piercing blue eyes and some stubble. She had fancied him from the start, but now she fell in love, or at least very deeply in lust.

"Come on, Maggs, Liam has seen you every day since last Monday," Alice pointed out.

"And what about you? Bill has certainly been around a fair bit recently!"

It was true Bill had been visiting her. But it was really to explain that he was a CIA agent working on secondment in Northern Ireland. He had been working with a team that had been tracking Terry Lomax. It had been a bit of a surprise, but it explained how he had got so friendly with Aunt Jean and why he had hung around the shop when Alice took over. He knew that eventually Terry would come looking for Alice and it was just a matter of time. She knew the homing device that Bill had given her disguised as the charm bracelet had saved her life. She also knew it had been out of necessity rather than because he cared.

"Here, let's see, is that a painting I spy?" Maggie sat up to take a closer look.

Isabel showed it to them shyly. It was a delicate watercolour of the front door of the cottage. "Well, I don't know if it's any good."

"It's lovely, Isabel!" said Maggie.

"The colours are just gorgeous!" said Alice.

"It's for you," she said to them both.

"For us?" Maggie said in delight.

"Are you sure?" said Alice. "Don't you want to keep it?"

"To be honest, I painted two – but this is the better one."

"We'll have to get it in a nice frame." Maggie studied the painting. "Thank you!" She gave Isabel a big hug.

Isabel blushed with pleasure. She had thought the painting was rather good too.

The doorbell rang again.

"OK, guys, before you start offering each other money to answer the door, I'll go," said Isabel, getting to her feet and going to answer the door.

"It's the police!" she said leading DI Henderson and DS McIlroy into the living-room, which was now a little cramped.

Alice jumped up, shoving the duvet down the back of the sofa in an attempt to make the place look a little tidier.

"Please don't get up." DI Henderson sat down in the only available seat in the room, leaving DS McIlroy standing beside him.

"Here, have a seat." Maggie got up off the sofa and sat cross-legged in front of the fireplace.

DS McIlroy smiled and took the offered space on the sofa. She smoothed her skirt as she sat down.

"How can we help you?" Alice asked. She was tired of questions from the police and hoped that they were now no longer suspects in the murder case.

"Well, we have a bit of good news for you and some information we thought you would be keen to know about, given your recent involvement in the operation to apprehend Terry Lomax," said DI Henderson.

"Did you catch him?" asked Maggie eagerly.

"He used one of his aliases in the last two days to enter Columbia so you can rest assured that the CIA agents in place there will apprehend him at their earliest convenience."

Alice knew that was where Bill had gone. He had flown out of Heathrow the previous night. He hadn't been able to tell her anything more at the time.

DI Henderson indicated that DS McIlroy should take up the story.

She sat up straighter and began.

"We have really come because we have news regarding the death of Malcolm Hewitt. The scene-of-crime guys have found some pretty damning evidence which places Alfie Nailor at the top of our suspect list."

"Who?" Isabel asked. It was a name she had not heard before.

"Alfie Nailor, one of Terry's partners in crime. We believe he was possibly one of the men that initially broke into the shop next door."

"OK, he was the guy we saw with Darren a couple of times?" Maggie asked, admiring the very good manicure DS McIlroy had recently had.

"Very possibly." The sergeant secured a loose tendril of her blonde hair behind her ear before continuing. "Anyway, as you may have been aware, from the outset it was clear that Mr Hewitt had not been killed in your garden – he had simply been dumped there in what we now believe was an attempt to frighten you and make you think you were targets. Which due to recent events we know you were."

Maggie and Alice caught each other's eye and smiled.

"Our main concern after we identified the body was to trace the scene of the crime. We initially checked out Mr Hewitt's home address and it was clear from our visit that Mr Hewitt had not left his home of his own volition. The house showed evidence of a struggle: lamps knocked over, rugs askew and television still on and so on. There was no evidence, however, that he had actually been killed there."

Isabel was nodding, totally rapt in what the police sergeant was telling her.

"Anyhow, we realised that Mr Hewitt had been quite

literally kidnapped from his own home and we set about finding out where he had been taken. We ran through the usual suspects and we came up with two possibilities: Alfie Nailor and Darren O'Brien. Then a call came in to our Bangor station: a complaint about noise in an apartment in a converted old house. The neighbour was concerned because the flat had been vacant and they were worried that the new residents were squatters. Two officers went to check out the complaint. By the time they had got there the flat had been vacated, but there were several signs that these had not been normal residents. The windows were painted black, so once inside one couldn't tell if it was day or night." DS McIlroy paused, looking up at DI Henderson to make sure it was OK to continue.

Alice felt sick thinking about what poor Malcolm must have suffered. She was so glad that Terry Lomax was out of their lives for good.

Given the nod from her boss, DS McIlroy continued her gory tale.

"Secondly, the smallest bedroom contained only one camp bed – and it had a lock on the door. In the living area, on one side of the room, the officers found what they believed to be blood-stains so the scene-of-crime officers from Bangor CID were called to the scene. The blood matched Hewitt's. So now we had evidence that Mr Hewitt had been abducted and held in the flat in Bangor."

"Bloody hell!" Alice whispered.

"Fibres collected at the scene correlated with fibres found on Malcolm Hewitt's body. A search of Alfie Nailor's house led one of the SOCO guys to check the filter in Mr Nailor's washing machine. Again similar fibres showed up, trapped in the filter. They were identified as carpet-fibres. Therefore we are presuming he was removed from the flat, wrapped in a carpet, and taken to another location where he was shot in the temple with a nine-millimetre bullet. We have been unable to recover the shell, but a Glock nine-millimetre was found under the floorboards in Mr Nailor's home."

Maggie shuddered at what could have happened to her and Alice – they could be lying under floorboards somewhere, undiscovered for years.

"He was then stripped of his clothes and washed or hosed down as the murders thought that would get rid of any forensic evidence. They had however forgotten the fingernails. That was where that the pathologist found an abundance of matching carpet fibres where Mr Hewitt had struggled to free himself."

Isabel was completely amazed at what the police could do with a couple bits of fibre. But then she thought about the trail of devastation the twins left in their wake and how she could tell what had happened just by looking at the paint/crayons/crumbs on the floor. She smiled to herself – she was a forensic mum!

"So Mr Nailor was apprehended by our CID officers and taken in for questioning. When he was told of the death of his cohort Darren O'Brien and that Terry Lomax was now on the run, he confessed that he had been involved in the murder with Darren O'Brien, Terry Lomax and Raj Persha. Both Mr Lomax and Mr Persha you met on Monday. They had been attempting to discover where the missing diamonds were as Mr Hewitt was known to be a one-time business partner of your aunt."

"But why kill him?" Maggie asked still unclear.

"Mr Hewitt must have threatened to go to the police," said DI Henderson. "And, of course, after spending time in their company he would be able to identify them."

"And then they dumped the body in the garden thinking that it would scare Alice into a confession!" Isabel added horrified.

"They didn't realise that at that stage you knew nothing about the missing diamonds," said DI Henderson. "So when the body turned up, unpleasant and harrowing as it may have been, the full force that they had intended was lost, as the man was a stranger to you."

"Why on earth did he confess?" Alice asked, as amazed as Isabel by what the police had been able to piece together from a few minuscule carpet fibres.

"The criminal mind is a strange one," said DI Henderson. "Mr Nailor was exceedingly proud of his involvement and couldn't wait to fill us in on the finer details. According to Mr Nailor once Terry Lomax realised that you didn't yet know of the whereabouts of the diamonds his idea was to wait until you did. Then all he would have to do was to scare you so much that you would hand over the diamonds without a fuss."

"What he hadn't banked on was Bill Hardy," DI Henderson butted in.

"We don't think Lomax even knew there were CIA

agents in Ireland looking for him. We didn't," DS McIlroy admitted.

"Why is he wanted by the Americans? I mean I know he's evil, but he's English," Alice asked.

"Mr Lomax is wanted on several counts of drug-smuggling and murder in different states across America," answered DI Henderson. "He worked for the Colombians for a while bringing drugs into America, but found the climate in South America not to his liking, after he had rubbed a few high-profile drug barons up the wrong way. He decided to come back closer to home. He couldn't go back to London – every officer in the city would be looking for him. He had killed several police officers before running off to South America. Ironically, he thought that he could slip into Ireland and go unnoticed."

"Nice bloke," Maggie murmured.

"So what about Aunt Jean?" Alice asked.

"This is where we draw a bit of a blank. DI Donnelly will hopefully have the answer to that shortly. We didn't know until relatively recently that Jean Maguire hadn't died in an accident. When we checked we discovered that the driver involved had disappeared soon after Jean's death, and was no longer working for the coach company. He had worked for the company for five years so is unlikely to have had any connection with the gangsters. But the fact that he disappeared suggests he must have witnessed something. We may have to autopsy the body of your aunt again to determine cause of death."

"Can you be sure it wasn't Lomax who killed her?" Alice persisted.

"Well, it's very unlikely. With Jean dead he couldn't get to his diamonds. You turning up was a stroke of luck for Mr Lomax. However we can't rule him out. The man is a cold-blooded killer, but as yet we can't see why he would have killed her. It could have been for the same reason as Mr Hewitt – she possibly knew too much. There is also the small point that there could be another member of Terry Lomax's gang still on the loose."

All three girls looked horrified.

"But we're certain we have them all," DS McIlroy added quickly, seeing their expressions.

"So she died for nothing," Alice said quietly. Isabel slipped her arm around her.

The two officers left shortly afterwards, refusing any of the chocolates or offers of cups of tea.

* * *

Several days later news came via Liam that Terry Lomax had been captured in Bogota. Bill had successfully completed his mission and would be returning to Washington where he was regularly stationed.

"So he won't be coming back then?"

"To Ireland?" Liam had asked. "No. As they say, his work here is done."

"Is he really your cousin?" Alice had asked, trying to keep her voice level. She was surprised to discover she was really upset at the thought of him not coming back.

"Yeah, he really is." Liam had laughed, not noticing that her voice had gone strangely high.

Since the decimation of Terry Lomax's gang, Liam had become a virtually different person. His attitude had relaxed massively. He was actually quite good fun to be around and had a very dry sense of humour. And he was a total gentleman. He had wined and dined Maggie and she was loving every minute of it. Alice tried hard to be pleased for them both, but deep down she was broken-hearted that nothing had come of her and Bill when she had so hoped that it would. Why hadn't she made the move when she had the chance? But he had a high-flying career in the States, and security of the state and espionage were much higher on his agenda than an ex-solicitor running a hardware shop in the arse-end of Ireland.

* * *

"I have an idea on how to cheer you up!" Maggie said, as she came running into the living-room.

It was Saturday, about a month after the hijacking, and Alice was lying on the sofa watching something that demanded very little of her brain cells on the television.

"I'm not miserable," she argued.

"You bloody well are. You haven't had your hair cut for weeks or gone out for a night. When was the last time you bought any new clothes? And you've put on weight." Maggie pointed at Alice's tummy.

"I have not! Leave me alone, you evil tart!" Alice sat straight up in her seat, sucking her stomach in as if to prove it wasn't really there. Horrified that someone had noticed.

"Oh really, so why do we keep running out of Jaffa Cakes? I haven't eaten one in weeks." Maggie looked at her accusingly, but she was smiling.

"That's because you're in love. Everyone knows that when you start going out with someone you can't eat because there are too many butterflies in your tummy. In any case, you're a skinny bugger all the time." Alice made a face and ran her hand through her greasy hair.

"Alice, comfort-eating is making you more miserable. Forget about Bill, he's back in Washington."

"I never even knew where he lived," Alice said, looking at her stomach as if it were the first time she had even noticed that it was there. She thought Maggie was being a bit hard on her.

"You've got to get on with your life." Maggie was standing with her hands on her hips.

"Yes, I know. Look at you! You have survived the break-up of your marriage. Got up, dusted yourself down and now you're contemplating moving in with Liam, only you don't know how to tell me." Alice slumped back in her seat, relaxing her stomach muscles, distressed that it did indeed stick out a little more than it used to. How had she managed to do this much damage in a matter of weeks?

Maggie looked stumped.

"How did you know?"

"It's pretty obvious really and the paint-colour cards from B&Q were a bit of a give-away."

"Well, he hasn't actually asked me yet. But I think he's building up to it. Though I think I may buy a place of my own for a while, see how things go."

"You just make sure it's what you want. You haven't known each other very long. Buying a place is probably a good idea whatever you do. Then you won't be caught out." Alice had mixed feelings about Maggie moving out. She would really miss her, but had known that they weren't going to live together forever. It had been a temporary mutual need for company until a better offer came along. It was just that Maggie had got hers first.

Maggie nodded seriously at Alice for all of one second.

"Anyway, back to what I was going to tell you."

"Oh yes." Alice dragged her attention away again from the painful chat show she was watching.

"How about we go on a trip to Spain?"

The two large women slugging it out on daytime television, in too-tight spandex and leather outfits, over a rather skinny dorky-looking moron called Duane were forgotten.

"A girls' trip?" Alice sat back up in her seat, her interest piqued.

"Yes!" Maggie nodded.

"Sounds like a fantastic idea. I haven't been abroad for ages. Would we be able stay in your place?"

"Of course."

"Can Isabel come?"

Maggie nodded again.

"Already ran it past her. All day lazing by the pool,

sunbathing and eating fabulous, yet healthy food." She eyed Alice's stomach again.

"Cheeky cow!" Alice laughed, but she sucked it in again anyhow.

Maggie feigned innocence.

"When are you talking about?" asked Alice.

"Soon. We're into the middle of June now so I thought if we can arrange it we'll go in a couple of weeks – if we can get cheap flights."

"Count me in." Alice stopped thinking about Bill and what might have been for a few moments.

"Now, you'll have to get yourself some decent clothes and get that bikini line waxed. I won't have you embarrassing me round the pool. I'll go and book the flights," Maggie bossed, then went back to her borrowed laptop to do what she did best – shop.

Alice, who had taken the afternoon off work, decided she would go through and see how Emlyn was getting on in the shop. He was with a customer when she walked in, so she took herself into the back office and put the kettle on.

What was she going to do with herself if Maggie moved out? Looking about the office she got a little depressed. Was this really what she wanted? Her six months were up; she was free to put the house and the shop on the market. Emlyn had recently been talking about her going back to London. Maybe going back wouldn't be such a bad idea after all. The only question that remained unanswered was who had killed Aunt Jean.

Maybe it had been an accident after all. All the evidence was circumstantial though compelling – even the police were convinced she had been pushed. Only no-one could find out who had done the pushing. The errant bus driver had never been found. In her heart she was sure the killer was Terry Lomax. Revenge killings were high on his agenda – as she and Maggie had almost found out to their cost.

"What are you up to?" Emlyn came into the office, his hair-sprayed hair a little bigger than usual.

"Not much. Busy this afternoon?" Alice had noticed that Emlyn hadn't become any less nervous around the shop in the past few weeks. Really since the diamonds had been found. She had been sure that, now that he knew about Terry Lomax, he would relax.

"I'm reorganising on the first floor. Brenda has been helping me. She has so many good ideas," Emlyn prattled.

"Oh, really, what are you doing?" Alice wasn't so much annoyed as a little bit put out. She had never even met Brenda and the woman was here reorganising her shop.

"Well, I thought since it's only used as a stockroom I would tidy and make more room. We've sold all the garden furniture so I've made another office upstairs for me, where I can do all the ordering and balance the books." He gave a half-smile and looked at the floor.

"But those are my jobs." Alice realised she sounded like a petulant child as she said it.

"No offence, Alice, but you haven't exactly been 'hands

on' in the past few weeks now, have you?" Emlyn gave her a very strange look, but then changed his expression so quickly she wondered if she had really seen it.

"Well, I'm back now. What needs to be done?" She stood up and put her hands on her hips as if to signal authority. She felt an almost undetectable shift in their boss/assistant dynamic.

"It's all done," Emlyn said simply, looking at the floor again

"Well, I'll go and have a look at your office then, shall I?"

"It's not much, really I wouldn't bother." Emlyn seemed almost annoyed that she wanted to go and look.

She didn't really want to go and look, but felt that she had to assert her authority somehow.

Climbing the stairs she could feel his eyes on her back. She turned round and he walked back to the counter.

Upstairs the stockroom had never looked so tidy. The floor had been brushed and in the corner Alice could see where Emlyn had set up a little desk for himself. There was a pile of catalogues that he used to order the stock from, a notebook and pen, and a file where he kept all the invoices that needed to be paid. Alice took a deep breath. She was getting paranoid. In her head she had almost convinced herself that Emlyn was trying to bully her. Now that she thought about it he had been quite right. She hadn't been hands-on at all. In fact, Emlyn had been running the place for ages.

She sat down on the chair behind the desk and looked

out the window. The sun was shining on the lighthouse, almost blinding her, the sea was calm and lots of people were out walking.

"It really is a beautiful place to live." She sighed, wondering why she had thought about moving back to London.

"It certainly is."

Emlyn's voice made her jump. He was standing at the top of the stairs, smiling.

"I didn't even hear you come up the stairs."

"So you don't mind about the desk then?" he asked, in his usual overly concerned way.

"Not at all, it's a much better view up here anyway." Alice didn't know what else to say: he was doing a better job running this place than she could.

Emlyn gave a weak smile and Alice thought she had been silly to imagine he was up to anything.

"Things are still good with Brenda then?"

"Yeah, getting quite serious actually."

His attitude was almost a little cavalier. This was something she had never witnessed.

"Well, when are we going to get to meet her?" She pushed the conversation forward.

"She's very shy," was all he would say.

He undoubtedly didn't want to be drawn into conversation.

"Emlyn, if you keep making up these excuses I'm going to start thinking that she doesn't exist," Alice joked, not sure why she was feeling so uneasy.

"Oh she does, she does," Emlyn assured her with a vigorous nod of the head.

"Why don't you ask her to come round to the shop when I'm here then. We'll just have a cup of tea and a chat."

"That sounds fine, I'll ask her." His expression was impassive.

The door jangled downstairs. Emlyn turned on his heel and went down. Alice mentally told herself to get a grip and followed him down.

It was Maggie. She had the flight confirmation which she had just booked over the Internet in her hand.

"Isn't it great? Isabel showed me how to work it. Liam lent me his laptop and I have just booked us all flights!"

"You, me and Isabel, right?" Alice didn't like the way Maggie had said 'us all'.

"Weeell, you, me, Isabel, Liam and Charles." Maggie didn't meet her eyes.

"Oh Maggie, thanks a bloody bunch! Now I get to act like a gooseberry while you lot sit and snog the faces off each other! No thanks! Count me out!"

"But the flights are paid for!"

"I'll pay you back."

"I don't want to be paid back. Look, I'm sorry. I got carried away. I thought Isabel and Charles could do with the break. They had to cancel their trip to Disney World, as they couldn't afford it. Isabel is sending the twins to stay with her sister and Laura is going with them. I just thought it would do them good. And I asked Liam because I'm a selfish old cow and I wanted him to go."

Alice felt a total heel. Maggs was right. Isabel and Charles did need a break; they deserved one. And so what if Liam was there? Even if he wasn't Maggie would talk about him non-stop anyway so what real difference did it make?

"What date do we go?"

"30th of June – back on the 7th of July."

"As long as the weather is good and we go out for lots of nice meals, I won't mind."

"So you'll come?"

"Yes, of course I'll come. Sorry for being a grumpy old cow."

"I love you! And you're going to love Marbella. It's is full of sugar-daddies and modelly types. The food is great and the weather is fabulous." Maggie clapped her hands and gave Alice and Emlyn a hug each before disappearing back out the door.

"Emlyn?" Alice turned to him.

"Yes, I'll look after the shop," he answered her before she even had time to ask the question.

Alice caught herself again – was that fear she had seen in his eyes? Like the last time, the look was gone before she could be sure.

Chapter 37

They met on Thursday for late-night shopping. Isabel was a little late because as she was leaving Henry had thrown most of his fish-fingers up all over her.

"God, I feel like a bad mother leaving him like that. I think he must have picked up a bug at school. God, I hope Amy doesn't get it too. That's the problem with kids – they pick up all the bugs of the day and then pass them round the whole family."

Maggie took a step back from Isabel as though she thought she would catch something by standing too close.

"Charles is looking after him though, isn't he?" Alice asked.

"Yes, and he didn't look too pleased about it! I think he was going to bath him, to rinse him off!"

Maggie and Alice both tried not to gag at the thought of the vomit-coated little boy.

"I want to ask you something, though it sounds a bit

mad," Alice said to the other two as they browsed the swimwear section in Debenhams. Maggie was holding an almost non-existent pink string-bikini up in her hand, admiring the tiny triangles, which were supposed to be the top.

Isabel shook her head. "Too young for you, my dear!"

Maggie faked a hurt shocked look.

"I can't shake this weird feeling that I'm getting from Emlyn. Have either of you noticed anything odd?"

"Well, he doesn't call round the way he used to." Maggie put the minuscule bikini back on the rack.

"You said he had reorganised the shop without mentioning it to you," Isabel said from behind a rather sturdy-looking bathing-suit in sensible black.

"Maybe he's having a rare fit of efficiency?" Maggie pulled a face at Isabel's choice.

"I can't put my finger on it, but I'm sure something is up. He looked practically terrified when I asked him to run the shop while we were on holiday."

"That does sound like Emlyn. He can be such a quiche-maker sometimes."

"There is absolutely nothing worth buying in this shop," Maggie announced within earshot of a loitering sales assistant who didn't seem to hear her.

"Why don't we have a look on the Internet?" suggested Isabel.

"We could look at Victoria's Secrets web page and have a look at all the local sites as well."

"But you can't try anything on. And if it's not right,

375

it's a total nightmare to try and return anything." Maggie spoke with authority – she had become a bit of a closet Internet shopper.

"Oh, let's just go to Marks!" Alice put down the blue and green bikini she had briefly considered.

They left Debenhams, leaving all the hangers turned the wrong way round on the bikini rail.

Marks & Spencer was not up to much either and the three, fed up now from trailing round the busy shopping thoroughfare, decided they would take themselves off for dinner.

They were sitting round a table in Christabel's ten minutes later, having ordered Portavogie prawns in a light curry sauce and a side order of chips.

"Shall we order a bottle of wine?" Maggie asked.

"Well, I don't know if it will suit my new diet now," said Alice. "Lots of calories in wine."

"Oh shut up! You don't need to lose any weight," Isabel said as she munched on an olive.

"Speak to your friend there." Alice pointed her bread-stick at Maggie who was engrossed in the wine list.

After the waiter had poured them all a glass of chilled Chablis, Isabel turned to Alice.

"So you really are OK about Charles coming on this holiday?"

"Of course I'm fine." Alice watched her glass mist up with the cold wine and sipped it.

"Thank God – we're really in need of this break. I won't be sorry to see the end of this year, let me tell you."

"Isabel, it's still only June – you've got another six months to go. They could be the greatest of your life to date." Maggie was managing to eat an olive and a bit of Alice's bread-stick at the same time.

"I know, I know. Jeepers, I hadn't even thought about fitting into a bikini until we went into Debenhams – oh, the shame! Beside you two I'm going to look like the Incredible Hulk." Her chestnut curls shook as she roared with laughter. Alice and Maggie joined in after feebly protesting, but the sight of Isabel in kinks of laughter was too hard to resist.

The rest of dinner was a scream. Spirits soared round the table. Getting out was just what Alice had needed to take her mind off Bill and Maggie and Isabel were both excited about the holiday. Maggie was telling them all the fabulous shops and restaurants that were there.

"Walking along the harbour with the totally amazing yachts on one side and the restaurants full of people on the other is one of the best people-watching places in the world. Last summer when I was there I saw Des Lynham and quite a few soap stars."

Isabel's eyes lit up at the mention of soap stars: she was addicted to *Coronation Street*, *Eastenders* and *Brookside* and meeting some of her idols would be heaven.

"Oh my God, not to mention the boob jobs! In fact, loads of women from the UK go over there for plastic surgery – I think it must be cheaper over there."

"So I could fit in a little liposuction while I'm there," Alice said sarcastically, lifting a handful of Maggie's chips as they were set down in front of her.

"Oi! Hands off my dinner!"

"Ladies, enough!" Isabel instructed.

Alice and Maggie both stopped and Isabel took the opportunity to stick her fork in the chips when they least expected it.

Maggie described her apartment to them.

"It has three double bedrooms and they all have an en suite, so it means that we won't all be in on top of each other. It has marble floors, of course, but then most of the Spanish apartments have that now."

Isabel and Alice looked at each other.

Maggie went on to describe the bougainvillaea growing on the terrace of the second-floor apartment with its view of the beach and the pool right below. She described lazy days of sunshine, driving along the coast in a convertible and turning as brown as a conker.

"Derek and I were there together this time last year." She stared off into the middle distance.

Her eyes threatened to mist up, but she caught herself quickly. This year I will have the pleasure of DI Donnelly for company, she thought, while Derek is still slogging it out in that pathetic excuse he calls a bar.

"Have you spoken to him recently?" Alice asked, her mind going back to the programme she had seen on Sky One, but never mentioned.

"He calls me every couple of months, but I knew about the bar because I saw it on the television late one night when I couldn't sleep."

"You never said," Isabel said cautiously.

"Well, I knew you pair must have seen it as you're the biggest watchers of crap I have ever come across."

Isabel and Alice looked at each other again, this time unsure of what to say. Neither of them had known the other had seen it.

"I saw it in London ages ago," Alice confessed, "but it was repeated a few months back. I didn't say anything as I thought I was the only one."

"I saw it one night when I was waiting for Charles to come home. I didn't think either of you had seen it."

"Wasn't it the biggest pile of crap you ever saw?" Maggie asked.

There was an awkward silence for a few seconds while the other two tried to decide what sort of response would be suitable.

This time it was Maggie who howled with laughter and the others followed, glad that she found the programme as funny as they had.

"So what are you going to do about Emlyn?" Isabel asked much later on as they paid the bill.

"What can I do? I might be imagining it all. I can't tackle someone because I suddenly find his or her presence a little unnerving. Well, it sounds really stupid to say it, but he's almost intimidating recently. Maybe it's just new-found confidence with his girlfriend but it isn't 'nice' confidence, if you know what I mean?"

"Maybe you're both just having more trouble getting over the whole Terry Lomax thing than you thought. I mean it was only four weeks ago. The holiday will be just what you need. Emlyn is probably just trying to assert a bit of authority in his life – you know, to impress the girlfriend with his business savvy."

"Yeah, you're probably right. But earlier in the week he told me that he had rearranged the stockroom. Not a big deal in itself, but it was more the way he told me. He didn't want my approval; he was just letting me know. He also accused me of not having a clue what was going on in the shop because I wasn't bothering my arse."

"That's a bit insensitive of him," Isabel agreed. "But remember how important the shop is to him. It's his last tie to Jean."

"Another thing, and now you will really think I'm getting paranoid, but he has stopped mentioning Jean's name at all. It's almost like her memory has ceased to exist."

"It's possibly just his way of dealing with things, though it does sound a bit out of character," Isabel conceded.

"That's just the thing. I get the distinct impression he's feeling guilty. I only noticed it after he admitted about the safety-deposit key."

"It's a bit odd," Maggie agreed, trying to think if she remembered anything unusual about him in the past few weeks.

"I think I'm seeing a different side to him. I wonder if it has anything to do with Bill being away?"

"You think his behaviour has changed now that Bill isn't around?"

"Yeah, like he can carry on how he likes now that Bill isn't watching."

"Do you think he knew that Bill was in the CIA?" Isabel asked.

"How could he have? We didn't have a clue," Maggie replied.

"Let's face it, Maggs, we don't really know what sort of relationship they had," said Alice. "They always seemed friendly. But if we had no idea about Bill, we probably have no idea about Emlyn."

"What are you suggesting? Do you think he's in some kind of secret police?" asked Maggs.

"No, I'm pretty sure that he's not. But I think something is definitely going on."

"You think he might have his own agenda?" said Maggs.

"That is exactly what I think. Now that my six months are up I'm free to sell the shop or the house or both. If I hadn't taken them on then they would have been sold and the proceeds given to Action Cancer."

"You think Emlyn wants the shop?" asked Isabel.

"I'm sure he doesn't want me in it any more. Every time I go in he has changed something without consulting me. I get the impression I'm becoming more of an inconvenience – every time I walk in one door he walks out the other. With Bill out of the picture Emlyn can start whatever it is that he has up his sleeve."

"Probably some good-luck beads!"

"Maggie, I'm serious!"

"So am I – his jewellery is appalling."

"Maggie Sullivan, sometimes I wish I had longer arms

so that I could reach over the table and poke you in the eyes!"

"Come on, guys, don't you think the idea of Emlyn plotting world domination is a little far-fetched? He would be too busy ironing a fresh cravat for the next morning!" Maggie was exasperated. Sure Emlyn was a little odder than usual, but that in itself was really not that strange. Alice had been in the house too long brooding over Bill.

* * *

The following morning was Friday. They were leaving for Spain in ten days! Alice had admitted to herself and the others the night before that she was nervous about leaving Emlyn on his own in her shop. She had never felt remotely possessive about it until Emlyn started throwing what weight he had around. She was up and dressed by eight thirty and was in the shop sipping her Earl Grey when Emlyn arrived.

"Oh, you're in." His tone couldn't have been less enthusiastic and he immediately started looking guilty again.

"Morning," she chirped as brightly as she could manage.

"What are you up to today?" he asked her with even less enthusiasm than his first remark.

"I'm here all day."

He nodded, but said nothing.

Alice deliberately put herself in his way as much as she could that morning and she could tell it was driving him mad.

Their relationship continued to deteriorate quite rapidly over Saturday and on Monday even Maggie, who had called into the shop with fresh coffee from the coffee house on the High Street, had to admit that all was definitely not well.

"What is his bloody problem?" she whispered to Alice as they sat behind the counter while some customers browsed quite happily among the shelves.

"Don't know, but it's clear that he has a real problem with me."

"Are you going to tackle him about it?"

"I'm going to have to. I don't want to leave him here in the shop in some strange state of mind – Christ knows what he would get up to."

Emlyn was upstairs in his office. Since morning his behaviour had been erratic, and as soon as Maggie came in he had disappeared up the stairs like a startled rabbit.

"Do it soon, we're leaving next Monday."

"I will, promise."

"Are you going to stay here all day?" Maggie asked.

"I guess so, I really should, shouldn't I?"

Maggie shrugged her shoulders; she didn't know what to advise, but Emlyn had gone from kooky, eccentric behaviour to downright creepy. Rather Alice than her.

After Maggie had left, Alice worked on the end-of-month figures and balanced her accounts. Everything seemed in order. At least Emlyn didn't seem to be siphoning money out of the shop. Emlyn went out of his way to avoid her and she ignored it for most of the day, but around five o' clock she couldn't stand it any longer and decided to have it out with him.

"Emlyn, do you have a problem with me?"

He had been brushing the floor and stopped. To give him a bit of credit he at least had the decency to look surprised, if not a little guilty.

"Problem? No, why?" His face was blank.

"We've hardly spoken in the last couple of weeks. You keep going up to the stockroom any time you think I'm going to start up a conversation. Has something happened that you haven't told me about?"

"Well, we have both been busy. I thought you didn't mind my office upstairs."

"I don't mind it, of course not. It's just that we don't seem to get on as well as we used to. We used to be friends."

"We're still friends," he said, looking suddenly sad.

"Emlyn, what's up? Surely you can tell me?" Alice attempted the sympathy vote to see if she could get him to tell her.

"Alice, you're imagining things, we're fine. Maybe you still aren't really over the whole Terry Lomax drama – it was pretty shocking after all." He didn't even sound like he was convincing himself let alone Alice.

"You didn't seem to be that shocked." She realised as soon as she said it that it had been the case.

"Look, I've got to head on, Brenda will be waiting for me."

He grabbed his velveteen jacket off the peg in the

back office and left before Alice had any time to argue. She was left standing in the empty shop.

Something occurred to her as she stood there – she locked the shop as she considered it. She went home to have a glass of wine and to think about what she would do next. She really missed Bill; his friendship was one she had come to rely on.

* * *

That evening Liam called round for dinner with Maggie.

Alice got up to leave shortly after he arrived.

Maggie walked into the living-room, with beads of sweat on her forehead from the heat of the oven and oven-mitts over her shoulder. "Won't you stay for something to eat? I've made lasagne."

"It smells great, but I have a couple of things to discuss with Emlyn, I won't be long."

"Are you going round to his house?" Maggie didn't think going to Emlyn's house was the greatest idea.

"Yeah, he did a runner on me earlier today so I want to make sure I have his full and undivided attention."

"Sounds serious?" Liam set his wineglass down on the coffee table and eased his shoes off.

"You make yourself at home," Alice teased, eyeing his feet.

Liam blushed and moved to put the shoes back on.

"I'm only messing. I'll be back in half an hour. You know where Emlyn lives, don't you, Maggs?"

"Yeah, why? Do you want me to pick you up?"

"Nope, just wanted to make sure you knew where he lived." Alice grinned.

Maggie cocked her head to the side like a confused dog.

"Is everything OK really?"

"Absolutely."

Maggie was spooning delicious mounds of lasagne onto two plates as Alice left. The smell of the garlic bread nearly put her off her mission, but she had something to put to bed tonight – something that she had been thinking about all afternoon. Things had started to click into place.

She waved goodbye and pulled the door shut behind her. In the hall she hesitated. She'd better take a jacket – it might be chilly on the way home. Her own jacket was upstairs so she grabbed a light fleece of Maggie's. Maggie wouldn't be going anywhere but upstairs to bed that evening!

It was actually quite pleasant and balmy outside. There were plenty of people out walking or just sitting on the sea wall. She smiled at a few of the people she recognised as she walked through the town. In her head she went over the questions she was going to confront Emlyn with.

She was suddenly conscious of a weight in one of the pockets of the fleece. She thrust her hand in and was dismayed to find that she had taken Maggie's mobile.

She dialled home and Maggie answered.

Maggie's only response was: "You dragged me away from Liam just to tell me that!"

Alice laughed. "OK, I won't interrupt again unless I'm being attacked by a knife-wielding maniac!"

Well, I hope it won't come to that, she thought, as she walked on.

* * *

Back at 20 Shore Street, Liam's mobile rang.

"Oh, not again! Just ignore it," Maggie pleaded as he put down his fork and got up to answer it.

"I have to answer, Maggie, it could be important."

Maggie shovelled a large piece of particularly garlicky bread into her mouth.

"Fhat wooll sherve yoou wwright," she said, her mouth stuffed full of the bread.

"Nice!" Liam grinned as he hit the 'yes' key to accept the call.

"DI Donnelly." His tone became business-like.

He turned his back on Maggie as he became embroiled in his conversation. She was still working on the chewy bread; she might have overcooked it just a tad, she thought, as she nearly lost a filling.

"Hi, right, yes, I wasn't involved in that, but I know the case well." Liam was nodding and looking about for something to write on.

Maggie jumped up and handed him a file block that was in the drawer of the coffee table. He nodded thanks and started to make notes, his dinner temporarily forgotten.

A couple of minutes later he concluded his conversation.

"I really appreciate you letting me know – come back to me and let me know how you get on, good to talk to you again." He ended the call and put the phone back in his pocket.

"They've just found the bus driver who hit Jean Maguire." He sat back down.

Maggie was agog for information.

"Well?" she nearly exploded as he calmly took a bite of his lukewarm pasta.

"He was caught a couple of hours ago. He's been living in Donegal for the past nine months. The Gardai just pulled him over for drink-driving. He was so plastered that when they questioned him he started to cry and told them he had been driving a bus in Donaghadee which had hit a woman and that he had run away. They, of course, had no idea of what he was talking about, but a guy I know at the station made the connection – I happened to have mentioned Jean's death to him recently. The police always thought it was suspicious that the driver had disappeared, but could never find him."

"Was that the guy you know on the phone?" Maggie's dinner was now forgotten.

"Yeah – Davey Mulligan, a good man."

"You guys don't hang about for pleasantries."

"No need, he'll ring me back if he has news."

"But why not just arrest him if he has admitted to it?"

"Eleven people have admitted to driving the bus that killed Jean. None of them actually did," Liam calmly explained.

"Oh. You mean people want to be blamed? How come?" Maggie was flabbergasted.

"Nutters! All want to be the centre of attention. I don't know, never could work out why. Most of these guys just saw it on the news and fancy a bit of excitement in their lives, a chance to be in the paper. Most of them have done it a few times so we know of them. But I have never heard of this fella. Davey is going to ring DI Henderson and let him know."

Maggie sat thinking what a strange world it was where the bad guys didn't want to admit to a crime while innocent men came forward and tried to take the blame, or the glory depending on your point of view. She looked down at her plate, her appetite gone.

Liam swapped their plates and swiftly finished hers off as well.

* * *

"Who is it?"

Emlyn opened the door a crack and peeked out.

"Oh! Alice! What are you doing here?"

"I have a couple of things to ask you and since you ran out of the shop earlier I thought I'd call round."

She was standing on his doorstep waiting to be asked in.

"Brenda's here," he hissed.

"Good, maybe she should hear this too."

Alice pushed her way past him, taking him by surprise. In Emlyn's small living-room a diminutive blonde sat, holding a glass of white wine. The Venetian blinds were tilted almost shut despite the fact it was still bright outside – Emlyn was clearly going for privacy! He had turned on the reading light in the corner, throwing shadows across the room making it a bit gloomy rather than romantic. The blonde stood up, seeming unsure whether to take Alice's hand or not.

Alice was thrown for a couple of seconds: 'Brenda' really was a Brendan.

"What's this about?" Emlyn demanded, clearly embarrassed at being caught out.

Alice ignored him.

"Brendan, pleased to meet you. I'm Alice, Emlyn's boss." She said it most deliberately.

"Hi, nice to meet you." His eyes darted from Emlyn to Alice and back to Emlyn.

"What's going on? What are you doing here?" Emlyn was visibly squirming and he practically shouted at her.

Alice turned to face him and asked almost casually: "Actually, Emlyn, I came round to ask you why you killed my aunt." She sat down in the nearest chair to give the impression that she was calm and in control, but her heart was pounding and she was sure Emlyn could hear it.

Brendan gave a little squeak as if someone had trod on his tail.

Emlyn was as white as a sheet.

"Bloody Hell! Have you lost your mind, coming here interrupting my evening with my friend with your wild ramblings! Get out, how dare you!" He was starting to shake.

"So you deny it?"

"You have no idea what you're talking about!" he yelled.

Emlyn was raging. He was pacing the room and appeared to be terrifying the shit out of little Brendan. Alice absent-mindedly thought their relationship wouldn't last much longer. Seeing Emlyn get so upset, she realised that her hunch may have been slightly off the mark.

"What don't I understand?" she bellowed back, trying to goad him on.

"You have no idea what pressure I have been under! Jean had no idea what was going on!"

"So you just decided to kill her off?" She said, riling him a little more.

"No! Alice don't be so short-sighted." He looked utterly desperate. "When she started getting involved with the whole Terry Lomax thing she had no idea what she was doing. She wanted to push it all the way. With so many stolen goods passing through the shop it was easy to shift a small table here, a chair here, a painting and whatever else they forced on her, a good way to supplement her income and make up for what was happening to her. When the diamonds arrived it was like manna from heaven. Jean couldn't help herself – Terry was driving her to distraction."

Alice stayed silent. Here at last was the whole story.

"I tried to convince her not to do it. But she sold four

of the diamonds to a guy she knew of in Dublin. She put the money into the shop, so it would be financially secure."

Alice fought the urge to punch him in the mouth. Why did he let Jean do it? Why hadn't he been stronger?

Emlyn sat down on the sofa, wringing his hands.

"Someone leaked news of the diamonds being sold back to Terry Lomax. I swear I don't know who it was. Jean was frightened, but she didn't know what to do. We had been passing stolen goods through the shop and she didn't want to go to the police. Terry was playing her."

He seemed to have shrunk in stature. He looked like a small strange tweed-clad bird.

"She panicked, putting the rest diamonds in the safety-deposit box and hiding the key. When the threats started I thought she would give it all up and admit what she had done, but she was prepared to go into battle against this gangster. Jesus, she had no idea what she was going up against. By then she was scared. That's when Terry got to me. If I didn't do what he wanted then he said he would hurt her. If I told her that Terry was threatening me she would have gone to pieces, so I fed her the stories Terry told me to try to get her to give the diamonds up – which is what I wanted her to do anyway. Just hand them over and be done with it all."

Emlyn paused – a nervous-looking Brendan had heard enough and was fumbling at the door.

"Please stay," pleaded Emlyn tearfully.

Brendan reluctantly went back to cowering in the corner of the sofa.

"She went out that afternoon. She was so beside herself she never noticed anyone was following her. She was meeting Terry or one of his henchmen and she intended to "confess" that she had sold all the diamonds and given the money to charity. She thought that he would have no choice but to accept the situation. Somehow she couldn't see that Terry was into revenge for the sake of it. She even took that basket and joked about picking blackberries as a cover. I followed at a distance, but I was too far away. She was dead before the bus ever got near her. The bus driver had no time to stop. All it took was a minute – she was hit over the head and thrown onto the road. It was over so quickly I didn't have time. I couldn't do anything. I ran back to the shop to call the police. One of Terry's guys was waiting for me. He said if I did anything I'd be next."

He paused, sobbing quietly at the memory.

"Alice, I swear I didn't know what to do. I thought if I stayed quiet Terry Lomax would go away. What choice did I have? I knew you would come. Jean told me the whole of the will, even the bit about you having to run the shop. God, I prayed you would take up the offer, though half of me hoped you wouldn't get involved in all this. I thought you might not want to come. I mean, you run a shop? What the hell did you know about anything? You had a high-flying career in London – Jean was so proud of you. But you came."

Emlyn looked wretched, staring down at his hands which he kept rubbing, reminding Alice of Lady Macbeth.

"Jean thought if you had something of your own, you

would find peace with yourself. Ha! What sentimental old cobblers!" He laughed weakly. "When I realised that there was no way Terry would just go away, I thought if I pointed you in the direction of foul play you could involve the police and get rid of him once and for all. I thought if the diamonds were returned then he had nothing to hang around for. Later, I changed my mind and I was going to try and talk you out of it, but then Bill got involved and I didn't want to look suspicious. He was as protective of you as he was of Jean, but he couldn't help her when she needed him."

His eyes had a faraway look to them and Brendan moved in his seat, as if he were trying to hide under the table – his night had definitely taken a turn for the worse!

"Lovely American Bill Hardy just seemed to materialise out of nowhere. I didn't think he knew what was happening. I'm positive Jean never told him the truth. Finding out he was in the CIA – we had no idea! I thought he was just some burned-out marine biologist or something. I don't think he had any idea about Terry threatening me, though he did still keep a close eye on the shop and always called in. I was very careful not to say anything to him – Terry seemed to have people watching all the time. Jean thought I was her devoted friend to the end. What would she have thought if she had known the truth?" He looked up at Alice with tears rolling down his cheeks.

Alice squeezed her eyes shut. How could she have got the situation so back to front? She had come to the conclusion that Emlyn was plotting against Jean – she had no idea that both their lives were under threat. It was nearly too much to bear. How could Emlyn have allowed Jean to do something so dangerous as meet Terry Lomax in an isolated place? But then she remembered how obstinate her aunt was – no, she couldn't blame Emlyn for what he had done, or not done. The whole situation was hopeless.

"But you and your friends, carrying on like detectives, you had no idea what you were doing. No idea how much danger you were in." Emlyn was talking again.

Alice stayed mute, thoughts whirling round in her head. She was aware of the frightened mouse in the corner and she felt awful that Brendan had to hear all of this. But this was her big chance to get the truth and she had to make the most of it.

But then the little mouse was off the sofa and walking into the middle of the room.

He fixed his eyes on Alice.

"After you failed to be lead us to the diamonds," said Brendan matter-of-factly, "Terry employed me to work on Emlyn who we suspected knew their whereabouts. With that policeman hanging round the house all the time making puppy-dog eyes at your friend it got a little awkward, but I was hopeful that you'd become sloppy and give us another chance. But no, you made no move. And now the diamonds are gone. Well, we have had enough – Terry wants you out of Donaghadee and out of Ireland for good. You didn't take the easy way out so now I'm going to have to help you on your way."

Emlyn and Alice stared at Brendan in horror. The mouse had turned into a rat!

"You too, Emlyn, I'm afraid – you've heard too much and you're not really my type after all."

Poor Emlyn looked so scared that Alice went over and stood in front of him. She couldn't believe that this evening had been turned on its head.

"We're leaving, Brendan. Don't try and stop us. The police know about you!" Alice made for the door, Emlyn scuttling after her.

"The police know nothing, you stupid bitch!" Brendan laughed.

Alice was tugging at the door-handle.

"Oh, I took the precaution of removing the key," said Brendan.

Alice turned to see him dangling the key smugly. She remembered his attempt to leave earlier and her heart thudded even faster as she realised how clever their enemy was. They were trapped. Alice's eyes flew to the window and in the same moment she remembered Maggie's phone in her pocket. As Brendan's eyes flicked to the window she put her hand in her pocket and wrapped her fingers round the phone. Home had been the last number called and Alice hit the dial button. Now all she could hope was that Maggie and Liam would hear what was happening. She prayed that they hadn't sloped off to bed already. She slid the phone out of the pocket surreptitiously.

But Brendan spotted her.

"*Bitch!*" he screamed. He hurled himself at Alice and she dropped the phone with the force of the blow.

"*Maggie! Liam! Help!*" she screamed as Brendan picked up the phone and hurled it into the fireplace: the tiny Motorola smashed into smithereens. Alice knew she had played her trump card: all she could now was hope like hell that the thirty seconds that the phone had connected was enough for someone to hear them and realise that they were in trouble. All she could do was try and keep herself and Emlyn out of harm's way until rescue arrived.

* * *

Maggie and Liam were just been about to start on the apple-pie that Maggie had proudly baked earlier on that day, when the phone rang.

"Oh, no, no more interruptions," said Maggie firmly. "The answer machine will pick it up. We'll hear who it's anyway." She handed Liam a bowl of hot apple-pie smothered in thick vanilla ice cream.

They both paused, startled as instead of a message they heard a shout, then Alice's voice a little muffled, a lot of background interference – then the line went dead.

"Do you think she hit the call button by mistake?" said Maggie. "She isn't used to my phone. Though, she would have to flip the phone open to make the call . . ."

"Sounds as if she's in a pub or something – with that background noise."

"The reception's probably bad. Maybe she'll go outside and call again?" Maggie looked at Liam. "Jesus, I hope she's OK."

"Can you rewind the tape and turn the volume up?"

Maggie looked at the side of the phone and slid the volume control to max. Liam held his finger up to his lips as he listened.

They clearly heard a strange male voice scream *"Bitch!"* Then Alice calling urgently: *"Maggie! Liam! Help!"*

"Oh, my God!" said Maggie.

"That wasn't Emlyn's voice, was it?" asked Liam.

"No, no, I don't think so!" Maggie was white-faced with shock.

"Take the tape out so it doesn't get recorded over," said Liam, getting to his feet.

"We should get round to Emlyn's flat immediately."

Maggie jumped up and took the tiny tape out of the machine. Then they rushed out to his jeep and set off for Emlyn's flat, Maggie shouting directions as they went.

It soon became clear that Maggie had no idea how to get there.

"For Christ's sake, Maggs, I thought you told Alice you knew how to get to Emlyn's flat!"

"Don't shout at me! I've only ever walked there with Alice – it's this bloody one-way system, I'm confused."

"Well, un-confuse yourself! Your friend is in hot water, again!"

Maggie eventually managed to find Emlyn's street. Liam halted and called the station for back-up. Then they drove cautiously up to Emlyn's front door. There was no sign of any disturbance or anyone lurking around.

"Is there a back door?" Liam asked as they got out the jeep.

Maggie screwed up her face as she tried to remember.

"No. I'm sure that there isn't. He has a window looking out into a communal garden at the back. But he doesn't have access – I think."

Liam rolled his eyes.

"I've only been there once!" she shouted, cross that she couldn't be more definite.

"Don't worry," he said, putting a hand on her shoulder. "Wait here and I'll go and talk to the local boys."

A police car pulled up in front of them, having come from the opposite direction. Three burly policemen got out. Maggie recognised one of them as one of the young constables who had arrived at the house when they had found Malcolm Hewitt's body.

Liam went over to them and they grouped around listening to him as he issued instructions. One of the officers ran round to the back of the block of flats while the other two stayed with Liam. They approached the front door.

* * *

Inside the flat, Emlyn, Alice and Brendan all jumped as they heard the ringing at the front door. Brendan had been sitting in the armchair, a poker from the fire resting in his hands. He had picked it up after smashing the phone and had corralled Alice and Emlyn in the corner of the room. He had been ranting for what seemed like hours and Alice couldn't understand what his intention was.

The ringing continued. Brendan made no move.

"Emlyn Gordon, open the door please – this is the police!"

Alice recognised Liam's voice and relief flooded through her. Colour started to come back into Emlyn's cheeks for the first time since Brendan had threatened them. "We'll be OK now," Alice whispered to Emlyn.

"Think so?" Brendan shrieked as he leapt to his feet, dropping the poker, and produced a gun from the pocket of his denim jacket, which was hanging on the back of one of the dining-room chairs.

"Oh God," Emlyn whimpered as Brendan brandished the pistol in their faces.

"Come on, Brendan, what good will that do you now?" Alice tried to reason with him, adding for good measure, "The police are here and they have the place surrounded."

"Oh yes, I forgot Detective Watson, the Know-it-all," Brendan jeered. "Terry told me you fancy yourself as a right little Nancy Drew." He was grinning maniacally. Alice just then spotted the policeman in the back garden through the Venetian blinds and she tried to move towards the window to block Brendan's view.

Constable Fraser could see through the window that the little blonde man had the other two at gun-point in the living room. "Donnelly, this is Fraser," he whispered into his radio.

"Go ahead, Fraser," the radio crackled back.

"There are three people in the living-room. One of the men has a gun. I can't make it out clearly, but it looks like a semi-automatic."

"Don't move a muscle, Fraser, I'm coming round the back to take a look." The radio went dead.

Liam appeared down the side-alley seconds after and assessed the situation through the tilted blinds, ducking as Brendan swung the gun round.

Inside, Alice and Emlyn tried to get as far away from the gun as they could, which was difficult considering that it was a small room. Bits of furniture stood between them and the gun-toting midget. He was muttering again to himself now. Alice glanced back out the window. She couldn't see anyone out there now – surely they must have seen her?

"Open the door, this is the police!"

It was a different voice that called now. Brendan turned off the reading light and room filled with darkness. The only light came from a window in a house behind the flat. There were no street lights.

It took Alice a few moments for her eyes to adjust to the dark. Emlyn was still whimpering beside her. Brendan was still on the other side of the room, muttering about death and that he was going to kill them both. Alice was petrified. She hadn't banked on a gun. As her eyes adjusted she saw him sitting in the chair, gun still in his hand, facing them. But he seemed almost to have forgotten that they were there. She and Emlyn hunkered down behind the sofa for protection while Alice tried to work out if she could break the window and get them both out without Brendan managing to shoot them. It was so dark he couldn't possibly see them clearly, but on the other hand if he started shooting randomly they could both be shot in the confusion. Alice and Emlyn didn't move a muscle, both praying that the police would do something soon.

* * *

"We'll have to go in the front," Liam said, reappearing back round the front of the building. "The bastard has Alice and Emlyn there and he has a gun. He has just turned off the lights so we can't see a thing."

Maggie was literally jumping up and down. Liam tried to get her to get back into the car, but there was no way she could just sit calmly while some murdering lunatic held a gun to Alice's head.

* * *

Brendan was suddenly shaken out of his reverie. He jumped off the chair and flicked on the main light-switch. His two hostages were still cowering behind the sofa.

"Up!" he instructed, his face twisted into a ghoulish smile.

They got to their feet, never taking their eyes off the gun. He opened the door of the room and pushed them out, Emlyn first. Then Alice felt the nose of the gun in her hair and Brendan pressed it into the back of her head.

They were frogmarched into the bathroom where he locked them all in.

"Into the bath."

Alice and Emlyn both scrambled into the bath, Emlyn getting a little tangled up in the shower curtain as he did so. The bottom of the bath was wet from the shower. Alice wrinkled her nose at the sight of the soapy trapped hair caught in the plughole.

They could still hear the banging of the door outside as the police continued to shout through the front door.

Emlyn and Alice crouched down in the bath while Brendan sat by the door listening. Alice's eyes fell on a salon-size can of hairspray sitting on the window ledge above her head.

"Let them go!" came Liam's voice from the front-door. "It's over! You can't escape now!"

Alice began to cry at the sound of his voice and even Emlyn's eyes filled up.

Brendan turned suddenly to Emlyn and pulled him out of the bath by his hair. Emlyn didn't utter a sound. Brendan pressed him up against the door.

"Get out! Do anything stupid and I'll kill him," he snarled at Alice.

"Please, please don't shoot me!" Emlyn pleaded, his cheek squashed against the door. Alice got out of the bath and Brendan let go of Emlyn who collapsed into a little heap on the floor.

"Move and I'll kill you," Brendan warned, gun still in hand.

He started clearing bottles off the windowsill as if he was preparing to escape. He set the hairspray down right in front of Alice. He cleared a space and then cautiously started to open the small window.

Alice saw her chance: she grabbed the can of hairspray and swung it round, giving her the force of a discus-thrower, except that her weapon was a salon-sized can of Elnett. Thankfully the can was relatively new so it was heavy. She crashed it into the back of Brendan's head. Brendan lost his balance and dropped the gun. Alice kicked the gun over to Emlyn. Alice brought the can down on Brendan's head again and he fell to the floor.

He tried to stand up.

"Don't move!" Emlyn had the gun in his hands, which were shaking like jelly.

"You wouldn't! You're just a pathetic little bastard – you even thought I fancied you!" Brendan sneered, ignoring Emlyn and continuing to get to his feet. He stood up straight and took a step towards them.

Emlyn kept the gun level.

"I'm serious, you bastard, don't come any nearer." His voice was stronger, but still unsteady. The tears had dried up.

There was no noise outside the bathroom.

Alice held her breath. She was standing beside Emlyn, and both had their backs against the door. Brendan was facing them, his back to the window, broken bottles and jars and a slightly bloody can of hairspray at his feet. He put his hand up the back of his head. Bringing it back down he looked at his fingers they were covered in blood.

"Fucking whore!" he bellowed at Alice and lunged forward.

Emlyn closed his eyes and pulled the trigger. The noise was deafening.

Brendan stopped almost in mid-air, a look of total surprise on his face. The force of the shot pushed him backwards against the wall and he slumped down it, leaving a smear of blood on the white and yellow tiles behind as he sat, legs spread, on the floor, blood staining his shirt round his midriff.

Emlyn dropped the gun; he was shaking so badly now. Alice, her ears ringing with the shot, unlocked the door and yanked it open to the sound of shattering glass from the living-room. A moment later, Liam appeared, gun in hand, at the living-room door.

He flattened himself against the wall at the side of the bathroom door and covered the quivering Alice and Emlyn as they ran down the hall on trembling legs.

Then he cautiously entered the bathroom. Brendan was sitting with eyes as big as saucers as pain flooded through him.

* * *

Maggie was dizzy with relief. She had been hiding behind some parked cars in case Brendan escaped, but when she heard the shot she had screamed out loud and come running out in time to see a very ashen-faced Alice and Emlyn emerge. A wave of relief swept over her, but then her heart nearly stopped when she realised that Liam was inside the house with the maniac. Fortunately, Liam appeared at the front door almost at once, calling to his colleagues to get an ambulance. She wanted to throw herself in his arms, but held back, conscious of the fact he was in police mode.

She saw Brendan being carried out with a stunned expression on his face. He was moaning and swearing mostly and the sight of her had made him swear even more.

The next hour was a blur to Alice, as paramedics treated her and Emlyn for shock, while another ambulance took Brendan away to the Ulster Hospital in Dundonald.

"You shot him in the stomach," Liam told Emlyn who was still unsteady on his feet.

"Nasty, but not fatal. We'll get that bastard to court yet. Membership of Terry Lomax's gang and two attempted murders – I think he can put his career in general thuggery on hold for a very long time."

Neither Alice nor Emlyn were harmed physically, but it could be a while before Emlyn invited anyone round to his flat for dinner. The effects of such an ordeal would be hard for either of them to get over in a hurry.

"Thank you." Emlyn took Alice's hand in hers.

"What for? Jesus, I put you in danger." Alice couldn't believe he was thanking her.

"He would have shown his true colours eventually and I'm just glad I wasn't alone when I got to see them."

"Well, I'm sorry we had to find out that way."

"At least we got our revenge for Jean."

Alice looked sharply at the quivering jelly she had spent the last couple of hours with.

"Gosh, that came out a bit harshly, didn't it?" Emlyn put his hand up to his mouth and started to giggle – then he burst into tears.

Alice hugged him. "We're going to be OK. Right? It's all over."

Emlyn nodded through his tears.

"He's going away for a long time. I think the best advice is get yourself a normal boyfriend."

"Where are they? Any man I meet has some major flaw. This was the first date I had in ages and definitely the most dramatic!"

He started giggling again; Alice was concerned that he would break down and was relieved when a kindly neighbour handed them both cup of tea. It shifted the focus and Emlyn seemed to calm down.

The police were going to want to question Alice and Emlyn. Liam managed to persuade DI Henderson and DS McIlroy, who arrived shortly after Brendan's ambulance had left, that it would be OK to question them the following day.

Chapter 38

After the whole debacle, even with Brendan in custody, Alice wasn't sure if she still wanted to go to Spain. She could close the shop, sure, but she was still trying to get her head round everything. Was going away the right thing to do? Emlyn was still shaken up and suffering terribly from the guilt of hiding everything he knew from her.

"The last thing you need is to sit here on your own and mope about. Come with us, the weather is brilliant over there and you'll have a laugh. You might even meet a man!" Maggie was doing her damnedest to try and convince her.

"That's the last thing on my mind at the moment." Alice laughed, but without any humour.

Maggie and Isabel had called into the shop to see Alice. Her wanting to back out of the holiday wasn't a complete surprise. Isabel wasn't sure she would still want to go if all that had happened to Alice had happened to her.

"Do come, Alice! Total relaxation is what you need

after all this," Isabel tried to tempt her. "Look at me, two kids and a puppy packed off to Donegal with my mother, my sister and her husband."

"I'm just finding it hard to come to terms with what has happened and I don't know whether Emlyn should be left on his own."

Alice was pale and drawn. She had stopped eating and, though the doctor told Maggie and Isabel it was simply a result of the stressful situation she had endured at Emlyn's flat, they couldn't help worrying and if they were totally honest they didn't want to leave her on her own either.

"I know it has been a really nasty few weeks," said Isabel, "but as some expert somewhere says, things can only get better."

"I think I'm going to sell the shop."

"No! Why?" asked Maggie.

"Why do you think? Knowing that little bastard Terry was scheming, driving Jean into an early grave and poor Emlyn going slowly nuts. It's all I can do not to go round to the hospital and haul Brendan out of his bed and give him a damn good kicking! I don't think Emlyn will ever date again."

"Well, think about it this way: the stress for Emlyn is over and it would be worse for him if you packed up and left," said Maggie. "You guys need to stick together. And just think: with a bit of luck Brendan might be sharing his cell with a huge guy called Bertha who likes a bit of company!" Maggie winked mischievously.

Alice giggled at the thought.

"Well, that would be some sort of justice," she agreed.

"Come with us! This will all still be here when you get back. At least this way you can put a little distance between you and the shop for a week or so. Remember, you'll have to face the whole thing again in court."

"After all that trailing round flipping shops trying to get a nice bikini or two?" said Isabel. "Taking all that crap from Lady Muck over there about your gorgeous figure? I personally wouldn't let her away with it."

"OK, you pair put up a very convincing argument. Let's hope Brendan's barrister doesn't have the same talent with all Lomax's money behind him."

"No chance! The bad guys never win!"

"Alright, you've talked me into it," Alice conceded.

"Right, now close the shop. The good people of Donaghadee are going to have to put their hose-pipe requirements on hold for a week while this proprietor gets herself a decent tan." Maggie rubbed her hands together. "Let's get packing!"

They hustled Alice out of the shop before she had time to change her mind, into the house and then Maggie and Isabel both sat on her bed to make sure she really did pack and remembered her essentials such as the little black dress she had bought in Oasis, and the slinky black sandals that went with it.

* * *

They all met the following morning at the check-in for Malaga. Liam had stayed the night with Maggie and Alice and had driven them all to the airport. Charles and Isabel had made their own way. They had more suitcases between the five of them than the rest of the queue.

Alice was leaning on her trolley, her suitcase and hand luggage in front of her. A neighbour who had a soft spot and fresh chicken for Gary was looking after him. In fact, the little feline traitor had been off having two meals a day with the kindly old gentleman before coming home and demanding Whiskas and attention from Alice. She was thinking of the positives. She hadn't been abroad since God was a boy and was looking forward to it. She couldn't wait to get a tan. She just wished as she looked at the two couples who were queuing in front of her that she had someone to share it with. Deep down she knew who she really wanted to share it with. No matter how much she kept telling herself just to get on with her life, she kept coming back to the same face in her mind.

Maggie was really excited; she had never been on holiday with Isabel or Alice before and she thought it would be the greatest laugh. She was also looking forward to having Liam all to herself.

Liam was looking forward to a break. He hadn't been away for over a year and it would be good to chill out with Maggie. He was really starting to fall for her. Her bright sunny smile was something he had come to depend on, with his job that so often exposed him to the seedy dark side of human nature.

Isabel was standing hand in hand with Charles and she couldn't keep the smile off her face. They were going away together for the first time in years without the twins, and though she would miss them like mad she was really looking forward to having no responsibilities for a week. Amy and Henry had skipped off with Laura and Crunchie without so much as a backwards glance. They were going to spend the week in Port Salon in Donegal in a cottage that Sophie her sister and her husband had rented for the summer. She wished that she hadn't panic-packed. Last night, trying to organise the twins and her husband, she had ended up tipping virtually her whole wardrobe into a giant suitcase and shutting it closed without too much thought. God only knew what was in there!

Charles was standing close to his wife, hardly daring to believe the turnaround that had happened within their marriage since March. Their financial situation was a whole lot better and they could afford to enjoy themselves this week. The idea of lazing in the sun with the latest John Le Carré thriller he intended to buy in the airport shop was more appealing right now than anything else he could think of. He squeezed Isabel's hand and she leant over and planted a kiss on his cheek.

The plane was cramped and full of package holidaymakers in their leisure wear, all looking forward to their annual fortnight in Fuengirola or Torremelinos. No amount of screaming children could dampen the spirits of the two happy couples, sitting side by side.

Alice was pissed off. Not only had everyone refused to let her mention Bill's name, but now she was squeezed into the window seat beside a rather pudgy twelve-year-old boy who kept farting and laughing and punching his younger brother who was in the aisle seat. Alice was sure she would have whiplash as every time the boys fought she could feel the impact through her chair. She leant into the window to prevent from becoming bruised herself. Thank God the flight is only two and half hours, she thought to herself, as she tried to immerse herself in *Marie Claire*'s interesting and life-altering reportage on women living up trees in the Congo.

The food was pretty awful: harassed air-hostesses flung trays at their charges as they served the meal as quickly as was humanly possible. For starters, small slices of melon floated in thick syrup with some even smaller bits of pineapple, all topped with a rather tired cherry. Alice peeled back the silver foil lid of the main course and poked the over-cooked pasta smothered in congealed tomato and something-small-and-brown sauce. Closer inspection revealed a rather sad-looking miniature chicken breast beneath the solid carbohydrate mass. She nibbled at a bit of pasta, but realised there would be more nutritional value in the back cover of her magazine. Her travelling companion eyed her virtually untouched dinner so she took the bread roll and cube of cheddar and offered him the rest. He wolfed down the pasta and chicken before Alice had finished chewing her first mouthful of bread. Next he pilfered the dessert, which was some sort of

413

blancmange with a slice of tinned mandarin on the top; it vanished in even less time than the main course. Alice hid behind her magazine again until the orange-faced unsmiling air-hostess in her acrylic ill-fitting uniform returned to offer her stewed tea or tasteless coffee. Alice plumped for the coffee and just managed to rescue her after-dinner chocolate before the eating machine next door got his fat little fingers on it.

After the food, the fight seemed to have gone out of her travelling companions and the last hour of the flight was bearable. They watched the cartoons that were being shown on small screens throughout the cabin. Alice read the whole of the magazine right through to the horoscopes and recipes. After that she worked her way through the in-flight magazine which seemed to have been there since last summer judging by its curled corners and missing pages. Thankfully they were now flying low enough that Alice could make out the patchwork fields and mountains of southern Spain; the earth was deep ochre and terracotta colours. Alice's mood lifted as she imagined exploring the tiny villages Maggie had told her about that were built into the mountains up behind the commercialised coastline. She was looking forward to the sun, the heat, and, like Isabel, it would be nice to leave the responsibilities behind for a few days.

* * *

The ground seemed to shimmer in the heat as the plane taxied to the gate. They had to wait for a while until steps arrived so that they could disembark. The two boys quickly got bored when they couldn't get off the plane immediately and started fighting again. Alice, driven nearly to distraction, couldn't understand why the parents didn't do something to stop them. Instead, they just stood calmly in the aisle with all their hand luggage and duty-free Malibu, like sheep waiting to be led away to the coach which would take them to their hotel.

Thankfully, soon after that steps were found before the body-odour situation reached crisis point. There was a great rush for everyone to get off the plane as fast as they could.

Alice sat were she was. She couldn't be bothered to fight her way up the aisle while people made desperate grabs for their hand luggage in the overhead lockers once there was a break in the people filing past them. She caught up with the others as they walked towards the terminal building. The heat was glorious after leaving Belfast, which had been overcast. Once inside there were short queues while the Spanish immigration gave a cursory glance at everyone's passports.

"That wasn't so bad." Maggie indicated back towards the plane.

"The food was pretty awful," Isabel commented.

"Neither of you were obviously sitting beside children from hell then?" Alice said as she pushed open the door into the building.

After passport control, their made their way along several long marble-tiled corridors and down the escalators to the baggage-reclaim area. Liam and Charles already had trolleys and had located which conveyor-belt their luggage would come in on. It seemed as if all the Spanish in the building were smoking and the Irish who had just arrived took this as an open invitation and practically all lit up en masse.

Maggie's bag was the first off, her Louis Vuitton motif case standing out from all the other standard suitcases. One by one, the other cases were spotted though getting them off the carousel was a bit traumatic as all the other passengers had their trolleys shoved up against it to make sure they got their bags first. They ignored the yellow line, which was painted round the edge advising the passengers not push their trolleys beyond it. Liam very nimbly managed to get between two chain-smoking women with tight curly perms and sovereign rings to grab Alice's bag. The bags were all present and correct and they made their way out of the airport down to the car-hire area, which was one level below. Maggie had rented a Ford Galaxy people-carrier to fit them all in with their bags. The heat was incredible and Alice could feel sweat trickling down her back, but with the air-conditioning on full she quickly returned to a more comfortable temperature.

Maggie successfully negotiated their way out of the airport, then bypassing Malaga itself they got onto the coast road to Marbella. They drove the new motorway which took them up into hills where they could see down to the sea and the towns that sat on the water's edge. Many of the buildings were high-rise blocks and there was a lot of building work going on. The right side of the road was much prettier, with the ochre and terracotta Alice had seen from the sky and white villas dotted along the hillside. The sky was brilliant blue and the water sparkled. She had been right to come.

The banter on the forty-minute drive was great. Alice, who had never really spent much time in Charles' company, was really starting to warm to him. He and Liam seemed to have hit it off and Alice could feel everyone relaxing and chatting as they neared their destination. They were staying ten minutes south of Puerto Banus in a small new development right beside the beach.

Charles parked the car in shade right outside the block that Maggie's apartment was in. Everyone took his or her own bags out of the boot, except Maggie who had cunningly run up to the second floor to get the door open. The steps up to the apartment were terracotta tiles and plants trailed down over the white plastered building. Alice looked at Isabel who grinned. The whole thing was just so – Spanish. When they finally dragged their bags up to the second floor, Maggie had left the door wide open. The apartment was cool and just how she had described it, down to the marble-tiled floors. They walked into the living area; two huge white low sofas were along each wall with a glass coffee table between them. Beyond that was the terrace where Maggie was winding the canopy shade down over the white patio furniture. There were brightly coloured geraniums and bougainvillaea all along the balcony. Alice set her bag down and went to have a look outside. Maggie was giving instructions as to whose room was where. Alice looked over the terrace wall, down to the azure pool below. There was only one deeply tanned woman in the pool and one man sunbathing, his book covering his face. It looked like heaven and Alice couldn't wait.

"Where is everyone?" she asked Maggie.

"Siesta time. Most of the Spanish do observe it. Come three o'clock this place will have filled up again. We should do a quick unpack and get down there. Mind you, there are a few pools in the complex so this one is never overly busy. Come on, I'll show you to your room."

Maggie led Alice back through the living-room. This time Alice could see the little kitchen through a large serving-hatch – in front of the hatch was a dining-table and chairs. The sideboard had a mini stereo system on it with CDs lined up beside it.

Maggie showed her into her room, which was painted white just like the rest of the huge apartment. A huge double bed dominated the room, facing a double patio door. One wall was taken up with built-in wardrobes and there was a door in the other wall. Opening it, Alice was in her private bathroom with more marble tiles – this time they were even on the walls.

"Holy shit, Maggs, this place is amazing!"

"Do you like it?" Maggie was clearly delighted with Alice's reaction.

"Like it? It's the nicest place I've ever stayed!"

Maggie beamed with pleasure.

"Oh, let me see your room!" Isabel came running in. "It's lovely! Have you ever seen beds so big in your whole life?"

"I know, I'll get lost in mine!" Alice joked, and thought of Bill.

The apartment was really spectacular.

"Now I know there was a good reason for being friends with you!" said Isabel.

"Anyone for a glass of freezing cold white wine?" Charles called from the kitchen where he was investigating the fridge.

"Yes, please!" was the chorused reply.

Ten minutes later Alice, having half unpacked, was sitting on the terrace sipping the chilled Vina Sol, wearing a pink bikini with a sarong tied round her waist. She had a pair of Maggie's Chanel sunglasses on, which were very fashionable – rimless with pink glass. Her blonde hair was squished up into a vague bun-type affair on top of her head. She felt she could definitely get used to this. The others were getting changed and Liam was already sporting swimming-shorts which showed his very fit body off nicely. Alice had a brief pang of envy has she thought about his cousin.

"Well, how is everyone feeling?" Maggie asked when she appeared in a black and sheer swimsuit that only someone as petite as her could get away with. Her raven-black hair was tucked into an Abercromie baseball cap and she looked like a member of the Spanish glitterati.

Isabel couldn't get over how Maggie just seemed to fit

into her surroundings as if she had been born there. She was feeling self-conscious in her swimsuit, which was a lovely shade of tobacco brown and complemented her chestnut hair – but she had an oversized tee-shirt over her swimsuit, as her tummy bulges seemed to have worsened since the plane journey and she felt a bit like Buddha. She had some platform flip-flops on which made her feel even more ungainly as they threw her a little off balance. She clasped Charles' hand tightly and he held on, smiling at her. She had brought her watercolour paints with her and hoped to get a bit of painting done while she was here. So far everyone had been quite complimentary about the little sketches she had done, but she really wanted to do something more dramatic. Maybe she would take the car into the mountains one morning and give it a go. Charles on the other hand was thinking how beautiful his wife looked, sitting there so quietly. He knew that when she was this quiet in company she was usually nervous about something. He made a mental note to tell her how beautiful she looked that evening when she was getting dressed for dinner.

Maggie was delighted that everyone seemed pleased with the accommodation. She had been so nervous about this trip with Liam, but the tension was starting to go, as he was so relaxed with the others and with her. She knew this was going to be a brilliant holiday.

"Let's go down to the pool when we've finished our wine. Did you all get a beach towel out of the cupboard?"

Alice pointed to the pile of brightly coloured towels

heaped on one sofa just inside the glass doors. Beach bags bulged with sun-creams, books and newspapers.

The wine glasses now empty, they made their way down to the pool. Maggie locked the front door and ran down the stairs to catch everyone up.

At the pool they quickly found empty loungers and moved them so that they were facing the sun, which was still quite high in the sky. No-one seemed to have come back from the siestas yet. The woman who had been in the pool earlier was now improving her enviable tan and the man was still there with his Tom Clancy hardback over his face.

Isabel quickly pulled her tee-shirt over her head and lay down on her lounger; she had already put her sun-cream on in her room. Charles and Liam swapped newspapers and settled back to read. Maggie got straight into the pool to do some lengths, still wearing her sunglasses and baseball cap.

Alice applied high-factor sun-cream to her pale legs and hoped that she would soon go the same lovely golden colour Maggie seemed to be all year round. Once she had rubbed cream over her arms and face and tummy she lay back on her lounger, her book in her hand.

"Fancy seeing you here!"

Alice gasped and dropped her book. She would recognise that voice anywhere. She spun round on her sunbed.

"Bill!"

"In the flesh." He grinned and got up off his lounger. The others stopped whatever they were doing and watched. No-one looked surprised to see him there. Isabel forgot to be self-conscious and sat up on her lounger to get a better look, the men cast their newspapers aside and Maggie trod water in the deep end of the pool with a big grin on her face.

Alice turned round to the spectators, her sun-cream not quite rubbed into her face, white globs on her eyelashes.

"You all knew?" She was astounded – she had to fight to keep her jaw from trailing on the ground.

They nodded in unison.

Bill was wearing long surfer shorts, his light-brown hair pushed back off his forehead, his face freckled with the sun. He looked a mix between sexy as hell and just the same Bill that had made her feel so safe and secure back in Donaghadee. He looked really good.

Alice stood up too. She didn't know whether to laugh or cry, hug him or shake his hand. She still couldn't believe that he was here.

"I thought you were in America?"

"Everyone needs a holiday," he said, his kind eyes twinkling as he walked the short distance to stand in front of her.

A million things were running through Alice's mind: "Bikini line – check. Cellulite – a bit too late to worry about that now. Protruding tummy – hold it in. Fuck it all, Bill is here, Bill is here!"

She stood awkwardly, not sure what to do, trying to position herself to look slimmer. Bill answered the question for her by taking her in a huge embrace and giving her a very big kiss on the lips. Alice tried to kiss him back, but she was smiling too much. She could hear a very gentle round of applause behind them.

When their lips separated, he hugged her tight again.

"I missed you so much," he whispered.

Alice couldn't believe that she was finally hearing the words she had longed to hear, but was sure she never would.

She stared into his clear, kind blue eyes and kissed him again.

"At long bloody last!" Maggie called from the pool.

THE END